WAR&PEACE

CONTEMPORARY RUSSIAN PROSE

The premier showcase for contemporary Russian writing in English translation, **GLAS** has been discovering new writers for over a decade. With some 100 names represented, **GLAS** is the most comprehensive English-language source on Russian letters today — a must for libraries, students of world literature, and all those who love good writing.

For more information and excerpts see our site:

www.russianpress.com/glas

GLAS NEW RUSSIAN WRITING

contemporary Russian literature in English translation

VOLUME **40**

This volume of Glas was made possible by the support of the Arts Council of England and New Writing North.

CONTEMPORARY RUSSIAN PROSE

glas
MOSCOW

GLAS PUBLISHERS
tel./fax: +7(495)441-9157
perova@glas.msk.su
www.russianpress.com/glas

Glas is distributed in North America by
NORTHWESTERN UNIVERSITY PRESS
CHICAGO DISTRIBUTION CENTER
tel: 1-800-621-2736 or (773) 702-7000
fax: 1-800-621-8476 or (773)-702-7212
pubnet@202-5280
www.nupress.northwestern.edu

in the UK and Europe by
INPRESS LIMITED
tel: 020 8832 7464; fax: 020 8832 7465
stephanie@inpressbooks.co.uk
www.inpressbooks.co.uk

Within Russia Glas is distributed by
JUPITER-IMPEX (www.jupiters.ru)
through the following bookshops in Moscow:
DOM KNIGI (8 New Arbat), MOSKVA (8 Tverskaya),
DOM INOSTRANNOI KNIGI (18/7 Kuznetsky Most),
BOOKBERRY (10 Kutuzovsky);
in St Petersburg: DOM KNIGI (9 Lomanaya);
and also www.ozon ru and www.bolero.ru

Edited by **Natasha Perova** and **Joanne Turnbull**
Designed by **Andrei Bondarenko**
Camera-ready copy by **Tatiana Shaposhnikova**

ISBN 5-7172-0074-9

CONTENTS

WAR AND PEACE IN TODAY'S RUSSIA

The two parts of this collection of contemporary Russian fiction are stories about the modern-day Russian army ("War") and stories by and about women ("Peace"). Together they provide an all-round picture of post-post-perestroika Russia.

WAR Army problems are currently much debated in Russian society in connection with the recent shocking revelations about the inner life of the army, including cruelty to young conscripts, use of soldiers as slave labour, lack of food and other supplies, poor organization and insufficient training. There is a vast online library of army stories by veterans of modern-day wars, but not many have been printed as publishers are reluctant to annoy the authorities with exposures of the grave situation in the army, particularly in the Caucasus.

The authors declare their anti-war sentiments but hatred towards "the enemy" bursts out from time to time as men forced to shoot each other from opposite sides of the frontlines inevitably develop hostile attitudes towards one another. Any war inevitably sows hatred among otherwise peaceful people – such is the message of these stories.

The theme of hunger runs through all these stories: soldiers suffer from constant malnutrition, so much so that they are even prepared to steal food or obtain it in exchange for munitions with which they are themselves later killed.

Alexander Terekhov, the first writer to speak openly of his army experiences, says: "The entire army system of relationships is built on a daily humiliation, both physical and moral, which amounts to savagery."

ARKADY BABCHENKO's *Argun*, a compulsively readable, autobiographical account of life as an ordinary young soldier in Russia's campaign in Chechnya, takes the raw and mundane reality of days amid guns and grenades and twists it into compelling, chilling, and eerily beautiful prose.

DENIS BUTOV's *Five Days of War* plunges you into the midst of fierce fighting and a miraculous salvation from sure death. His *How Dreams Don't Come True* is about an ex-serviceman's inability to reintegrate into peaceful life after his army stint in Chechnya and society's mistrust of men who only know how to kill.

ROMAN SENCHIN's autobiographical story *24 Hours* relates the events of one day in his bleak existence as a border guard on the Russian-Finnish border. He depicts vividly the soldiers' longing for discharge from the prison-like army set-up.

DMITRY BYKOV's *Christ* shows the army as a harsh male world with crude practices and sadistic hazing that drives young men to suicide and insanity. The two episodes from his new novel JEWHAD, a futuristic anti-utopia about imminent ethnic conflicts and the inevitable crisis of democracy and liberalism as we know them today, are drawn from present-day army life.

JULIA LATYNINA exposes corrupt administrations in the Caucasus. They openly disregard the law and even resort to contract murder in maintaining their totalitarian rule, but they have to comply with the local mafia lords and rebel chieftains, who actually control business enterprises and whole territories.

PEACE Women's stories are a sharp contrast to the "War" section. They immerse you in a world of basic human values such as love, children and family, but also of aging, generation gap, and violence to women. Female readers in the West will be surprised to discover many common issues – the setting is different but the problems are essentially the same.

The stories reflect the current stage in the evolution of Russian women's fiction from near non-existence during the Soviet period, through several stages of vigorous development in the 1990s, to current confident craftsmanship, wide thematic range, and high stylistic standards.

OLGA SLAVNIKOVA's *The Secret of the Unread Note* paints a life-like portrait of a small provincial town where a modern young woman, who is not pretty or outstanding, still yearns for love and tries various ways of getting it.

In **MARIA GALINA**'s *The End of Summer* the mysterious appearance of a little clairvoyant girl wreaks havoc on the leisurely life of a childless couple. The wife's longing for motherhood turns out to be stronger than her love for her husband.

MARIA RYBAKOVA looks at the eternal drama of aging in her finely-crafted psychological narrative *A Sting in the Flesh* in which an old lady inadvertently kills the emerging love between two young people.

MARIA ARBATOVA's *My Last Letter to A.* conveys the modern woman's rebellion against the traditional dependency implicit in male-female relationships. Arbatova's forte is her frankness and precise characterisation, which has won her the admiration and gratitude of many newly liberated Russian women.

As evidenced by **MARINA KULAKOVA**'s story *Alive Again*, "peace" is not so peaceful after all, and violence towards women is very much a part of it. In her story, based on personal experiences, she investigates the psychology of the rapist and the victim as well as showing the roots of such phenomena and the public's indifference to the problem.

ARKADY BABCHENKO
DENIS BUTOV
ROMAN SENCHIN
DMITRY BYKOV
JULIA LATYNINA

ARKADY BABCHENKO
ARGUN

We halt for the fourth day at the canning factory in Argun. It's the best place so far during our deployment and we feel completely safe inside the fence that skirts the perimeter.

The trouble with this war is that there are no rear positions and no base where you can be withdrawn for rest and recuperation — we are in a permanent state of encirclement and can expect a shot in the back at any moment. But here we are sheltered.

Two automatic mounted grenade launchers are positioned in the administration block and cover the whole street from the direction of the gates. There are two more launchers on the roof of the factory's meat packing section and a machine-gun nest on the second floor of the entrance block. This way we completely control the surrounding area and feel relatively secure. We relax.

April has arrived and the sun is already beating down. We walk around practically naked, wearing just shorts made from cut-off long johns and army boots, and we are alike as brothers. And brothers we are, for there's no one in the world closer than emaciated soldiers with lice-bitten armpits and sun-browned necks on the rest of their white, putrefying skin.

The battalion commanders leave us in peace to get our fill of food and sleep. Yesterday they even fixed up a steam bath for us in the old sauna room in the guardhouse and we sweated away there for almost an hour. They issued us with fresh underwear into the bargain, so now we can enjoy two or three blissful lice-free days.

Fixa and I sit on the grass by the fence and wait for two Chechen kids to appear. Our bare bellies upturned to the sky, we bask in long-forgotten sensations of cleanliness and warmth. Our boots stand in a row and we wiggle our bare toes and smoke.

"Bet you five cigarettes I can stubb out this butt on my heel," he says.

"Think you'll wow me with that one, do you?" I reply. "I'll do the same trick but for two cigarettes."

The skin on my soles has grown as hard as a rhino's from the boots. I once drove a needle into my heel for a bet and it went in more than a centimetre before it hurt.

"You know, I reckon the brass is being too wasteful in handing over our guys' bodies to the families," Fixa muses. "They could put us to far better use after we're killed, like make a belt sling from a soldier's hide. Or you could knock out a pretty good flak jacket from the heels of a platoon."

"Uh-huh. And you could make a bunch of them from the guys who died up in the hills. Why don't you tell the supply officer, maybe he'll give you leave for the smart idea?" I suggest.

"No, I can't tell him, he'll just sell the idea to the Chechens and start trading in corpses."

A gentle breeze plays over our bodies and we laze ecstatically as we wait for the kids to show up.

The knot of nervous tension inside just won't loosen up after the mountains and fear keeps churning away somewhere below my stomach. We need to unwind. Two signal flares are stuffed into the tops of Fixa's boots that we'll swap for marihuana. We already gave three flares to the Chechen kids as an advance and we're waiting for them to come back with the promised matchbox of weed.

There's a small gap in the fence at this corner and a small market has sprung up. The kids sit all day on the other side and soldiers come up on ours and offer their wares: tinned meat, diesel, bullets. Half an hour ago the battalion cook stuffed a whole box of butter through the gap. Fixa wonders if we should give him a beating but we can't be bothered to get up.

We get an unexpected treat of meat. The infantry caught and shot a guard dog, roasted it over a fire and gave us two ribs. It turns out some of them are from Fixa's home region. It's a fine thing to have common roots with guys in your unit. Only when you are far from home do you realise what a bond you have with someone who wandered the same streets and breathed the same air as a child. You may never have met before and are unlikely to meet again later but right now you are like brothers, ready to give up everything for the other, a Russian trait through and through.

We chew the tough meat and bitter-tasting fat runs down our fingers. Delicious.

"Spring onion would be good now, I love meat with greens," says Fixa. "But most of all I love pork fried with potato and onion. My wife cooks it just how I like it. First she fries the crackling until the edges curl upwards and the fat oozes out. It has to be well fried or the fat will be stewed like snot and not tasty. And when the fat starts to sizzle in the pan she adds thinly sliced potato, fries it lightly on one side and then the first time she stirs it she adds salt and onion. The onion has to go in after the potato or else it burns. And then..."

"Shut up, Fixa." I suddenly have a craving for fried pork and potatoes and can't listen to his gastronomic revelations any more.

"There's no pork here, they're Moslems and don't eat it."

"Just noticed, have you? You won't find pork here in a month of Sundays. How are they supposed to have pork fat if they can't even wipe their backsides with paper like human beings, I ask you?"

This aspect of local Chechen culture engenders particular hostility in Fixa and the rest of us too. Quite apart from anything else, our soldiers resent the Chechens because they wash themselves after doing their business, rather than using paper.

In each house there are special jugs made from some silvery metal with a long spout inscribed with ornate Arabic script. At first our boys couldn't figure out their purpose and used them for making tea. When someone finally told them they freaked out. The first thing they do now when they occupy a house is kick these jugs outside or fish them out with sticks.

Actual faith doesn't matter one bit to us, be it Allah, Jesus or whoever, since we ourselves are all a godless lot from birth. But to us these jugs embody the difference between our cultures. It seems to me the political officer could distribute them instead of propaganda leaflets and we'd rip Chechnya to shreds in a couple of days.

"My cousin served in Tajikistan and told me the Tajiks use flat stones after the toilet," I say as I inspect the dog rib in my hand. "It's still the Stone Age there, they don't know about toilet paper or even newspaper. They gather pebbles from the river and use those. Each outdoor bog has a pile of stones beside it like a grave."

"So what's it like in Tajikistan then? Bound to be better

than here. What else does your cousin say about it?" asks Fixa.

"Nothing. He's dead."

My cousin died just two days before he was due to be demobilized. He volunteered for a raid at the border. The patrol was made up of greenhorn conscripts who still didn't know anything and so my cousin stood in for some young kid. He was a machine-gunner and when the shooting started he covered the group as they pulled back.

A sniper put a round into his temple, a rose shot, as we call it: When the bullet hits the head at close range the skull opens up like a flower and there's no putting it together again. They had to bind up my cousin's head for the funeral or it would have fallen apart right there in the coffin.

"Yeah," says Fixa. "It's all just one war, that's what I think. And you know what else, Chechnya is just for starters, the big war is still to come, you'll see."

"You think so?"

"Yes. And I also think I'm going to make it through this one."

"Me too," I say. "Maybe since my cousin was killed I believe I'm going to survive. Two Babchenkos can't die in battle."

We finish the ribs. We've gnawed off all the gristle and soft tissue and all that's left in our fingers is five centimetres of hard bone that we can't chew down any further. We put the stumps in our cheeks like lollipops and, lying on our backs, suck out the last traces of fat. Our chomping is the only noise for the next fifteen minutes. Finally even this pleasure ends, the ribs are empty.

Fixa wipes his hands on his shorts and gets out a notebook and pen that he brought along specially.

"Right, tell me where we've been then. I just can't remember the names of these villages."

"OK. You joined us at Gikalovsky, right? So, Gikalovsky, then Khalkiloi, Sanoi, Aslambek, Sheripovo, Shatoi, and..." I pause for a moment, trying to get my tongue round the next one. "... Sharo-Argun."

"That's right, Sharo-Argun. I remember that all right," Fixa mutters.

"You don't forget something like that in a hurry."

"I'll draw a gallows beside Sharo-Argun," he says, sketching awkwardly in the notebook. His fingers are not comfortable with a pen, he's more used to handling steel. Before the war he wielded a trowel and spade as a builder, now a rifle and grenade launcher.

I lean over and look at the crooked gibbet and the figure hanging from it. Sharo-Argun. What a dreadful name. We lost twenty men there, Igor, Pashka, Four-Eyes the platoon commander, Vaseline, the list goes on.

There are lots of places like that in Chechnya: Shali, Vedeno, Duba-Yurt, Itum-Kale, all names of death. There's something shamanistic about them, strange names, strange villages. Some of my comrades died in each one and the earth is drenched in our blood. All we have left now are these odd, un-Russian words, we live within them, in the past, and these combinations of sounds that mean nothing to anyone else signify an entire lifetime to us.

We take our bearings from them like from a map. Bamut is an open plain, a place of unsuccessful winter assaults, a place of cold, of frozen earth and a crust of bloodstained ice. Samashki — foothills, burning cars, heat, dust and bloated corpses heaped up by the hundred in three days. And Achkhoi-Martan, where I had my baptism of fire, where the first tracer rounds flew at me and where I first tasted fear.

And not forgetting Grozny, where we lost Fly, Koksharov, Yakovlev, and Kisel before them. This land is steeped in our blood, they drove us to our deaths here as they will continue to do for a long time yet.

"You should draw an arse instead of a gallows," I tell Fixa. "If you imagine the Earth as an arse, then we are right in the hole."

I shut my eyes, lay on my back and put my hands behind my head. The sun shines through my eyelids and the world is tinged orange. Hell, I don't even want to think about it, the mountains, the snow, Igor's body. I'll get to it later but for now everything has stopped, for a while at least. Right now we are alive, our stomachs filled with dog meat, and nothing else matters. I can lie in the sun without fearing a bullet in the head and it's wonderful. I suddenly recall the face of the sniper who was gunning for me in Goiti. For some reason I wasn't afraid then.

Then I remember the photo of the little Chechen boy we found near Shatoi. He's only about seven but he's showing off with a rifle in his hands while mum stands alongside, beaming at her grown-up son. How proud she is of him, so full of joy for the holy warrior who already knows how to hold a rifle.

There will be even greater pride in her eyes when he severs the head of his first Russian prisoner at the age of seventeen. At twenty he'll attack a column and kill more people, and at twenty-two he'll run his own slave camp. Then at twenty-five they will hunt him down from a helicopter like a wolf, flush him into the open and fire rockets at him as he darts between shell craters, splattering his guts all over the place. Then he'll lie in a puddle and stare at the sky with half open, lifeless eyes, now just an object of disgust as lice crawl in his beard.

We've seen warriors like this, grown up from such boys, into wolves from cubs. And to think, my mother would have flayed the skin from my back with a belt if I'd ever thought to pose with a weapon when I was a kid.

Enough, no sense in dwelling on this now. Later. Everything later.

Fixa and I lie in the grass in silence, neither feels like talking. The sun has tired us out and we daydream, maybe doze off for a while, it's hard to say — our hearing stays as sharp in sleep as when we're awake and registers every sound, from the twittering of the birds to soldiers' voices, stray gunshots and the chugging of the generator. All harmless noises.

We don't rouse until the sun sinks beneath the horizon. It gets chilly and the ground is still damp. I'm covered in goose bumps and I want to get under cover. My cold stomach aches, I get up and pee where I stand. The stream of urine quickly wanes but I get no relief, my belly still hurts. I'll have to go to the medic.

The Chechen kids never showed up. We wait another half an hour but they still don't come. Evidently our signal flares went to the fighters' beneficiary fund free of charge.

"Some businessmen we are, Fixa," I say. "We should have got the grass first and then paid. We've been had, come on, let's go."

"We should have brought our rifles, that's what, held one of them at gunpoint while the others went for the weed," he says.

"They still wouldn't have showed up! They're not fools, they know we won't do anything to them. Would you shoot a boy over a box of grass?"

"Of course not."

We follow the fence back toward our tent, brick debris and shrapnel scrunching under our boots. There had been fighting here at some time, probably in the 1994-96 war. Since then no one had worked at the factory or tried to reconstruct it. These ruined buildings had only been used for keeping slaves.

I suddenly remember Dima Lebedev, a guy I transported coffins with in Moscow. His armoured car ran over a mine by Bamut and the whole unit except Dima died instantly. He said he saw his platoon commander fly up like a cannon ball as the shock wave tore off his arms and legs and dumped his trunk on the ground, still in the flak jacket.

Dima was heavily concussed and lay there for almost a day. The Chechens that emerged from the undergrowth after the blast thought he was dead and didn't bother to put a bullet in him. He came round at night and ran straight into another group of fighters who took him with them into the mountains and kept him at a cottage with six other conscripts.

Their captors would beat them, cut off their fingers and starve them to get them to convert to Islam. Some did, others like Dima refused. Then they stopped feeding him altogether and he had to eat grass and worms for two weeks.

Each day the prisoners were taken into the mountains to dig defensive positions and finally Dima was able to escape. An old Chechen took him in and hid him in his home where Dima lived with the family like a servant, tending the cattle, cutting the grass and doing chores. They treated him well and when Dima wanted to go home they gave him money and a ticket and took him out of Chechnya to the garrison town of Mozdok, moving him at night in the boot of a car so the fighters didn't get them.

He made it home alive and later corresponded with his old master, who even came and stayed with him a couple of times. That's what Dima called him, master, just like a slave. He was scarred forever by captivity. He had submissive, fearful eyes and was always ready to cover his head with his hands and squat down, shielding his stomach. He spoke quietly and never rose to insult.

Later his master's nephew came to his home, knocked his

mother around, abducted his sister and demanded a ransom for her release. Maybe he even kept her here in the basement of this factory with dozens of other prisoners, I wonder.

"Tell me, would you really have finished off that wounded guy back in the mountains?" Fixa suddenly asks. We stop walking. Fixa looks me in the eyes and waits for an answer.

I know why this is so important to him. He doesn't say so, but he's thinking: "So would you finish me off then if it came to it?"

"I don't know. You remember what it was like, it was snowing, the transport couldn't get through for the wounded and he was going to die anyway. He would just have screamed — remember how he screamed, how awful it was? I just don't know..."

We stand facing one another. I suddenly feel like hugging this skinny, unshaven man with the big Adam's apple and bony legs sticking out of his boots.

"I wouldn't have shot anyone, Fixa, you know that, and you knew that then in the mountains. Life is too precious and we would have fought for it to the very last, even if that lad had puked up all his intestines. We still had bandages and painkillers and maybe by morning we could have evacuated him. You know I wouldn't have killed him, even if we had known then for sure that he would die anyway."

I want to tell him all of this but don't manage to. Suddenly there's a single shot and a short burst of rifle fire immediately followed by a powerful explosion. A cloud of smoke and dust envelops the road by the entrance block, right where our tents are pitched.

My first thought is that Chechens have blown up the gate.

"Get down!" I shout and we dive face down onto the asphalt. We freeze for a moment and then hurl ourselves over to the wall of the transformer box where we lie motionless.

Dammit, no rifle, idiot that I am I left it in the tent, now of all times. I'm never without my weapon! Fixa is also unarmed. We completely dropped out guard at the factory, thought we could take it easy and go a hundred metres from our position without rifles.

Fixa's eyes dart around, his face pale and mouth agape. I can't look much better myself.

"What do we do now, eh, what do we do?" he whispers in my ear, clutching my arm.

"The flares, give them here," I whisper back, petrified with fear. Without a weapon I am no longer a soldier but a helpless animal, a herbivore with no fangs or claws. Now they'll pour through the breach, take us right here in nothing on but our shorts and butcher us, pin our heads down with a boot and slit our throats. And there's no one else around, we are alone on this road by the fence. They'll get us first and kill us before the battalion comes to its senses and returns fire. Dumb holidaymakers we are.

I look round. We'll have to make a run for it behind the warehouses where the vehicles are parked and where there are people.

Fixa pulls the flares from his boots and hands me one. I tear open the protective membrane and free the pin. We hold them out in front us, ready to fire them at the first thing that appears on the road and we freeze, holding the pull-strings.

It's quiet. The shooting has stopped. Then we hear voices and laughter from the direction of the entrance block. They are speaking in Russian, no accent. We wait a little longer and then get up, dust ourselves off and go round to find the battalion commander, supply officer, chief of staff and some other officers milling around, all half drunk. They've dragged a safe out of the admin block, fixed a stick of dynamite to the door and blown it in half. It's empty. One officer suggests blowing up a second safe in the building in case there's anything in it but the battalion commander is against the idea.

"Morons," Fixa growls as we pass by. "Haven't they had enough shooting yet?"

Our own damage is not so bad. I tore up my knee slightly on a piece of brick when I threw myself down and Fixa has a long scratch on his cheek. What bothers us more is that we are filthy again and the steam-bath has been a waste of time. We go into our tent and bed down.

That night we come under fire. A grenade flies over the fence near the transformer box where Fixa and I had prepared to defend ourselves. A second grenade explodes, then tracer rounds illuminate the sky. A few bursts pass over our heads and the bullets whine in the air. It's not heavy fire, maybe two or three weapons. The sentries on the roofs open up in reply and a small exchange ensues.

Three signal rockets rise from the other side of the fence, one red and two green. In the flickering light we see the figures of soldiers running from tents and clambering up to the tops of the buildings. While the flares hang in the air the fire in our direction intensifies and we hear a couple of rifle grenades being launched.

We crouch by our tents and watch the sky. No one panics as it's clear that the only danger from this chaotic night shooting is a random hit. The fence shelters us and there are no tall buildings near the factory, and since our attackers can only fire from ground level the bullets just go overhead. Our tents are in a safe place so we don't run anywhere. We can only be hit by shrapnel from the rifle grenades but they explode far away.

The fighters could inflict far more damage if they fired through the gates but they either didn't think of this or they don't want to risk it. Our lookout post is in the admin block where the two grenade launchers and a machine-gun are set up, and it would be hard to get close on that side.

We sit watching the light show as green streams of tracer fire course across the sky. Then the guns fall quiet as suddenly as they started up. Our machineguns on the roofs pour down fire in all directions for another five minutes and then they also cease. It's now silent apart from the background chugging of the generator.

We have a smoke. It's great outside and no one wants to go back inside the stuffy tents where the kerosine lamps are burning. We are almost grateful to the Chechens for getting us out. The moon is full, it's night time, quiet. Garik comes down sleepy-eyed from the roof of the meat-packing shop where our grenade launcher is mounted. He slept right through the shooting, the silly sod. Pincha was on duty with him but he stays up top, afraid that Arkasha will give him a thrashing.

"Why weren't you shooting?" I ask Garik.

"What was I supposed to shoot at, you can't see anything beyond the fence. And we didn't want to drop any grenades, we might have hit you."

He knows it sounds unconvincing but he also knows we won't do anything to him, none of us were wounded so there's nothing to get worked up about.

"Enough of your stories," says Arkasha, the oldest and most authoritative among the privates in our platoon. "Do you want to spend two whole days up there? I can arrange that for you, no sweat."

Garik says nothing, knowing he can land himself in hot water. Arkady can indeed see to it that they spend two more days on the roof.

Fixa nudges me. "Those were our flares, did you notice? One red and two green, just like I gave the boy. Definitely ours. Return to sender, you could say."

"I'd have preferred if they'd just tossed the matchbox to us," I mope.

The commanders step up the guard for the rest of the night and we sit like cats up on the roof. Fixa, Oleg and I join Garik and Pincha, while Arkasha, Lyekha and Murky head over to the admin block.

I know they'll just crash out to sleep as soon as they get there. We also have no intention of peering into the steppe all night and we take our sleeping bags up to the roof and bed down between two ventilation shafts.

The generator chugs away below us. In Argun lights glimmer at a few windows, seems they already hooked the place up to the electricity. All is quiet out in the steppe, not a single person is to be seen, no movement. Chechnya dies at night, everyone locks themselves into their homes and prays that no one comes for them, that no one kills or robs them or drags them off to the Russian military detention centre at Chernorechye. Death rules the nighttime here.

On the horizon the mountains stand out as a dark mass. We only just came from there. That's where Igor was killed. I fall asleep.

Replacements arrive, about 150 crumpled-looking guys who are trucked in to our battalion from Gudermes. They stand huddled in a crowd on the square in front of the entrance block that we dubbed the parade ground. They carry only half empty kitbags: all the things they had with them had been bartered for drink on the way.

This lot are no use as soldiers, there isn't a single bold or cocky one among them, or even one who is physically strong. Each new batch of replacements is worse than the last in quality. Russia has clearly run out of romantics and adventurers and all that's left is this worthless muck that has nowhere to go apart from the army or prison. This lot on the parade ground have darting, lost eyes set into swollen, unshaven faces, and seem to blend into one monotonous, grey mass. And they stink.

We stand by the tents and bluntly survey the new recruits. It's a dismal sight.

"Where the hell do they get them from," says Arkasha. "We've no bloody use for this sort here, all they can do is guzzle vodka and pee in their pants. We have to talk to the commander so he doesn't take on any of them — warriors like these we can do without."

"What do you want then, for them to send us linguists and lawyers?" replies Oleg. "That kind are not very keen to come here. All the smart, good-looking ones managed to wriggle out of this war, but since the draft board has to meet its quotas they just shunt whatever's left this way."

We're short of people in the platoon but Arkasha is right, there's no place for this rabble, we'll manage somehow without them.

Two are assigned to us anyway, slovenly specimens of an indeterminable age, rat-like, unreliable. They immediately dump their kitbags in the tent and make themselves scarce, mumbling something about vodka. We don't hold them up.

"Maybe they'll get chopped to bits at the market, it'll be less hassle for all of us," says Pincha, digging dirt from between his fingers with his bayonet.

Arkasha has the idea of breaking into the trailer wagon that the supply officer tows with him all round Chechnya behind a Ural truck. It's constantly guarded by cooks and what they keep in it is anyone's guess, but you can be sure it's not state bank bonds.

To effect the burglary we plan a full-scale military operation. Arkasha's plan is simple. It came to him at night while we were being bombarded and in this instance the arrival of the replacements will only be to our advantage.

When it gets dark we emerge from our tents, turn left

along the fence, make our way to the fence opposite the vehicle park and jump into one of the useless sentry trenches the cooks dug for themselves there.

In front of each trench a firing slit had been cut in the fence and the embrasure lined with turf. Judging from the fortifications they are preparing to defend the stocks of tinned meat to the bitter end.

Lyekha and I get two hand grenades and pull the pins while Arkasha wraps his rifle in three ground sheets and aims it into the bottom corner of the trench.

"Ready?" he whispers.

"Ready."

"Now!"

We toss the grenades over the fence and they explode with a deafening clap in the night silence, or maybe it just seems that loud, such is the tension. Arkasha looses a few bursts into the ground.

The muzzle flash is invisible inside the ground sheets and the sound seems to come from the earth. It's impossible to tell where the firing is from, it seems like it's coming from all sides at once.

Lyekha and I throw two more grenades and I fire a signal flare.

The overall effect is extremely realistic.

"That'll do!" says Arkasha. "Let's get out of here before they wake up!"

We manage to run about ten metres when the machine-gun on the roof comes to life. I'm suddenly afraid that in his stupor the gunner will take us for attacking Chechens and cut us down in the wink of an eye.

Meanwhile, cooks emerge from every nook and cranny and lay down a withering barrage of fire. We also fire a few bursts in the air, our faces hidden in the crook of our arms and averted from the illuminating muzzle flashes.

No one pays us any attention. The whole battalion is now dashing round in disarray and within a minute firing issues from all corners of the factory grounds.

The new recruits stoke the confusion, shouting "Chechens, Chechens!" as they run toward the fence with their rifles and indiscriminately spray bullets from the waist and generally behave like children. To make matters worse, they are firing tracer rounds, which ricochet and whiz all over the place, perfectly creating the impression that we are being attacked.

We freeze for a moment, dumbstruck. Little did we suspect that four grenades and a couple of rifle bursts could stir up such pandemonium. It must be said, a battalion is a force to be reckoned with.

We make our way amid the chaos to the wagon. There's no guard. Arkasha breaks the lock.

It's pitch black inside and we hastily grope around the shelves, chancing upon tins and small sacks and packages that we sweep into an open ground sheet. I come across a heavy, bulky object wrapped in paper. I stuff it inside my tunic and fill my pockets with more tins, spilling something in my haste, sugar maybe. Speed is of the essence.

"Give me a hand lads, I've got something here," says Arkasha. I feel my way over to him. He is holding something by two handles, big and heavy, covered with a tarpaulin.

"It's butter," exclaims Lyekha. "Just look how much that bastard has stolen."

"Right, let's get out of here," Arkasha orders. It's almost as dark outside and only small sections of the roof are lit up by muzzle flashes. There's still a fair bit of shooting but the commotion is gradually dying down.

Someone is approaching the wagon, panting his way towards us with a stench of onions on his breath. Looks like some sneaky character also decided to take advantage of the melee. Arkasha lashes out blindly in the dark with his boot and the man yelps and falls.

"Leg it!" I hiss and we bound and stumble our way back. The wooden chest with the butter is unbelievably heavy, it painfully thumps my ankle-bones and slips from my fingers but we're not leaving it behind. It's impossibly awkward to run with all this stuff — apart from the chest we have those tins bouncing around in our pockets and I have to hold the package inside my tunic with my spare hand to stop it falling out.

We reach the warehouses and find a small ditch that we dug earlier and lined with ground sheets. We dump the chest in with our tins and packages and cover it all with more ground sheets that we brought with us. Finally we scatter chunks of brick and lay a sheet of metal over the top. Then we hasten back up to the roof.

The shooting has almost died down. We race across the roof toward the entrance block, jump down to ground level by the meat-packing shop and wander leisurely back to our tents. I jab Arkasha with my elbow and he bumps me back with his shoulder. We grin at one another.

The next morning they fall in the whole battalion on the parade ground. The commander tells us how last night, while the battalion was repelling an attack, some swine broke into the transport park's store wagon and stole food from his comrades. There is to be a search of all personal property and vehicles while we remain on the square.

"Like hell it was from our own comrades," says Arkasha. "Our comrades would never have seen this butter. We should regard ourselves as battalion delegates for sampling food products intended for us. Later we'll tell the guys how delicious the food is that we are supposed to get."

They keep us standing there while the supply officer personally shakes down every tent and armoured car,

throwing everything out onto the ground as h
bunk beds and knocks over cooking stoves.

His lower lip is swollen and he is in a foul tem
the one Arkasha kicked, right in the face. We were
lucky that he didn't grab his leg and pull off his boot. y'd have beaten us half to death for this, but now it's impossible to identify us.

We gawp impudently at the contorted face of the supply officer and smile among ourselves. The stolen goods are well hidden in the ditch and there is no evidence.

The search continues for six hours and we grow thirsty as the sun beats down. I read somewhere that the Germans used to force concentration camp inmates to stand in the sun half the day for fun, much like this.

But we're in good spirits nonetheless. Covered in ground sheets in that ditch by the warehouses awaits a chest full of butter and we'd happily stand on the square a whole week for that.

"OK lads, I invite you all for tea," says Arkasha. "I promise each of you a butter sandwich that weighs a kilo. Pincha even gets a double portion."

"Wow," says Pincha. "But where's the butter from?"

"Let's just say there's no more left where that came from," grins Arkasha, winking at Lyekha and me.

Eventually they fall us out. As was to be expected, the supply officer didn't find a thing. Nor did he expect to — any fool knew that no one would keep the stolen stuff in his tent. He just wanted to get his own back for the split lip.

The rest of the day we wander idly around the factory but stay away from the hole. That night we are all put on guard duty again. Toward morning we leave our positions and make our way to the warehouses. Arkasha shines his torch in the ditch as Lyekha and I retrieve the booty.

Our raid yielded 18 cans of various foodstuffs, bags of sugar, four sets of dry rations, a hefty chunk of pork fat that must weigh about three kilos — the package that was in my tunic — two loaves of bread, six blocks of cigarettes and... a generator! The exact same one we looted near Shatoi, a beautiful, plastic-cased Yamaha, complete with that crack in the housing. It stands in the ditch, covered with ground sheets as if this was its rightful home.

"It's butter, it's butter!" Arkasha says, angrily mimicking Lyekha. "Can't you tell the difference between butter and engine oil?"

"Actually I can't, I've been pretty much unable to tell the difference between any smells recently. My nose is probably bunged up with soot. And anyway it was in a case and doesn't smell too much of anything."

He's right, the supply officer has kept the generator in good condition, clean and dry and not one new dent in it.

"Never mind, we can sell it," I say. "The Chechens would give their arm for something like that and still think it was a bargain. For them a generator is like manna from heaven, and this one will power up twenty homes. Have you seen how they mount a Lada engine on a stand and turn it into a dynamo? And this is a factory-made generator and a diesel one at that."

"Risky," says Arkasha. "We can't get it past the fence and it won't go through the gap. We'll leave it here for the moment, maybe we'll think of something."

Until dawn we carry some of the stolen goods to our tent and stash the rest in a personnel carrier driven by a mate of ours. We put two tins in our armpits at a time and walk through the yard with a bored air, yawning as if we were just out for a stroll and a breath of air. We carry the pork fat and cigarettes inside our tunics.

Later we divide the spoils equally. We also give Pincha a

tin of condensed milk to make up for the lost butter. It's his birthday in a week and he stashes the tin away, almost swooning with happiness — it's the best present he's ever had in his life. He says he won't open it before five a.m. Friday, the time he came into this world. He's lying of course, he'll wolf it down tonight, unable to wait.

That evening we have a feast for our stomachs and no one goes to the vehicle park for the usual gruel. Pincha eats his fill of pilfered canned meat and noisily stinks the tent out all night.

The kombat (battalion commander) has caught two recruits from the anti-tank platoon up to no good. It turns out they had passed some boxes of cartridges through the fence to the Chechen kids, then drunk a bottle of vodka and fallen asleep by the gap.

Half an hour later the kombat chanced upon them and gave them a beating before keeping them overnight in a large pit in the ground. Today their punishment is to be continued and they fall us in again on the parade ground. We know too well what will happen now.

At the edge of the square they dug an improvised torture rack into the ground, a thick water pipe that has been bent into the shape of a gibbet. At the kombat's orders, the platoon made it during the night by placing the pipe against two concrete piles and using an armoured car to bend it in the middle. Two ropes now dangle from it.

The anti-tank gunners are lead out, hands bound behind their backs with telephone cable and dressed in ragged greatcoats and long johns. Their faces are already swollen and purple from beating and there are huge black haematomas where their eyes should be, oozing pus and tears from the corners. Their split lips can no longer close and pink foam bubbles from their mouths and drips onto their dirty, bare feet. It's a depressing sight. After all, these are not tramps but soldiers, ordinary soldiers, half of the army is like these two.

They stand the soldiers on the square. They raise their heads and look through the gaps in the swelling at the ropes swinging in the wind.

The kombat grabs one by the throat with his left hand and hits him hard in the nose. The soldier's head snaps back to his shoulder blades and emits a cracking noise. Blood spurts. The commander kicks the second one in the groin and he falls to the ground without a sound. The beating begins.

"Who did you sell the bullets to?" screams the kombat, grabbing the soldiers by the hair and holding up their swollen faces, which quiver like jelly from the blows. He traps their heads in turn between his knees and lashes them with blows from top to bottom.

"Well, who? The Chechens? Have you killed a single fighter yet, you piece of shit, have you earned the right to sell them bullets? Well? Have you even seen one? Have you ever had to write a letter of condolence to a dead soldier's mother? Look over there, those are soldiers, 18-year-old lads who have already seen death, looked it in the face, while you scum sell the Chechens bullets? Why should you live and guzzle vodka while these puppies died instead of you in the mountains, eh? I'll shoot the fucking pair of you!"

We don't watch the beating. We had been beaten ourselves and it long ceased to be of any interest. Nor do we feel particularly sorry for the gunners. They shouldn't have got caught. The kombat is right, they have seen too little of the war to sell bullets, we're the ones entitled to do that. We know death, we've heard it whistling over our heads and seen how it mangles bodies, and we have the right to bring it upon others. These two haven't yet. What's more, these new recruits are strangers in our battalion, not yet soldiers, not one of us. But most of all we are upset that we can no longer use the gap in the fence.

"Cretins," spits Arkasha. "They put the gap out of bounds, got themselves caught and ruined it for all of us. So much for selling the generator."

He is more bothered than any of us. Now he'll have to go to the local market to satisfy his passion for trading. We don't like it at the market, too dangerous. You never know if you'll come back alive. You can only buy stuff from the Chechens at the side of the road, when one of you jumps down from the armoured car and approaches them while the platoon trains their rifles on them and the gunner readies his heavy-calibre machine-gun.

The market is enemy territory. Too many people, too little room to move. They shoot our guys in the back of the head there, take their weapons and dump their bodies in the road. You can only walk around freely if you take the pin out of a grenade and hold it up in your fist. It was a whole lot more pleasant to trade through the fence on our own ground. We were the ones who could shoot people in the back of the head if need be.

"Yeah," says Lyekha, "Shame about the gap. And the generator."

The kombat works himself into an even greater rage. There's something not right with his head after the mountains and he is on the verge of beating these two to death.

He lays into the wheezing bodies with his feet and the soldiers squirm like maggots, trying to protect their bellies and kidneys, a vain hope with their hands tied behind their backs. The blows rain down one after another.

The kombat kicks one of them in the throat and the soldier gags, unable to breathe. His feet kick convulsively and he fights to gulp in some air, eyes now bulging through the swelling.

The rest of the officers sit in the shade of a canvas awning near the entrance block, watching the punishment as they take a hair of the dog from a bottle of vodka on a table in front of them. Their faces are also swollen, but from three days of continual drinking.

Our political education officer Lisitsyn gets up from the table and joins the kombat. For a while they flail in silence at the gunners with their boots and the only sound is their puffing from the exertion.

We understood long ago that any beating is better than a hole in the head. There had been too many deaths for us to care much about trivia like ruptured kidneys or a broken jaw. But all the same, they were thrashing these two way too hard. We all thieved ! and every one of us could have wound up in their place.

Thieving is both the foundation of the war and its reason for continuing. The soldiers sell cartridges, the drivers sell diesel oil, the cooks sell tinned meat. Battalion commanders steal the soldiers' food by the crate — that is our tinned meat on the table that they snack on now between shots of vodka. Regimental commanders truck away vehicle loads of gear, while the generals steal the actual vehicles themselves.

There was one well-known case when someone sold the Chechens brand new armoured cars, fresh from the production line and still in the factory grease. Military vehicles are still riding round in Chechnya that were sold back in the first war and written off as lost in battle.

Quartermasters dispatch whole columns of vehicles to Mozdok packed with stolen goods, carpets, televisions, building materials, furniture. Wooden houses are dismantled and shipped out piece by piece, cargo planes are filled to bursting with stolen clutter that leaves no room for the wounded. Who cares about two or three boxes of cartridges in this war where everything is stolen, sold and bought from beginning to end?

And we have all been sold too, guts and all, me, Arkasha, Pincha, the kombat and these two he is beating now, sold and written off as battle losses. Our lives were traded long ago to pay for the generals' luxurious houses springing up in the elite suburbs of Moscow.

The blows eventually cease. Those two jackals step back from the gunners, who lie gasping face down on the asphalt, spitting out blood and struggling to roll over. Then the armaments officer steps forward and helps Lisitsyn lift one up, raise his arms and tie his wrists in the noose. They tighten the rope until his feet dangle a few centimetres above the ground, suspending him like a sack, and string up the second guy the same way. They do it themselves as they know that none of us will obey an order to do it.

"Fall out," the kombat shouts, and the battalion disperses to its tents.

"Bastards," says Arkasha. It's not clear who he means, the gunners or the kombat and Lisitsyn.

"Pricks," whispers Fixa.

The soldiers hang there all day and half the night. They are opposite our tents and through the doorway we can see them swaying on the rack. Their shoulders are pressed up to their ears, their heads slumped forward onto their chests. At first they tried to raise their bodies up on the rope, change their position and get a little more comfortable. But now they are either asleep or unconscious and don't move. A pool of urine glistens in the moonlight beneath one of them.

There is a hubbub inside the command post as our commanders down more vodka. At two in the morning they consume another load and all tumble out onto the square to administer a further round of beatings to the dangling gunners, who are lit up in the moonlight.

The officers place two Tapik (TA-57) field telephones under the men and wire them up by the toes. The units contain a small generator and to make a call you wind a handle, which produces a charge and sends a signal down the line.

"So, do you still feel like selling bullets?" Lisitsyn asks and winds the handle of the first phone.

The soldier on the rack starts to jerk and cry in pain as cramps seize him.

"What are you yelling for, you piece of shit?" Lisitsyn screams and kicks him in the shins. He then rewinds the Tapik and the soldier howls. Again Lisitsyn lashes at his shins. And so on for maybe half and hour or more.

The officers of our battalion have turned into an organized gang that exists separately from the soldiers. They truly are like jackals and so that's what we call them, us contract soldiers, who in turn are called 'contras', or sometimes 'vouchers', as we are there to be spent. And the two camps hate each other for good reason.

They hate us because we drink, sell cartridges and shoot them in the back in battle, because every last one of us yearns to get discharged from this lousy army. And since we want nothing more from it than the money it pays us for each tour of duty, we don't give a damn about the officers and will screw them over as the opportunity arises. They also hate us for their own poverty, their underfed children and their eternal sense of hopelessness. And they hate the conscripts because they die like flies and the officers have to write letters informing the mothers.

What else can you expect of the officers if they themselves grew up in barracks? They also used to get beaten as cadets and they still get beaten at their units. Every other colonel of ours is capable of little more than screaming and punching, reducing a lieutenant, captain or major into a moaning, dishevelled wretch in front of junior ranks. And the generals too no longer bother meting out penalties to the colonels but simply hit them.

Ours is an army of workers and peasants, reduced to desperation by constant underfunding, half-crazed with hunger and lack of accommodation, flogged and beaten by all, regardless of the consequences, regardless of badges of rank, stripped of all rights. This is not an army but a herd drawn from the dregs of the criminal masses, lawless apart from the dictate of the jackals that run it.

Why should you care about soldiers when you can't even provide for your own children? Competent, conscientious officers don't stay long and the only ones left are those with nowhere else to live, who cling on to empty assurances that they will be allocated an apartment some day. Or those who cannot string two words together and know only how to smash in the teeth of some young kid! They make their way up the career ladder not because they are the best but because there is no one else. Accustomed from the very bottom rung to beating and being beaten, they beat and are beaten right to the top, teaching others to follow suit. We learned the ropes long ago, the ways of the gutter are the universal language in this army.

Lisitsyn gets bored of winding the Tapik. He puts a flak jacket on one of the gunners and shoots him in the chest with his pistol. The round doesn't pierce the jacket but the impact rocks the body on the rope. The soldier contorts and gasps, his lungs so close to collapse that he is unable to draw breath. Lisitsyn is about to fire again but the kombat averts his arm, worried that in his state of drunkenness he will miss and hit the wretch in the belly or the head.

We don't sleep during all of this. It's impossible to doze

off to these screams. Not that they instil fear in us, they simply keep us awake.

I sit up in my sleeping bag and have a smoke. It was much the same in Mozdok. Someone would get a beating on the runway and I would sleep with a blanket over my head to keep out the light and muffle the cries and I'd think, great, it wasn't me today. Four years have passed since then and nothing changed in this army. You could wait another four years and forty more after that and it would still be the same.

The yelling on the parade ground stops and the officers go back to the command post. The only sound now is the moaning of the gunners. The one who was shot at wheezes heavily and coughs as he tries to force some air into his chest.

"I'm sick of their whining," says the platoon commander from his sleeping bag. "Hey, shitheads, if you don't settle down I'll come and stuff socks in your gobs," he shouts.

It goes quiet on the square and the platoon commander falls asleep. I pour some water in a flask and go outside. Arkasha tosses a pack of cigarettes after me.

"Give them a smoke."

I light two and poke them between their tattered lips. They smoke in silence, no one speaks. What is there to say?

An illumination flare rises in the sky over the police post near the grain elevator, then a red signal flare. A firefight starts. Short, chattering bursts of rifle fire echo across the steppe and then a machine-gun on the roof of the elevator opens up. Our eighth company is holed up on the 22nd floor and from there they can cover half the town. The fighters have no hope of dislodging the police after one of our guys, Khodakovsky, mined the stairs for them.

The machine-gunner has spotted some fighters and looses off short, targeted bursts. After a while the exchange peters out and the police troops send up a green flare to give the all-clear.

The cigarettes burn down. I stub them out and give the gunners a drink of water. They gulp it greedily. I remember that we still have some rusks in our rations — they'll have to suck them now like babies as they probably have no teeth left. The battalion sleeps.

At the morning parade the two gunners are beaten again but not so viciously as yesterday. They no longer squirm and just hang there, moaning quietly. Afterwards the armaments officer unties the ropes and they fall to the ground like sacks of flour. They can't stand or lift their swollen arms. Their hands have gone black and their fingers are twisted. The kombat kicks them a few more times then takes their military ID cards and tears them into shreds.

"If I catch one more son of a bitch with cartridges I'll shoot him without trial. That means every last one of you, old and new. Is that clear?"

No one replies.

"Throw this refuse out of the gate," he orders, nodding to the two prostrate forms. "Don't give them money or travel documents, they don't deserve it. They can find their own way home. I don't need shit like that in the battalion."

The gunners are carried out and dumped on the street. They turn their heads and look up at us as the gates close behind them. They have no idea where to go or what to do. There's no way they'll make it to Mozdok. The fighters will probably get them right here in Argun. If I were them I'd try to reach the police block-post and ask the guys there to put them on a convoy to Khankala, the main base outside Grozny.

The police troops won't refuse since our guys helped them last night. But even then they'll be unable to fly out of Khankala and they'll be left to wander around until they get taken prisoner. We stand in silence. The kombat turns and goes back to the command post.

The gunners sit at the gates like abandoned dogs until

night falls. At dawn I take up my lookout shift in the admin block and the first thing I do is glance onto the street. They're gone.

One morning the battalion gets a visit from the top brass. We've just got up and are washing ourselves from hollow support blocks, knee-high piers for propping up the metal walls of the unfinished meat-packing shop. Each one holds about five litres of greenish water from melted snow, no good for drinking but fine for a rinse.

A captured Mitsubishi off-roader belonging to the regiment commander Colonel Verter drives in with two armoured personnel carriers loaded with humanitarian aid packages.

Colonel Verter steps down from the silver jeep and the battalion is hastily ordered to fall in as if the alarm had been sounded. We come running, still dressing.

"I wonder what's up?" says Pincha, leaning on Garik as he wraps a puttee around his leg. The cloth is black with filth and stinks to high hell. Used to all manner of stench as we are, we wrinkle our noses, unable to fathom how he managed to foul his puttee so badly. We'd only recently had a steam bath and all this time we did nothing except sunbathe half-naked. Then again, Pincha always walks around in several layers of clothing and boots and his feet are usually so dirty you could plant potatoes between his toes. Arkasha tells him he should scrape off the dirt from his feet for blacking his boots and just sell his polish. We never fail to laugh at that one.

It's 45 minutes before morning parade time and no one knows why we have been fallen in. We stand for a while, guessing what might have happened, then a rumour spreads along the ranks that the regiment commander has brought medals and will decorate those who have distinguished themselves.

Medals are good news and we brighten visibly. We don't say as much but we all hope to get one and return to our homes in full splendour. We didn't give a damn about this in Grozny or up in the mountains where the only thing we wanted was to survive. But now peace is within reach and we want to go back to Civvy Street as heroes.

I nudge Lyekha and wink. He'll certainly be able to hang a 'For Bravery' gong on his chest today after being twice commended by the platoon commander before we had even left Grozny. He grins back.

They carry a table covered with a red cloth onto the centre of the parade ground and arrange lots of little boxes and award certificates on it. The medals cover almost half the surface, enough, it seems, for all of us to get one.

It starts to drizzle. A few drops spatter on the covers of the booklets and smudge them. Two soldiers pick up the table and move it up to the wall for shelter, placing it next to the torture rack. We are to be decorated with a gallows as a backdrop!

Pincha thinks our first award ceremony might have offered a little more pomp and ceremony and that the colonel could have arranged a military band.

"I've seen medal presentations on TV and there's always a band playing a brass fanfare," he says. "Otherwise there's no sense in awarding the medals. The whole point is that you get them to a fanfare."

"Yeah, right," I scoff. "And maybe you'd also like the president to kiss your butt while they give it to you?"

"That's not a bad idea," says Pincha, a thoughtful look appearing in his eyes. "I reckon every last one here should be able to pin a medal on his chest. Ever been in Chechnya? Well then, dear private, please accept this 'Merit in Battle' medal. Were you there during the storming of Grozny? Then have 'For Bravery' too. What, you even served in the mountains? Then you must also have the 'Order of Courage'."

"You know they only give 'Courage' to those who were wounded or killed. The most you can hope for is "'Merit in Battle, First Class'."

"Well, that's not bad either," Pincha concedes. "But in that case I expect a fanfare with it."

"D'you know how many regiments there are in just our army group?" Garik asks. "No band could attend all those medal presentations. And how do you know they even have a band?"

We then argue whether the army group has a full military band. Pincha and Fixa are adamant that such a large formation must have one, or at the very least a small company of musicians. How else could they have celebrated the February 23 Defenders of the Fatherland Day in Khankala? There was bound to have been a parade of some kind and you don't have a parade without a brass band.

Garik and Lyekha don't think there is a band in Chechnya. But either way, everyone agrees with Pincha that some extra sense of occasion is appropriate today.

Still the question arises: If there's no band, how do they give generals a proper send off if one of them gets killed?

"Generals don't get killed," says Oleg. "Have you ever heard of even one of them dying here? No, they all sit tight in Moscow."

"What about General Shamanov?" objects Pincha. "He's down here and drives around the front line. He could easily get blown up on a mine. And Bulgakov, he was up in the mountains with us, wasn't he?"

"Shaman won't get blown up," I chip in. "I've seen how he travels. He has two armoured personnel carriers riding with him and two choppers buzzing round overhead all the time. And even though he rides in only a jeep you can be sure the sappers have swept the road ahead. No, Pincha, it's not so easy to blow up an army group commander. Colonels, sure, they get whacked. I've seen a dead colonel with my own eyes and even heard about colonels being taken prisoner. But generals are another matter."

"But they come down from Moscow for inspections here, don't they?" persists Lyekha. "Some generals or other from GHQ fly in and bunches of them get flown around in choppers. They could easily get shot down in the mountains."

"I somehow don't recall a single inspection by generals in the mountains," I say. "Seems to me they just come down in order to collect their war-zone per diem, and even then no further than Khankala or Severny, those places also count as forward positions."

"How is Khankala a forward position?" asks Pincha, confused. "It's well in the rear."

"It might be the rear for you but in the generals' expense claims it's the front line all right. Each day they spend there counts as two, and then they get the presidential bonus of 1,500 roubles a day in wartime, and extra leave. Three trips to Chechnya and they get another "Courage" for their chest."

"I stopped in Severny on my way back from hospital," Lyekha tells us. "It's great there now, not like a couple of months ago. Nice and peaceful, green grass, white-painted kerbs, straight roads. They hooked it up to the electricity recently and now Severny lights up like a Christmas tree in the evening. They even have women there, officers get posted there with their wives. Just imagine, in the evening couples wander round the lanes under streetlights, just like back home. The soldiers there don't carry weapons with them and they get hot food three times a day and a steam bath once a week. They don't even have lice — I asked while I was there. They built a modern barracks there, you know, just like in the American movies. They even have porcelain toilets with seats, white ones, I kid you not! I went specially to use them. And lads, you won't believe me, but they even have a hotel for the generals' inspections we were talking about. Televisions with five channels, hot water, showers, double-glazed windows..."

We listen, mouths gaping, spellbound by Lyekha's description of the Severny base and airport on Grozny's outskirts, as if we were hearing a fairy tale. White porcelain toilets, mess-halls, double glazing. It seems fantastic that Grozny can have a hotel. We saw this city when it was dead, when the only residents were rabid dogs that fed on corpses in the cellars. And now it has a hotel — that surely can't be true?

Severny is only a stone's throw from Grozny's Minutka Square, where the heaviest fighting took place, and from that cross-shaped hospital where we lost hordes of guys. This is a city of death, and as far as we are concerned there should never be any luxury there so that what happened is never forgotten. Otherwise this whole war amounts to nothing but a cynical slaughter of thousands of people. It's not right to build new life on their bones.

We just returned from the mountains where our battalion took fifty per cent losses, you couldn't even raise your head without being shot at. Up there they are still killing and shooting down helicopters while in Grozny our commanders are supposedly taking hot showers and watching TV. We are willing to believe in white porcelain toilets but a hotel for the generals is going too far.

"You're making it up," says Murky. "It can't be true."

"Oh yes it can, I saw it myself."

"Saw it yourself, did you? You, the same person who tells us that herds of generals prance around in the mountains like antelopes? Well that at least can't be true, they'd never leave the hotel."

"I still want to know what happens when they bump off a general," Pincha says, returning to the topic. Lyekha's account has made no impression on him, he took it all for a fairy tale and nothing else.

"If a general dies, do they pay his widow an allowance or not? And how do they pay it, do they bring it round to her home or does she stand in line with the rest of us at the cashier's office at the bases and write letters to the newspapers saying 'please help me, my husband was killed and the state has forgotten me'. There were lots of women like that back at my regiment, struggling through all the red tape after their men got killed."

Pincha's right. When we signed our contract to serve in Chechnya we also saw such women. We got an advance before we moved out and we stood in the same line as them for money. We always let them go ahead in this queue for the state's attention, to receive some elementary compassion and sympathy, out of respect for a mother who gave up her most precious possession for her country, the life of her son. And who got nothing in return, not even money for his funeral.

These women always got brushed off everywhere by the bureaucrats. Now the mothers of Fly and Yakovlev and the others are probably also fighting their way through red tape to get some basic rights.

"Of course they don't stand in the same queue. You can be sure a general's widow gets her payments in full and straight away," says Fixa.

"After all, we're talking about a general, not some worthless Pincha, the like of which they can heap up a hundred a day and not care. But we don't have that many generals. They have to be bred, trained in the academy, educated. I dare say the president himself knows them all by name. Yes, I bet he does." Fixa pauses to consider his latest revelation. "Hmm, I wonder what it's like when the president shakes your hand in greeting..."

Arkasha finally puts an end to the discussion.

"It doesn't matter if you are a general or a colonel," he says. "What's important is the position you hold. To be the widow of the chief of the military accommodation authorities and the widow of a general in command of some military district deep in Siberia are quite different, even though the district commander is higher in rank. And like hell does the president know them all by name, we have countless numbers of generals. Up there in the Defence Ministry they wander round like orderlies and clean the latrines — since there are no ordinary soldiers there the generals have to get on their knees with rags and mess up their dress trousers. I heard this from a colonel who asked us to help file a complaint on his behalf. A general beat him up and broke his tooth so he grassed on him, told them how the general was using stolen materials to build himself a house and had soldiers sweating away for him on the building site. They have their own system of hazing in the ranks, you can rest assured."

I don't believe him, it seems unlikely that they have violent hazing even in the ministry. Then again, why not? Generals are not made from pastry, they were once lieutenants themselves. A couple more wars like this and our kombat will also become a general, get promoted and cudgel us all from up there instead. And what's so special about it?

At last regimental commander Verter comes out onto the parade ground accompanied by the kombat. We fall silent.

"Greetings, comrades!" he shouts, as if addressing a parade on Red Square and not some depleted battalion in Argun.

"Greetings sir," we reply half-heartedly.

"At ease," he tells us, even though it hadn't occurred to anyone to stand to attention.

The colonel talks to us about drunkenness. He calls us bastards and pissheads and threatens to string us all up by our feet from the rack so ingeniously devised by our kombat. He fully approves of this innovation and will advise commanders of other battalions to draw from our experience. And just let any soldiers dare complain to him about non-regulation treatment, for he intends to fight drunkenness and theft in the ranks!

After this he goes on at length about the duty we have fulfilled in the mountains and how the Motherland will not forget its fallen heroes, and such nonsense. He strides up and down on stiff legs, his beer belly thrust forward, and tells us what fine fellows we are.

"Calls us crap, then sucks up to us," Murky comments.

"You know what?" says Arkasha, narrowing his eyes. "He's on his way up. He just got appointed deputy division commander and that means he'll be a general. And for a successful anti-terrorist operation in Chechnya, Colonel Verter has been put forward for the 'Hero of Russia' medal. A guy I know in the GHQ saw the letter of recommendation."

"No way!" exclaims Oleg. "He's a coward! He's only been to the front once. Got half the battalion killed for some lousy hillock and he still didn't manage to take it. His sort should be shot, no way can he become a general and get 'Hero of Russia' to boot."

"Sure he can. It may be a lousy hillock to you but in his reports it's a strategically important height, defended by superior enemy forces. And we didn't throw ourselves at them head on for three days, we executed a tactical manoeuvre as a result of which the enemy were forced to abandon their positions. It's all a matter of presentation.

Don't be so naive. The war isn't fought here but in Moscow. What they say goes — don't you agree that you are a hero? I suppose you'll refuse a medal now?"

No, no one intends to turn down any medals. If each of us helps heave a handful of colonels and generals up the career ladder then let them give us something for our trouble in return.

"I wonder what Verter will do with his Mitsubishi after the war?" Pincha says.

"Don't worry your pretty head about it, he's not going to give it to you," replies Arkasha.

"Now that would be a fine thing. I wonder how he'll get it out of here, on a transport plane probably."

After the colonel's address the awards begin. He stands at the table below the rack and in a wooden voice starts to read out the decoration order of the army group commander.

We wait impatiently, who will be first? Who does the Motherland see as the best and worthiest among us? Maybe Khodakovsky, he never got a scratch but was one of the first to reach Minutka Square during the assault on Grozny. And he fought like a true warrior in the mountains. Or Emil, our Daghestani sniper who crawled fifteen metres one night to the enemy trenches and fired on them at point-blank range. He killed thirteen and came out unscathed, earning himself a commendation for 'Hero of Russia' from the kombat. Or maybe one of the mortar-men, they heaped up more dead than all of us?

After he reads the order, the colonel takes two steps back and lets the kombat forward to the table to hand out the decorations. He takes the first box, opens up the medal certificate and draws a deep breath. We freeze in anticipation, who will it be?

"Private Kotov, step forward!" he announces loudly and solemnly.

At first I don't have a clue who this private Kotov is. Only when he passes through the ranks and trots up to the table with an embarrassed smile and raises a clumsy salute do I realise it's Kot, the cook from the officers' mess. He cooks for the kombat, lays the table and serves up the dishes.

The kombat probably just happened upon his medal first by chance. He might have shown a bit more care, the first person in the battalion to get decorated should be the best soldier or officer.

The next medal goes to the staff clerk, then the transport chief, and then someone from the repair company. We lose all interest and ignore the ceremony, it's clear enough what this is all about.

"Everyone who was in this stinking war should get a medal," says Lyekha. "Cooks, drivers, clerks, everyone, just for being here. Every last one of us has earned that much."

"Right enough," says Arkasha. "And Kot above all."

Standing beneath the gibbet, the kombat awards the next medal to the next 'outstanding' soldier. It suddenly strikes me that he perfectly embodies our state, a gibbet behind his back and medals in his hand for lackeys. For he is the highest authority on this strip of land inside the fence. For us he is judge, jury, prosecutor and parliament rolled into one. Here and now, he is the state. And so it turns out that the state has screwed us over yet again, heaping favours on those who are closest to it and who sucked up to it best.

Khodakovsky and Kot now both wear the same 'For Bravery' medal, although the first could have been killed a hundred times in the mountains and the second risked only dying from overeating.

The only one in our platoon to get even 'Merit in Battle, Second Class' is Garik, and then only because he worked as a clerk for a month in the headquarters. After he is decorated he resumes his place beside us, shifting with embarrassment.

He wants to take off the medal but we don't let him, he earned his gong.

We no longer believe in these decorations, to us they are now just worthless metal. We are far more likely to receive a smack in the mouth from our country than an award that actually means something.

"Hey, Fixa," I say, elbowing him. "It's a right shitty country we live in, isn't it?"

"Yep, it's shitty all right," he answers, picking a blister on his palm.

After the decoration ceremony we are addressed by a representative of the Soldiers' Mothers Committee. A feisty, cigarette-puffing woman of about 40, she is bubbly, big-framed and still pretty. She has a commanding, chain-smoker's voice and can hold her own with us swearing.

We take to her at once and smile as she tells us simple things like how this war has ravaged all of us but how peace is not far away, how we must hold on just a little longer, and how folk back home are thinking of us and waiting. And as proof of this, she says, she's brought us presents. She then distributes to every one of us a cardboard box with lemonade, biscuits, sweets and socks. It's a grand haul.

Later they prepare a sauna for the regimental commander, the officers and the female guest. They steam away a long time before the procession finally troops out and the half-naked officers sit in the shade beneath the tarpaulin and start on the vodka. A sheet periodically falls from the representative of the mothers' committee, giving us a flash of her ample white body. She's not in the least bit shy and soon we forget our own shyness.

Even Arkasha refrains from joking. We like her and no one dares to cast judgement on this woman who came to war bearing gifts for the boys. She is the only person in months who has spoken to us like people and we unconditionally forgive her for the things we'd never forgive the regimental commander: the half-naked fraternization with the officers, the drunkenness, the box with aid intended for us that stands on their table. After all, she could sit tight in Moscow and not risk taking a bullet here. Yet she chose to rattle her way down here in a convoy from Mozdok without expecting anything from us in return.

Before she leaves she gathers phone numbers and addresses, offering to call home or write for us and tell everyone we're alive and well.

She calls us all boys and even "sonny". Arkasha's pockmarked face creases in a smile and he gives her his phone number, tells her they might even meet after the war.

I also come up to her and give her my home number. When she hears I'm from Moscow she snaps off a quick photo of me, hugs a dozen nearest soldiers and then leaps nimbly into an armoured vehicle as the convoy pulls out.

A cloud of dust swirls for a while beyond the fence and settles and we stand like orphaned children by the gates as they close. It really does feel like our mother has left, our common mother, and we soldiers, her children, have been left behind.

"Fine woman," says Arkasha. "Marina's her name. Her son is somewhere here and she's driving round different units looking for him. I feel sorry for her."

The regimental commander is still here and they put us on the roofs on reinforced guard — the brass must see that we are carrying out our duty properly.

We clamber up onto the meat-packing shop, kick away rusty shell fragments that have lain here since some barrage and seat ourselves on black tarred roofing sheets that are baking hot from the sun. We have four of the aid boxes with us and spread the grub out on jackets.

"In the name of the Russian Federation the flesh of

private Fixa is hereby decorated with the Order of the Stoop, Second Class with lifelong entitlement to dig near electricity lines, stand under crane booms and cross the road when the light is red," Arkasha announces ceremonially, and presses a biscuit onto Fixa's chest.

Lyekha sings a fanfare, wipes a tear from his eye and gives the grinning Fixa a fatherly clap on the back as we salute in unison. Then we get stuck into the food, scooping condensed milk into our mouths with biscuits and washing it down with lemonade. Our fingers get sticky and we wipe them on our sweaty bellies, munching away with smiles on our faces. Emaciated, unwashed soldiers in huge boots and ragged trousers, we sit on the roof and gorge ourselves. We've never had it so good.

"Enjoying that?" Fixa asks me.

"Not half. Are you?"

"Couldn't be better."

Two tins of condensed milk, a bag of biscuits, a dozen caramel sweets and a bottle of lemonade. That's our sum reward for the mountains, for Grozny, for four months of war and 68 of our guys killed. And it didn't even come from the state but from mothers like our own, who scrimp and save the kopeks from their miserable village pensions that the state still whittles away to raise funds for the war.

Well to hell with the state, we're contract soldiers, mercenaries who fight for money and need nothing more from it. We'll go into battle right now if need be and they can pin their medals onto their backsides to jangle like baubles on a Christmas tree.

Fixa wipes his milk-smeared hand on Pincha's britches and daintily takes a postcard from one of the boxes. It bears the Russian tricolour and the gold-printed words "Glory to the Defenders of the Fatherland!" Afraid to smear it, he holds it in two fingers and reads aloud:

"Dear Defenders of the Fatherland! Dear Boys! We, the pupils and teachers of sixth class B of school 411, Moscow Eastern District, extend our heartiest congratulations to you on the Defenders of the Fatherland holiday. Your noble feat fills our hearts with pain and pride. Pain, because you are exposed to danger every minute. Pride, because Russia has such courageous and strong people. Thanks to you we may study in peace and our parents may work in peace. Look after yourselves and be vigilant. May God protect you. Come home soon, we await your victorious return. Glory be yours!"

"Are we supposed to be the strong ones here?" Pincha asks, spraying crumbs from his mouth.

"Yes mate, it's about you," answers Garik.

"Good postcard," says Fixa.

"Bad one, it's on glossy paper," I disagree.

"I mean it's well written, you fool."

There is a slight tremble in Fixa's voice and his eyes are misty. What's up with him, surely he's not touched with emotion? Can it be that this tough guy from Voronezh, who usually has no time for frilly sentiment and understands only the most basic things like bread, cigarettes and sleep, things that are as simple as he is, has been moved by a postcard from some children. Well, I'll be damned.

I take the card from him and look at it. It's nothing like those despicable cards they sent us before the presidential elections in 1996. For a while they stopped calling us bastards and sons of bitches and started to refer to us as 'dear Russian soldier' and 'respected voter'. These were the first elections in our life and for three of us in my unit they were the last ones. They didn't get to cast their ballots and died in the first Chechen war before they could fulfil their civic duty.

"This school is in the east of the city, not far from where I live. If you like, after the war I'll drop by there and thank them," I tell Fixa to make him happy.

"We'll go there together," he says. "We'll go to the school together. We have to, don't you see? They remembered us, collected money, sent us aid packages. What for? Who are we to them?" He pauses. "It's a shame Khariton is gone, I shouldn't have driven him on at the hill, shouted at him. Nor should you," he tells Arkasha. "What did you hit him for? He was just a kid. Why did you hit him, eh?"

Arkasha doesn't reply. We sit in silence. Fixa is crying. I fold the postcard in half and put it in my inside pocket. At that moment I really believe I will visit that school after the war.

After the glut of sweet food we suffer a fresh epidemic of dysentery in the battalion. Our stomachs were unaccustomed to normal food and we are stricken twice as hard as last time. The inspection pits in the garage are full to brimming and black clouds of flies circle above them.

Oleg says this outbreak is our bodies reacting now that the danger has passed, we relaxed and sickness is now kicking in.

"The same thing awaits us at home," he says. "You'll see, we'll come home from the war decrepit wrecks with the A to Z of illnesses."

I think there's another reason. The battalion is squeezed into a small area and those same flies buzzing over the pit settle on our mess tins when we eat.

We crouch half-naked in the meat-packing shop, the only place left we can still use. We sit this like half the day, there's no point in putting on our trousers since dysentery sends you running continuously. Sometimes you can't force anything out, other times you jet blood.

"False alarms are a symptom of acute infectious dysentery," says Murky, flipping through a medical encyclopaedia he found in Grozny and carried with him across Chechnya, establishing erroneously that we have symptoms of typhoid, foot and mouth disease, cholera and plague. Now the encyclopaedia itself befalls a terrible fate, being made of soft pages like newspaper, and within two days only the binding is left. Dysentery is the last disease that this fine medical reference book diagnosed in its time.

"Remember how they made us crap on paper?" Garik asks with a grin.

"Oh God, yes," Oleg laughs back.

Before we were sent to Chechnya, the regiment would file out of the barracks twice a week and, company by company, drop its pants after placing a piece of paper on the ground. While a pretty young woman medic walked through the ranks they made us defecate and hand her our excrement to be analysed for dysentery. The cattle must go to the slaughter in good health and our shame at this act bothered nobody.

Now no one shows us such concern. All they do is give us some kind of yellow tablets, one pill between three of us. We take them in turns but this treatment has no effect whatsoever.

"Heavy calibre, take cover!" warns Fixa before loosing off a deafening burst in the pit. Arkasha responds with a smaller calibre, Murky fires single shots. But Pincha outguns us all, straining long and hard before producing a report that would shatter all the window panes in the area if any had still been intact.

"Tactical nuclear warhead with enriched uranium, explosive power equivalent to five tons of TNT," he says, smirking.

"That's prohibited weaponry, Pincha," protests Arkasha with a belly laugh.

At night the battalion resounds to deep rumbling and moaning. The sentries do their business straight off the rooftops, it's too exhausting to run down 20 times a night.

The night sky is illuminated by bright stars and gleaming white soldiers' backsides. Walking under the roofs is hazardous.

My bleeding starts again and my long johns are permanently encrusted with blood. We all have it. Your rectum swells up and protrudes several centimetres. Half your backside hangs out and you sit resplendent like a scarlet flower. Where are we supposed to find wiping material? We strip the remaining scraps of wallpaper from the storerooms and rasp at our poor backsides, inflicting further harm on ourselves, sending blood gushing from our trousers.

War is not just attacks, trenches, firefights and grenades. It's also blood and faeces running down your rotting legs. It's starvation, lice and drunken madness. It's swearing and human debasement. It's an inhuman stench and clouds of flies circling over our battalion. Some of the guys try to heal themselves with herbal folk remedies that end up making many of them only sicker.

"This is our reward from the Almighty," Arkasha says. "The whole battalion has flowers springing from their arses, that's our springtime!"

"What did we do to deserve this?" moans Pincha.

I find a roll of kitchen towel in the admin block and hide it in a pile of rubbish, using it only when there is no one else around. It wouldn't last the platoon even half a day but this way I'm OK for a while at least.

In a bid to fight the dysentery the battalion commander imposes a strict regime of mess tin cleaning. Now after each meal a duty soldier washes the platoon's mess tins. There's no water here and we wash them in the same water we wash ourselves in each morning. Flakes of soap and grease float in the green water with mosquito grubs and we have to scoop away the flora and fauna with our hands to gather enough water for tea.

People start pilfering water again amid the shortage and our position by the gates gives us a strategic advantage. As soon as the water truck drives in we block its path until we have filled every container we have.

Arkasha and Fixa found an old bathtub somewhere and we also use that. The supply officer threatens to have us shot but we still carry out the tub every morning as we go water collecting.

In the recesses of the unfinished meat-packing shop we find more concrete support piers with dips full of murky water. We keep the find secret but people cotton on and we have to mount a guard. It comes to blows as we jealously protect our source.

"It would be better if we were fighting again," says Fixa. "At least there's no problem with supplies then."

That's true enough. The commanders only think about the soldiers when we are being killed by the hundred. After each storming operation they fall us in and tell us what heroes we are and give us normal food and water rations for two or three days. Then once again we get half-cooked gruel for breakfast and a smack in the mouth for lunch.

"But these lulls are still good," says the platoon commander, washing his feet with "dry-fruit water" they call "compote" that we are supposed to drink.

"Warm, dry and nowhere to go. Not even for washing water — look at this brew, it isn't even sticky because it's peacetime."

Peacetime compote is indeed different from the stuff they serve during the fighting. What they give us now during this slack period can be used for anything. You can drink it, wash in it or soak your underwear because it doesn't contain a single gram of sugar or dried fruit, the supply officer traded both commodities for vodka. He does the same during combat phases but not so often, the conscientious fellow.

One day a jeep carrying police officers is shot up near the village of Mesker-Yurt. We are alerted and set off in two armoured personnel carriers, a platoon of infantry and our three gun teams.

The first vehicle churns up great clouds of dust behind it, making it impossible to breathe or open our eyes. The dust grates on our teeth, blocks our noses and coats our eyelashes, eyebrows and hair in a grey film. We cover our faces with bandanas but they don't help and we still can hardly breathe. Bloody weather, impenetrable mud in winter and vile summer dust that turns into dough when it rains.

The jeep stands on a road between fields and has been almost completely destroyed. The fighters waited in the undergrowth and hit it with a rocket launcher. One side has been blown apart; mangled metal and a seat hang out with a pair of dangling legs and some other lumps of flesh. The four guys inside were torn to pieces. The attackers evi! dently raked the jeep with several rifles after the explosion and the other side is peppered with holes where bullets and shrapnel exited.

The local police arrive and there is nothing for us to do except guard the investigators. We leave after a couple of hours.

That evening we are sent again in the direction of Mesker-Yurt. A paramilitary police unit has located the same rebel group that killed the officers earlier. They holed up in the village after the attack and were waiting to ambush us but we never came.

I can't mount my grenade launcher on the personnel carrier, my hands don't respond and the bedplate won't go onto the bolts. My body is like cotton-wool, my fingers can hardly feel the nuts and I fumble to tighten them. I look at them and can't focus properly. I sense that I must not go to Mesker-Yurt today. I'm scared.

Fear fills me gradually, rising in my body like a wave and leaving an empty space behind it. This is not the hot, rushing fear you feel when you suddenly come under fire, this is different, a cold, slow-moving fear that just doesn't recede. Today, near Mesker-Yurt, I will be killed.

"Go and get two cases of grenades," the platoon commander orders.

I nod and go to the tent. The cases weight 15 kilos each and I can't carry two at once, they are slippery and there's nothing to hold them by. I empty my knapsack and stuff one case inside and put the second under my arm and run out of the tent to see the column already driving out of the gate. The platoon commander motions me to stay behind.

I watch them disappear toward Mesker-Yurt and suddenly I am seized by furious trembling. I feel chilled to the bone, my arms are weak, my knees give way and I sit down sharply on the ground. Blackness clouds my sight, I see and hear nothing and sit uncomprehendingly, on the verge of vomiting. I haven't felt such terror in ages.

Fixa is standing near the gate.

"How come you didn't go?" I ask.

"I got scared, you know?" he replies.

"Yes, I know."

He gets his cigarettes out. My hand is trembling so hard I can't even strike a match. What the hell is the matter with me, nothing like this ever happened before? I have to get a grip. The column left while Fixa and I stayed behind and are out of danger.

Our guys come back at night. Mesker-Yurt was taken but our battalion was deployed in the second security cordon around the village and didn't take part in the fighting. The police paramilitaries did all the work and lost ten men.

We didn't take any casualties that night but I still feel that it would have been my last. I want to go home.

I live with fear constantly now. It began that day and doesn't abate. I am scared all the time. The fear alternately turns slowly like a worm somewhere below my stomach and floods through me with a hot flush of sweat. This is not the tension I experienced in the mountains but pure, animal fear.

One night I beat up Pincha for leaving the lookout post before he was relieved and then did the same to two new guys. They didn't hit it off with our platoon and sleep separately in the cook's armoured car. Then the pricks go and brew tea right on the windowsill of the lookout post. Their fire flickers away for all to see and is visible for several kilometres, giving away the position and maybe drawing the attention of snipers. And I'm the one who has to relieve them.

I can no longer sleep these days. I don't trust the sentries and spend most nights in the admin block or on the parade ground. I always wear my webbing yoke stuffed with loaded magazines that I traded for food and cigarettes. I have about 25 magazines and it still seems too few. I also empty a few clips of bullets into my pockets and hang about a dozen grenades from my belt. It's still not enough. If they storm us I want to be fully armed.

One night I relieve the guys on the lookout. I stay away from the window and stand in the room round the corner, motionless for four hours, freezing at the slightest sound outside.

It seems I am alone and that while I am skulking in the admin block the Chechens have silently butchered the whole battalion and are coming up the stairs for me. I hate the generator as it drowns out every other sound. I try not to breathe and strain to hear what's going on in the building.

Sure enough, they're already inside. Brick chunks grate under foot as someone makes his way up the stairs. The

Chechen turns on the stairwell and puts his foot on the last flight. Nine more steps and he'll reach my floor. My heart stops beating. I don't want to shoot because I'll give away my position. I may take one of them out but the rest will know I'm here and will get me with grenades. I won't be able to run away or hide anywhere, they are all around.

"I want to go home," I say out loud and draw my bayonet from the top of my boot. The blade gives out a dull gleam in the moonlight. I clutch the weapon with both hands in front of my face and tiptoe slowly to the stairs, keeping my back close to the wall, trying to step in time with the Chechen.

He's now on the second step. I also take a step. We move our feet simultaneously. Third step, fourth, fifth. He has four more steps to go, three, two... I leap forward and lash out wildly with the bayonet round the corner, striking a deep gash in the wall and scattering crumbs to the floor. A chip bounces down the stairs and hits an empty tin with a clink. There's no one there. I take several deep breaths.

The stairwell is deserted. The Chechens are of course already in the room. While I was fighting ghosts in the stairwell they occupied my position, climbed up the heap of rubbish outside and swung themselves stealthily through the window. Now they are fanning out to the corners. I can't hide any more and so I unsling my rifle, slip off the safety catch and tramp my way noisily toward the room. I kick a brick and it flies off to one side with a deafening crash. My footsteps are probably audible from the street. I give a sharp shout.

My plan is simple. They will hear me coming along the corridor and run out of the room one by one only to be picked off by me. But then I beat them to it, burst in, squat down and circle round like a wolf, training my rifle ahead of me. No one. I'm still alive, thank God!

I stand in the corner again and listen into the night. I

can't see anything from here but snipers can't see me either. And in this corner I have a better chance of surviving if a grenade comes through the window. I crouch down, cover my head with my jacket and switch on the light on my watch. Thirteen minutes of my shift have passed. Another three hours and forty-seven minutes at the lookout.

I hear footsteps on the stairs and freeze. Five more steps. I draw the bayonette from my boot.

I stop talking to people altogether. I don't laugh or smile any more. I am afraid. The desire to go home has become an obsession. That's all I want and I can think of nothing else.

"I want to go home," I say as we have supper in the tent.

"Shut up," says Arkasha.

He gets more wound up than the others by the mention of home. He is not due for demobilization, he has no medals, and in any case if he goes home they'll likely lock him up because of an old bribery charge against him from his civilian days.

We've been halted in Argun for too long and the tension is now being displaced by fear. This spell of rest and recuperation can't last forever, something has to happen. They'll either send us home or back into the mountains.

"I don't want to go back into the mountains," I say. "I want to go home."

"They can't send us back into the mountains," Fixa assures me. "We've done our stint. There are so many different units and so they just send new brigades up there. No, we won't go into the mountains any more. And we can annul our contract any time we like, don't forget."

"I want to go home." I repeat.

Arkasha throws an empty tin at me. I don't react.

We wait.

I pay my daily visit to the medics to get the ulcers on my

thigh dressed. They refuse to heal and continue to grow, having now reached the size of a baby's palm. Smaller ones dot my arms.

There are two new nurses at the first-aid point, Rita and Olga.

Rita is a red-headed broad, well-built and with a drink-toughened voice that was made for firing off her earthy barrack-room jokes. She's one of us and the lads go crazy over her. But I like Olga more.

Olga is small, quiet and over 30 but her figure is still good. She hasn't had an easy time here — women like her have no place among drunken contract soldiers. She's a real lady and remains one even in the midst of war. She hasn't started smoking or swearing and doesn't sleep with the officers. The little white socks she wears under her shoes never fail to fascinate me, femininely dainty and always clean. God only knows where she manages to wash them.

I visit her every day for treatment. She removes the old bandages and inspects the wounds, bending down over my thigh. I stand naked in front of her but it doesn't bother either of us. She's seen countless unwashed guys encrusted in blood and I am in no condition to flirt with a woman anyway.

But it's still pleasant when her cool fingers touch my thigh and her breath stirs my body hair, bringing me out in goose-bumps. I close my eyes and listen to her tapping gently on the skin and I will my leg to rot further so she will have to care for me a little longer. Olga's tender touch is so much like peacetime and her palm is so like the palm of the girl I left behind in the pre-war past.

"Why don't you wear underwear?" she asks one day.

"They don't issue us any," I lie. In fact I am simply ashamed of my lice-ridden long johns and before each visit I remove them and hide them in a corner of the tent.

She sprinkles streptocide on my festering thigh ulcers and spreads pork fat on my arms to contain the others. Two weeks later they start to heal.

We hear a three-round burst of fire. Someone screams over at the infantry personnel carriers.

"Rifles on safety!" I hear Oldie shout. We run over.

It turns out some drunken driver forgot to put his rifle on safety and accidentally pressed the trigger. All three rounds hit home. One ripped off a contract soldier's jaw. He sits on the ground, blood streaming from his smashed mouth into a large, fatty pool on the earth. He doesn't make a sound, just sits there and looks at us, arms hanging limply before him. The pain hasn't set in yet and he doesn't know what to do.

The staff commander tends to him, injects him with painkiller and tries to bandage what's left of the jaw. Jagged splinters of bone tear the gauze as he binds the wound. The soldier starts to jerk so Oleg grabs him by one arm and pins him to the ground while Murky holds the other.

The other two bullets did far more damage, hitting Shepel in both kidneys. He lies on top of the armoured car while Oldie bandages him.

The soldier's breathing is laboured and uneven but he is conscious. Even in the light of the moon his face look deathly pale.

"Pity," he gasps. "Pity it ended like this, I almost made it home."

"Nothing has ended, Shepel," Oldie tells his friend. "Do you hear me, nothing has ended! We'll get you to hospital now and everything will be OK. Come on mate, you'll see."

He applies bandage after bandage, several packets, but he can't stop the bleeding. The blood flows thickly, almost black in colour. It's bad. Shepel no longer speaks. He lays with closed eyes and breathes heavily.

"I'll kill that son of a bitch," Oldie screams.

The personnel carrier leaves for Khankala with the injured men and Oldie goes with them.

"That's the most goddamned unfair death of this whole war," Arkasha says as he watches the vehicle disappear into the darkness. "To go through so much and die here, in the rear, from a stray bullet."

His fists clench and unclench and the muscles in his cheeks twitch.

"What an unfair death," he whispers into the darkness. "So unfair."

They don't let the carrier through at the checkpoint into Khankala. Shepel lies on the top dying while some duty lieutenant demands the password, saying he can't open the swing-gate otherwise. This rear-unit rat who spent the whole war in this field wants the password and couldn't care less that our comrade is critically wounded.

He is afraid to let them through, afraid that the brass will find out and that there will be consequences for him. They are all afraid that for any screw-up they will get sent to the front line. And then they will be the ones bleeding to death on top of a carrier while someone else bars the way to the hospital.

Oldie doesn't know the password and starts shooting in the air in fury, sending tracer rounds over this safe, snug Khankala with its cable television and double-glazing. He fires and screams and begs Shepel to hold on a little longer. They get through the checkpoint and to the hospital but Shepel dies a few hours later. We had failed to stem the bleeding.

They don't let Oldie out of Khankala and would surely have thrown him in one of the infamous "zindan" pits in the ground that captives are often kept in. But there aren't any pits in Khankala because there are plenty of journalists here and they consider it an inadmissible form of torment to keep soldiers in pits, although torment in my opinion is something quite different.

So to avoid antagonising civilians the command has generously allocated some wheeled wagons as detention cells. There are lots of these wagons here, a few for holding our soldiers and the others for captured Chechen fighters.

One of the Chechen ones was dubbed 'the Messerschmidt' after some bright spark painted a white swastika on the side. At night harrowing screams rise from the Messerschmidt as our interrogators extract confessions.

Oldie has landed himself in an unenviable situation. Shooting in Khankala is a serious blunder. The rear commanders were scared witless when he unloaded tracer rounds over their heads and now they want to avenge their embarrassing display by pinning a drunken rampage charge on him.

We manage to visit him in Khankala after talking our way onto a transport run with sick cases. While our medic delivers them to hospital we look for the wagon where Oldie is locked up.

This place is completely different to how we remember. Khankala has grown to an incredible size. It's no longer a military base but a town with a population of several thousand, if not tens of thousands. There are untold numbers of units here, each with its own perimeter fence, and you can get lost here if you don't know your way around. But it's remarkably quiet, as if you are on a farm. The soldiers wander round without weapons and standing upright, now rid of the habit of stooping like they do at the front. Maybe this lot never even heard a shot, their eyes betray neither tension nor fear, they are probably not hungry and have no lice. This really is the rear.

It's a cosy little world, segregated from the war by a

concrete wall. This is the way the army should be, ideal, astounding order. And it's just how Lyekha had described Severny to us, although we didn't believe him at the time. Straight, tarmac roads, green grass and white-painted kerbs, long parades of new one-storey barrack houses, a metal Western-style mess hall with a gleaming semi-circular corrugated roof, clubs, toilet blocks and saunas. Everything neatly swept and sprinkled with sand, a few posters here and there and portraits of the president gazing down at you every other step.

And streetlamps that work, casting light onto officers as they stroll with their wives. Lyekha was right, they actually bring them down here to live.

"I'm off to work, dear, be a love and hand me my bayonet," of a morning. And in the evening: "Have a good day, darling?" wife asks. "Yes, dear, excellent, I killed two Chechens." Some of them even have children with them, and they grow up here in Grozny.

We walk around Khankala, calling out Oldie's name. People stare at us, we are superfluous here in this place in the rear, where everything is subordinate to strong army order. The neatness of it all infuriates me. We walk around like plague victims and survey these well-fed soldiers with hatred. Let just one of them say a single word or try to stop or arrest us and we'll kill the lot of them.

"This place is a goddamned rats' lair," spits Fixa. "Pity we don't have a grenade launcher, we could stroll around and take care of this lot with a few bursts. Oldieee!"

"Oldieee!" I follow.

Finally Oldie's unshaven face appears in a tiny barred window. Fixa gives the sentry some cigarettes and we have a few minutes to talk. We can only see half of his face. We smile at one another and light up. I climb up on the wheel and pass him a smoke and the three of us puff away in silence.

We don't know what to say, loathe to ask how it is in there and what they feed him. What does that matter now, it has to be better than in the mountains.

As it happens, it's quite bearable in there. There are a few mattresses on the floor, he has a roof over his head, it's warm and dry, what else do you need? They don't even beat them here because of the journalists. They should have brought a few journalists into the mountains or to us in Argun when Lisitsyn shot at the soldier on the rack — that would be a hoot. Then they would know what real torment is. But with them it's all zindan this and zindan that. I think they just like the word.

"It's a rest home here," Oldie says with a grim smile as he tells us of his existence. "Mountain air, three meals a day. Pincha would love it. No oat gruel here, they give us proper food from the officers' mess hall. Today, for example, I had meatballs and pasta for lunch."

"Oh really, nice set-up you have here then," says Fixa.

"Can't complain."

I look at his face through the bars and smile. I don't have any particular thoughts, I'm just happy to be here with him and that we are together again. I can't imagine being demobilized without him, or how I will live later without all of them, Oldie, Fixa, poor Igor.

"Shepel died," Fixa tells him.

"I know. I'll find the guy who did it."

"We'll find out who it was, Oldie, I promise."

"No, I'll find him myself. I have to do it, don't you see? If I don't find him, then the deaths of Shepel, Igor, Khariton, Four-Eyes, all of them, will cease to have any meaning? Then they've simply died for nothing, do you see? All of them could just as easily have been killed by some drunk with no retribution, no one bearing any responsibility. If I don't find him then all these deaths are some kind of dreadful crime, plain murder, slaughter of grey soldier cattle, do you understand?"

He is absolutely calm as he says all of this, his expression hasn't changed and retains the same good humour as if he were still telling us about the meatballs he had for lunch. But I know this is not just talk. He will find and kill this guy and he is fully entitled to do so.

The value of a human life is not absolute and Shepel's life in our eyes is far more valuable than the life of some drunken driver who never had a single shot fired at him, was never pinned down by sniper fire, never used his hands to staunch flowing blood, and who never saved anyone's life. So why should he live if Shepel died? How could it be that this person who never experienced the horrors Shepel did was able to go and kill him in a drunken stupor and stay alive himself?

It doesn't seem right. There is no other punishment apart from death because anything less is still life, and so it's no punishment. To shoot a swine of an officer in the back is in our eyes not a wicked deed but simple retribution. Swines shouldn't live when decent people die.

Oldie and Shepel were good mates, they immediately hit it off though they weren't from he same town.

"I understand. We won't touch him," I tell him.

"Did you come here with the medic?" he asks.

"Yes."

"Have we got many wounded?"

"None, just sick. The war is coming to an end now."

"Too bad, I really wanted to go home," Oldie says.

"We won't leave you behind. If need be we'll tear this shitty Khankala to pieces, but we won't leave you. You're coming home with us."

Oldie makes a tired gesture. He has let himself go since he's been here. Maybe Shepel's death broke him somehow or maybe he's just worn out by it all.

"To hell with the lot of them," he says. "It doesn't matter any more. The main thing is that we are alive. I don't care about anything else. After all, a few years behind bars is still a few years of life, isn't it?"

"They can send you down for seven years on these charges, you know."

"So what...It doesn't matter any more."

We smoke another cigarette and then it's time to go. We push a few packs of smokes through the window and head back to the hospital where the transport is waiting for us. Fixa and I turn and see Oldie watching from the window.

We won't leave him behind.

The battalion leaves for Kalinovskya where we are to be discharged. For us, the war is over.

It starts to rain. The tyres of the vehicles squeal on the wet asphalt and rainbows glimmer in spray thrown up by the wheels. I open the hatch and stick my face out under the rain. Large drops fall straight and evenly on my skin. The sun hangs heavily on the horizon and our column casts long shadows in its rays.

And that's it. Peace. This warm, damp day is the last day of our war. Shepel's dead. And Igor, Khariton, Four-Eyes, Pashka, Vaseline, Fly, Yakovlev, Kisel, Sanya Lyubinsky, Kolyan, Andrey...Many of them, a great many.

I remember all of my comrades, I remember their faces, their names. At last we have peace, lads, we waited for it so long, didn't we? We so wanted to meet it together, go home together and not part company until the whole platoon has been to everyone else's home. And even after that we should stay together, live as one community, always close, always there for each other.

What will I do without you? You're my brothers, given to me by the war, and we shouldn't be separated. But we'll always be together. We still have our whole lives ahead of us.

I stand up to my waist in the hatch. Large raindrops roll down my cheeks and mix with tears. For the first time in the war I cry.

Hey Kisel, Vovka! How's it going Igor, Shepel? Hi guys.

I close my eyes and cry.

The runway is deserted. Warm rain falls.

Translated by Nicholas Allen

DENIS BUTOV

FIVE DAYS OF WAR

(August 1996)

To the memory of all the Russian soldiers killed in Chechnya. May they rest in peace.

DAY ONE

A grenade launcher is no joke. The first shot knocked off the radio station. Along with the operator. Good that there was another radio in the fighting vehicle. Bad that the vehicle caught fire after five minutes. I had been asleep and the whole action seemed to happen in discrete bits.

Hands shaking, I pushed another clip into the gun and aimed – the clip fell on the ground. It must have gone in better the second time. I suppose. I don't remember. Lieutenant Sadykov sobbed, slipped down a wall and curled up. When I ran out of ammunition, I turned him over on his back and feverishly searched his cartridge vest for clips. Judging by his smashed chest and open glassy eyes he was beyond help. I've known worse lieutenants. I got a camouflaged figure with beard and clenched teeth in my sights and gave a long burst of about twenty rounds. My palms, stained with Sadykov's blood, stuck to the gunstock.

There'd been twenty-six of us at the checkpoint. Earlier that morning. And then, for some reason, the Chechens decided they needed that mashed, corpse-stinking wreck of a town that had once been Grozny. After one hour of attack there were only ten of us left, and only eight who could still fight. There probably weren't more of them than us to begin with. They just used the element of surprise to good advantage. And their fighters are more experienced. At least, they never walk into fire. Not like Sanya Krivolapov who was lying with a smashed skull alongside Sadykov and some other lads, who'd been inside.

The checkpoint was well placed. Relatively speaking, of course. Well-placed for us, that is. It'd been some kind of office. A smallish, one-floor building made of concrete blocks, with five or six rooms. It had a lot of windows, most of which we'd closed with sandbags. The others made decent firing posts with a good field of vision. The nearest building was 150 metres away. The ruins 50 metres away had been a building too until a self-propelled gun went to work. We weren't too worried about the ruins – they were well mined. We used nearly all our claymore mines there, so we had to use grenades on trip wires for the building. And you can't be sure of them. So we had someone watching that building all the time. We'd been watching it before the attack too. But not hard enough. Now there were two Chechen machine guns there. Maybe more, but we'd counted two for sure. And those machine guns were working us over. Heavy Kalashnikovs, judging by the noise.

Our sniper got hit with shrapnel early on. He died of loss of blood wrapped round his rifle. I am not a bad shot, so I decided to try being the sniper. Curious. I thought before that sniping was an easy job – you look in the sights, train the cross roughly where the heart is, or on the forehead, or wherever, so he is full height and in your sight, line it up, and pull the trigger. Then you put a notch on your rifle butt. But it's not so damn easy when you try. There's no cross as such – there are angles and divisions... I pretty much got the idea of the curve. It's a distance measure. If you shoot from four hundred metres, the figure is small, and you're lucky to hit it anywhere, let alone in the head or heart. And if you're aiming from eight hundred metres? A man is no more than a nit's egg. In size.

Despite the problems, I edged out bit by bit and decided to pick off those machine gunners. I looked down the sights, and thought I saw one of them. I shot and missed. I shot again, and missed. I tried four times and missed every time. Then he opened up with the machine gun – he didn't need to snipe. I only just had time to hit the deck. I figured that sniping was a tough way to earn a living, left the sniper rifle and picked up my own gun.

We were besieged. The Chechens weren't about to try storming us again. We'd shown some fight – got about eight of them. I have a strong suspicion that even Muslims aren't in a hurry to meet the paradise maidens, or not unless they're real fanatics. And we weren't giving them much trouble, as far as I could see. So they'd left those machine gun nests and a few more men on the other side, and cleared off. We weren't about to go anywhere. We didn't know the town, had no idea where our side was. We'd been brought here in an IFV. The driver was now smouldering in its remains and the Loot was lying in the corner with a smashed chest along with the others who had copped it. None of us had a clue where the gun-layer was. Some of ours had copped it outside, from the grenade launcher. He was probably there. There was no map. We'd found a plan of the area around the checkpoint on the Loot's body. But we needed it like a fish needs an umbrella. We were stranded.

We had seven wounded, but most of the wounds were light, except for Rashid Khusnutdinov. He had taken shrapnel in the stomach and his guts were hanging out. We bandaged him and injected him with promedol, but he still died two hours later. He said something in his Tatar, smiled, and died. The most seriously wounded of the others was Tiny – one eye had been blown out and the other blinded. He sat in a corner, saying nothing, crying. There was no one to comfort him, no time and no reason. Pointless. The others had nothing much wrong with them. An arm grazed by a bullet, a scratch on the hip...

No one knew what to do. The machine gunners occasionally gave a burst at our windows. Luckily the building didn't stand too well for them, there were dead zones. The other Chechens, who had gone round the other side, were better placed. As we realized when Murza caught a round in the chest... "and then there were eight". Tiny was out of action. Murza was still alive but obviously not for long. We shot the second-last tube of promedol into him, bandaged him up and put him beside Tiny.

We had a meeting, a quick exchange of views, damn it... a tense exchange. There were four of us. The others were at the windows keeping an eye on the Chechens.

"Well," I said, "what do we do?"

Sanya Kikin (we called him Kika) said:

"What do we fucking do, we break out and go look for ours."

"So you know where ours are?"

"We'll find them."

"Like fuck you'll find them, you dumb arse!"

That was Vagiz getting wound up. He had sat ten years at the same school desk with Rashid in Naberezhniye Chelni. They'd been called up together, served together. Now one of them had copped it and the other was in deep shit, as we all were. We were all wound up.

"Have you got a map? Do you know the town? Where are you going to look?"

"Well, what the fuck are we going to do here?"

"Here we still have a fucking chance. We haven't made contact on time, the brigade will realize something's wrong, they'll come and fetch us."

"Yeh, if the brigade hasn't been fucked over too."

We stopped and thought. No one seriously believed that the brigade could have been "fucked over", but the situation didn't encourage optimism.

"They'd get what's coming to them if they tried that. Anyway, I say we stay here and sit it out."

That was Bull putting his weighty word in. Bull was an optimist.

I agreed with him one hundred percent. We were better off with a slim chance on familiar territory than crawling off Hell knows where with no chance at all. What scared me most was being taken prisoner. Better like Rashid. Or even better like Sadykov. Bang, and you are up there. Lads in the brigade told us how they were at a checkpoint once and got chatting with the locals. The peaceful locals. Yeah, yeah. "Don't be scared of the hand grenade – it's kind to hands." These peaceful locals promised them whatever they wanted: "We'll send you home, give you money for the trip, just quit fighting..." Two idiots believed it and went off at night, took their guns with them. The Chechens sent one of them back later. His nose and lips were cut off and his eyes had been poked out. If that's what the Chechens do with people who surrender of their own accord, what would they do if they caught us? To Hell with that, to Hell with that.

"I agree," I said.

"Me too," said Vagiz.

Kika just shrugged.

"Dumb arses. What are we going to do at night? What about water? What about ammo? What are we going to eat? How long are we stuck here for, anyway?"

"As long as it takes," Bull snapped. "As for all the rest, we'll have to look."

I went off to look in the kitchen first – it had a big water container that got filled once every few days. The kitchen window happened to look straight onto that damned building and the lowest of ten bullet holes in the container was eight or ten centimetres off the bottom. The floor all around was soaking wet. I crawled up to the container, trying not to show myself, and nudged it. Water splashed out of the holes. So it had about ten centimetres of water in it. About six or eight litres. Shared between all of us, it wouldn't even fill our canteens. Bad news.

Psychology... As soon as I realized how short of water we were, I felt thirsty. I tipped a bit into my canteen – about half full, or a bit more. I thought a moment, and decided to wait. I crawled to the corner, where there was a crate of corned beef. There were about twenty cans. Not so bad.

I got carried away and exposed myself. The Chechen gave a burst with his machine gun and it's a miracle he missed. Or maybe he wasn't aiming at me – just decided to give a burst. Anyway, he didn't hit me. Here, you can't help believing in fate. If you are born to hang, you won't drown. You might blow yourself up on a trip wire, but you won't drown.

I curled up in the corner and waited for the Chechens to calm down, covering my balls and head with my gun as best I could. Luckily it wasn't a corner room. In the corner rooms there was a mighty ricochet off the other concrete wall. But here the partition walls were probably made of uncooked bricks, or God knows what. Maybe some sort of homemade bricks. They crumbled and absorbed the bullets.

I crawled back to the central room, to our headquarters... told them how it was. Vagiz and Bull got some more canteens together. I said:

"We need to get the container in here – much more shooting from that fucker, and we'll have no water left. There's less than he's got rounds as it is."

We dragged it in. It wasn't so difficult really. Kika gave a couple of bursts from the other window and got down behind the sand bags. While the machine-gunners worked his window over, we pulled the container out of the kitchen and must have spilt at least a litre on the way. We grabbed a few cans of beef as well.

I sat down, fell back against the wall, and was about to open a can with my bayonet. Suddenly I started shaking. I dropped the can and the bayonet and wrapped my arms round my shoulders. I was shaking as if I'd got malaria. And I wanted to shit like anything, but I couldn't get up. Kuzya noticed, felt in his cartridge vest and passed me a half-pint. I took it and remembered instinctively where we'd tucked the vodka. By my reckoning, we had a lot more vodka than water. Some cause for cheer in this crappy life.

I tore off the seal with my teeth, and took a couple of long gulps. I felt better straight away, picked up the can and opened it. The Chechens were shooting now and again, lazily. The others sat round, chewing. I chewed as well, though I didn't particularly want to. No bread and no water. Well, a bit of water, but not much. Almost none. And God knew how much longer we'd have to sit there. We should go easy on the meat too. I said so to the lads, and they agreed, but carried on eating. I put my can on one side, still two-thirds full. It was surprisingly good beef, not the string and jelly they brought us last time.

I went for a shit. It must have looked funny – I wiped my backside and moved off squatting all the way to the door. I looked in at the wounded. There was only one of them now. Murza wasn't wounded any more. He was dead. Tiny was unconscious. The corpses were still there. And it was

August, not the coolest month in Chechnya. There would be a stink soon.

I ducked over to Bull. He was watching the machine gunners. We watched them in pairs. So there were four of us on guard in total – two in each corner room. And five relaxing.

We smoked.

"Murza's dead," I said.

"It's his own fault." Bull sucked on the cigarette. "He shouldn't have fucking strutted about like on parade."

None of us liked Murza. He was greedy and dumb. Even the other Tatars didn't mix with him. No one remembered his first name. Just called him Murza. I think his surname was Murzayev.

"We could do with an extra man, though."

"No shit," Bull agreed. "We could. But not Murza. How's Tiny?"

"Unconscious."

"It's a shame about him."

It really was a shame. He was a good soldier and a good lad. He would have a hard time being blind.

"OK, go eat. I'll be here."

Bull ducked down and went, and I stayed with Vasya-Altai. I used to think, almost in earnest, that Vasya-Altai couldn't speak Russian. Then I decided that he couldn't speak at all. He hadn't said a word for the two weeks I'd known him. He was silent now. And I was silent. The Chechens were silent too. We were all silent. Grey silence.

DAY TWO

Tiny shot himself that night. Blew half his head off. I was on duty, watching the building. I heard shots inside and rushed to the room where the The heat was overpowering. By evening we'd drunk nearly all the water we had left. There was a definite smell of decay from the room where the corpses were. Vasya-Altai broke his silence. He swore in Russian, and something that wasn't Russian, for an hour. Then he was silent again.

DAY THREE

The third day without sleep. I was dozing off towards morning when the Chechens started firing like mad. I sprang up all haywire, not realizing that the Chechens weren't shooting at us. There was a battle going on out there. And who could be fighting the Chechens? Only our side.

I rushed into the corner room, with windows on that damned building where the Chechens were. We decided to give our side some support, if only moral. We started firing all the guns we'd got at the windows where the machine gunners had been. I fired off two clips and slapped my pockets, but found no more. I had to run to the morgue room, where we had spare guns, the sniper rifle, and cartridge vests from the dead men. You had to breathe through your mouth in there.

The battle ended while I was looking for ammunition. An IFV came out from behind the building and accelerated towards us. I just had time to think how we would fight back if it was full of Chechens. But the vehicle came racing up, turned sideways-on, and a scruffy soldier looked out of the hatch and shouted: "Who the fuck are you?!"

It turned out to be a mechanized regular army unit. They were on their way to relieve their own checkpoint and ran into us. Or rather into the Chechens, who had us pinned down. We were lucky.

DAY FIVE

I flew from Khankaly to Mozdok. From there, they say, they'll send us home. On board we had equipment, fifty air force and army, and thirty dead lads. We'll be flying home soon. All together.

HOW DREAMS DON'T COME TRUE

Fire! Smoke cutting my eyes. The APC is burning. I'm burning! Cartridge boxes bursting. Must get out, jump now! I can't! My legs! My legs are caught! I'm burning!!! The pain!!! No!!! Harley! Harley, you fucker!!! Pull me out!!! No more!!! No more!!!

"Denis! Denis!"

I sit bolt upright on the bed. At home. The sheet is wet, I'm wet too. I'm drenched in sweat, damn it.

"You're keeping me awake again. You're shouting in your sleep."

It's my brother. We share a room. He hasn't had a quiet night since my discharge. Unless you count the nights when I don't come home. But that isn't often.

"Sorry, Sergei."

"It's OK..."

I go to the bathroom, put my head under the tap. I don't want to sleep any more. I wouldn't sleep at all if I had the choice. Mum asks why I drink so much. Because when I collapse drunk, I don't dream. That's why.

It's cool in the kitchen, the top window is always open. I stand by the window and light a cigarette. I look out at the night.

"Good luck, Mucks!"

"Good luck, Den!"

"Hope it all works out for you!"

"Good luck, Den!"

"Good luck!"

"Good luck..."

Mucks, they called me in the regiment. First it was Mucker, and then they shortened it to Mucks. I was respected in the regiment. For what? Maybe because I tried to be... well, fair, I suppose... to be reliable... to be... It didn't always work, but at least I tried. To be human. Not a Rottweiler. Many in our brigade turned into Rotts, real beasts, who didn't care what they savaged – a wolf, another person, their own puppy. Rotts were respected too – respected because feared. I saw how the faces of the young conscripts changed when they heard Mamai's voice. Though Mamai isn't really a bad lad. He has just lost it. He was shell-shocked three times, not badly, but still three times. The slightest touch sets him off, like a good motorbike. There was some bullying in our regiment but nothing like what I found when I first joined the brigade. I had done four months by then. And I waltzed my way to the brigade, like a dork. There weren't many Rotts in our regiment, most of them were in the SpecOps: the Special Operations Group. Their commander was a real Rott.

I got the send off... They gave me a good send off. I remember vaguely how they opened the gates, put a clean towel under my feet. To wipe my feet clean. A daft tradition, really. They took me all together to the bus station, put me on the bus. I remember getting off for a slash in Budennovsk. I was nearly sober by Pyatigorsk. My head was thumping, so I went to the station buffet and had some more vodka. I wasn't going straight home. I was going to relatives in Cherkessk first. When I was ready to go home, striking miners in Rostov blocked the railway, knocking their helmets on the rails in protest. So I figured that if I took the train I'd maybe only get home in three months. I wished I could go by train. But that would be much too long, so I went and got a ticket for the plane. A silver bird with silver wings.

At the airport in Minvodi I went out on the porch for a smoke. There was a captain there. He said:

"Hello there, rekky."

"Hello," I said.

"Going home?"

We got chatting. He turned out to be the chief military officer at the airport.

"A quick hundred grams?" he said.

"Why not?"

I had four hours till the plane. They had to load me on, like special cargo. I slept the whole flight. Got out of the plane, walked to the terminal. And as I came out of the terminal, walking to the bus stop, I heard them call me. My father and brother. Crikey. My brother had grown up so much in two years... I didn't even recognize him at first.

We went home. Home! Where we all wanted to go, where all our dreams were. Home, home! "The wind'll whistle it behind the barracks, the carrier clanks its tracks: 'Home! Time to go home!'" What a lovely song. Home...

I wandered around the flat like a lost soul, remembering how I had lived there two years ago. In a past life.

"Can't sleep?"

My mother. She smelt the tobacco smoke. I forgot to shut the kitchen door.

"Yes, Mum, can't sleep."

"Another bad dream?"

"No, Mum, I'm fine. Just don't feel like sleeping. Everything is OK, Mum. Go to bed."

"You've been in the army?"

"Yes, here's my service card."

"That's good, we need people with army experience. Where were you?"

I had come about a job. To a private security company. A job as a security guard. I saw the advertisement. The first month I drank non-stop. Then the money ran out. I was ashamed to take money from my parents, but I took it anyway. Not for vodka – for cigarettes and other little things. I got about four calls in the month from various police branches – the beat, home and office security. I told them all the same thing – sorry, I have given the Interior Ministry two years and that is enough, I'll look for something else.

"In the internal troops."

"Where exactly?"

I didn't want to go back to college, but Mum persuaded me. Objectively, I'm no longer fit to be a student. But she persuaded me. I re-registered. For an accounting course, for fuck's sake. I finished two years of the economics faculty and went back to fourth-year accounting. I don't envy the firm that takes me as accountant.

"In reconnaissance."

"A-a-a... Reconnaissance? Special training, hand-to-hand?"

"Yep. Special training and hand-to-hand."

"Meaning... you were on combat missions as part of a unit...? You fought?"

"Sure."

"Sorry, we can't take you."

My mouth fell open

"Why?!"

"You all come back from there funny in the head, and we handle firearms. Who knows what crazy stuff you might do with a real pistol."

I looked at this jerk in specs without saying anything. He started to fidget, seemed to feel awkward. I suppose he thought that he was about to get a dose of behavioral inadequacy "from there." I burst out laughing. I remembered the crazy stuff I did with machine guns. A REAL pistol... as if those machine guns were toys. I slept with my rifle and went to the toilet with it. And he talks about a real pistol, by God! I was bent double, crying with laughter. The jerk must have thought I was having hysterics. What if he tries slapping my face, I thought. The thought bent me even further. I took out a handkerchief and wiped my eyes. The twat offered me a glass of water, meaning "drink this you'll feel better". I got up, thanked him for our interesting and rewarding conversation, emptied the glass over his neatly combed head, took my documents and left.

"I want to go home! Mucks, do you know how good it is at home? Do you know how they miss me there?"

"I know, Harley, I know. They miss me too."

Bullshit. No one missed me. Except family. Civilian life, which I had been dying to get back to for two years, which I thought and dreamt of, turned out shitty. You haven't got any money? You haven't got what it takes. You were in the army? You couldn't get out of it, you thickhead. You were in the war? You total loser.

There were friends, who were glad to see me back, but we don't understand each other any more.

"What's war like?"

"Is it frightening?"

"Did you kill anyone?"

"What is that like?"

"Tell us......"

I told them. When I was drinking, when I was half-numb. During one session I told them why it's better to strangle a guard than to cut his throat, and after that the girl I liked stopped seeing me. She just put the phone down and didn't answer the door. I suppose she didn't like the physiological details.

Once we were drinking in a student hostel on the edge of town. We went to the neighbouring room for some reason, and the neighbours turned out to be Chechens. I was sitting bare to the waist, drinking vodka, not saying anything. One of the Chechens poured wine in my glass and I threw the glass out of the window. I don't remember why I didn't leave. Probably because my friends were there. I suppose that's why. I sat and took it. One of the Chechens pointed to my identification badge – "death tickets", we called them – and said: "Next time you come, take it off at the door". I snapped. They had to drag me out. Good job they did, or I'd have killed him and gone down. For a Chechen.

I switch on the kettle, light another cigarette, remember to close the door this time.

When I got to Cherkessk I went for a walk around the town.

I used to go there every summer, until 1994. It is a quiet, green place. It has its charm. You walk down the street lined with apricot trees, plum trees, mulberry. You can climb up a tree and eat as much as you like.

I was waiting at the stop for a trolleybus. Bang, bang! The diesel backfiring on a lorry. I reacted like one of Pavlov's dogs – jumped into the bushes straightaway, feeling for my gun. I was ten seconds feeling for it before I realized how stupid I looked. There were several people at the stop, all staring at me. I can imagine how it must have looked – a lad is standing there, suddenly he jumps in the bushes, like he is having a fit, and peeps out at them. I got up, dusted my trousers, put on an indifferent look, as if I had done it on purpose. I didn't get on the trolleybus, I walked instead. My ears must have been glowing red.

In my hometown I was walking in the park with a girl. The one who didn't like hearing about knobbling guards, as I learnt later. She didn't understand why I suddenly stopped, said to her "Don't move!" stood like that a few seconds, then laughed and walked on. I didn't explain: I had taken a rusty bit of metal with wires coming out for a booby trap.

At least dogs like me. And I like them. The more I get to know about people, the more I like dogs. I don't like people, at all. People in general. With very few exceptions. I can't like people who say to me: "You couldn't get out of the army? You must be poor, and if you're poor you're dumb." I can't like people who say to me: "You're still young and wet behind the years. When you been around as long as me..." I can't like people who eat in expensive restaurants every day. Even if it's only me being envious, even if I'm told that they earn their money honestly. All the same I can't like them. I can't like people who can hit a dog. I can't like people with empty eyes.

I won't die young, I know that. Because it is too late for me to die young. I am not young any more. We're twenty seven, and you can't wash us clean (with vodka or water) of what we've seen. I haven't even got to twenty five. But I'm not young any more. I don't say that to anyone because they would laugh. I don't like those people. And I don't like people who feel sorry for me. I don't like myself either.

But, please, no pity. Give yourself a chance.

Translated by Ben Hooson

ROMAN SENCHIN
24 HOURS

I

"Hey, Rom, wake up! Time for you to get up. Senchin!" Terenty is in a tizz, his voice lowered to a hoarse whisper. "Do you hear?"

■ "I hear. Piss off..."

Five seconds of silence, then again:

"Ro-om..."

I open my eyes. A blinding white light is making them hurt. I shut them tight and shield them with my hands.

"Take that torch away, you daft bugger!"

"The electricity's off."

"So that means you have to go around blinding people with a torch?"

Sleep is banished. My wakening has come between me and the warm, colourful images I was seeing in my dreams. They are no more.

"You stinking, subhuman, half-witted baboon..." I mutter as I pull on my trousers.

Terenty, a very young sergeant, shines his torch for me and takes this in.

"What's the weather doing out there, Little Pig?"

"Raining."

"Shit..."

"Okay if I go? I need to get back to the control room."

"Piss off, brown-noser."

Letting the beam of light precede him, Terenty leaves the dormitory. I grope around under the bunk and find my boots. My foot wrappings haven't dried at all, and neither have my tunic or trousers. The bedding feels damp and slimy, as if a gigantic slug has been wallowing about on it. The rain finds its way into everything and turns it into a glutinous, stinking mush... Everything reeks of rot and decay, of rancid sweat and putrefaction from unwashed foot wrappings.

Pellets of December rain rattle against the window. The scrawny birch trees round the drill square creak in the wind.

Reluctantly, but with a rapidity born of practice, I get dressed and roughly make the bed — in four hours' time I'll be back to catch up on my sleep.

Walking past the utility room, my eye catches the dark shape of a full dress uniform hanging on the mirror. Of course — Baldy is getting out today. That will leave just two from our draft: me and Melon.

The drying room is cool and damp. My parka, which I had carefully spread over the radiator, is barely warm and in no way has it dried out. How could it have? The perpetual dampness keeps even the firewood from burning properly, and there's no paraffin or petrol. Baldy isn't being driven to the station in our Skull off-roader: instead a communal truck is coming round all the border posts to collect demobbed guards. Sal said we have just enough petrol for a couple of sorties if the alarm goes off.

"You've got four minutes, Rom," Terenty announces sententiously the moment I appear in the duty room.

"Shut up and give me the magazines."

Our little sergeant gives them to me already full of rounds, along with a flare pistol in its holster and a torch. I help myself to an assault rifle from the cupboard, thread the cartridge pouch and holster on to my belt, and shove a communications receiver inside my jacket.

"Right, time to report for duty." Terenty adjusts his uniform, tightens his belt, checks that his cockade is directly aligned with the bridge of his nose, and heads for the office. You'd think he was on parade.

"You really are a daft bugger, though, Terenty," I shout after him.

Never mind, the sharp corners of his military college training will be knocked off soon enough. He'll charge around saluting everything for a month or two yet, then he'll wise up and aim only to eat and sleep as much as he can, while slogging his guts out as little as he can.

Lieutenant Piksheev, a short, scraggy little fellow, rolls eyes still bleary with sleep and barks out the orders. In two years I have been able to make out only the beginning: "You are to proceed to guard the state border..." He explains where I am to proceed to and how, what is to be done in the event of discovering the enemy, which installations are to be guarded with particular vigilance, etc. As he drones on, I start drifting back to sleep, hearing not his monotonous voice but the babbling of a brook with soft tall grass all around and cold water splashing in the sunlight. How I long to lie down in the grass, to bury my face in it, to dream... I am just about to topple over to my right on to the plaster model of a border marker when Piksheev's recitation comes to a halt.

"Orders received and understood," I respond robotically. "Proceeding to guard the state border..."

By the porch, directly beneath the water streaming from the roof, stands Vovka Shatalov who looks after our livestock. Evidently sloping around outside for four hours in weather like this is too much even for a tough peasant lad like him.

He can't wait to dart back in to the, admittedly only relative, warmth and comfort of our post.

Terenty perfunctorily supervises the unfastening and fastening of magazines and Vovka, his sodden boots squelching, his parka bloated with water and his fur hat awry, rushes inside. He is no longer on duty: I am.

My one consolation is that any day, a week from now at the outside, this will all be over. It will be my turn to sprawl drunkenly on the top bunk in a railway compartment as every passing minute brings me nearer to home. The wheels will drum, the carriage will sway, smoothly, gently, and I will be feeling on top of the world. The demob-happy ex-conscripts will be bawling songs, and the stations flying past will at first have Finnish names: *jarvi*, *ljuli*, *pohji*; and then Russian names, and finally I shall see Devyatkino, Petersburg, Metro. Home!

The one good spot for sheltering from the rain without losing sight of the door of the border post is the unloading booth on the edge of the drill square. A James Chase novel is concealed behind one of the roof beams, but I'm unlikely to be able to read it: my torch battery is low. The torch will only function on continuous beam for another twenty minutes or so before it goes out completely.

We have power cuts nearly every night. The electricity doesn't stay on long enough for Melon to recharge the batteries supplying the Border Security System, let alone all the other electrics. Life without electricity is dull, and if you're the cook it's one hard slog. Poor Lydia Alexandrovna, the warrant officer's wife, keeps the stove fuelled herself and swears endlessly: the firewood won't burn, the water won't boil, and the kitchen is full of smoke. Our former cook, Fly, was long ago reclassified as a marksman and by now has probably forgotten even how to cook pasta. Not counting the two officers and Warrant Officer Khomutenko or, as from today, Baldy, there are twelve of us to man this border post. Ideally there would be twenty, and we could just about manage on sixteen. There aren't enough of us to do the work. We kip for three or four hours, go on sentry duty, get a couple of hours sleep, kit on again, grab a rifle, and patrol fifteen Ks of the System at the double. Sometimes the regulation eight hours of sleep gets spread thinly over a whole day.

The unloading booth isn't much help. The roof leaks, of course, but not too badly, and yet the air itself is so laden with moisture that your parka soon feels as if it had been dipped in a puddle. Your hat gets sodden and starts pressing down on your head. I lean against the brick wall and begin to drift off. Warm, gentle waves raise me up as a long-awaited guest and carry me away to a place where, I know for sure, I am going to feel good. And then, amazingly, I find myself back in my room, my own little room as narrow as a pencil-box with the window looking out on to the main road. I'm standing by the window watching the passers-by streaming along the pavement and I start counting them but soon give up. What a lot of splendid cars in bright colours, powerful four-wheel drives which put our Skull to shame. Blocks of flats stretch endlessly away to the horizon, seven, nine, twelve storeys high: a far cry from the pathetic two-storey shack of our border post. It's a miracle! I cast my eyes round the room: my television, my tape-recorder, my telephone — they're all there. And my divan! I'm going to collapse on to it now, at long last I am going to sleep and sleep and sleep!

Even before the door has creaked behind me I am out marching over the square with my eyes shut. I can't unglue them immediately, can't drag myself up out of that sweet vortex. The divan reluctantly comes apart at the seams and the insistent little hammer blows of icy raindrops dissolve my room.

"Hey, Rom!" Terenty yells from the porch.

"What?"

"The transport's on its way from 'Aphrodite'. D'you hear?"

"Fuck the transport!" My instinct is to loose off a short burst straight at him. "Get lost, moron!"

"Piksheev ordered..."

"And fuck him too. Bugger off!"

Terenty shifts from foot to foot on the porch, mutters something that escapes me and disappears. The bastard! I was miles away. I was in heaven! What's he on about anyway? Everyone will be wide awake half an hour before the transport gets here without my having to do anything. They will spill out on to the porch. You don't just say "So long" to someone who's being demobbed. There are songs to be sung, the demob guy's farewell cigarettes to be smoked, the truck to be pushed out the gates. Mind you, that's not going to be so easy when we're this short on manpower.

On the one hand, I feel envious — of course I do — that another of our intake is heading back to freedom while I am left behind to languish here, but on the other hand, bidding farewell to Baldy will help to break up my stint of sentry duty. I'll get to spend almost one hour of the four in the company of fellow human beings; I'll smoke like a chimney, maybe sing a bit, get to shove the truck. Being with other people does make time pass faster.

Smoking is your greatest craving, and the desire most difficult to satisfy. Smokes are a constant hassle, and you dream about them more often than you actually smoke them. The mobile shop arrives a couple of times a month and the cigarettes it offers are nearly always the expensive sort, so that you can afford to buy only ten or fifteen packs, which only last a few days. Of course, you also fancy getting your teeth into something tasty: biscuits, vacuum-packed frankfurters, chewing-gum... But when they have cigarettes those are the first off the shelves.

What would I like to do right now? Chain-smoke, obviously, only I'm clean out of cigarettes: not even a fag-end for a black moment. I can only dream. Okay, I do have three packs of Bond in my briefcase, but those are sacrosanct. They're reserved for my demob send-off.

"Hey, Rom, still alive?" Melon appears round the corner of the hut.

"Just about. Are you stoking today?"

"Oh yes..."

"Not exactly hot, is it? In fact, it's freezing in the dormitory."

"The boiler keeps going out." Melon sighs. "We could use a couple of litres of paraffin."

I want him to stay for a bit longer, to chew the fat.

"What's the time?"

He shines a torch on his watch.

"Twenty-five to."

"Fuck, I've only been out here for half an hour." I scowl. "Wake them all up in there. The truck will be here soon."

"You want me to get them out to entertain you?" Melon grunts understandingly, and disappears into the hut.

He's a really great guy, good-natured in spite of all the crap of army life. The others turned nasty long ago. They're as like as not to fill you in, if they don't think up some greater evil. Melon is virginal and child-like, he reminds you of home. Perhaps that's why I'm drawn to him. He does his job, doesn't arse-lick, and doesn't try too hard. Right now he knows more about the System than anyone else, which is why they aren't letting him go. Our Technician Commander is pretty raw; he needs to teach himself the basics before he can teach them to anyone else, so Melon is being held on to until the last possible minute, to keep the entire security system from packing in. Even so, I don't think the army will last much longer anyway. There simply won't be anyone to draft.

We used to have eleven Dads here, conscripts completing their last year of service. Then there were seven Pheasants (the spring draftees), and a total of nine guys in our intake. There are three new Pheasants now who have passed the twelve-month mark, five of our Sons from last year, and two very new lads from just last spring. When Melon and I are demobbed, touch wood, there will be just ten men left. To make matters worse, one of our Sons is on compassionate leave now on family grounds, and another is in hospital (the dickhead slipped and broke his collarbone). But, for Christ's sake, to do the job we need three sentries to cover the twenty-four hours (each on duty for two four-hour periods), two men to patrol the right flank of the monitoring strip, and two for the left. That's already seven. Another two on duty in the border post itself, monitoring the equipment for twelve hours at a stretch. That makes nine. In theory, two stokers. It's not too cold at the moment so Melon is coping on his own, only heating the place at night. We need a cook, a stockman, a couple of drivers... They shuffle us around, but when the alarm sounds there's sometimes nobody to send to check it out.

And we get alarms, the siren sounding, all the time. Then we have to race out in the Skull to the System: the station CO, the Technician Commander, Melon, a driver (needless to say), and there's supposed to be a dog handler with an alsatian, only we haven't got a single alsatian left: they've all died. We can't even scrape together five guards to send in the off-roader to hunt down an intruder. What sort of a dragnet is it anyway if five men are spread out over several kilometres? An intruder could easily slip across, no sweat. If he knew how few of us there are, he would just stroll it.

They're finally stirring. In the windows of the office and the dormitory I see the faint glimmer of torches and cigarette lighters. They have woken up and are getting ready to see Baldy on his way. To civvy street. Well, no. Actually it's a long way yet to civvy street. He can look forward to being put through the wringer back at the Unit: turning in his belongings (as listed in the inventory), getting his discharge certificate from HQ, this and that. And you can simply end up in a cell at the last minute. The bloody-minded officers in the Unit can put you on a charge for the least thing, and instead of riding off on the train you'll be sitting in a cellar, and being marched around in your demob full dress uniform under guard.

I'm in no hurry to leave the unloading booth. I keep an eye on the door of the main building. Even if Piksheev did catch me dozing off in here, or wangling a hot potato in the kitchen (and if the electricity was working I surely would be in pursuit of scoff), there is nothing all that terrible he could do. He could rant and rage, or at worst give me an extra four hours on duty, although that's unlikely: we're all so shagged out we might make a right balls-up of everything. Our sad little officers know that perfectly well. To be fair, they don't have such an easy life themselves.

I can't remember when I last got the regulation eight hours of sleep without interruption. There was a time when we occasionally had Sundays off. On Saturday we scrubbed the rooms, cleaned our weapons, then took ourselves off to the scorching steam room of the bathhouse with a cold fruit drink to follow, and on Sunday crashed out all day or watched the box. When the numbers are up to strength you get to take it easy now and again. The way things are now, though, we don't even scrub the duty room that often. We crawl into the bathhouse only to sluice off the dirt, and the TV stands in the Lenin Room covered in dust and forgotten. All we want nowadays is to get something in our bellies and fall into bed; we don't even have the energy to spruce up our dress uniform properly. You can forget inserts in the epaulettes, aiguillettes, stripes, charms made from rounds, cap peaks stylishly curved, fit for a general! We don't care what rags we wear: we just want to get out of here as soon as possible and back home. What we're going to find there, we prefer not to think for now. We'll find that out soon enough.

A group of the lads have piled out on to the porch carrying torches. They're all smoking, puffing away loudly, inhaling, enjoying. A guitar clonks against the railings, the strings resonating piteously. Among the grubby parkas and shapeless pancakes of the perpetually wet fur hats, Baldy's greatcoat stands out, and the green peaked cap dangling from his left ear.

There is a quiet but excited babble of voices husky from drowsiness or colds. They are staring at Demob Man like lepers eyeing someone in good health, as if they want to tear the clothes off him and put them on themselves. Baldy is conscious of the envy. He feels embarrassed. These minutes are trying for him, but he can put up with it — they are, after all, his last few minutes in this place.

"Any smokes left?" I ask, crossing to the porch. "Where's the demob stock?"

Makar gawps at me, blinking idiotically and hiding a cigarette butt in his fist. He is a young, lanky lad, as scrawny as someone with dystrophy, conscripted only last spring and eternally bewildered, scared and hungry.

"Come on, Makar, bring that stock here at the double!"

"Oh, okay!" He rushes off to the main building. The door's new springs slam it shut.

"All right then, Baldy? Kit all packed?"

"Well, yes..." He glances at me. "Perhaps it'll be your turn tomorrow," he offers in consolation.

"Perhaps," I agree curtly.

Balton, our admittedly rather shitty guitarist, flicks away a fag he has smoked down to the filter.

"Well, guys, how about a song?"

"Let's do it," Melon endorses the suggestion. "Let's raise the roof, Baldy, one last time."

Balton plucks the strings, tightens the pegs.

Makar reappears carrying a wooden rack that usually houses fifty rounds, primers uppermost, in specially drilled holes. When you report after your spell of duty you return the rounds you've removed from the magazines in this rack, the idea being to show the officer that everything is hunky dory and you have not used your weapon. Now, however, the holes hold cigarettes rather than rounds. This is the demob stock. The soldier leaving treats those left behind to the smokes.

"Oh, thanks guys for leaving a whole three for your Dad." I shake my head reproachfully as I pull out the cigarettes, tuck two away in the inside pocket of my tunic, and avidly light up the third.

The song, which is actually pretty stupendous, trails along, ragged and uncertain. Only in the chorus do the voices become confident, predicting with vindictive mirth:

If you haven't yet, you surely will,
And if you have, you'll not forget
Those seven hundred thirty days
The army made you grunt and sweat.

Surrounded by the group and standing next to our guitarist, Lyson watches Balton's fingers repetitiously strumming his unsophisticated three-chord accompaniment. Baldy sings along half-heartedly, the look on his face mirroring that of Lekha Orlov, whose teeth are giving him hell. Orlov is our Son and we have nicknamed him Canary because his surname means 'Eagle'. It's implied he can call himself Eagle after he has seen us demobbed. Right now, with his swollen cheek half closing his eye, he is doing his best to join in the singing, his eyes riveted on Demob Man. Hard luck, Canary, you've got one more year to go. Only a year... only one more infinitely long, never-ending year.

Our little Pheasant chicks really are not to be envied. I remember seeing off their granddads, indeed their great granddads, when there seemed no prospect of surviving the more than one and a half years which lay ahead, and when those who had suddenly found they had survived through to demobilisation seemed superhuman, fabulous heroes who had been through fire and water and ordeal by sounding brass and all manner of murderous misbehaviour.

And yet, these years of purgatory will pass, have no fear, and like me you will look back in amazement, hardly able to believe it's all over. Almost all over.

The main thing then will be just to make it through those last two or three weeks, somehow to hold out, somehow to endure to the end. You will be far from certain that you are going to hold out through those last weeks, right up until the moment you hold in your hands the telegram confirming your demobilisation. Your disbelief about sticking it out will be even stronger than your earlier disbelief about surviving those two long years now behind you. Two years, of which three months were muddled through in the Unit on so-called "basic training", and the other one and a half years and a bit at this border post. Day after day in the same place, surrounded by the forest and the marshes, seeing always the same twenty or so people. Every day going through the same routine, tabbing twenty or thirty Ks, eating crap scoff, snatching a few minutes kip at a time, becoming stupider and coarser. Every day trying to hide away from what matters most to you, concealing it from yourself behind obsessive thoughts of food and sleep and how best to skive off: your constant thoughts of home, of your parents, of the girlfriend you might have had but who, thanks to the bloody army, you don't. For all that, the day will come of your wretched, long awaited demob. A transport will come, and I too will be driven away from this place.

I can hear a low rumble on the left flank. It is far away, behind the hillocks, behind the wall of the forest. I have heard it well before the others. Even now, when the people around me are chatting and I am joining in the singing, I am listening out. Even while I am trying hard to free myself from the feeling that I am on duty, I reluctantly remain first and foremost a sentry, instinctively paying attention to shadows, sounds and movements outside.

"Quiet! I think it's coming."

The lads stand still, straining to hear.

"You're not wrong."

"It's creeping our way, our dear old pal."

Our driver Sal, an elder Pheasant, says apologetically.

"I'm really sorry, Baldy, it's not going to be me whisking you to the station. I can tell you, you'd have felt the breeze in your hair."

"Sure..." Demob Man sighs, registering distress, although actually he doesn't give a toss who drives him as long as somebody does.

Gradually the low rumble becomes a growl. We can tell it's a truck, most likely a ZIL.

"Oy, Makar," I say, "Go and tell Terenty: vehicle approaching from the left. Tell him to report it to Pixie."

Baldy is on edge. He grabs his briefcase and stares avidly towards where the growl of the engine is growing louder and clearer.

"It's miles away yet. We've got plenty of time for the demob anthem." Balton strums out the prescribed solemn and plaintive melody and we provide the words:

And now my final duty as a soldier,
How grand it is, like rituals of old...

The song doesn't really get off the ground, however. It trails off, crowded out by the increasing sense of anticipation.

"Oh, rat shit, Baldy, when's it ever going to be my turn?" Melon bursts out. "I'll never live to see the day."

"You will," Baldy says, and gives him a reassuring hug.

Now everybody else goes over to Demob Man. They put their arms round him and wish him all the best in civilian life, plenty of money and a prick that never wilts; Baldy replies equally traditionally, hoping time flies like a bullet for them, and that they get excused as many details as possible.

Piksheev comes strutting out on to the porch, holding himself very erect. He is still drugged with sleep, but peers at the lads with an authoritativeness which grows as his vision clears.

"They're on their way, then?"

"Yes," Baldy breathes, trying to hold back his jubilation.

"Well, jolly good."

Piksheev straightens his cap and lights up a cigarette. He looks in the direction of the left flank, and Balton runs his stiffening fingers over the strings of the now redundant guitar.

Then the tops of the pine trees are raked by the distant, faint beam of headlights, the engine roars with a change of gear as the truck comes to the last of the hillocks. On the porch of the border post stand a pathetic bunch of little people all gazing in the direction from which the vehicle will shortly appear. Baldy swings his briefcase, impatiently shuffling about on the damp, dirty matting in his polished shoes. God, how long, how infinitely long he has been waiting for this moment, and now it is coming nearer with every revolution of the wheels, with every breath, with every drag on the last cigarette he will ever smoke here. Even Piksheev, a hopeless satrap, even he is moved by the moment. Yet another of his soldiers is leaving. Off you go then, lad. You've earned a rest.

A GAZ-66 bounces out from behind the trees by the gates, roaring and careering over the ruts and potholes which cover the track, its headlights poking the road. Before it is in the courtyard Baldy is rushing off the porch into the rain and about to head towards it. Then he realises he's in too much of a hurry and turns back. He removes his cap, shakes off the raindrops and hooks it over his ear again.

"Well, Baldy, on your way!"

"Say hello to civvy street!"

"Hey, fuck some fillies there... Some for you and a few for us..."

"Don't forget to drink to the guys out on guard duty!"

The farewells rain down on him from every side. We hug him tightly, shake his hand, slap him on the back. Guys from neighbouring posts who have served their time smile out from the tarpaulin covering the back of the truck, wistfully, knowingly.

"Vaka! Don't say they're even letting you out?!" I yell in astonishment, recognising one guy famed for his breaches of military discipline who seems to have been moved round every post in our unit, been held in the Unit guardhouse for not far off a hundred days, and even (a rare achievement) spent ten days in the cells of the regional Head Shed. "You lucky bastard!"

"I'm the last from 'Windlass'. I've been on duty on my own there for a week. The rest all left a while ago," Vaka explains apologetically.

"Well, fuck you. Good luck!"

"You too. I hope they soon..."

Piksheev extends to Baldy his dry little hand.

"All the best, Lysenko. Thank you for your service. I wish you every success in, erm, civilian life."

"Oh, well, and I hope you too, er..." Demob Man can't think what to say.

Some chirpy chappie from the Unit sticks his head out of the cabin of the truck:

"Fellows, time's up! Climb aboard anyone who's homeward bound."

Baldy jumps into the back of the truck, Makar passes him up his kitbag, Canary his briefcase. Baldy casts a farewell glance over the square, the main building that hasn't been whitewashed for ages, the garage containers, the bathhouse, the sports square.

"Hey, Rom!" He remembers something and beckons to me. "Over here, mate!"

I pull myself up on the side and he whispers hurriedly:

"In the kennels, you know, that place behind the stand where the boards are coming off..."

"What about it?"

"I squirreled a bottle of Florena away. Completely forgot about it. Knock it back with Melon."

"Cheers!"

The truck revs, but the driver is in no hurry to move. By tradition those seeing their comrade-in-arms off should push the vehicle out the gates to speed him on his way.

We lean against the sides and push.

"What's he doing? Hasn't he put it in neutral?" Sal grunts.

"Even out of gear, five tons is no joke," Balton replies.

Sal dissents:

"This floozy is more than five tons."

I halt the debate:

"Stop bellyaching and shove!"

Somehow or other we manage to get it moving. Luckily the road slopes away. The 66 reluctantly trundles out of the compound. If it had been a ZIL there's no way we'd have got it moving.

It rolls on down, gathering speed. The driver puts his foot on the accelerator, the gearbox wheezes painfully and the truck moves off down the road. Baldy waves his cap and we all wave back.

The vehicle reaches the turn in the road, the trees. Unsteady white beams flicker in the damp and darkness of the night. The lads, round-shouldered, flapping their freezing arms, head quickly back to the border post.

"Hang on," I say, catching Melon by the shoulder. "Are you going off to stoke?"

"I'd better fuel her up."

"Well," I murmur, "Baldy stashed away a little poison in the kennels behind the stand where our pedigree pooches..."

"Seriously?" Melon is childishly delighted. "Let's go!"

"When I get off duty... Go and check it out. Perhaps you can even filch some scoff. Case the kitchen, okay?"

"Okay!" With a spring in his step, Melon high tails it towards the fence in front of the dog handlers' shack and the empty cages for the alsatians.

II.

It's four in the morning and dawn is still very distant. It will get light at about nine, a weary, pallid, lethargic dawn. Slowly, arduously, a grubby, joyless haze will thin the darkness. The sun will be far, far away behind layers of leaden cloud, and there will be no telling where exactly it is: the whole sky will be uniformly, densely grey. Just after three in the afternoon it will start getting dark, and by four night will almost have fallen again.

My hours of guard duty are over. Now it is Makar's turn to pace the slippery square. He will be mulling over something in that slow-witted way of his. Actually, he isn't slow-witted all the time. When he is thinking about things that matter to him, the things that mattered during his first eighteen years of life, I can believe he is quick-witted and clear-thinking. While he is trudging to and fro, he is most likely thinking about his village. One time I heard Makar talking to Vovka Shatalov in the smoking area about horses. We have two horses here — occasionally we have patrols on horseback, and they are needed to run the place, bringing in hay from the mowing, logs and other loads; we have a constant problem getting fuel for our machinery. They got so carried away, Makar and Shatalov, giving each other advice, arguing. It got quite heated, but in a good way, the way two experts argue in order to check out how much the other knows, and to learn from him. In terms of his military duties, Makar is so far completely clueless, and seems unlikely ever to be an effective soldier. To tell the truth, I hope he never is.

"Bottoms up, Melon. Here's to the good!"

We are sitting in the boiler room, which is unwontedly warm and dry. Fire is slowly consuming the sodden firewood and water is slowly gurgling through the pipes.

The boiler room is quite a hospitable place. There are comfortable seats, a bench behind the boilers, pictures cut out of magazines on the walls, which are blackened with soot. The most important aspect of its hospitability is, however, that here you can warm up properly and dry out.

We are sprawling on tractor seats. There is a little table with sawn-off legs between us. On the table reposes a small bottle of Florena aftershave, a plastic bottle of water, a piece of bread, and a sliced onion.

"Let's do it!" Melon exhorts, breathes out and abruptly tosses his head back to get the aftershave down his throat as quickly as possible.

I watch enviously as he gasps for air, greedily washes the fluid down, winces and twitches.

"A hit?" I glug some for myself into a mug kept specially for this purpose.

Like Melon, I breathe out deeply before tossing the caustic liquid down my throat. I gulp wide-mouthed and the fireball proceeds down my gullet, scorching and bringing me to life. My tongue is instantly numb, I can't breathe, and my body shudders as the aftershave explodes inside.

I reach for the water, take a few gulps, wipe away the tears.

"Okay, that!"

"Not bad! Cheers, Baldy, for this warm feeling."

"A worthy leaving present."

Melon gets off his seat, extracts a hand-rolled cigarette from somewhere in the tangle of pipes, and lights up.

"Very soon, Melon, it'll be you we're seeing off."

"That would be good," he replies flatly, as if he really doesn't believe it will ever happen.

We share the cigarette and drink a bit more until the small bottle is all but empty.

"Could have done with a bigger bottle."

"Never mind, we'll soon be getting so-o hammered, we'll more than make up for the past two years," I promise. "I really will come to visit you. I suppose you do have pubs in Malaya Vishera?"

"Su-ure. We got everything."

We munch the bread and onion. There was a time I couldn't stand onion; just the sight of it made me feel sick, but now I put it away without a second thought. I'm pleased we even managed to find an onion.

"What I really wanted," Melon informs me in a quiet, confidential tone, "What I really wanted was to get back home while I was still nineteen. My birthday's the seventh of December. I could still make it. What do you think?"

"Well, sure, who knows. It just depends how the cards fall out."

"But now," he goes on, not listening, "Now I'm worried I might even end up seeing the New Year in here."

"Don't talk crap! They'll let you out."

"But what if something goes wrong?" Melon looks at me with his big, girlish eyes. He seems to be begging me, as if there was something I could do about it. "They might intensify border patrols, or invent something else."

"What would they want to do that for? Stop bellyaching. We would do better to..." I hand him a mug. "We'll get out. Nothing is going to go wrong. Get this down you."

"Hang on a moment."

Melon jumps up from the seat and busily throws some more roughly chopped spruce logs into the boiler. A mixture of smoke and steam billows out of the furnace.

The combination of weariness and inebriation has really messed my body up, and it lurches and bends. There's something wrong with my legs, and I totter along, my head lolling forwards like a great cast iron weight. I'm expecting at any moment to collapse and clutch at the brittle branches of the scrawny birch trees, at the display stands which surround the square with their boldly marching soldiers doing acrobatic high kicks practically up to their foreheads.

"M-Makar!" I bawl, stopping at the porch and clutching at the railing. "Hey, sentry, where are you, you mother-fucker?"

Makar appears, standing to attention in front of me.
"What?"
"Well, now! You listen to what I'm saying, little man. Are you listening, or what?"
"Yes, sir."
"You," I poke him in the solar plexus, "The army's gonna blow your fucking mind. It is. And how. You ain't seen nothing yet. Know what I mean?" I know perfectly well that I'm talking pathetic drivel and disgust even myself, but I can't stop. I carry on pestering Makar. "Count the days, laddie. Count the days! Then you might start being a real soldier. So how many have you got through? Eh?"
"It'll be seven months soon."
"How many days, I said, how many days?"
"I don't know."
I take a swing, beat my breast, and proudly bark out:
"Seven hundred and forty-nine here! Can't do it, eh? Can't count like that, can you, laddie."
"No, sir."
"Well there. You see? If they'd sent a ZIL for Baldy we couldn't have done it. We couldn't have shoved it out. Know what I'm saying?" I suddenly sense that I'm on the verge of tears. "No. We wouldn't have been up to it. Got that? No-o." I give myself a shake and sober up a bit. "Okay, Makar, stay in the unloading booth. Not so damp there. We can't afford to let ourselves get cold!"

I'm dreaming, seeing coloured lights.
Yet again I hear that nauseating half-whisper of Terenty's.
"Rom! Rom, do you hear? Get up!"
"What?"
"You have to go out on patrol."
"What patrol? What's the time?"
"Something's registering on the System."

"In a minute you're going to register a bunch of fives!" I say, waking up. "You've gone barking mad! I've got two details today! I'm warning you, if I get out of this bed it's curtains for you, asshole."

He mumbles something and I start drifting back to sleep.

"But there's... Piksheev's waiting... The patrol's ready... Come on, get up. Rom!" Terenty timidly shakes my shoulder.

"You moronic fuckface!" I explode. "Crawl up your arse, you stupid git!"

"Pixie's orders. Something wrong with Sal. He can't get out of bed."

"Neither can I, wanker."

I am wide awake now, with a raging thirst. Sitting up in bed I ask, by now rather more calmly:

"What's up with Sal, then?"

"Rom, I feel like shit," Sal groans from his bunk. "Really shitty."

I realise the light is on.

"Great, at least we've got electricity," I mutter darkly. "We should be grateful for that, at least."

"I've been shivering since yesterday, and now I'm really feverish. I've got blisters bursting on my skin."

Piksheev comes into the room.

"Get a move on, Senchin, you can catch up on your beauty sleep afterwards."

"For Christ's sake!" I pull on my damp, stinking uniform. "Which flank is it, anyway?"

"The right."

"Oh, well..."

Things could be worse. The left flank is three Ks longer, and hilly. There's even a marsh in one place which you have to tiptoe across on planks, like a tightrope walker in the circus. The right flank isn't quite so bad, although even so it's fourteen there and back. Not much fun either.

"And am I going to be on guard duty after that?"

Piksheev nods affirmatively.

"Aren't you worried I might just croak? And never live to see my demob?"

"Well, what can I do about it?" our sad little lieutenant snaps. "There's nobody else. Salnikov has contracted chickenpox, or so it seems. We have orders to get him to hospital by the first available transport. By the by, Salnikov," Pixie goes over to his bed and whispers behind his hand, "Get yourself to another dorm. Chickenpox is infectious. Understand?"

We have three dormitories, but currently all sleep in this one to keep warm, and anyway, life is marginally more fun when you're all in together.

We hastily breakfast on barley porridge and plenty of black bread, and have a mug of tea. I leave the fresh milk (Shatalov has just milked our cow) to drink when I get back. After a tab that length I'm going to be hungry, and glad of any crust.

"Do be quick," Terenty says, peeping timidly into the canteen.

"Shut yer face!"

Lydia Alexandrovna is clattering about with the pots and pans in the kitchen and from time to time you hear the hiss of her swearing. She's a pretty woman of around thirty from Ukraine. Her husband, Warrant Officer Khomutenko, is also Ukrainian; they come from somewhere near Lvov but, as people say, destiny has ordained that they should now be living in the forests of Karelia. To a man, the officers and other ranks can't keep their eyes off Lydia Alexandrovna. Actually, in this place you couldn't keep your eyes off anything in a skirt. In the twenty-one months I have been stuck in this border post we have had two visits, on Border Guards' Day, from the schoolchildren in the nearby village;

they included some pleasant girls. I even managed to touch one up a bit. But, for Christ's sake, out here even the cartoons in Krokodil give you a hard-on.

The briefing room is crowded. Almost our entire complement is assembled. Terenty hands over command to Sergeant Gurian, who has grown into the job in his just over one year of service. Gurian is probably the only real soldier there will be here after we have gone. All hopes rest on him, but anyway, what the hell do I care? Fuck this border and fuck this shitty border post and everything associated with it. What fucking use is it? Apart from elks and bears nobody ever tries to break through the System: anybody who needs to go abroad without the proper documents can stroll through the customs post for fifty bucks, and the locals are allowed through without formality. They can drop in on each other for tea.

The left flank is being taken by the Technician Commander and Fly, and the right by me and Canary. Balton is on sentry duty. Makar goes off to get his head down after his spell of duty. Melon, I imagine, is dreaming dreams in the boiler room.

Piksheev is breathlessly spouting his memorised orders. Those commanding the border details dutifully reply: "Proceeding to guard..." Terenty takes us to load the Kalashnikovs. Gurian checks the logbooks, counts the weapons and the ammunition.

Unclipping the magazine, jerking the bolt, and pulling the trigger, Makar, lifting his long thin legs high, races across to the porch. We, however, clip our magazines in. Our slog is just beginning.

The sky is no longer so relentlessly dark, the blackness now slightly shot through with a dense, inky blue. Without a torch you still can't see a thing.

Looking from the rear, that is, from the territory of Russia, our border post is on the far side of the System. Accordingly, we're separated from the rest of the country by a barbed-wire fence. We're located in a strip of Russian soil some five kilometres wide, beyond which is the contiguous state of Finland.

We arrive at the Monitoring and Tracking Strip. Canary and Fly cross it, smooth over their footprints with rakes, and throw them back to us. The sapper hides the rakes in a clump of heather. Canary and Fly will walk along the narrow strip between the screen of the System and the MTS, and the Technician Commander and I, in command of the patrols, will walk along the other side of the strip.

"Okay, so long," the sapper bids us a dour farewell, lighting up a short, grubby cigarette butt.

I nod and set off briskly along the track whose every tussock and hollow I know. I make no attempt to avoid the stalks of dead grass covered in water (my clothing can't get any damper than it is already); they shower you with droplets if you so much as touch them. I focus on one simple idea: the sooner I get to the end of our stretch the sooner I can get back and fall into bed. I probably won't be able to get any sleep before my next stint, but it would be good at least to lie down for an hour or so.

Canary is a few paces ahead of me, his torch beam probing the barbed wire while mine sweeps over the ploughed and harrowed strip.

From time to time he stops, takes a flask out of his jacket and rinses his mouth.

"What's your tipple, dude? Looks like whisky," I banter.

"Mmm," Canary moans, then furiously spits the liquid out. "It's my tooth... It's killing me! My whole jaw is agony. Soda solution keeps it just bearable, otherwise...

"Okay. Take it easy. You'll survive to demob day, no sweat."

The MTS seems endless, and so does the line of creosoted posts with barbed wire stretched between them. If a single strand is breached the alarm goes off at the border post, a siren wails, and we all rush to action stations. In the autumn and spring the false alarms are never-ending as elks just barge their way through the System. Perhaps this is when they migrate. Sometimes it goes off for no good reason at all: the wires are short-circuited by snow or wet leaves, or a diode blows in one of the drums.

It really is endless. The whole country is enclosed in barbed-wire fence with its adjacent strip of ploughed land to register the footprints of man or beast, and hundreds of border details are patrolling the System at this very moment, from Nikel in the North to Korea in the South for all I know. But right now what matters is that our stretch is not endless, and it's up to the neighbouring border guards to worry about the stretch after that. We stand at our end point, pretend to light up, and head back the same way, only faster.

III.

Where we split this morning to check out the left and right flanks there is a small gate in the System to enable patrols to go out on a task in the hinterland. There have been no such patrols for a very long time and the track is completely overgrown.

Beside the gate is a watchtower which is supposed to have a sentry posted in it during the hours of daylight. To my delight I hear Vadik, as our CO is known, announce, in that quick-fire rattle which makes him sound like a state prosecutor or a church deacon, that he is sending me up there. All right! It's not the worst place to kip, or just sit in a cabin which shelters you from the wind and rain. And the rain is getting up again. Nature seems to be trying to do everything she can to finish us off, to drown us in marsh water, or at least force us out of this place. Every depression turns into a lake, anywhere that hasn't been trampled down hard becomes a swamp. Whatever you touch is covered in a film of moisture, your clothing is constantly sodden and stinking, and the air so laden with moisture that at times you're afraid you're going to drown in it.

Almost running, drenched by sheeting rain, blown by gusts of icy wind, I hasten to the pylon-like watchtower, climb the ladder: the first flight, a landing, the second flight, another landing, the third, the fourth. I butt the plywood trapdoor open with my head and climb up into the cabin. How unbelievably warm and dry it is here! With horror I imagine myself marching at this moment round the square, churning up the courtyard mud as I pound out my beat. There's no hiding during the day. Before you know it, Vadik or Piksheev will pop up from nowhere, and even Khomut when he's the wrong side out can have you on a charge for unsatisfactory performance of your duties.

The watchtower cabin is not that badly furnished. An iron chair with no legs stands on a crate of sand. How many times our superior officers have thrown it out during inspections, but we just drag it back up. There is an apology for a table, with a field telephone and a logbook in which to record our observations: what kind of vehicle went where and when; what kind of patrol went out along the System and when; what suspicious activity was observed in the Finnish watchtower. You can't see it with the naked eye, but with powerful binoculars on a clear day you can make out the Finnish border guard sitting in a cabin which looks just like ours.

I lean my rifle against the wall, take off and throw to the floor my belt with the cartridge pouch and flare pistol holster threaded on it. I shake off my hat the raindrops which have not already soaked into the fur, and beat it against my parka.

Spray flies all over the cabin; in those few minutes outside I have almost got soaked to the skin. What state would I be in if I was out there for the full four hours?

"Gurian, this is Rom," I say into the telephone. "Are you receiving me?"

"Loud and clear," the guard replies.

"If there's a problem, call through. I'm just going to... You know."

"Sure."

I put the receiver back on its cradle and extract from their hiding place behind the cladding a pile of well-thumbed magazines, *Soviet Soldier* and *Krokodil* from God knows how many years back. I sit on the chair and browse through them. I have read them all, studied every photograph and drawing. I know every caption by heart. I should have taken that Chase novel from the unloading booth. Well, to hell with it. I should just kip while I have the opportunity.

No sooner have I settled down nicely, preparing to drift off into the cosy realm of dreams, to feast my eyes on something soft and light and good and desirable, when the telephone squeals. "Oh, fuck!" I grunt, scowling, driven out of dreamland and back to cold, damp reality. "What?" I shout intemperately into the receiver.

"Senchin," I hear the Warrant Officer's voice, "Come down."

"What's up?" I try to resist. "My orders are to..."

"We're out of firewood and the forecast is for a sharp drop in temperature. Look lively, get yourself down here."

"On my way..."

I slowly put my belt back on, sling the rifle over my back. I return the reading matter to its hidey-hole and look one last time round the cabin like a knight leaving the beautiful palace where he had hoped to take his ease, to warm himself by the fire, to drink his grog, but now, alas, obliged to set out once more into the storm and perform deeds of derring-do which are of absolutely no use to fucking anyone.

Behind the bathhouse is an imposing pile of tree trunks which were evidently brought here ten years ago or thereabouts when new cuttings were being made through the forest, the old cuttings maintained and roads laid. To this day we saw up this detritus with its peeling bark for firewood.

To one side a circular saw stands under cover. Its huge disk looks capable of dealing with any amount of timber no matter how hard, but it doesn't get sharpened very often, to put it mildly.

There is a lever for raising and lowering the disc. A tall shelter was built to store the firewood, but it has long been empty: sawing firewood is a slow business and you need three people at least.

Vovka Shatalov and Makar are poking around in the woodpile looking for manageable trunks.

"Greetings, prisoners of war!" I say as I walk towards them.

They give me a wry look and nod. They would have preferred to see somebody a bit more junior. They don't have much hope that I'll be particularly helpful. Slithering in the mud, they drag a trunk rotten at one end towards the saw.

I take off my rifle and belt and put them down on the chopping block.

"OK, shove it under the saw blade. I'm ready for work."

Makar and Shatalov slide the timber along the ground until it is under the disc and Makar moves round to receive the logs. I switch on the saw and our ears are assailed by its shrill, oscillating screaming, which becomes harsh and grating when the saw teeth bite into the wood.

The sodden wood is not easy to work. The disc gets stuck

and has to be raised from time to time to make a parallel cut for a wider notch.

Gradually the pile of logs grows. The main difficulty is finding a suitable tree trunk or other timber in the woodpile. Most of what is left is huge pieces, which ten men couldn't shift.

"We need a chainsaw. We could slice this little lot up in five seconds if we had one," Makar grumbles, struggling to dislodge a fir tree whose trunk, as far as we can tell, is not unduly heavy and which is sticking out of the pile. "We've got one of them back home. My dad and I used to do the sawing for the whole village."

"We've got a chainsaw," Shatalov says. "We just haven't got any petrol."

While we're working time passes by unnoticed, or faster at least. Sometimes I can forget I'm on duty. That's good. Time really hangs heavy when you're on sentry duty. You have to invent all sorts of distractions to kill those four endless hours. I even took a liking to reading because of sentry duty. It means you're not just hanging around. You can get quite into it sometimes. If you kept on the march, as the regulations stipulate, you would go crazy after a dozen details. You have to save your sanity by thinking up something to do, or just dozing off.

To be fair, today's lunch was quite passable. There was even, believe it or not, something resembling a salad: grated beetroot! We had cabbage soup made from blackened, half rotten cabbage with a knob of army margarine. This margarine is odd stuff, a close approximation to plastic: while the food is hot you can get it down, but if it cools slightly the fat congeals and coats the inside of your mouth and throat as if you really had had melted plastic poured in. You have to drink mugful after mugful of hot water to wash all the fat down into your stomach. It's monstrous stuff, but the main course today was cause for celebration: tinned stew with rice. That's more like it! For a moment Khomut has been feeling generous and released stew from the reserve rations.

Fresh meat is a great rarity. We get enough sent from the Unit to last an average of one week per month. Sometimes they send us tinned food, but that's a rarity too. Last autumn Khomut slaughtered a bull calf, but this year our cow had a female calf so it's been left to grow, and the pigs haven't been stuck yet. They look really puny, though, more like poodles. I remember Kudrya, one of my generation's Dads, once felled an elk which had blundered into the System with his rifle butt. Of course, he was in trouble for that, not least because the butt splintered, but we were glad of the elk. The officers grabbed the best cuts for themselves and their families. One winter the Head Shed officers came hunting on our territory. They brought in elks one after the other on their Buran snowmobiles and piled them up beyond the paddock. I reckon they killed more than twenty, skinned them there and then, and roasted the joints on a spit, just like in films about the Middle Ages. Some of that elk meat came our way too. Occasionally we manage to go fishing. There are plenty of bream in the lakes, and with a spinning rod you can land pike.

To tell the truth, though, the scoff here is the pits. We plant our own potatoes on an old, abandoned monitoring strip; we've made two cold frames for cucumbers; in a hollow by the stream we've established a cabbage patch. The state farm where we used to get vegetables has gone to the dogs. It went bankrupt and now you can't buy anything there even for cash in hand. All the land around here is ownerless and overgrown, but you can see it hasn't always been that way. If you go a lot further to the rear, you have to tab back thirty

Ks or so, you come across the remains of a lot of ruined Finnish farmsteads.

You'll be sloping along and suddenly, in the middle of dense forest, you come across a clearing overgrown with bushes and scrub fir trees, and there you suddenly find the stone wall of a house, like a broken tooth, and near it twisted, half-withered trees with sour little maggoty apples. They say cultivated trees gradually revert to the state of their wild cousins if they aren't properly looked after.

There is one strange, rather disconcerting track in the rear. We call it "The Road to Demob". It's level and as straight as if it had been drawn with a ruler, and who knows how long. We patrol it for about five Ks. God knows where it starts and finishes. All that grows on it is low grass, and even in downpours the surface stays firm. Trees, of a variety I don't recognise, grow along the verges. They have straight trunks and slender branches growing not outwards but upwards, and the leaves are narrow and thick, fleshier than you expect in the North. If you look up, you see the crowns of the trees meeting, almost intersecting, creating a kind of vault above the roadway. This means the road is in shade even on hot days, relaxing and pleasant to walk along. You'll be proceeding along it, though, and suddenly on your right or your left you see the spooky ruins of homes and neglected orchards which look like dry, grey skeletons. Underneath the scrub you can still picture neat plots of land, and you realise you are passing through a place where once life was good. No doubt time was when carts trundled down this road laden with grain, and open carriages sped by. It would have been a noisy place in those days, but now there is only an eery, graveyard silence. It is disconcerting but also interesting, and you can picture yourself as an explorer who has stumbled upon the remains of a lost civilisation; until you are hit by the oppressive and unpleasant recollection that your own grandfather, an ex-serviceman rewarded with a personal pension, took part in the destruction of this civilisation not, when you think about it, all that long ago. What was the point of destroying it, of crushing the way of life here, of depopulating these regions?

But, hey-ho, the way things are going it won't be that long before the Finns start to return; they will wait until everything in Russia has rotted away completely, and then return to the land of their forebears, knock down the defunct System, build farmsteads here again and live a good life.

Sleep, sleep. I can look forward to another two hours of sleep before tomorrow comes. After that, briefing, dinner; and duty and sleeping, working and eating in fits and starts.

I come out of the dining room, vainly trying to force out a sated belch. Canary, a towel wound round his cheek (evidently his abscess is driving him mad), is sluggishly mopping the floor of the briefing room. Gurian is dozing at the desk with the radio playing quietly. A breathless young woman is communicating the conditions of the station's latest competition: "Only the first ten listeners to ring in..."

I go up to the first floor. From the washroom, which in the winter doubles as a smoking room, come the sounds of Balton's nasal dirge:

Again today you have not come;
I had so waited, hoped, believed
That all around the bells would ring,
And you walk down the aisle to me.

Terenty and Fly are beside Balton. They are gazing with dull, sad eyes at the guitar, their lips trembling, as if they want to join in but are afraid to do so. A fag-end smoulders between Fly's fingers.

"Leave some for me."

He takes one final deep drag and passes me the pathetic stub of his roll-your-own. I greedily fill my lungs with the acrid smoke from smouldering wool fibres, breadcrumbs, dust and tobacco. After I have drawn on it a few times the butt is finished.

"Okay, put a sock in it, I'm going to sleep," I say when Balton finishes his song. "I'm hoping to get a couple of hours' kip."

"While we head out to the flanks," Terenty responds plaintively.

Fly peers under the bench in the hope of finding something that can be smoked.

It's dark and stuffy in the dorm. The stuffiness could make you believe it isn't actually all that cold in here. Without getting undressed (I take off only my boots and belt) I throw myself down on the bed.

First I hear a hoot: "Ooh!" and then silence, but it's enough to banish slumber. I lie there, blinking my eyes and waiting. I can just imagine the scene in the duty room at this very moment.

The number of a section has lit up on the wall panel, and the silence has simultaneously been rent by a siren. If the alarm is on the main System, that really does mean, "Scramble!" There is a secondary, inner System for a few kilometres, where the main System runs too close to the border and a supplementary fence creates an additional obstacle for a *yashka*, or intruder. Gurian is a pro and knows to kill the siren immediately in order not to wind people up needlessly. He goes to Admin to report. Vadik is in there at present, our CO, quite young to be a Senior Lieutenant. He will certainly order us all out. A real bastard, keen as mustard, which is why he is in command of a border post when he's not yet thirty. Pixie gets us all out too, trying to get himself promoted. He's understandably bitter about still only being a Junior Lieutenant when he's knocking forty. I ponder these things, and gradually sink back into a state of drowsiness. The words of a children's song come to mind: "That button isn't our button! – all the children said. Tra la la la la la. Four days they galloped, four days they searched..." Now, however, the merciless siren wails again, this time assertively, evenly, and at full blast.

When the fuck is all this crap going to be over?! Shit! How much of this bollocks can you take for Christ's sake?

Soldiers are milling around the duty room, getting ready to go out, jostling each other, getting in each other's way. Their rifles clatter and they shove loaded magazines into cartridge pouches. Melon replaces the batteries in the walkie-talkie. Torches blink on and off as they are checked. Section 8: the left flank, then. The clock is showing twenty minutes to six. I have managed to sleep for a little over an hour, and should be grateful for that.

"Move it! Move it!" Vadik is standing in the middle of the duty room, ready to leave. He has the slightly predatory, excited look of a puppy ready to play as he impatiently straightens first his holster, then his neat little officer's walkie-talkie.

Poor old Canary, meanwhile, is lumbered with lugging the ranks' walkie-talkie, which weighs about ten kilograms. It's a bloody great metal case with a long flailing antenna which he, rather than Shaitan the alsatian, has to carry now.

Hooting from the courtyard tells us Balton has driven the Skull into the square.

"Arbuzov, Belikov, let's go!" Vadik skips outside in the wake of the Technician Commander and Melon.

Piksheev appears looking grumpy and hastily chewing

something. The alarm has probably parted him from his dinner. His thin little voice, which actually sounds quite like a siren itself, chivvies us along in imitation of Vadik:

"Let's get out there at the double! At the double! The intruder isn't going to hang around waiting for us." We climb into the back of the GAZ-66. At the wheel, enveloped in a sheepskin coat, his skin covered in blotches of green ointment, is Sal. I wonder who's going to drive us when he goes into hospital. Khomut, presumably, since the rest of us can't drive.

We speed along the left flank over the squelching dirt road, ploughing through the puddles. Alarms on the left flank are not too bad. Although it's a long, bumpy ride, at least you don't have to run too far to mount a dragnet. You don't drive so far on the right flank, but you have to tab umpteen fucking Ks! You sometimes face a forced march from the border post practically to the far end of our stretch. There is no road for a vehicle to drive along in the search for an intruder on the right flank.

We cling to the benches as we lurch from side to side. Beyond the end of the truck, quivering darkness is mitigated slightly by the faint glow from searchlights on the border post's roofs. When we plunge down from the top of a hillock the darkness deepens instantly. At the bottom the vehicle splashes into an enormous puddle and, straining, roaring angrily, assaults the next mound.

We pass a smoke round, taking a couple of drags each. (Vovka Shatalov managed to cadge it off Piksheev in the turmoil.) Its living glow makes me feel a bit better, slightly less ill. The warm, cheering stream of smoke enters your throat. You long to inhale it, to force it deeper and deeper into yourself, as if it can get you out of this, make you warm, take you far away. In fact, however, it can do none of these things. All it can do is try to pull the wool over your eyes for a minute: soon, brother, any minute now things are going to get better. Just take one more drag and I'll help you. But tobacco isn't strong enough for that. You need something heavier. I remember, crestfallen, how prodigally we squandered that vial of Florena. The high it could give Melon and me, bollockbrain that I am, I wasted by going to sleep.

We turn off one track which runs along close to the System and on to another, less trammeled and hence slightly more even. We will be jumping out any minute now. I run a finger over the holes in the worn sides of my tarpaulin boots. I should have done a swap with Baldy yesterday when he offered me his better ones. I moronically brushed it aside, saying I'd stick it out in these. Seconds from now I'm going to have very wet feet.

The GAZ-66 brakes, skidding on the slippery grass. It halts abruptly as Sal pulls on the handbrake. We jump down one after the other and head off along the cutting, along the final frontier, to man the dragnet. To our right, some one hundred metres away, is already Finnish territory.

My position on grounds of seniority is closest to the car, not counting the driver. I still have to run along. After a few steps my left foot sinks into a hole and marsh water pours briskly into the boot, freezing me. I pull my foot out and run on, squelching and swearing. Canary is wheezing along in front of me, bent double under the weight of his walkie-talkie, the whippy antenna catching on ice-coated branches. The poor sod has to run further than anyone else, rounding us all up again after the all clear.

Right, I can hide here. Very suitable. I dive into the bushes and hang my rifle on a branch. I have the cutting in front of me. My task is to stand and observe, to lie in wait for the intruder. Admittedly you can't see a bloody thing, just a black wall of forest straight ahead. Above us is a black, starless sky.

Some laggard runs by (I thought I was the last); he stops

five metres away and I hear the rustling of branches. "Occupied," I state unambiguously. His squelching boots full of water, the unknown soldier runs panting on.

I pass the time as best I can. For starters I take off the boot, pour the water out of it and scrape out the rubbish with my fingernails. After that I wring my foot wrapping out thoroughly, wind it back on my foot, and put the boot back on. Now, if I wriggle my toes energetically, it should soon begin to warm up. I rub my hands against the lining of the parka and feel in my pockets for something to smoke. No luck. How could there be anything there? I investigate the bottom of every pocket several times, the flaps of my fur hat: not a shred of tobacco anywhere. I make no attempt to peer into the darkness: doing that only hurts your eyes. I realised long ago that there aren't any real *yashkas*, at least not any stupid enough to clamber through the System and run headlong through the forest into a foreign country. There may well have been in the past, I don't deny that, but nowadays the most troublesome intruders are elks and bears. After them come racoons and foxes (which like to tunnel under the System, but even there we have barbed wire, and if you disturb it you set off the alarm). After that come wet leaves, snow, and faults in the alarm system itself.

And so it is today. Some component went awry in one of the drums (gadgets located in every section to monitor the voltage in the wires) and set off the alarm. Melon poked around and fixed it and we get the all clear.

We return in a bad mood, soaked and hungry. Sal drives the truck back so furiously we are tossed all over the place in the back. You can understand how he feels: he can hardly stand, he is feeling completely terrible. He has dabbed his sores with green ointment, but he ought to be in hospital. He's been promised a lift only after lunch tomorrow, he isn't allowed to mix with us, and he's lying in a cold, empty dormitory which is more like a mortuary.

"Right, time for dinner, if it's ready. Briefing at eight," Vadik says, taking the loudhailer from the duty officer.

Now he, Pixie and Khomut will spend an age ingeniously shuffling the duties around so as to get ten people to cover tasks which are supposed to be done by twenty.

"Good evening, Lydia Alexandrovna!" I am the first to shove my head into the serving hatch. "What culinary delights do you have for us this evening?"

"Ah, Senchin," the cook smiles wearily. "Still here?"

"Yup. I'm not going anywhere for a while yet — probably the best part of a week."

"That's not long, believe me," she demurs, handing out a bowl of millet porridge and an opened tin of sprats. "Here, you're welcome to what we've got," she says, and adds in a strict voice, "That tin, by the way, is between two of you!"

"Any butter?"

Lydia Alexandrovna replies with a wry smile. I'm incensed:

"Come on, we've had no butter for almost ten days now! The regulations say we get thirty grams a day."

"Listen, don't give me that, okay?" A frown darkens Lydia Alexandrovna's kindly but exhausted face. "When they deliver it you'll get all there is straight away."

"I'm going to really pig myself when they do. That's going to add up to..." — I try to multiply — "God knows how much! That could make it worth staying in the army."

IV.

We are standing in the duty room in a straggly line. First, Section 1: those engaged in houskeeping duties: the stockman, drivers, cook. This section is under the command of

Gurian. Section 2 is exclusively the sharpshooters, supposedly the most numerous, except that right now there are only two people in it: Junior Sergeant Terentiev and me. Section 3, the technical section, consists of Commander Belikov, the Technical Officer, and Melon. Section 4 is the dog handlers, whose sole representative is Canary: there is no sergeant and, come to that, no dog as it died of exhaustion. When Shaitan died the Unit sent a vet specially to perform an autopsy. They threatened us with sanctions for the loss a military dog, but the vet found no criminal liability. He concluded that the dog had, quite simply, been worked to death. It's easy to see how: patrolling the System twice a day meant Shaitan covered around thirty kilometres, and also had to race through marshy forest whenever there was an alarm. He was fed oatmeal porridge with a meagre dash of margarine. (We hadn't had dog food sent for a thousand years, and even when it was we were more likely to eat it ourselves. You would salt the meat and eat it, just crunching through the gristle.) Given that kind of life, it was easy to die. Nothing surprising about it.

"Dress ranks. Atten-shun!" Gurian orders as Khomut, Pixie and Vadik file out of the Office. The CO halts in the middle of the duty room and inspects the line with dour contempt. He clears his throat and greets us. In a robust bass we chorus:

"Greetings, Comrade Senior Lieutenant!"

First, a few announcements: a reminder that we are to clean our personal weapons after the briefing; that Lance Corporal Salnikov is suffering from chickenpox and will be sent to hospital tomorrow and that in the meantime all contact with him is forbidden, even for those who have already had chickenpox; that in the near future we are expecting reinforcements to the tune of three to five persons, among whom there should be a driver; and that in view of the frequent disruption of the electricity supply and the imminent drop in the ambient temperature, Lieutenant Khomutenko is ordered to commence preparation of firewood, and that all personnel not engaged in military duties are at his disposal. After that, a slightly shamefaced Vadik finally reads into the microphone the duty roster for the next twenty-four hours.

After every name and task a low, agonised groan is heard from the ranks. When I hear my duties, I most certainly also groan. I have two details tomorrow: in the morning the right flank, and in the evening the left. The other way round would have been better: getting the left flank over with while I am still fresh, and afterwards muddling through the right flank somehow or other. To add insult to injury, I'll have Khomut grinding me down at any time of day with his log sawing. There is, however, some cause for celebration: I should get eight hours of uninterrupted sleep. A rare treat.

"There's a bi-ig freeze back home." Vovka Shatalov gives a long preoccupied sigh as he forces the ramrod up and down the barrel of his Kalashnikov. "They said on the radio — below minus twenty, and snow..."

You feel an urge to respond to this with some annihilating put-down, but Shatalov is such a special guy that everybody instinctively respects him. He is thickset, tough and dependable, with large, coarse features and big, strong hands. He moves unhurriedly but in a confident, purposeful manner, and seems to fit everything in without having to rush. Right now, unlike the rest of us, he has his boots and belt buckle polished, his undercollar is clean. We are dozily polishing the parts of our rifles with a rag, while he has all but finished cleaning his. He will assemble it next and then go to milk the cow.

He was put in charge of the paddock to care for the livestock the moment he arrived; he delivered the cow's calves, looks after the pigs, and keeps the horses in good shape. He puts up with all the bullshit of army life uncomplainingly, but looks sad sometimes and tries to tell us about life in his village.

"It's very quiet there in the winter, everything covered in snow, smoke rising straight up out of the chimneys. Mother bakes a whole batch of kalach loaves. I wish I could go hunting right now, grouse in the pine forest. Nothing better!"

"Hmm," I smile, unable to resist giving him a pinprick. "Why not grab your rifle, Vovka, and go and do it. A couple of elks wouldn't come amiss."

One or two chuckles. Shatalov pushes home the bolt he is checking and throws a glance in my direction. I see regret in his eyes, and a longing for something, and I'm left with a feeling of not knowing something that matters a lot, something essential, which he does know.

Piksheev pedantically checks how well the rifles have been cleaned. He criticises but doesn't send anyone back to do a better job. It's after firing practice you really have to slave. Fire a dozen rounds, and the next morning your Kalashnikov is like the firebox in the stove. That's when you have to work yourself stupid. Sometimes you feel like loosing off just for the hell of it, just so you know this lump of wood you hump around on your shoulder every day really is a rifle, a weapon of war; but when you remember about having to clean it afterwards, all you think about is how to get out of having to fire it. You'd sooner take a couple of hikes the length of the left flank.

When you're off duty, your time's your own. You're expected to mend your clothing, attend to matters of personal hygiene, write letters home, watch television... Right now, however, we can't be bothered with the telly, let alone the length of our toenails. We all have but one desire, and Vadik, bless him, understands and allows those who so wish just to sleep.

I ask Technician Commander Belikov, who has just assumed command of the border post, to put aside a couple of mugs of milk for me. At the same time, just on the off chance, I ask whether he might be able to find a smoke for me.

"A chance would be a fine thing," he fires back, scowling, and swallows loudly like a child who has been reminded of something tasty that he can't have.

Khomut comes out of the office.

"Comrade Warrant Officer, I don't suppose you would have a spare cigarette?" I ask. "To help me sleep."

"You're like a swarm of locusts! You've filched a whole pack off me in the course of the day!" He does, nevertheless, put his hand in his pocket and fumbles around there for a long time, evidently fishing one cigarette out of a pack which is stuffed full; he finally hands it over.

"Cheers! I'll be able to sleep now."

"You mean, without it you wouldn't?" Khomut winks. "You couldn't just churn yourself off to sleep?"

Feeling more cheerful, I go up to the smoking room, but before I can toke I hear from all sides:

"Rom, leave us some! A couple of drags!"

I sit down on the bench and click my lighter. The envious, greedy eyes accompanying every inhalation are an embarrassment poisoning my pleasure.

"For Christ's sake, will you take your eyes off me!" I finally snap. "I can't even enjoy it. Balton, play something, will you?"

"'The Photograph'?" Balton eagerly takes up his guitar.

"Let's hear it."

This is the anthem of our border post. It is said to have been devised long before my arrival by Sidor, a legendary cook. My Dads had not known him either, but they had heard about his exploits from their Dads. The story went that he would run off at nights with his guitar to the nearby village (now almost uninhabited) to his girl. He would trick the System by throwing a blanket over the barbed wire. The alarm would go off, the border guards would be called to arms to track down the intruder, and Sidor would rush straight on through the forest to his tryst. It's an unlikely story, but perhaps we can't get by without such legends. We want to believe that in days gone by there were fearless, madcap heroes. It is only we who are so lethargic, constantly weary, unmotivated, half-dead. But, the story goes, in days of yore...

The same three chords, Balton's nasal voice grating on your soul:

Your photograph hangs on the wall,
Making me wish you were with me tonight.
Your photograph promises love yet to be,
Reminds me right now you are not far away...

Between verses I shove the cigarette between Balton's lips. He sucks the smoke deep into his lungs, lets it out and continues with the song. I pass the cigarette butt to Terenty who takes a few hasty tokes before passing it on to the next in line, Makar.

I hold a small calendar in my hand, scuffed and well thumbed and almost completely riddled with tiny holes. Only underneath the heading "December" are two columns intact. I take a needle out of my fur hat. Every evening I pierce through another date, expunging one more day lived through. I pierce it as if driving an aspen stake through the heart of a vampire, to make sure it can't come back to life, can't drag me back, can never be repeated.

I open my eyes. From force of habit I was going to get up straight away, pull on my trousers and tunic, but nobody is haranguing me, no duty officer is standing over my bed. All is calm and still, apart from the lads wheezing and snoring nearby. The dormitory is warm. I stretch out a hand and feel the radiator: it's hot. Fly is doing his best. It doesn't feel right. I feel uneasy, as if something I need is missing. It's not cold enough, I'm not being woken up by an intrusive "Time to get on duty! Move it. Hey, wake up!"

The night lamp filters through the red-painted lampshade, softly lighting the dormitory.

I'm not sleepy. I'm free of that constant state of stupefaction from lack of sleep and exhaustion. I lie with my eyes open, looking at the ceiling. If you watch closely you can see pale shadows slipping lazily across it. I follow them with my eyes and my thoughts come to life, break free and grow into dreams. Vadik said they were sending reinforcements. Three or five men. It's perfectly possible that my demob telegram will arrive in a few days' time, perhaps even this morning. It will come just like that. For Melon and for me. And the day after tomorrow we will leave this place in the night. Completely. Forever.

I'll put on the dress uniform which has long been readied for the occasion. Admittedly it's rather plain, without all the extravagant ornamentation it might have had. I will pack my things and:

Away back to their native haunts
The border guards, the champions demobbed...

The lads will shove, straining, against the sides of the truck, and I shall finally shout to them: "Keep it up, golden guys!" and wave my cap.

Yes, fuck knows, demob is inevitable, as a young

conscript said, wiping away a reluctant tear with the floor cloth.

Stop! Stop! No dreaming: it's too scary. I evoke instead, in succession, other scenes from the past two years. There we are, still in civilian clothes, many of us even with long hair, being led into the Unit. Buzzing and groaning, the gates close behind us. The five-storey building of the barracks, and bloodthirsty faces laughing at us from the windows, and a mischievous, ominous shout from above: "Hey, greenhorns, go hang yourselves!" The first wash in the bathhouse, disinfections. The uniform, foot wrappings, and some fat warrant officer plonking a huge fur hat on my shaven head and saying, "Go, serve your country!" Every morning began with the hysterical shriek of the orderly: "Company, reveille!" We leap up, puny, scared, upset. People jump down from the upper bunks on to the lower bunks. We dress, confused by the unfamiliar items, bumping into each other in the narrow passages between the bunks. Anyone who's still in bed gets knocked to the floor by the sergeants. You have one minute to get dressed, then run to the square, then a three-kilometre run, morning fitness exercises, fifty press-ups, and only after all that can you run to the toilet. Polish the floors till they shine like glass, make and remake the beds, kitchen duties where you wash the dishes endlessly, never able to get them to a state which satisfies the orderly, then straightening the tables to perfection. In the evening, two free hours for watching the news programme, 'Vremya', while half asleep, writing tearful letters home, tending to your feet raw with blisters. In the night the inevitable practice alarms; and every day and evening the dirty tricks of the Dads. It seemed then that every day must be your last, that you would die of weariness and despair or, at best, go mad. But it didn't come to that: I survived, and have almost retained my sanity.

And now I can say I have stuck it out to the bitter end.

"Belikov, can I have the key to the storage room? There's something I need to get."

"By the way, I left your milk in the canteen, in the cupboard."

"Oh... You're welcome to it."

My kitbag is right beside the door. It's been waiting there for a month. All I need to do now is strap on my parka and boots, shove my winter uniform and dirty underwear inside, and depart. First, of course, I'll be taken to the Unit. I will hand in my uniform, and get my discharge papers and travel pass to my place of residence.

Right next to the kitbag is my demob briefcase. My parents sent me it at the end of September just when the order came. What a long time ago that was: the order demobilising into the reserve soldiers of my intake. Soon it will be three months, almost ninety days. Ninety extra days.

I undo the locks on the briefcase, break into a pack of Bond cigarettes. It's one of three. For the demob stock I need fifty cigarettes, so there are a few to spare. I pull out one, then another two. That still leaves fifty-seven. I can't possibly not smoke now. This is one of those rare moments, as if the wheel has stopped turning and, inside it, you have stopped too, stock still, and you look around in amazement. We had a game like that when we were kids. We would drag the tyre of a Kirovets tractor up the dam, one of us would climb inside where the inner tube should be, pressing his feet against the rubber, clutching the edges of the tyre. "Ready!" And the tyre together with its daredevil rider would be pushed off the dam and roll, spinning furiously, bouncing up on the stones and flying into the water. I have just the same sensation at this moment. For long seconds, hours, days I have been spinning, bouncing around, clinging on in order not to be thrown out and break my neck. Now it has all stopped, stock still, unexpectedly flopped over to one side, and you look around, freaked out by the sudden stillness, staring at everything around as if seeing it for the first time, and waiting in terror, but also with longing, with eagerness, for everything to start turning again, flashing by, blurring into whirling commotion.

Spitting often, I draw in the acrid, choking smoke of the stale, dried-out tobacco. It's a strange sensation — usually you are smoking damp cigarettes; in order to inhale properly, you need to suck with all your might, even giving yourself a headache. Now, suddenly, everything seems altered at this moment into something I want, something positive and good. For some reason, right now I know I am going to miss this hated border post which has so pissed me off, these lads the like of whom I will never meet again in civilian life, because there they will be different. I will miss being homesick too, and even this longing to get the hell out of here.

I jab the melted filter into the metal side of the urn at great length. I really do need to get to sleep. Tomorrow is going to be a hard day, like most of the days that preceded it.

I go down, give the key back to Belikov, and go to the toilet. How many times have I scraped the chipped enamel of these troughs set in concrete until they shone. I got into plenty of trouble: one time perhaps caught in the kitchen angling for a hot potato, another time not bothering to march all the way to the end of our section of the System, another time telling Piksheev to go to hell. Well, farewell, shitholes, soon I shall be seated on a comfortable pedestal toilet with a soft seat, a cigarette in one hand and a cup of coffee in the other. I will make up to myself for everything.

The air in the dormitory is fetid. As always, it reeks of damp, dirty foot wrappings, unwashed bodies, acrid sweat. I leave the door to the corridor half open. I lie down on my bed and stretch myself.

Time and again, with minor variations, I picture my departure, the day I finally bugger off. I try to drive away these frighteningly real images of what is soon to happen, must happen. But then, why drive them away? Why not just imagine it, and fall asleep to the accompaniment of these wondrous visions.

I hear a rhythmical, cautious rustling, as if a rat is gnawing at a rotten beam in the wall. I listen more attentively and detect murmuring and muffled sighing. I raise myself on an elbow and look over to where the sound is coming from.

Two bunks from mine a blanket is moving regularly, and the rustling and murmuring are coming from there.

"Hey, Terenty, stop wanking!" I say loudly, in order to put the wind up him. "There are people here, for heaven's sake. Go to the toilet and relax yourself there!"

"But I'm not..." Terenty wheezes, half asleep. "My leg has gone to sleep, it's like a log."

"You are like a log!" I feel with relief that I'm getting angry, returning to my normal state, that that strange, disturbing mood is being dispelled, the tyre is spinning round again, carrying me onwards, and I cling to it and shut my eyes tight. "You're a half-wit, Terenty, a monster, a baboon!"

I pull the blanket over my head and curl up in a ball. I try to hypnotise myself, whispering over and over again, "Sleep! Sleep! The more you sleep the sooner you will be demobbed. Sleep! Sle-eep!"

Translated by Arch Tait

Dmitry Bykov
CHRIST'S COMING

"It is that very one, resembling the faces of all the others, that must be the face of Christ."
Ivan Turgenev: "Christ"

20 September. 75th checkpoint duty.
192 days to demob.

What's remarkable about a company is that everything happens at the same time to everyone. Presumably they'll discover an explanation for this phenomenon, as for instance when everybody gets a toothache simultaneously and you, a sprog on night watch duty, see one squaddie after another go up to the mirror, examine his aching tooth, run off to the MO for drops and rub his gums with the stuff (which is a fat lot of good anyway, it just delays the hurting). It's the same for tummy-ache, and not through any fault of the cook but because of this very same rule. And with catching flu. Last winter there were days when not more than thirty showed up for reveille, all the rest were either flopped-out in the billet (there are only five beds in the infirmary) or if they had the milder sort then they got up late and were kept apart, left behind to overhaul their quarters and do some house-painting — come spring a big inspection was due. So everything turns out synchronised. Of an evening everybody feels well-disposed and placid — the day is over. In the morning, sullen and tetchy — the day is still ahead, they are short on sleep, they bawl out the sprogs (most particularly, of course, Chuvilinsky) and indeed everyone is going to get it in the neck.

It's like that now. The day after some slick story has got about the whole company hums with rumour. Before today's duty detail (in the course of which I am writing this) Sergei Maksimov came up and told me that the end of the world was at hand. It seems like some scientists have worked it all out or that some sort of meteorite is on its way. In the evening Vanka Kolodny, a lanky Ukrainian clodhopper from the transport drivers' platoon, said he had heard talk of it on leaving town: "It'll soon be curtains for us, chaps, a comet's flying in!" Finally when the unit orderly dropped by during the night to check that we were on the ball — I was with Valentinov, a sprog on his third checkpoint duty assignment — he said, "Sure thing, Sergei, there really is some sort of comet coming in and if next month it collides with the earth then pieces will end up all over the shop. Even allowing for the way reports get muddled there must be something in it."

Actually I don't remember a time when tales of this sort weren't doing the rounds, in fact these days they'll talk here about anything you can think of — the rising price of sugar; the end of the world; the effect of the world's ending on the price of sugar; the effect of the price of sugar on the ending of the world.... By and large one can always live in expectation that maybe the end's just round the corner. It's annoying that demob's now such a short way off and along comes this comet.

Perhaps it will miss.

Right now it's night: at two Valentinov is to relieve me if his orderlies manage to get him up on time, and if they don't I'll make it hot for them tomorrow. Not the way they came down on us in our time, just a verbal dressing-down.

I don't have any books here at all, just this notebook I brought back from leave so that I wouldn't altogether forget how to write. Before, I was mostly on in-house duty detail and in the mess, but now after my second year it is generally VCP — vehicle checkpoint guard duty. True, it comes much too often because we have fewer men after staff cuts and so on. The cuts are OK by me, but one gets sick of all the flying about on details. One good thing is that my demob is getting close. When there were two hundred days to go not one of us got a taste of butter. Then it was a hundred and fifty, then a hundred, and soon it'll be all over. They promised we wouldn't be kept on after discharge. For my last weeks I'll be choosing VCP.

I've already written my letters home and all that's left is to have a smoke (the drivers have brought some packs of Astra from town), to write all this down, to listen to the rustlings of the mouse under the floorboards. Come daylight Valentinov will be sweeping leaves and I'll sort-of give him a hand. It will be funny reading all this over later.

I really would like to know: the end of the world, what will signal its coming? On the one hand they all said that the falling star called Wormwood signifies Chernobyl because "Chernobyl" means "wormwood" and because from it "bitterness flowed into the waters". It certainly gives one the horrors, the whole of the Apocalypse — even though all I know of it is from re-renderings and not from the original which must be even more frightening. Furthermore there are to be insects of some sort, which will eat people up. There will be three horsemen... then three angels... I can't remember. I ought to get hold of something and read it up: there's a whole shelf on atheism in the library. But the main thing — the crux of the matter comes to me — is that there's bound to be a Second Coming of Christ. If he has not come yet rumours about the end of the world are so much hot air.

That mouse under the floorboards has been getting on my nerves. Pitch black all around. It's just started raining. Half past one. I am bored and want to sleep. What more is there to write about?

In three days I become a "Dad"[1]. Hoorah for that!

28 September. 77th checkpoint duty.
184 days to demob.

I drew the Sayings of the Apostles (as rendered by Kosidovsky) from the army library. Very absorbing. Christ existed (which I had never doubted) but here to be sure he is nothing like he was in *The Master and Margarita*.[2] Kosidovsky gives evidence according to which he most certainly was not "the most beautiful of the sons of Israel". They wrote (and surely without any intentional slander?!) that he was both short and ugly, that he provoked something close to loathing and that he had filth thrown at him — so the discrepancy was all the stronger between the way he looked and the way he spoke. I think he might indeed have been just such a one, and he didn't even need to say anything since his very appearance aroused compassion. But there you are, it is a fact that in the army someone like that, with his looks, would absolutely be eaten alive — to put it mildly. With us for some reason personal neatness is considered the greatest virtue, and that's not so much by the command as by the rank-and-file. "Just take a look at yourself, you're bloody shambolic" — I often heard this during my first year and now I'm saying the same to that

[1] a serviceman who has completed two and a half years of his obligatory three-year term (*tr.*)
[2] the novel by Bulgakov (*tr.*)

there Chuvilinsky. He is on duty with me today. Chuvilinsky is worth describing.

For who and for what am I describing Chuvilinsky? For posterity? I'm going to do all I can to see that this notebook doesn't come down to them, I'm going to burn it ceremoniously at the dacha after demob. (Yes, that's coming! And fairly soon too!) Is it for myself? That way I won't forget him as long as I live. Actually I am writing because there is nothing else to do.

Night. Mouse. Hush. Chuvilinsky won't be getting here for an hour and a half yet.

They call Chuvilinsky "Little Chuvy" or just "Chuvy". He is elongated like his surname — not tall but extended. He's got warts and there are warts like them on his mother too. She somehow got down to see him once and Chuvy offered little treats to everyone but they were reluctant to accept even treats from him. Everything about Chuvy makes one feel squeamish. It's not that Chuvy is dirty. He has a puffy face with small eyes and an expression of humble, imbecile adoration. This isn't coming out as a very rounded description. I need practice and I'm no writer. They train us how to teach literature but not how to write portraits.

Chuvy is hopelessly thick. He has no idea how to get on with people. One time they beat him up in the drying rooms — our "Dads" hadn't left yet — and like an idiot he was making a great fuss, bleating without a shred of self respect, behaving like an absolute schmuk! And he had enough wit to yell: "What's your gripe? I've done nothing to you!" They were splitting their sides. Chuvy's fellow recruits said not a word and kept out of the drying rooms although if it had been someone other than Chuvy... Oh well, they wouldn't have gone in anyway, there's our swinish nature for you. But anyway there Chuvy was, and absolutely nobody wanted to stand up for him. They said at first that he was a sneak, then they came to realise that he hadn't the mother-wit even for that. The army on the whole encourages informing, it's hard to stand out against it here. They do all they can to you to make you grass but if, which God forbid, you do grass you've had it for good and all. But luckily for him Chuvy is too dim even for that. In his dimness there is something demonic, supernatural, he doesn't react to anything, his sense of personal pride has been reduced to zero. One day the boys were having him on: "Hey, Chuvy! You got a girlfriend?"

"Yeah," he says with a timid self-satisfaction (an incongruous combination).

"So what's her name?"

"Olya."

"Well, how do you do it with her?" Chuvy gave a hesitant snigger.

"She hoists you up on top, or do you manage to clamber up on her yourself?" Again he sniggered.

Both Chuvy and this sort of horseplay are equally disgusting for me. I'd often say, "Oh, stow it, lads!" or simply decline to have any hand in it — that's as far as my resistance went. After all, in the army that's the way it is: right now everything may be more or less hunky-dory, you've got your friends and there are no open enemies in sight, but just stand out from the others in some small way and you'll find yourself occupying the niche Chuvy is in. When there are a hundred healthy snouts, when there's work, drill every day and hunks of lard for breakfast, lunch and supper, then inevitably you'll find there is jeering, taunting, meanness. The niche is occupied now by Chuvy but any one of us (and I repeat, anyone!) could in an instant land up in it. Here you've got to tread a knife edge between eating one's self up out of conscience or being eaten by the rest. I'm muddling things somewhat in the words I use, it comes out jerky. I badly want my sleep.

I would just have to say tomorrow that Chuvy hadn't relieved me on time and he would see even less of checkpoint detail than of his own saggy behind, which sticks out oddly as he walks. He'd go flying back to Company the softie. He's been mostly rostered for them as it is. Checkpoint detail is an easy option, a job for Dads: they put in an old hand as sentry and to help him out there's some sprog. Just now Valentinov who is usually with me and is quick on the uptake is off sick, so now it's got to be Chuvy cooling his heels on the lookout stand the way we all once had to. When I'm quit of the army I'd like to set fire to that lookout stand. If Chuvy's late I'm going to tear the tits off him. No, that's foul. I won't tear the tits off him. I'm writing down any sort of trash just so as not to snooze. Trash. Hush. Snooze. Mouse. One could make up a story just using those words.

If Chuvy doesn't relieve me I don't know what I'll do to him — I'm bound to fall asleep, the duty orderly will catch me snoozing and chuck me out of the detail. Then I'll make Chuvy... No I won't come down on Chuvy, he has enough on his back without me. I'm not up to it, besides which I get all queasy at having any dealings with him. Chuvy is clottish and dirty. I'm repeating myself. And just what am I to do so as not to drop off?

In the distance I can see Chuvy coming, his arms dangling in a silly way.

Bedtime.

15 October. 80th checkpoint detail. 167,
or after base withdrawal 166, days to demob.

The Company is being withdrawn. Soon it will be down to 150, and by-and-by close to 100 days to demob.

From there home will be really close. All through life you're trying to slow down time — who wants to die? — but in the army it's the other way round. Here you want to be through with it. As in the song, "Jump aboard and full steam ahead!"

Those sorts of sentiments had been scratched all over the table at checkpoint — mine had been among them — but yesterday or the day before they changed the table. I'm sitting and writing.

There is an interesting idea in Kosidovsky: apparently Christ was seen by many to have had a diabolical, a devilish origin. He exorcised demons and evil spirits, which meant he was connected with them. The notion that they had simply submitted to him was unbearable for the mindset of that era. Then it was easier for them to suppose that he was their Prince. Especially if you assume his appearance to have been deformed — pathetic or frightening, as you will. But in him one could really sense some demonic quality.

It is a curious thing how in extreme examples of ugliness and stupidity there is something mystical, awe-inspiring. I will never forget seeing in the Timiryazev Museum an anencephalon preserved in a bottle of spirit, a brainless foetus. That is to say, there was a head, but it was somehow triangular without a roof to its skull or else it just had something or other sticking out from there. Brrr... It seemed to me (and it was all grey, submersed in spirits, the colour of putty) it seemed to me that it was aware of some awful mystery, with those rolling eyes, somehow very protuberant, with the look that it had... Afterwards outside the museum when the excursion was over and I'd been left behind by my classmates I ran home in a fearful funk. It was dark, the area almost unknown to me, though it was only about seven at night, and then to top it off I tripped over a drunk. I have long been aware that there is some sort of Train of Destiny — once something scares you then all sorts of other things are going to creep up to frighten you some more, one after another. A happy man attracts happiness and an unhappy one the reverse. It's like that in the army: if you are feeling jolly everyone is nice to you, if you are gloomy they will pile on more gloom. For Chuvy they pile it on.

As a matter of fact in Russia people have always both feared and revered village fools and simpletons. In Leonid Andreev's stories[1] the idiot is a symbol for fate, I remember that from school, that's what they told us and I've read it myself. There's something frightening in all this. All my life I've shied away from Down's syndrome people, and in Chuvy there is something of it in his submissiveness, his tiny eyes, his vapid smile, his ceaseless stomach-rumbling, in the foul smell of his breath (I try to turn away when he speaks to me), in his naivete verging on God knows what. At the last bath time he came up to me (would you credit it? A yearling to a Dad!) and says with the grin of some holy fool: "Seryozha, rub my back for me, do!" His eyes are shining with meekness and imbecility. (No, shining with imbecility, that's not possible.) And what is more, on the lads soapsuds are just soapsuds but on him they are all grey and patchy, beastly to look at. He's got a hairy, round-shouldered back and a sticking-out paunch (he's not fat but he looks fat), thin little arms on a lanky, ungainly torso. "What's got into you, Chuvy?" I said, "Are you out of your tiny mind? Get out! And don't think you can sweet-talk some sprog into it or I'll twist off those lop ears of yours!" He gave a guilty smirk, said not a word and took himself off all wet to rinse himself away from the tub (for bathing we go to the village: there are tubs there and showers but the sprogs aren't allowed to use the showers). Whether or not I was being a shit I felt

---

[1] a popular writer of sensational horror stories in the period leading up to the revolution (*tr.*)

not the slightest sympathy for him, for that hairy rump, skinny legs, idiotic way of walking. I comfort myself with the thought that he's got it coming, but, after all, any of us might quite easily find ourselves in his shoes. And I also comfort myself with the thought that Chuvy is a typical peasant and if there was anyone more degraded than him then he'd be the first to cuss out the wretch, applying to him all the refined torments which he'd experienced on his own hide.

That's why I have no sympathy for Chuvy, I'm never sorry for fools and I myself have no call for anyone's pity. I'm in the mood for writing today, I don't even feel like sleeping, but then — have I got to sort out this thing about Chuvy, if only for myself? Not long ago I was in the Quartermaster's and late for lunch. I'd been chatting up a young storekeeper girl — we have a lot of civvies in the unit — and in came Chuvy at a run wobbling ridiculously in his ill-fitting boots with this ingratiating silly smile of his. He said, "They're calling you out on parade." His voice was low, drawling, oh so doleful... And how I yelled at him! That was because for being late on parade they would have my balls, also because he was grinning in a stupid way — could it be he was glad I was about to be landed in it? He didn't stop grinning, and there really was something diabolic in that grin: demon Chuvy! Too funny for words. But there you have it — a mystical figure, this demon Chuvy!

Last time he was with me on guard duty — or was it the time before? I get all mixed up about times — he left a scrap of paper there, a letter, and, I, shameful to relate, read it right through. It began with an affectionate "Darling Olya" — stiff, tall letters, the handwriting of a simpleton. "How are you getting on, I'm just fine." He's a devil, that Chuvy!

25 October. 82nd checkpoint detail.
158 days after base withdrawal to demob.

I finished reading Kosidovsky during the night. The Vet was just leaving our unit. The Vet is our Colonel and why they call him that is something one can't fathom — perhaps on account of his bright red mug, perhaps on account of his great strength: they said he pretty well wrestled down a bull, and though I consider that to be pure bullshit it has the attraction of a legend. No one wants to be completely subordinate to some prick of a nonentity so one has to invent some qualities for him, it seems to me this could be the subconscious explanation. So the Vet drove out from the unit. I was so immersed in my reading that I hardly managed to get the gates open for him. Crikey! How little things can trip you up in the army! But I did manage, even made a show of bustling about, so he sketched a salute and left. With Vet's departure there is perfect peace in the unit.

I've lost the thread. I read all through Kosidovsky and something peculiar came home to me: that Christ did not come in order to preach about this and that. In the final analysis all those Gospels had already been laid down in the Old (an interruption here, the duty orderly arrived) Testament, yes, in the Old Testament. His appearance had been predicted there. That is... to be sure he made it all human, brought it home and so forth, he preached splendidly and was very fascinating no doubt, but I still think it was this way: a purposely ugly, wretched, idle good-for-nothing arrived purely to put to the test people's reverence for the Old Testament and, most importantly, to find out to what degree they can be considered human beings. I mean, I don't know much about the morality laid down in the Old Testament but I'm supposing that he was sent to check whether there are rules applicable to all humankind or not. And generally, I wouldn't call myself a believer but, all the same, like in the Strugatskys,[1] I often have the impression that certain things are sent to us so as to test our reaction. It seems to me that this was the case here and that humanity had failed to pass the test because, in the first place, what was sent down to them wasn't like one of themselves (which would have been bad enough); and in the second place, he was different from them in a nasty way, that is, filthy, ragged and so on. To be sure, had he been the handsome fellow that had been promised the story would have turned out no different. Incidentally, if he was so very pathetic was it worthwhile crucifying him? But perhaps he really did preach to his followers that that was how it had to be, that there was no getting around it? Here something else really staggers me: "Ye know neither the day nor the hour wherein the Son of Man cometh." That is, you must keep watch. That is, he might arrive at any moment.

That is, he can arrive at any moment.

Somehow I'm beginning to repeat myself, or rather, I get to pondering and then I write down the very same thing. This is because my head is aching badly and I'm permanently short on sleep.

I was always convinced people aren't alike, that no two are identical, but now I see that there are certain things about them. One has got to hide them away inside oneself, especially in the army; subconsciously I did hide them away and by now it is hard for me to say just what those things are. Why do they hound Chuvy? (Well, all right, to be honest, why do we all, me included, hound Chuvy?) I can also understand why it is necessary that somebody has got to be

---

[1] the science-fiction writer brothers whose works examine problems of amorality and aimlessness in a completely materialistic society. (*tr.*)

hounded, and he is, inherently, abject. But what if he was able to lash out in retaliation? Then they would torment not him but somebody else and for this lot here I could easily fit the role — and then nothing could save me (or anybody else for that matter).

That's the essence of this nightmare: we torment Chuvy and in fact we are tormenting not him but the niche he occupies, and in that niche could be any single one of us. So we are tormenting ourselves: it turns out to be absolutely the way it was for Christ.

One thing I can say with complete certainty: Chuvy repels me. He is so thick that it looks as if he is skiving. But if it's a matter of skiving, and maybe it's not, I don't know... however that may be, if Chuvy has been sent to try us then we most definitely are failing the test.

All the same they found just the right place to send him to — to the army! After they had seized Christ the soldiers beat him all night in the guardroom (there were already guardrooms then! There is some mention of that, or else this is another thing I read about in Andreev.) One shouldn't turn anyone over to a lot of soldiers, they'd finish off not just Christ but all the Apostles to boot.

It's enough to send one crazy, the monotony of our existence.

Valentinov's brought a smoke.

Misha Kovalchuk said I'm getting odd. He said that with a chuckle. That means, if I get a bit odder yet I could fill the niche. Once I realised that the niche existed I began to be scared of it and once you start getting scared — that's asking for it.

It's nothing to me. I'm almost down to a hundred and fifty days before home. I don't give a damn.

First thing, all the same, I'll burn this notebook. Then I'll take a proper bath.

29 October. 83rd checkpoint detail.
152 days from base withdrawal to home.

Yesterday Chuvy didn't leave his boots in the drying rooms, he got tired and fell asleep because they'd sent him to unload wagons with furniture for the military township and he got knackered. He put his boots by his bed. They crucified him... God, what have I written! What I mean is, they kicked him awake and kept kicking him until he had fetched his boots and then junior-sergeant Vanka Melnikov, one of his co-draftees from somewhere or other near Voronezh, ordered him to sniff his feet. Four men sat on Chuvy (though they wouldn't have had to hold him down) while Vanka shoved his foot into his nose. Chuvy howled a bit, in a contemptible sort of way.

I broke it up but to little purpose: they were already taking the mickey out of me, even.

"There goes a fan of Chuvy's!" Vanka said today.

One of our lot put him in his place, but our lot too can't understand why I shield Chuvy. They don't see that it's not him I'm protecting — what is he to me? It could be that I'm saving my soul: down in town, all over the place, they are talking about the End Of The World. The End Of The World... If Chuvy is really sounding us out then indeed we're for burning, every one of us. Well, a joke's a joke, but small things cast long shadows.

Of late my head's been aching atrociously. I'm really cheesed by this life, this strain, this sleeplessness. I don't talk of it to anyone and I don't mention it in my letters but I can tell myself about it. I started talking to myself on checkpoint duty. One time Valentinov was on duty with me, I didn't notice him coming in after lunch (I had mine earlier on my own) — he said I was talking to myself about something. He was chuckling too.

In the army after the first year there's no new sustenance for the mind and like a hungry stomach it begins to digest itself. The same thing happens as with a stomach ulcer but this is a mind ulcer. It's awful. In general if someone suspects that he is going crazy that means he is still sane. But the Dads were right, the last six months are hell. Like the first. That's because your thoughts are only about home, you're incapacitated, your brains eat themselves up. Perhaps that's why my head aches so much.

And my handwriting has changed. Having finished a word I'm always reluctant to take the pen off the paper, I sort of embellish it, complete the drawing of it, put in little dots and hooks. It seems to me that were I to lift the pen sooner than I ought to something would happen. Chuvy's example makes me scared. If we are all going to be burned up (the orderly just came up and asked me why my eyes are red), if we are all going to be burned up that's a real shame.

5 November. 85th checkpoint detail. 146 a.b-w. to home.

He had no father and Chuvy too has no father.

I also don't have a father but that's irrelevant.

Chuvy's mother isn't called Mary. I don't remember her name but it was definitely something else, the Deputy Political Officer greeted her by name and patronymic. Chuvy isn't Jewish.

If he were Jewish that would really be it.

But they couldn't care less about little coincidences like that, it's the principle that matters. It's better for them that there should be no resemblance. Watch out, for Ye know neither the day nor the hour. Nobody is supposed to know.

Two thousand years have gone by and we haven't changed, we've boobed again.

But who gave the order that it should be the army, that he should be sent into the army? Before the army he was a student and he was just fine. But what sort of student would that have been? Might it have been some trade school? No, I just can't...

Did I really come to believe in all this? After all it's not me who started talking about the end of the world...

When all is said and done, the fact that I started reading Kosidovsky was hardly accidental either. I myself would never ever have thought of reading Kosidovsky. Something or other INSPIRED me. I had to. So I would understand. So I could give warning. I didn't do anything. I'm standing guard in my Number Two khakis ready for the holiday. What a stupid remark if you think about it, introducing myself as a man all dolled up for tomorrow.

A truck has just gone through with the special holiday food.

I got a letter from my Institute.

I'd go on writing anything so that I don't have to think. My head is splitting. The back of my head hurts worst of all, it feels like it's going to burst. God, how my head hurts! He knew how to cure head pain.

But Chuvy has no abilities at all. That doesn't prove a thing. Could be it's simply that their headaches passed off of themselves and they credited him with it. I've asked our MO for a couple of aspirins, he'll bring them when he's finished his rounds.

I've got to distract myself with something right away or else I'll be thinking up all sorts of rubbish.

But all the same, something of the sort actually is flying in — yesterday there was this program on local TV. It seems it isn't all tosh. So it really is me that has got to speak out.

Then the aspirins. Scoffed them and feel a bit better. Read all through. It's terrible, the stuff I'm writing.

7 November.

NO, ALL CORRECT. UNDERSTOOD! THANK YOU, LORD, FOR APPOINTING ME. I WILL TELL THEM ALL.

These words concluded the notes in the sketch book found on the bedside table of Private Sergei N. (whose name for obvious reasons is being withheld). On November 7, at the time that the holiday detail was being drawn up, while Private Chuvilinsky whose holiday leave had been cancelled and who had to report for company fatigues had arrived and just taken up his position on the lookout stand, Sergeant Melnikov who was passing by gave him a kick. Everyone laughed. At that moment, to the surprise of all, Sergei N. in whose earlier demeanour certain peculiarities had already been detected, pushed Chuvilinsky aside, jumped up onto the stand and shouted in all directions "Don't you touch him! He is Christ!"

At first it was taken to be a novel bit of clowning and Melnikov even suggested crucifying Chuvilinsky. But N. was absolutely serious, he was terribly agitated, his eyes were shining. He was shrieking about a revelation of some sort. He kneeled down in front of Chuvilinsky beating his head on the ground in obeisance. He gave thanks to God for his predestined task and appealed to the servicemen present to repent, threatening them with hell fire. All attempts to pacify N. — who had never seemed particularly religious — came to nothing. He broke free with an astonishing display of strength and all the while was begging the forgiveness of those whom he was hitting. He rushed around screaming that Chuvilinsky was the new Christ, sent down to earth as a spiritual test. Chuvilinsky, terrified, huddled up in the corner, afterwards taking refuge in the Lenin Room. He was shaking all over.

They took Sergei N. to town, to the district military hospital where he was diagnosed with severe reactionary psychosis, the result of extreme exhaustion, lack of sleep and mental stress. An investigating commission was sent out to the unit but it did not find any violations.

In December of the same year, three months ahead of his scheduled discharge, Sergei N. was examined by a medical board and sent for treatment to Moscow. He is now altogether normal and remembers almost nothing of what happened.

And neither in the Company nor in the unit did it occur to a single soul that he was the one man who, like Christ, had shown pity to that most contemptible of wretches.

JEWHAD

The two episodes below come from Bykov's new novel, JEWHAD, a futuristic anti-utopia about imminent ethnic conflicts and the inevitable crisis of democracy and liberalism as we know them today. Although the novel is set in some distant future the events and situations described are drawn from the present-day army.

Facing Company Commander Funtov in the Sixth Company HQ, currently located in the village of Baskakovo, sat a woman in her fifties of that indeterminate social position which now characterizes the country's intelligentsia, marginalized by society but none the less still retaining some breeding. The head of this petitioner was covered by a patterned cashmere scarf such as was often sported in the seventies, at the time of Soviet-Indian fraternization. Her hands were folded humbly on her knees and her face expressed entreaty. The woman was deeply agitated. This was Gorokhova, a soldier's mother.

The Company HQ was distinguished for its exceptional cheerlessness. Everyone who landed up here had it somehow brought home to them that all effort was in vain. Dreariness emanated from the yellowish stools, the scrawny brochures of regulations and the sullen gaze of Marshal Zhukov from his portrait above. The floor was scrubbed three times a day but was still grubby. From the ceiling hung three sticky tapes thickly speckled with fly corpses. On the windowsill a potted plant was drying out: the orderlies watered it regularly but something or other outside the control of the orderlies, permeating the very air, gulped up moisture from the dripping plant's pot, fed the flies and covered the windowsill with dust.

The white curtains on the windows would soon be yellowed by the dreariness. Much use would it be to dream of victory if the fate of the army was decided in offices like this! Were one to draw a picture on the wall, a rabbit, say, or a mole, the unbearable depression might be dispelled — but no doubt the rabbit and the mole would turn out every bit as sour and crooked as the animals depicted on the walls of children's clinics and day nurseries. In the Sixth Company HQ any decent human being would want to hang himself. This ineluctable tedium was further amplified by Funtov's voice, monotonous as the buzzing of the flies — but the sticky tape for a Captain Funtov has yet to be devised.

Even flies encountering Captain Funtov wanted to do

away with themselves. Some couldn't hold out and — zhzhzhik — flew smack into the flypaper unable to withstand the boredom of the place. They must have simply envied Funtov, nonplussed by his flyishness: he was clearly outbuzzing and outcrawling them — out-heroding Herod. Whatever way it was, from envy or from boredom, the flies threw themselves onto the flypaper as onto barbed wire but there death was drawn out, adhesive: their ending was not a pretty one and long they lay twitching on the gum. Serves them right. One must die when one gets the order, not from one's own initiative.

"Look here, this is your third time here" — this in a monotone from Funtov, a short, almost rectangular man whose age was in fact not more than twenty-seven though he looked all of forty, portly, somnolent, as it were sprinkled with dust. It would be impossible to think of a topic one could discuss with Funtov after five minutes of being shut up with him in the same space. He could smirk lewdly over a mention of women, could lament the effeteness and puniness of the new intake, could yawn dreamily and enunciate his favourite saying: "Oh-ah, if ignorance was cash I'd buy me some country hussies so as to knock 'em about a bit." But there was absolutely nothing else in him.

The presence of this sort of person is particularly unbearable in moments of melancholy or anxiety when one eagerly awaits a kindly word and would gratefully welcome a single glance of understanding. But as far as that went Funtov was like a lump of clay, destitute of emotion from birth. At school he always dozed on the back benches but was famed for his ability quickly and efficiently to wring the neck of a pigeon. He wasn't much of an officer — a slacker, without initiative and with negligible tactical or technical abilities — but it was precisely his complete indifference to the fate of his troops (these to his understanding were not humans at all) which rendered him priceless in the eyes of the Command. Funtov was always put forward as a model at officers' meetings at which Colonel Zdrok gave hour-long speeches a la Fidel Castro. Funtov was in no sense a combatant, understood nothing of geopolitical briefings and most likely hadn't a clue as to with whom and why he was at war, but he did exhibit, to a degree that was even excessive, the most essential quality of an officer, namely obtuseness. To such a degree did it fill his entire being that it left room for nothing else, and on this account Colonel Zdrok loved him with a fatherly love and even General Paukov had said on occasion that Funtov was an able officer.

"Listen, this is your third time here," he drawled languidly, "Why do you keep coming? Your son, I mean, well, your son, see, he's being seen to. He's, like, under supervision, that is. You come up here and that's, like... annoying for others who don't have people coming for them. Him, he's not served six months yet. He's getting favours. He's still got the ways of civvy street. He's not a soldier, not yet. Him, he's a gherkin, a cabbage. And you keep on coming up here. What makes you come here?"

"Please understand," Gorokhova, the soldier's mother, was speaking nervously in the sincere belief that if now she found some really convincing words Funtov would know how to mitigate her son's sufferings. No he would not, to be sure, send him back from the front. It was wartime: they were more and more reluctant to admit her to the unit's location, she had to pull strings, to ring up a former classmate of hers whose replies were increasingly curt. Humiliation. Terror. But then, if only some soft duty could be found for him, something at headquarters or maybe in the rear, nearer to home... She had no doubt that the officer sitting opposite her must have a heart and she needed only to find some way to move it... But Gorokhova did not know how. She had come up to Baskakovo for the third time in four months because her son was driving her wild with his complaints and pleas, yet there was nothing she could do to help him and ahead was still a year and eight months of torment. In the three years prior to his call-up and in the first four months of his service she had aged twenty years and her face acquired the permanently woeful, suppliant expression of a person who has lost all self-respect.

"Do please understand. He writes he's got boils and can't walk but they make him run."

"They all write they've got boils," droned Funtov. "Nobody is made to run. There are slippers. Everyone walks in slippers. There's a medical centre, see. With the medics everything's as it should be. You didn't get him ready for the service, see? So he writes, like. If you'd got him ready, see, to serve, see, he wouldn't be writing, get it? But there it is, he writes and you come up. What's the point of coming?"

"He asked to be allowed socks," Gorokhova gabbled on, "He can't wrap his footcloths, doesn't know how, well couldn't he, surely, have socks, if only to start with..."

"Footcloths, see," said Funtov, "Footcloths let the feet breathe. A foot sweats. Feet get sweaty. In a boot a sweaty foot rots, it rots because it's sweaty, get it? And so as it doesn't rot from sweating they apply the appropriate regulations about footcloth, military, made of cloth. Also cotton, regulation kind. It lets the foot breathe, and then there's those ancestors too."

"What about our ancestors?" asked the alarmed mother.

"Those ancestors of ours," Funtov explained limply, putting on the sorrowful face of a peasant woman, "always fought in footcloths. There's Marshall Suvorov now: 'Serve by the rulebook and win honour and fame.' There was Stalingrad — they fought in footcloths. Kursk — in footcloths. The feet don't rot and you can do anything. Even route marches like. But you must have the know-how. Know the trick of it? You got to put the sole of your hoof down on one corner, then stretch it tight so's there's no wrinkles, and then wind it round quick. And afterwards wind it round a bit more so it clings to the foot. It lets the old sweaty hoof breathe. Then after it's tucked back under like this," he lazily sketched in the air exactly how to do it, wrapping up one stubby-fingered hand with the other as if the soldier's mother Gorokhova, right away, here in the Company HQ, would be needing to wrap her feet in footcloths in readiness for a training exercise. "And that's all there is to it. It's a matter of fifteen seconds, give or take. You stamp on it to firm it up. A sock doesn't let the foot breath, it'll go mouldy in it. You'll get an abscess starting and all." (Funtov himself went about in socks at his training school and got put on duty rosters for it but he just couldn't master the trick of winding on his footcloths.) "The footcloth is the Russian soldier, it's so very Russian that invention of ours. You got a Russian soldier, you got footcloths, everyone knows that. Europe knows it, Australia, er..." His voice slowed, then, remembering where else there was, "Africa knows it."

"But please understand," Gorokhova repeated, all the more despairing, "he's not able to. Perhaps it is not possible for everyone. He can't run. He writes nicely, quite a calligraphic hand. Perhaps you could pick him an occupation of some sort. I don't know, I'm not a military person, what sort of duties you would have. Perhaps something using biology: he's a biologist, second year..."

"I'm telling you," said Funtov flatly, "he's got to go through Basic Training like everyone else. What's this biology stuff got to do with us? He'll go through Basic Training and then he can have his biology. After Basic Training anything you like, demagology. We've got our smart chaps too, students. We've, like, got a warrant officer of that sort, he knows words your son wouldn't have heard of most likely. A modern army, that's what it is. All one family. The lads eat together, doss down together... It's a male collective, that's what. As for boils, every man-jack of 'em's got a boil. When it's parade drill they've all got boils, and when its greasy-spoon time then they'll be ready to dance dances."

"What's greasy-spoon?" soldier's mother Gorokhova asked stiffly.

"Greasy-spoon. The soldiers' canteen," explained Funtov. "They call it the greasy spoon. It's all proper there, there's gingerbread, sugar to buy if you want. We've nothing against it, that place. But ahead of the greasy spoon comes, like, the Fatherland, see. Got to Serve the Fatherland. You take a little morning run in the fresh air and then you can have your greasy spoon. And a stroll in the evening. But if your mother keeps coming up all the time with saucepans, see, what sort of a soldier will you be then? Especially in wartime."

Hearing about wartime Gorokhova snapped out of her stupor and lost all self-control.

"Wartime!" she cried. "Your soldiers can't even fire a shotgun, in wartime! My son was saying how in four months service he'd been to the range only once! With you, soldiers peel potatoes in wartime and scrub the floors and are made to run round the perimeter until their feet are worn down to the bone! You all keep saying that we didn't prepare our sons properly, and who are you preparing? You've been fighting four years and where has your fighting got you? Don't tell me we've failed to prepare them! You just want dumb cattle, cannon fodder, to send where you want and to hell with them!"

At that moment the soldier's mother realized that she had irretrievably lost her son any chance of a transfer to the HQ or of some other freeloading assignment: she had done something uncalled-for, unthinkable, she had raised her voice and bawled out the officer on whom everything depended. She slid from the stool onto her knees and beat her forehead on the incessantly scraped and still dirty floor of the Company HQ.

"Forgive me, I beg you," her voice turned into a wail, "I implore you, forgive me. His father's ill, he can't stand on his feet, my husband, his father! I'll do anything you want. He's our only son. For God's sake. Anything you say, just whatever you say. Forgive me for God's sake. I have no more strength left."

Funtov sat unstirring. "Woman," he drawled, "Mother Gorokhova, get up! What's got into you? Seems like, well, seems like you think as you're in your own home! This is a military place, see! What you've been saying, as how his father can't stand up — for all of them it's 'he can't stand up', any one of 'em will sing that tune.... Look here! For you this here may be a circus. This isn't a circus. This here's the office of a military company. Really, look at you, it's like you're getting married for the first time or something. Give over!"

"I'm not going anywhere," babbled the mother Gorokhova. "I'll do anything you want. I'll clean your shoes for you. Money, anything. I implore you. I won't go..."

"Orderly!" yelled Funtov. The orderly came in, a tubby soldier called Dudukin whose face never lost its expression of imbecile happiness. Dudukin was considered a model soldier despite his stoutness. He was a poor runner but they often gave him domestic work details, he adored washing floors, he squeezed out the rag with dexterity and generally would manage the incessant cleaning as easily as a woman. For cutting hair, shaving the back of someone's neck, carving out with his little knife the figure of a peasant with a bear, for these Dudukin was a true expert.

"Orderly Dudukin reporting and ready for duty!" he roared out with satisfaction.

"This here, look," said Funtov. "Pull that woman up, like. See she gets seen off from here. Give her some water. Put the reserve guard on watch duty. It's OK. Seems like soon this won't be Company HQ so much as a real number 14 madhouse." Why 'number 14' nobody knew, but to Captain Funtov this was a popular adage.

Soldier's mother Gorokhova felt really frightened. She finally realized that before her was a person with absolutely nothing inside him and that it was precisely for that reason that he was now in command of her son. She realized how terrible it must be for her son to be surrounded by this altogether inhuman mass of people, messing with them, dossing with them, winding on footcloths. A fly would feel likewise, persuaded of the uselessness of appealing to the flypaper for human or flyish feelings. Making requests was pointless, one might have to kill if kill one could, but nobody had taught soldier's mother Gorokhova how to. There remained only one outcome: to let her son be turned into that same sort of crude human biomass, for in no other way would survival be possible. He would have to become as they were, or else he would still be wearing his feet sore, sobbing, writing pitiful letters. Surrendering him to that biomass was even more frightful than sending him off into the army but there was no alternative: the soldier's mother felt as a homely adolescent feels on being beaten up by hooligan thugs. He knows that his entreaties are totally useless, that this is for real, that they are really determined to smash him up and will indeed do so, and no matter what he does nothing will deflect them from it. The soldier's mother came out of the Company HQ reeling. There would be no point in her going there any more.

Her son Gorokhov knew nothing of it yet, he was hoping

for an easing of conditions, was angry with his mother for taking so long and with himself, that she had to humble herself because of his own inability to be like the others. Besides which Gorokhov was hoping for a treat, he knew his mother had come with some patties but she went straight in to the Company HQ first. In civilian life he would never have thought that on the day of his mother's arrival, at the hour when his fate was being decided by her talk with his commander, his mind would be focussed on meat patties. But so it was. He saw the patties clearly; even if the Commander would not agree to anything at all at least there would be some food, only it would have to be eaten quickly, it would never do to take it back with him to the unit. The spectacle of his mother's patties being devoured by his barrack-mates would be quite unbearable. Gorokhov thought his mother would be coming over to see him right away and that on that account they would let him off 'geopolitics' and perhaps even the next day's duty detail.

He did not know that at that time his mother, all bent over, was trudging back through Baskakovo to the bus stop, further and further from the former school where the company was stationed. Soldier's mother Gorokhova did not have the strength left to see her son again, to look into his eyes and to promise a change for the better. He must not harbour hopes. Having landed here he must become part of the biomass. The bag with patties swung against her legs. After a half hour the bus came and with a wailing sound carried soldier's mother Gorokhova to the district town from which there was the prospect of 24-hours travel to get to Moscow by the only train. The bus was wailing, Gorokhova was wailing, the slimy scenery beyond the window wailed.

It was at this very time that on the parade ground, now tumid from three days of rain, a group of writers, who had come to

Baskakovo at the behest of the newspaper *Red Star*, were undergoing combat training. The writers had been sent to General Paukov for two reasons: first, because he was believed to be one of the best combat generals and, moreover, had a resolute ideological outlook. He could seriously and with thoroughness expound the objectives of the war, the morale of the troops and the inevitable triumph of the Russian cause. Second, Baskakovo was a relatively safe sector, they had of course long ceased to mollycoddle writers but an empire can't call itself an empire if it doesn't look after its bards. War is war but there should be some culture too.

The writers' unit had been put together in Moscow and despatched to the South-Russian front, but there they had got holed up once the fighting began, the High Command categorically refusing to allow their return to the rear. To be sure they were in no direct danger. They hardly ran the risk of being killed by the Jewhadists but they might be seized as hostages and to this the High Command was mightily averse. All too many minor writers, the swine, had deserted to the Jewhadists in this way, seduced by the promises of freedom. They never got any freedom and on the whole the ethnically alien elements in the Jewhadist army were openly mistrusted: Channel One had even shown film on how the turncoats were treated there as prisoners of war. However among writers the commonplace myth about liberty-loving ways in the Khazar army was widespread, which was why it was worth protecting this group of loyal citizens. And so it was that a posse of patriotically orientated writers numbering eight was inflicted for three weeks on General Paukov, to chew on army rations and to get to know the soldiers.

It was first decided that the writers would all lodge together at HQ but a directive came from Moscow to pitch them into real army life. After that directive the guests were dispersed among various lodgings and made the acquaintance of the Company's officers while those officers were ordered to facilitate contacts between the Moscow literati and any particularly gallant privates. Puzzled, the Company Command declined, it would have been difficult to tease out from the ranks of Paukov's division heroes worthy of gracing the pages of *Red Star.* The army was occupied in achieving excellence at square-bashing, geopolitical instruction and the cleaning of weapons. It diversified its days with increasingly frequent shootings of its own men.

"Take, for example, private Krasnukhin, he's a good soldier." With an embarrassed smile platoon sergeant Kasatkin was offering his help. "He hasn't performed any great heroics as yet, but while on guard duty he let off a warning shot when the NCO checking on him purposely failed to give a password. He almost shot him too. A good soldier."

"Hullo then," the selected one was being addressed ingratiatingly by writer Kurlovich, a half-Khazar by birth but still a convinced statist. Seated opposite in the Lenin Corner, his huge hands reposing on ample knees, was ginger-haired Private Krasnukhin. "Tell me something please about your achievement."

"Well, what's there to it?" said Krasnukhin in some confusion. "That is, I'm standing there and somehow I'm dozing off, but I'm telling myself — no, you mustn't!"

"And what was it you were guarding?" Kurlovich was anxious to get things right.

"Why that, whaddyercallit, I was guarding the watch mushroom."

"Um, quite so." Kurlovich, the writer, gave a slight nod, hurrying to show his familiarity with military life. However his story demanded precision, and why the watch needed a mushroom was something about which Kurlovich had no notion. Maybe it was a matter of foot-fungus having struck the watch which now had to be put under guard lest the infection reach epidemic proportions?

"Excuse me," continued the writer after a brief moment of indecision, "but all the same what is a mushroom for?"

"Well, as for that..." Private Krasnukhin gave his explanation unwillingly, fearing that here there was some sort of trickery, perhaps this was a crafty way of testing him for knowledge of the regulations? "According to Section Five of the Code for Guard Duties... the built up area attached to a rural location where is billeted a platoon, company, regiment or other military formation must be protected by night-time patrol of sentries spaced at fifty metre intervals and equipped with sentry mushrooms, each in conformity with the specifications for such mushrooms. The mushroom specification according to regulations are five in length, three in width and the height of the base two meters to ensure protection of the perimeter patrol post against rain, squally wind, snow storms, drifting snow and severe hail and with the intention of preserving personnel from colds, suppurating boils and other undesirable conditions." Krasnukhin had run out of breath while Kurlovich scribbled away. "Well there you are, the mushroom's standing there. All according to specifications, we put it up ourselves. And the rain was teeming down, 'like to God and my mother', it was."

"You love your mother?" Kurlovich asked with a warm smile.

Again Krasnukhin suspected a trick question.

"Excuse me, but that's a way of speaking."

"I understand," exclaimed Kurlovich, "after all, I'm Russian, aren't I!" (As was mentioned above he was not). "But I would like to fill in the details, you understand. So you are standing there in pouring rain at the guard post thinking about your mother."

Private Krasnukhin on that night and indeed very frequently did remember a mother but one with no relationship to his own parent, a tall, bony woman from near Voronezh. Rather, to him the word referred to the secret mother of all creation, she who had engendered the night, the rain, and the sentry-mushroom that was constructed in accordance with specifications.

"My mother's a hospital nurse." Krasnukhin spoke confusedly in a deep bass. "We don't have a father, but mother's O.K. She writes."

"Well, what was it you were remembering?" Kurlovich was insistent, having sensed that here there was some vivid, juicy detail to be had. "Perhaps the smell of home-cooked cutlets? Don't be shy, home cooking is also a part of our domestic life, our love for our native land!"

"No, with mother it was rather things made from spuds," averred Krasnukhin, "little flat cakes, know what I mean?"

"I know, of course I do," the writer was joyfully nodding in assent; potato-cakes are not mushrooms, here he was on familiar ground.

"Well there you are," the private was pensive. "Cabbage rolls too, sometimes."

"Tell me, can you remember what your mother's arms were like?"

Krasnukhin recalled his mother's long arms, her swollen joints and her flat fingernails. He felt sorry for his mother from whom to be sure he had had little tenderness but he felt no resentment on that score. After all, she had not beaten him although she should have done. Out of youthful folly he had several times been slung into the juvenile detention cells of police stations and once he had had a hand in robbing a trading stall and only by a great stroke of luck had not been caught. Altogether, if it hadn't been for call-up it would have been only too easy for him to have landed up in one of those "not so distant places", that is to say, a prison camp. His mother had been just a mother like any other, no worse, so what was this bespectacled nit banging on about?

"Well, yes," he replied with irritation, "But what about her arms? What's my mother got to do with this anyway?"

"But it was you who brought her up."

"Only in the sense that I said it was raining like to God and my mother."

"Tell me, do you believe in God?"

"Believe? In God you mean?" Krasnukhin asked. "According to the rulebook Holy Russia is a divinely chosen power, appropriately and symmetrically laid out over a sixth part of the world's land surface and gloriously arrayed through the munificence of Father, Son and Holy Ghost, her protection being the sacred charge of the Orthodox Army which has been provided expressly to preserve, uphold, guard, and with conscientious vigilance keep watch over her."

"Was that your own?" Kurlovich was startled. "Those are your own words?"

"Why mine?" — from puzzled Krasnukhin. "That's what's written in the Sixth Epistle from Sophronius the Eremite in the General Military Rule. Haven't you read it?"

"Of course, of course," spluttered Kurlovich, "Just, you understand, you had it so pat. I was wondering whether maybe you did any writing... verses perhaps, poetry?"

"No, that's just not my thing. I'm one of the platoon sentries. Standing orders is to swab the floors, smarten yourself up, put up a mushroom shelter when it's called for..."

"All right then," Kurlovich was disappointed. "You were standing there then, and so what happened next?"

"I heard a rustle," Krasnukhin was speaking slowly, "I shouted out: 'Halt! Who Goes There?' and according to regulations I should have got the reply 'Horse in Underwear', but seeing as I'm not getting the reply I slaps a cartridge into the breech and repeats the question 'Who Goes There?' And when I doesn't get an answer on the third time of asking I fires into the air and then Sergeant Glukharev as was going the rounds checking up shows himself to me and gives the order 'Attention!' But as I hadn't been given the password I turned my rifle on Sergeant Glukharev and loaded another cartridge into the breech and told him to give the password. And then Sergeant Glukharev said the right words and after that I lowered my rifle and replied in proper form."

"Tell me," Kurlovich asked with a degree of nervousness, "What if Sergeant Glukharev had not given the password?"

"Well, then," and it seemed as if Krasnukhin was himself astonished by his own words, pronounced with some perplexity: "Well then. Then I would have let off a round into the chest of Sergeant Glukharev according to regulations, even if that meant killing the Sergeant stone dead."

"But look here, he was your duty-sergeant, you knew him perfectly well, surely..."

"So what of it, that he was duty-sergeant?" Krasnukhin, still perplexed, answered with an enquiry of his own. "He was doing the rounds. Some enemy might infiltrate on pretences. Or suppose he'd been recruited by one. Or he was drunk, so as he couldn't remember the password. He'd broken the rules, right? Breaking rules means getting shot. And then I had asked three times, I'd cocked the rifle. If he was Sergeant Glukharev he should have reacted, but what if he was a zombie? They had shown us *Night of the Living Dead*. You've seen *Night of the Living Dead*?"

"I have," said Kurlovich in a low voice, "But surely

Sergeant Glukharev had not been coming from the direction of outside the perimeter? He had come from the village side, yes?"

"That's right," acknowledged Krasnukhin, not grasping the relevance of the question.

"In that case," Kurlovich launched into an exposition in proper rule-book style. "He was approaching your position and his direction of movement was not from the region outside but from the area of the unit and he gave no indication of any intent to capture and carry off anybody or anything anywhere?"

"So?" Krasnukhin conceded. So much was the obvious.

"Then what would you have killed him for?"

"But what difference does it make to me that he was coming from the inside bit or from the outside? He was breaking the rules so I had to act in accordance with regulations. It could be that he was intending to run away from the unit. How about that?"

"Yes indeed," said Kurlovich. "I hadn't thought of that. And then what next, if you had killed him?"

"I'd have got some leave." Krasnukhin smiled, distending wide lips which could have been made of rubber.

The writers passed a fortnight engaged in interviews such as this at the end of which Zdrok and Paukov were sick of them. These people were living alongside the soldiers but getting up at any time deemed appropriate by themselves and were altogether oblivious of military discipline. They had been told to immerse themselves in army life but this was turning out less an immersion than a quick dip. Furthermore, a directive had been sent from Moscow to lay on literary question and answer sessions in the evenings with the personnel, but the personnel had not read the works of the writers in question and had used up all their questions on the very first day. They had asked the writers how much they got paid, and what for, and inquired about their "creative plans", but the specification had been to devote an evening of questions and answers to each one of the writers and in the group, it will be recalled, were no less than eight. Something had to be done with these writers; all things considered they might stay holed up here for a long time and General Paukov made a decision which the Jewhadists' legendary figure Solomon might well have envied. For the first half of each day the writers were required to march, keep in formation, carry out loading and unloading exercises, in a word to emulate the drudgery of a soldier's life to the utmost degree. Then in the afternoon when the troops were kept busy with geopolitical instruction or were preparing kit for parade they recovered their writerly status, met the privates, put questions to them about the service or provided answers about their own literary labours.

After a week of pack-drill the writers fell out among themselves. Prior to this they had not been particularly fond of each other (as might be expected considering their rather putrid profession) but after the first bout of square-bashing and respirator drill and with the ending of their relatively untrammelled life on an officially approved posting they began really to detest one another. The notion of disobeying Colonel Zdrok, still less General Paukov, never for a moment entered their heads — they were politically-correct "cultural representatives" enlisted in time of warfare at the disposal of the *Red Star*, apportioned special rations, and to each was assigned the suitable military-style designation, one that is reserved for cultural workers after an outbreak of hostilities: Second-Class Kultrep. (First-class was conferred only on those in the performance arts: film actors and the stage comics or anecdotalists touring the front lines with specially sanctioned repertoires about Jewhadists.)

The writers conscientiously performed their route marches, donned their gasmasks and ran cross-country in full kit, beginning to puff after the first hundred metres. Their sergeants, in a fatherly way, steered them onwards with kicks and when Honoured Author Osetrenko fell to the ground and started wheezing that he could go no further the others had to drag him along on their backs, that being what was expected on normal cross-country runs.

After that the writers took it out on Osetrenko no less than the sergeants had and indeed a healthily ruthless spirit began to manifest itself amongst them. Colonel Zdrok listened with approval to the NCO's reports of the route-marches and screw-drills (as chemical warfare practice was termed by the army). For the second half of the day the writers, who had hardly yet come to their senses, met again with the personnel to answer questions from those very sergeants who had just been laying into them on the parade ground. So was achieved a balance between military service and homage to the muses.

Just now Sergeant Gryzlov was dressing the line of the team of writers in front of the Baskakovo school building beside some rickety basketball goal posts and a tilting wall of parallel bars.

"Stretch your feet out!" he shouted menacingly. "Pull the arse in! Your arses, pull them in, you egg-heads! You've been gorging yourselves on civilian grub. This is the army, not a farm! Why have you got that shitting-dog look? AttenSHUN! Ra-aight TURN! About TURN! By the right, qui-ick MARCH! Secshun, HALT, one two. We'll have it again! Left leg, RAISE. LOWER! Is that a leg or a lump of shit? Kultrep Second Class Strunin! I can't hear your answer!"

"A leg," the aged writer Strunin's lips formed the answer.

"I don't see a leg! What I see is a lump of shit!" Sergeant

Gryzlov was enjoying himself. "Others stand fast, Strunin will do commands on his own. Leg, RAISE. Leg, EXTEND. Stretch your foot out! Halt! I said HALT, you skiver!"

Strunin, standing on one leg, staggered and collapsed into the mud. Not one of the writers tried to help him, each fastidiously keeping his distance. Strunin, truth to say, was a poor writer, none of his colleagues liked him and his collection of essays about Russian army writers *Nightingales of HQ* was considered excessively sycophantic even by the patriotic camp.

"Pick yourself up!" said Gryzlov disgustedly. "What's this then, Kultrep Strunin? If your wife were to see you now what would she have to say? You don't tumble over when you're on top of her? Leg RAISE!"

"All the same, this is the devil and all." Grushin, a big and imposing "patriotic" writer, spoke with a deep sigh over a bowl of thin, over-salted bortsch — or rather beetroot-water with the occasional rotted cabbage leaf — sitting in the canteen among the soldiery. "How long do we have to stand for it? We could have been back in Moscow long ago!"

"So who put this brigade together," this to Grushin with loathing from the gaunt and bilious satirist Gvozdev. "Who was it had us all brought in?"

"Well, look here," Grushin shrugged his shoulders, "I always considered that the place for a Russian writer is in the ranks."

"So what's the grouse? Every morning you're out there, in the ranks."

"But everyone serves in his own fashion. I serve with my pen..."

"Well, you can stick your pen in Zdrok's backside," said Gvozdev. Grushin gazed at him in silent reproach and turned over in his mind the terms in which he would write a note of denunciation that evening. All the writers wrote accusing notes about each other. The Secret Service officer Evdokimov kept them in a special file and they constituted the pearl of his collection. These writers knew how to write, the expressions they used were elaborate and colourful. Grushin excelled, calling Gvozdev first a tame hyena, next a rabid fox. The playwright Shubnikov wrote well too in a firm rounded hand with a lapidary style honed on the composition of serial episodes. His words were mostly monosyllabic — louse, swine, scum — for in serials two-syllable words had long become exceptions and trisyllabic ones were crossed out by the producers.

After lunch, as was required, the writers answered questions. That same Sergeant Gryzlov who had just been comparing Strunin's leg to a lump of shit and concerning himself with how he used to bed his wife now asked in servile tones: "Comrade Second-Degree Kultrep! Please tell us about your creative plans."

There was nothing of pretence about his demeanour. Sergeant Gryzlov was what is termed an "eager-beaver", that is to say he went by the book with the intention of winning himself rank and renown. Following instructions and the rules applicable to sergeants he applied himself to the writers in the first half of the day as he did to any new draft which had to be ground down so that these rookie reinforcements would understand just where it was they had landed up. And for the second half of the day he regarded them as writers on a visit to the unit. In essence, the chief military virtue was and is (Gryzlov to be sure was unable to formulate this for himself, lacking certain necessary words, but he felt it in his very vitals) behaviour one-hundred percent appropriate to the role required of one, whereby all other affinity other than what is determined by rank is abolished.

Gryzlov no doubt would treat his mother with affection should she come to the Company base on what was called 'parents' day', the annual occasion when parents were officially permitted to visit the soldiers. But supposing it possible for her to arrive as one of the draftees he would have made her drill and haul herself over the assault-course obstacles, she in that context being not so much a mother as human raw material. The political officer Ploskorylov thought highly of this sergeant and paid close attention to him notwithstanding that Gryzlov was not really one of the traditional warrior breed. Gryzlov to be sure was a real product of the old-fashioned, intellectually backward indigenous population, but he had taken up the true spirit of military life: not merely its outward appearances but its essential spirit. Gryzlov would take on the shape of any mould into which he had been poured, or in this case confined.

Strunin had often in former times answered questions about his "creative plans". He was almost never asked anything else. He gave a cough and began ponderously:

"You see, the Army has always played a large part in my creative work. I consider that if you stand a teacher, let's say, side by side with an officer the officer turns out to be the better teacher of the two. Or if it is a driver and an officer. Or, say, a trainer and an officer. In every case the officer turns out the better man. I have always been an admirer of the Russian officer caste, it has, you will agree, a special bearing and poise. And so I'm thinking of writing a book now about the officer class, about how it has come about, about how it has become a real military aristocracy, about the best Russian officers from the time of Ivan the Terrible. I would like to give some sort of composite portrait or even a laurel wreath to crown the Officer of Russia who, chest held high, fought out a road to the sea, who with his whole body shielded his brotherly fellow Slavic peoples, who is always distinguished by his remarkable decency. So if I consider myself worthy of it I shall soon be launching myself into this book. I think that a deserved place in the gallery of brilliant Russian officers will be occupied by General Paukov, Commander of this very division who is now hosting us. Have I answered your question?"

"All correct!" Gryzlov replied joyfully. "Contingent! Ask questions!"

"Comrade Kultrep Second Class," in an uncertain voice from Private Saprykin, "tell us please of your creative plans."

Strunin gave a cough.

"You see," he began "the Army has always played a large part in my creative work. I consider that if you stand a doctor, let's say, side by side with an officer, the officer turns out to be the better doctor of the two. Or for example a conjurer and an officer, the officer turns out to be the best conjurer. The Russian officer is a Jack of all trades — he has been taught this. And so I am thinking of writing a book about the characteristics of the officer class, how it has turned into a special caste: the Knights of the Sword. About how by and large not just anyone can become an officer but only one picked out as worthy of the title. I would like, you know, to weave a wreath or garland to crown the Russian Officer who was in the vanguard of fighting out an outlet to the sea. Who with his breast shielded his brotherly fellow Slavic peoples and who is always distinguished by a remarkably pleasant scent.... So if I feel I have the strength I shall soon be launching myself into this book. I think a prime place in the gallery of brilliant officers will be taken by General Paukov to whom our writers' brigade is now entrusted. Have I answered your question?"

"All correct!" answered Gryzlov on Saprykin's behalf, he being more conspicuous. "Contingent! Questions for the Comrade Kultrep!"

"Comrade Kultrep Second Class," rapped out another

know-all, plainly Under-Sergeant Sukhikh, "Your creative plans?"

"And what's the magic word?" Gryzlov growled threateningly.

"Please," barked Sukhikh.

Strunin gave a cough.

"You see," he started, "the Army has always played a large part in my creative work. I consider that if you stand a mother, let's say, side by side with an officer, the officer turns out to be the better mother of the two. Or for example a camel and an officer, the officer turns out to be the best camel. The officer has been taught to be a Jack of all trades. In the Russian officer there is some sort of special roundedness, cosiness. And so I am thinking of writing a book about the officer class, how it has become an ivory tower. About how not just anyone can become an officer and I would like to weave a network... Whose foot opened Russia's door to the sea and whose backside... whose backside covered up his fellow Slavic peoples. So when I get worked up, as I should be, I'll set about it. I think it wouldn't do to leave out General Paukov. Hah, mm. When would things get done without Paukov? Our whole writers' collective is grateful to him... Have I answered your question?"

"All correct," waking from a brief doze (in the Russian army they all know how to drop off during any spare moment) Sukhikh briskly answered.

"Com-pany!" commanded Gryzlov. "In single file, to the doors, March! Thank you Comrade Writers!"

That evening, before bed, the writers bickered.

"You are still living in nineteen ninety-nine," began Grushin.

"Fancy you remembering," yawned Gvozdev. "I could recall what you were writing about Banan at that time..."

"Oh, I can remember all right. I remember what I was writing and what you were writing. And that there Mr. Strunin, what he was writing. Remember, Strunin? I could inform the Political Officer of the issue number and even send him a copy..."

"You always did envy me," Strunin yelled, almost hysterically. "Always did! You're not special for cleanliness neither. Your feet stink!"

"You're special in a nasty way. I know your real name's Stryutski."

"Gentlemen, gentlemen!" Kurlovich was trying to make them see reason. "We are intelligent people, creative artists. Gentlemen..."

"And you shut up, don't mess in a Russian quarrel!" Grushin shouted him down, forgetful just then that Strunin himself was not altogether ethnically pure. But in comparison to Kurlovich Strunin was practically an ally. I'll show the Political what you wrote about Khazars in ninety-six!"

"Stop it! You should be ashamed!" Kozaev joined the fray, one of the writers in the tandem that signed KozaKi, writing thrillers about the adventures of the Russian special assault units.

"Don't forget we're at the frontlines," assented his co-author Kirienko.

"Yes, you're at the frontlines," roared Grushin, "Puny little warriors, peddlers of pulp fictions..."

The KozaKi didn't listen and left for their own hut where they had the prospect of sitting up until dawn cobbling together the sixteenth sequel of the exploits of their hero: Secret Service agent Sedoi. The book was supposed to be submitted to the publisher no later than the fifteenth of August and a delay could result in their being struck off the special rations list.

And for a long while Grushin, Gvozdev and Strunin continued to exchange abuse in the darkness while, as if in duet, the dogs of Baskakovo yelped away and lazily scratched themselves.

Translated by Francis Greene

JULIA LATYNINA
NIYAZBEK

In Russia, when they say "the Caucasus", they almost always mean "Chechnya". In the West, when they talk about "Russia's problems in the Caucasus", it's usually Chechnya they have in mind.

However, the Caucasus is not just Chechnya. It is Dagestan, Kabarda, Karachaevo-Cherkessiya, Ingushetia and Ossetia – completely different republics, which nonetheless have one feature in common: customs, manners and morals that are inconceivable not only in the West, but also in Russia.

Russia's weak, hopelessly corrupt and incredibly venal state authority is gradually slipping down from the Caucasus Mountains — as grease slips off a dirty plate under a jet of hot water — exposing what has been there for thousands of years: a culture of mutual assistance based on clanship and family ties, barbarous cruelty, a cult of individual honour and blood vengeance – with the simple difference that now the blood vengeance is exacted using grenade launchers and Kalashnikovs.

There are many regions in these republics where Russian control is weak or even non-existent. In many of them the corrupt local presidents, who themselves are quite happy to use professional hit men for contract killings and have no regard whatsoever for the law, are obliged to deal with the local "strong men" – in effect the leaders of gangs or armed units which control business activity or territory.

This book is about one of these "strong men" and his relations with a republican president, whom he had elected with the help of his own gunmen. It is also about his relations with the Russian President's special envoy, whom he once freed from captivity in Chechnya.

This is a book about duty and honour, love and betrayal, re-emergent Islam – and about Russia, balancing on the edge of a precipice.

The road ran along the side of the mountain in a white stripe, and below the road, the brilliant green of the forest was punctuated by reddish cliffs. At the very edge of the road, beside a fence festooned with ribbons, sat an old Chechen man in a long shirt, with a face as wrinkled as a walnut. The man looked sad and he was holding a car bumper in his hands.

A rumbling sound ran through the bushes like a hail of shrapnel, sending startled birds scurrying, and a moment later a column of vehicles appeared from behind the cliff, led by an armoured personnel carrier. It was followed by two Ural trucks, and then a petrol tanker, and after that, a Geländewagen that looked like a black coffin. At the back of the column there was another armoured personnel carrier.

With a gentle hiss of brakes, the Geländewagen stopped beside the old man, and a man in a camouflage suit jumped down into the dust of the road, holding the automatic rifle slung across his shoulder. In terms of mountain time, the man was very young: he was thirty years old, and a black curly beard as thick as lamb's wool ran from just below his eyes to his plump lips.

"Salaam aleichem, Charon! What are you so sad about?"

"Valeichem assalaam, Arzo! My car went off without me, and I've lived with it more years than I have with my last wife. That's why I'm sad."

"Did it go a long way down?" Arzo asked.

"All the way to the bottom," the old man answered with a sigh and put the bumper down on the ground.

"What kind of car was it, then?" asked a third man, jumping down from the personnel carrier. He was also dressed in a camouflage suit and armed.

"A Volga. It was a good car," Charon sighed. "When your mother was carrying you, Arzo, your father and I took her to the hospital in that Volga."

Arzo Hadjiev walked over to the very edge of the road and looked down, as if hoping to spot the thirty-two-year-old Volga, and the world that had disappeared into the abyss with it, a world of Soviet automobile plants, tobacco fields and red flags on the village soviet on public holidays. But he couldn't see anything, apart from the clumps of prickly plants covering the surface of the cliff, which was almost vertical at this point, and the forest rising up from the bottom of the gorge.

"Get in," said Arzo. "If you're going to Sekhol, I'll give you a lift."

But Charon only shook his head.

"No," he said, "I think I'd better go back home. And then, the jam was in the car. I was taking my father some jam. I probably ought to go down to get the jam. Maybe it's still all right."

Arzo shrugged, walked over to the Geländewagen and

opened the rear door. The whole boot of the Geländewagen was crammed with sacks. Arzo slit one of them open at the side and took out three wads of Russian rubles.

"That's for you, to get a new car, Charon," he said. "And don't you go climbing down after that jam. Everything's smashed to pieces anyway. Better ask your father if he wants a Russian to look after his cattle. I'll let him have one cheap."

A minute later the column set off, leaving a translucent cloud of yellow dust hanging in the air. Old Charon carried on sitting there at the side of the road, holding the bumper in one hand and the Russian money in the other. The money was absolutely new, and Charon wasn't sure it was genuine. Who knew where Arzo had got the money? The guns that men like Arzo carried were real enough. But their money wasn't likely to be.

When the column had driven by, Charon got up, set the bumper down carefully beside a rock, cast a final glance at the gorge that had swallowed up his Soviet Volga and went home.

■ ■ ■

The sun was high in the sky when the column drove into the long mountain village that twined like a liana round its only street. The trucks and the Geländewagen turned in at the tall black gates. The armoured personnel carriers stayed outside.

Arzo's men took their dead comrades out of a truck and heaved the sacks of money out of the Geländewagen. There was a man lying behind the sacks in the boot. His hands were tied behind his back with sticky tape. They threw the man on the ground and he lay there like a pile of fallen leaves; one of the chickens wandering around in the yard went up to him and started pecking the blood on his sleeve. Even the chickens in this yard knew the taste of blood: there was so much of it at times.

■ ■ ■

The man they'd brought in the Geländewagen opened his eyes at about four in the afternoon. He was small and skinny, and although he was dressed in dirty camouflage gear, he didn't look like a soldier. In the first place, he was obviously too old, at twenty-seven or twenty-eight, and the long fingers on his slim hands looked as if they belonged to a pianist, not a fighting man. He had grey eyes and brown hair, and his face had that rounded softness you often see in the children of parents with important jobs, who take a responsible attitude to life, but have never encountered any real difficulties.

The basement in which the prisoner was lying was a small, dirty store room with a low ceiling, filled with an intolerable stench from the cess pit that had been dug in the right-hand corner. On all four sides of the basement, wooden boards had been laid on the floor, too short for anyone to lie on them without bending his legs, and too narrow to lie on with your legs bent. A few rays of golden sunlight slanted into the basement through a narrow little window.

In the centre of the basement a section of metal rail was sunk into the concrete floor, with four chains welded on to it. The chains were too short for anyone to reach the pit if he was sitting in the furthest corner, and so there was also a bucket in the basement. The bucket made it quite clear that everything in the basement had been carefully arranged to cater for prisoners, just as a good housekeeper arranges her basement to store her pickles.

The grey-eyed prisoner was not alone: there were three other men in the basement.

"Vladislav," said the Russian.

"Gamzat," said one of the prisoners.

"Gazi-Magomed," said another.

The third original resident didn't say anything: he lay on the planks, face upwards, and the flies crawled all over his face.

Gamzat was about twenty-five: he was lean and well-built, with incredibly large, black eyes and a little triangular chin, overgrown with black stubble. If not for the odd shape of his chin, he would have looked like an angel. Gazi-Magomed was maybe eight years older; he was a stout man with black hair and a stupid face as grey as emery paper. Vladislav realized the two of them had not been there very long: their beards had not had time to grow, and Gazi-Magomed hadn't lost any weight yet.

"Are you Chechens?" Vladislav asked.

"No," answered Gamzat, "we're Rutuls. A Chechen wouldn't steal a Chechen, would he? They'd fix him if he did. But no one's going to retaliate for someone like him." Gamzat nodded at the man who was being eaten alive by flies.

"What's happened to him?" asked Vladislav.

"A dog bit him," answered Gamzat.

Gazi-Magomed explained:

"They dragged him out of here and said: 'If you fuck a dog, we'll let you go'. So he fucked it. In front of everyone. But the bitch was in heat, and something inside her jammed tight. They got stuck together, and they couldn't get unstuck. The soldier was yelling, the dog was biting him, and the Chechens just laughed. So if they tell you to fuck a dog, don't do it. They won't let you go anyway."

Vladislav squeezed his eyes shut, and when he opened them, the copper stripe of sunlight on the floor had disappeared, and the only things glittering in the basement were the chains.

"Is he Russian?" asked Vladislav, looking at the man bitten by the dog.

"Yes," said Gamzat, and Gazi-Magomed added:

"They wouldn't do that to a Rutul, would they? Or a Lezghin? Or an Avar? If they did that to a Rutul, the whole clan would avenge him. But who's going to take vengeance for a Russian?"

■ ■ ■

They took Vladislav out of the basement early in the evening. The village was holding a wake, and he was ordered to clear away the remains of two Russian soldiers who had been shot as part of the ritual.

The yard echoed to bursts of automatic gunfire, and the steaming cauldrons of meat were big enough to boil a man in. They ordered him to take what was left of the Russians to the dogs.

When the prisoner had done his job, one of the Chechens prodded him with his automatic rifle:

"That way."

There was a personnel carrier standing under an awning, and curly-headed Arzo was sitting on its armour plating. They flung the Russian on to his knees in front of the Chechen.

"What's your name?" asked Arzo.

He spoke Russian quietly, with surprisingly good pronunciation, except that his speech – the speech of a man who had lived half his life in the Russian city of Grozny – seemed to tumble from one consonant to the next, like the river Terek rushing over its stones.

"V-vladislav. Vladislav Pankov."

"Are you a soldier?"

"N-no. I just... I was travelling with the cargo. I mean the wagons."

"Are you in the Federal Security Service?"

"No. I... I work for the Central Bank. By education I'm a financial specialist, I have my documents... all my documents with me."

"Did you shoot at my men?"

Vladislav involuntarily touched the bridge of his nose, bearing a dark horizontal scar. When he was taken prisoner, the butt of an automatic rifle had smashed the bridge of his spectacles into his nose: Vladislav was short-sighted.

"Yes," said Vladislav.

"You're no financial specialist," said Arzo. "You're with the Federal Security Service. You studied at Harvard, all right, but that's because you're Avdei Pankov's son. The minister Pankov. I knew you'd be travelling with the cargo. I was asked to shoot Pankov's son, as a special favour. And they told me there'd be money in the wagons. A lot of money. Two trillion, they said. One trillion's yours, they said."

The fair-haired prisoner shuddered. From the very beginning he'd thought it was strange that the fighters had entered Grozny and gone straight to the railway station. And that the trainload of cash for the reconstruction of Grozny had arrived just two hours before they attacked.

"Only there wasn't any money in the wagons," said Arzo.

"That's impossible! I..."

"It's very convenient. You load two trillion in cash into railway wagons, and off they go to Chechnya. Where's the money? The guerrillas stole it. But I left three men back there. What for? What am I going to tell their mothers?"

Vladislav didn't answer.

A young guerrilla holding a video camera appeared behind Arzo.

"Talk," said Arzo.

"What shall I say?"

"Say that you're being held by Arzo Hadjiev. That you're being well treated. Say that there were only five sacks in the wagons and the men who sent you with the wagons wanted me to kill you. And say that if your father wants you to live, he has to find the missing sacks. He's the minister of finance, after all."

When the guards had led the skinny Russian away, Arzo listened to the recording again and ordered it to be copied on to an audio cassette. Then he dialled a number on his satellite phone. Instead of saying hello to the person at the other end of the line, he switched on the cassette deck.

"What do you think is best," he asked when the cassette finished, "for me to get the money, or for Avdei Pankov to get this tape?"

■ ■ ■

The soldier who had been badly bitten by the dog died during the night, and when Vladislav woke up, he saw he was lying head to head with a corpse.

"So what did they steal you for?" Vladislav asked.

"We have a distillery in Torbi-kala," said Gamzat. "We got the seed money from him."

"Five million dollars," said Gazi-Magomed.

The young Harvard graduate found the idea that the bearded man with the automatic rifle could loan anyone money quite incredible.

"From Hadjiev?" he asked.

"Sure. And then he committed a massacre at Bochola and we didn't pay him back."

"If we'd paid him back, your Federal Security Service

would have said we were financing terrorists," Gazi-Magomed added.

Vladislav was intrigued. It was an interesting legal puzzle. If someone you've borrowed money from became an international terrorist, did that mean paying him back fell into the category of "financing criminal activities"? But of course, Vladislav didn't really think these men had been trying to avoid committing a crime when they didn't pay back the debt. He realized they'd just tried to take advantage.

"So what's he going to do with you?" asked Vladislav.

"It's hard to say," Gamzat answered, "he won't let us go until we give him the money back."

"And as long as we're stuck in here, we'll never be able to get that much together," Gazi-Magomed added sadly.

■ ■ ■

The paying of condolences carried on for a second day, and a third. The dead men were well known, and many people had come from distant villages when they heard they'd been killed. Two men had even flown down from Moscow.

On the morning of the third day, they cut off Pankov's finger. They dragged him out of the basement again, but this time they didn't record anything, just told him to phone his father. When some clerk's baritone voice came from the mobile phone the furious Arzo punched Vladislav in the face, and then he was stretched out on the ground, like an animal skin being dried, and they chopped off his little finger. It actually hurt less than the blow to his jaw.

■ ■ ■

On the evening of the third day the gates of Arzo's house swung open and two silvery jeeps drove in, crammed to overflowing with armed men.

The man in command of this new group of visitors was much younger than Arzo. He was tall – half a head taller than the Chechen – and he had the smooth, balletic movements of a wrestler or karateka. Unlike Arzo, he was clean-shaven, and a fresh cut from a safety razor looked strange on the plump cheek that merged into a powerful square jaw. His hair and his eyes were the same colour as his Kalashnikov, which he was not holding in his hand, like the rest of his men. It was hanging over his shoulder on a long, grey strap, like a postman's bag.

The new arrival embraced Arzo's father and set off towards the awning, under which the field commander and his brother were sitting. Arzo stood up to meet him.

"You have stolen my relatives. You have acted wrongly, Arzo. Give them back to me."

Unlike other visitors, the new arrival did not address Arzo in Chechen, but in Russian – as the mountain dwellers of the Caucasus always address someone of a different nationality. And his Russian was considerably less precise than Arzo's – the syntax and grammar were fine, but his pronunciation was harsh and guttural, as if every consonant in every word had been roughened with sandpaper.

"They owe me five million, Niyazbek," Arzo replied, "and another two for moral damage."

Niyazbek's eyes, the colour of Coca-Cola, swept the yard as if it were an opponent he was about to meet in the ring, or a car that had to be blown up. They probed into every point of space unhurriedly, like a probing rod in the hands of an experienced sapper, examining with identical indifference the puddle of blood spreading under a slaughtered sheep and the broad stain on the gates. The maroon stripe ran precisely halfway between two nails hammered into the gates. It seemed unlikely to have been a sheep that was crucified on those nails.

"That's a fair figure, Arzo. I acknowledge this debt. They'll pay you back every last kopeck. But these men are my relatives. No one can boast that he has stolen any relatives of mine."

"As a mark of respect for you I will release Gamzat," said Arzo, "let him get the money together. But Gazi-Magomed will remain a hostage."

"I want them both."

"Then you stay as a hostage," Arzo suggested with a smile. "You can stay with me for a while, and your brother-in-law can get the money together."

"I've never been a hostage, and I never will be," was the reply. "Sometimes I have stolen people, but no one will ever steal me. I give you my word – they will pay back the money."

"It won't be easy for me to shoot your word," said the Chechen, "or cut its ears off. These two are mean, greedy men. You know that as well as I do. Who knows what might go wrong? If you want them both, go away and come back with the money."

■ ■ ■

When the skinny prisoner woke up the next day, he was alone, apart from the corpse. Gamzat and Gazi-Magomed had disappeared and the sun was already high above the village. Somewhere in the distance cows were lowing, a mullah was shouting the call to prayer. A boy about ten years old was sitting outside the barred window, observing the exhausted fair-haired Russian through eyes the colour of blackberries.

"I'm Arbi," said the boy. "Who are you?"

"Vladislav," the Russian replied.

If he stood up on the planks, he could glance into the yard: the Geländewagen and the Ural trucks weren't there any more, but there were two abreks sitting by the gates, with the sun glinting on their Kalashnikovs. Arbi noticed the prisoner looking and said:

"My father's gone away. But you'll stay here until they pay for you."

"And what if they don't pay for me?" Vladislav asked.

"My father doesn't like Russians," said Arbi. "That is, he likes slitting their throats, otherwise he doesn't like them. He's very angry with them for what they did to me."

"And what did they do to you?"

Arbi turned and went towards the house, and when he moved away from the window, Vladislav saw that the boy had no legs. He moved about on a small wooden board with wheels, pushing against the ground with his hands.

■ ■ ■

Vladislav was hauled out of the pit so quickly, that he woke up properly only in the yard. The round-faced moon was shining in the middle of the sky, and one of the sentries was lying in its shadows. His throat had been slit from ear to ear. The other sentry was lying beside him, with the barrel of an automatic rifle pressed into the back of his head.

Two men were driving an old Niva out of the garage. Vladislav was flung to his knees before a tall man moving with the grace of a lynx. The man's face was clean shaven and his eyes were like two pieces of the night.

"Where are Gamzat and Gazi-Magomed?" the man asked.

For a second Vladislav did not understand the question – the man's harsh accent was so different from the Chechen accent he had almost got used to in the last three days.

"Who are you?"

"You haven't answered my question."

"They're not here. Arzo's gang took them with them."

The tall stranger picked Vladislav up and threw him on to the back seat. A moment later a grey-haired Chechen man was tossed at his feet. Vladislav realized it was Arzo's father. One of the kidnappers jumped into the driving seat, and the gates in front of the Niva slowly crept open.

They met no obstacles driving through the village. There was a war going on and the neighbours had learned from experience not to be curious: it was simply that for some reason in the middle of the night some cars were driving out of the house that belonged to the father of one of the influential field commanders.

The cars didn't stop until they reached the same spot in the gorge where two days earlier Charon had sat mourning his Volga. Now there were two silver Land Cruisers standing on the broad platform, with armed men beside them. They dragged Vladislav out of the Niva and tossed him into a Land Cruiser. Arzo's father was pushed beside him. Niyazbek got into the front seat, holding the ten-year old boy with no legs.

Ten minutes later the cars rumbled across a bridge over a river. Niyazbek got out and bargained for a while with the soldiers who came down to him from their tower at the guard post. After that, the cars pulled over on to the side of the road and Niyazbek dialled a number on his phone.

"Salaam, Arzo," said Niyazbek. "You remember the place we exchanged prisoners the last time? I'll wait for you until dawn. When you give me Gamzat and Gazi-Magomed, you'll get your father and son back."

The phone croaked something in reply.

"If you kill my relatives, I'll give the phone to your son," Niyazbek answered, "and he'll tell you how your father died. Then he'll die too."

■ ■ ■

The guard post where Niyazbek had stopped had a bad reputation. Everyone who needed to buy back relatives or find the people who were selling, came here, and during the day there were so many cars and negotiators that it was more like a market than a place of exchange.

But now it was night, and there was no one at the guard post apart from the soldiers and Niyazbek's snipers. And there was a tank half-buried in the ground. Some house-proud warrant officer had planted peonies and marrows around it.

Arzo Hadjiev arrived three hours later with four cars, after letting his own snipers out on the far side of the river. Niyazbek and Arzo got out of their cars and stood in full view of the sharpshooters lying in hiding, thereby guaranteeing the rules of exchange with their own lives.

They stood like that for about three minutes, and after Niyazbek's gunmen had put the two brothers in one of their cars, Niyazbek said:

"They don't have any more debts on them now. All the debts are mine. If you want to be paid, come and collect."

Arzo paused before he answered.

"Give me the Russian," he said, "and we'll be even."

"We're already even. If you'd trusted my word, you'd have been paid back. You said my word counts for nothing, so now you'll get nothing."

Then Arzo rummaged in one of the flap pockets of his jacket and took out a small plastic bag with a little finger sealed inside it.

"Give this to the Russian from me," he said.

■ ■ ■

Three hours later the cars stopped at a bend in the road. It was barely beginning to get light. The red-hot sun was rising swiftly from behind the mountains, the morning mist was curling over the parched land, and the gleaming white road wound round and down the slope, like a piece of string that had been dropped there, towards the dusty town curving in a crescent along the line of the bay.

There were little white houses standing to the right of the bend in the road, behind bushes that looked like a coil of barbed wire, and one of them had a limp Russian flag hanging on it. There was not a breath of wind, and the dawn smelt of the sea, heat and freedom.

Niyazbek jumped down lightly on to the scorched grass and the other passengers climbed out at his sign.

"You see the police station?" Niyazbek asked, pointing to the little house with the flag. "Go there and phone your father."

"And what shall I tell him?" asked Vladislav.

"Tell him the truth. Someone stole you and you got away."

Gamzat was startled.

"Niyazbek, he's not a soldier! He's some sort of bigwig! He's from the Central Bank! Why don't you give him to us? They'll pay a lot of money for him!"

Without saying a word, Niyazbek hit the Rutul in the stomach with the butt of his gun so that he howled and went flying into the blackberry bushes at the roadside.

"I swear by Allah, Gamzat, if you ever try to tell me what to do again, I'll forget that you're my brother-in-law. You live like a parasite, you borrow money and don't pay it back, you step in every piece of shit that's lying in the road and then you whine and beg for help. I call everyone here to witness, if you get into one more filthy mess, I'll kill you myself! You've just been hauled out of a pit and you're already digging a new one for someone else!"

Gamzat stared out of the blackberry bushes, and the whites of his eyes were glassy with hate and humiliation.

"Go, I said," Niyazbek told the fair-haired prisoner.

"Listen, Niyazbek," said Vladislav, "you saved my life. At least tell me who you are."

"I'm a hunter, and you're game," was the reply. "Go, Russian. Before you get stolen again."

■ ■ ■

It was the summer of 1999, June. Vladislav and his friends were sitting in one of Moscow's finest restaurants when the door slammed and out of the corner of his eyes, Vladislav caught a glimpse of men dressed in camouflage suits. A firm hand was planted on his shoulder and a voice with a light, gurgling accent exclaimed:

"Will you look at that! Could it really be the little pup from the Central Bank?"

Vladislav looked up and instantly recognised Arzo. The Chechen hadn't changed at all. He was wearing black trousers and a black turtle-neck sweater under his jacket. There were armed men in military camouflage suits standing behind him.

The Chechen flopped down on to an empty chair opposite Vladislav. He was obviously drunk.

"We stole him from the railway station in Grozny," Arzo

continued in a voice loud enough for everyone in the restaurant to hear, "him and some sacks of money. Five sacks of money. I kept him with a young guy called Nikita. What happened to that Nikita was very amusing. I had a dog in the yard, Mashka, a bitch, and she was in heat. I told Nikita I'd let him go if he screwed the bitch. So he went and screwed her."

The faces of Arzo's military escorts turned to stone.

"But you know, when a bitch is in heat, something happens... Well, anyway, he got stuck inside her. They got jammed together and couldn't get unstuck. She chewed off half his side before they were separated."

Arzo burst out laughing and started gesturing with his hands to show how much the bitch had chewed off the Russian.

"Who are they?" Vladislav asked Arzo, indicating the men in camouflage suits with his eyes.

"Them? They're Alpha Group. They're guarding me," said the Chechen, "looking after me, I mean. Making sure nothing happens to me. Listen, major, if I stole you, would you fuck a dog or not?"

The man the Chechen had spoken to simply stood there rigidly erect.

Arzo poured himself some wine from the bottle standing in front of Vladislav and raised his glass in the air.

"Let's drink," said Arzo, "To your good luck. I've never let any Russians go in one piece. You know why?"

"Because we crippled your son."

"No," said Arzo, "that's not right. Because the most terrible loss inflicted on the enemy isn't the dead. It's the cripples. A dead man stays in the ground, where no one can see him. But a cripple sits in the underground and begs for alms. So let's drink, Russian, to the fact that you still have your nose and your prick."

Vladislav gulped convulsively. The Chechen gave a drunken laugh and dropped his head on the table.

Two members of the Alpha Group lifted him up by the armpits and carried him carefully to the door. The major carried on standing there without moving, except for his hands, which were fiddling with a fork they'd come across on the table.

"Why don't you shoot him?" Vladislav suddenly asked in a trembling voice.

"We haven't been ordered to," the major replied.

■ ■ ■

It was the end of June. In Hyde Park the white and red rhododendrons were in blossom, the taxis looking like ladybirds were stuck in traffic jams on Piccadilly, and in the "Nobu" Japanese restaurant at Hilton two men were having lunch in the corner farthest from the door, beside the window: Vladislav Pankov, deputy head of the presidential administration of the Russian Federation, and his old friend Igor Malikov, Russia's representative to the World Bank.

They had first met ten years earlier, when Malikov was a deputy in the State Duma, but they had become really close in Washington.

After his terrifying ordeal in Chechnya, Vladislav Pankov had spent six months in an Austrian clinic, and then his father had sent him to the US, to take up the same post that Igor Malikov now held. Igor had been Vladislav's deputy, and he'd also been the first to notice that there was something wrong with his boss. Vladislav often came to work with a strange gleam in his eyes, he giggled in meetings and flew into senseless rages, and once Igor had found him in his office completely naked, sitting on the windowsill and eating an orange, complete with the rind.

Malikov quickly realized that his boss took to hard drugs. But instead of acting like any normal careerist Soviet official and betraying his boss to the secret services, Malikov did something else. He came to an arrangement with one of his friends, and they took Vladislav to the friend's house in Maryland. There he forced his boss to write an application for leave and handcuffed him to a bed. "You'll relieve yourself where you are until you're cured," said Malikov. Two days later Vladislav managed to get to a phone. Fortunately for Malikov, he didn't phone the police, but his pusher. Malikov met the pusher half way to the house and beat him unconscious.

Malikov and the private doctor he'd hired spent two months with Vladislav. He was the only man who knew his full story. He heard Vladislav crying in his sleep, "No, Arzo! No!" but he never talked to him about the Caucasus.

Just two months after he came back to Russia, Vladislav had learned by chance that Igor's real name was Ibragim, and he'd been born in the mountains, only eighty kilometres from the village where Vladislav had been held in a basement. And also that his surname, which Vladislav had always pronounced M***a***likov, was really pronounced with the stress on the second syllable – Mal***i***kov, because it didn't come from the Russian word "malenky", meaning "little", but from the Arabic word for "king".

The conversation between the two important officials was mostly friendly small talk. They'd already finished the marinated cod and soft crab, and the second bottle of sake had already been emptied when Vladislav said:

"I'd like to offer you a new position."

"In the president's administration?"

"No, I'm leaving the administration. Tomorrow I'll be

appointed the president's special envoy to the Caucasian Federal District. I'm offering you the position of president of North Avaria-Dargo."

Igor said nothing for a few seconds.

"I didn't think you knew I was an Avar."

"I read your personal file."

"I can't accept this offer," said Igor.

"Why?"

"How much time did you spend in the Caucasus, Vladislav?"

"Three days."

"And how long were you under treatment afterwards?"

"A year, if you count Washington."

Igor gave a grim chuckle and a harsh vertical fold appeared under his soft, remarkably vulnerable lips.

"I spent seventeen years there, not three days. When I was eleven, my uncle killed his sister. She had an affair with a young man, and my uncle took a very rational approach. 'It's impossible,' he said, 'my daughter's growing up, and how will I be able to marry her off? Everyone will say her aunt's a loose woman.' Everyone thought my uncle acted like a real man. When I was sixteen, my uncle was shot dead by the guy who had the affair with my aunt. And one day, when I was thirty-two and already a deputy in the State Duma, my younger brother came to see me. He embraced me and asked me to go with him straight away, that very minute, to a certain person's birthday party. We set off in his car, and since those were troubled times, the cops kept stopping us. I showed them my Duma deputy's pass and we carried on. We reached the Rublyovskoe Highway and turned into the woods. I asked: "Where's the birthday party?" and they told me "Further on". Then we reached a clearing and the car stopped. My brother opened the boot and began unloading guns out of it. The entire damn boot was crammed full of weapons. He'd just needed my pass, so he could smuggle them right across Moscow. And then they switched me to another car and my brother asked me what restaurant I'd like to go to for dinner. I'm a European, Vladislav. I've spent twenty years of my life learning to stop thinking about who is whose father-in-law and how much I ought to pay for a position."

"That's exactly why I want to see you as president of the republic. Because you're not worried about who is whose father-in-law."

"I don't want to go back into that zoo."

Vladislav waited before he answered.

"For the last few days, I've been studying the situation in the Caucasus. I knew it was bad. But I didn't know just how bad. And one thing I do know: if this zoo is ruled by the jackals, the Caucasus will soon break away from Russia."

"And if I take charge of the zoo, they'll kill me."

"Hang on, you..."

"No. No under absolutely any circumstances. I'd rather ask for political asylum in Uganda."

Vladislav sighed.

"All right. But can you at least do me a favour? Can you fly down to the republic? Just to give me some advice?"

"To tell you who is whose father-in-law?"

Vladislav nodded.

"All right. I'll come."

They were already saying their goodbyes at the doors of the hotel, to which the long black embassy Mercedes had delivered them, when Igor suddenly said:

"There's another reason why I can never accept your proposal."

"What's that?"

"That old business, when you were stolen. You were freed by a guy called Niyazbek."

"Yes. My father tried to find him. Afterwards, about six months later. He was killed. In some shoot-out or other."

"He wasn't killed," said Igor. "His name's Niyazbek Malikov. And he's my younger brother."

■ ■ ■

Magomedsalikh Salimkhanov, the construction minister of the Republic of Northern Avaria-Dargo, was beating Salaudin Bamatov, the vice-speaker of the republican parliament.

The leading sports channels would have been happy to show the fight, because the construction minister was a double world champion in Wushu-Sanda, and the vice-speaker of parliament was a three-time world champion in the pentathlon.

It should be said that the sports channels had quite a good chance of getting the recording, because the minister was beating the vice-speaker on the square in front of the republican House of Parliament, and this enthralling spectacle was being recorded by three cameras that had been sent to the economic forum going on there. In addition to the television cameras, the fight was observed by the combatants' bodyguards, about twenty parliamentary deputies, the minister of internal affairs and a two-metres-high statue of president Aslanov that stood in the middle of the square.

The minister feinted as if he was going to trip his opponent with one foot, the vice-speaker leapt back and received a blow from the same foot to his ribs. Then the minister swung round and struck the vice-speaker an impeccable blow to the temple with his heel.

The vice-speaker collapsed on the granite slabs that

ringed the monument. The minister pounced on him, grabbed hold of his tie and started choking him. At that moment the circle of parliamentary deputies surrounding them was parted, and a Russian official about thirty-five years old leapt forward to the pedestal of the statue. He was wearing a black suit with the maroon stripe of a two-hundred-dollar tie on his white shirtfront. The official was fair-haired and pale-faced, and the thick lenses of his tortoiseshell spectacles made his eyes look bigger than they really were.

"Stop that immediately!" the man in spectacles demanded.

The construction minister straightened up in amazement. He was a good head taller than the uninvited guest and his figure was reminiscent of a Michelangelo statue – not of David, but Goliath.

"And who are you?" the astonished minister asked.

"I'm the new special envoy," the fair-haired official declared.

Just at that moment the vice-speaker of parliament got up off the ground and, seeing that his opponent's attention was distracted, he made a run for it.

"I'll kill you like a dog!" Magomedsalikh cried and darted after him.

One of Salaudin Bamatov's bodyguards instantly tried to block his way. There was the loud roar of a gunshot and the bodyguard collapsed on the ground with a bullet through his shoulder.

The vice-speaker leapt over the wrought-iron railings separating the square from the little park on the right and scurried off along the wide oak-lined alley spread with yellow sand. The minister chased after him. When the representative of the executive branch finally became convinced that the legislative branch was running too fast, he yelled, "Rotten lousy sprinter!" then raised his silvery "Beretta" gun and started shooting fiercly. The vice-speaker wove between the trees like a hare. It was easy to see that in his recent sporting past he must have taken the hurdles in great style.

When the vice-speaker had disappeared among the trees, Magomedsalikh Salimkhalov shrugged, looked at the "Beretta", which still had a couple of shells left, so for good measure he fired them at a television camera that was shooting the opening of the economic forum. Magomedsalikh was a sensitive man and cameras made him feel embarrassed.

At this point Vladislav Pankov caught up with him again.

"What do you think you're doing?" he yelled. "Arrest this man! Immediately!"

The guests of the forum shuffled their feet awkwardly.

"What for?" asked the minister of internal affairs, who just happened to be there.

Pankov gestured indignantly at the gun.

"What do you mean?" he asked. "Is this an investment forum or a trap and skeet shoot? There was supposed to be a serious economic discussion here!"

"But what have I done?" asked the construction minister. "That bastard cut our budget by thirty per cent!"

"Arrest him," said the special envoy. Then he glanced at the minister of internal affairs and added:

"You, Arif Abusovich, are personally responsible in this matter. Do you understand?"

The minister nodded sadly.

"I understand," he said. "Let's go, Maga."

That evening all the central television channels broadcast reports about the progress achieved at the economic forum taking place on the northern shore of the Caspian Sea, in the town of Torbi-Kala. Channel One showed a live interview with the special envoy, who said that the investment climate in the Northern Caucasus had improved and noted, without going into any details, that the most animated discussion at the forum had flared up between the vice-speaker of the republican parliament and the minister of construction.

■ ■ ■

The economic forum was supposed to have begun at eleven o'clock, but the unplanned dispute between two highly placed officials delayed it by forty minutes.

Vladislav Pankov sat in the presidium of the economic forum. Sitting on his right was the president of the republic, Akhmednabi Aslanov, and on his left was Sir Geoffrey Olmers, an old friend of Pankov's and the head of one of the world's largest petrochemical corporations. Pankov had lured Olmers to the forum by telling him that the light offshore oil and Torbi-kala's unique seacoast position made it the ideal place to build a super-modern oil refinery.

The president of the republic was a little over sixty, but he looked younger. He was grey-haired, but impressively fit, with a hint of bronze in his voice and a glint of steel in his eyes. He had the dignified bearing possessed only by dictators and butlers.

President Aslanov introduced Russia's special envoy to every one present and expressed his conviction that the latter would help the republic to overcome poverty, terrorism and a servile, grovelling attitude to authority.

"All last week it rained," said the president, "but with your arrival the sun rose over our republic. You are the sun, Vladislav Avdeevich!"

At about twelve o'clock Pankov excused himself to go to

the toilet, and on his way back into the hall he met a short, plump Kumyk with black eyes as lively and cheerful as rooks in the spring.

"Arsen Isalmagomedov," the man introduced himself. "I literally need just a moment of your time, Vladislav Avdeevich. Concerning the ministry of construction."

"What do you mean?"

"As I understand it, this position is now free. I wanted to let you know that my brother has dreamed of working in construction all his life. And if we could discuss this matter later, at the banquet..."

Pankov turned away without saying a word and walked through into the hall.

In the meantime certain changes had taken place on the presidium. The president had gone away somewhere and his place had been taken by a stocky man of about fifty with broad cheekbones and blue eyes that contrasted strangely with his swarthy complexion.

"Sharapudin Ataev," the man introduced himself in a whisper, "the mayor of Torbi-kala." He paused, then leaned across and whispered in Pankov's ear. "You acted very courageously. I mean with Magomedsalikh. What an outrageous scandal! Do you know how many people he's killed? He has blood feuds in Chechnya. And with the public prosecutor of the Left Bank District. But you're taking a great risk, it won't make any difference to him that you're the special envoy. You need support. If you were just to appoint my son minister of construction..."

"Then what?" asked Pankov.

"A million," said Sharapudin Ataev.

During the five-minute break between sessions, Pankov received another two requests concerning the ministerial post. Both requests were accompanied by figures.

But Pankov received the most unpleasant surprise of all

at five in the afternoon, when the forum was nearing its end and president Aslanov had resumed his place at the rostrum.

"I think I'll be going," whispered Sir Geoffrey Olmers, gathering up his papers from the table.

"No, wait! We were going to view the construction site..."

"I've changed my mind," said the head of one of the world's largest petrochemical concerns, "and perhaps instead of a refinery, you might build something a bit more... in character. Perhaps a travelling circus."

The president declared the forum closed and walked across to the presidium table with a smile. A crowd had already gathered around the fair-haired Muscovite.

"Well, Vladislav Avdeevich," he said, "congratulations on a good start! We've worked really hard, now we could do with some rest. I've made arrangements for an informal continuation... I should tell you that the fish here is quite excellent. I expect you must be hungry..."

"Very," said Pankov. "Where's the canteen here?"

■ ■ ■

The head of the government of Northern Avaria-Dargo arrived at the former sanatorium of the Central Committee of the Communist Party, where Pankov was staying, at eight o'clock in the morning. He had a conversation with the special envoy that lasted half an hour, in the course of which the head of the republican government expressed the hope that the new envoy would put an end to terrorism, poverty and corruption, and also he put forward a proposal for improving the work of the government. He suggested dividing the ministry of construction into three new ministries: the first to build schools and governmental institutions, the second to build industrial projects within the terms of federal investment programs, and the third to deal separately with rural construction work. According to the head the government, this was necessary in order to reduce the level of corruption. So that there would be greater control over each minister and he wouldn't act like a racketeer.

"Yes, and the most pleasant thing I have to say," the head of the government continued, "is that on behalf of our entire people and the president of the republic in person, I would like to congratulate you, Vladislav Avdeevich, on your birthday, and..."

"Today is not my birthday," said Pankov.

The head of the government was taken aback.

"What do you mean, not your birthday?" he said. "When we've already got you a present!"

"What present?"

The head of the government gestured towards the window. Pankov walked over and saw a magnificent armoured Mercedes standing on the small asphalt patch beside the building. There was a pink ribbon tied round the Mercedes, and the head of the special envoy's bodyguard, Sergei Piskunov, was sniffing at the bonnet of the car like a cat at a tin of Whiskas.

Pankov called him over. "Sergei, how much does a thing like that cost?"

"Four hundred and twenty thousand dollars," said Piskunov with unhesitating precision.

"Are there any children's homes in the republic?"

"Yes."

"Sell it and give the money to a children's home. And remember, Saigid Ibragimovich, it's not my birthday today. Tell everyone that."

The head of the government left the sanatorium feeling very discouraged.

"Strange," he said, "when the Prosecutor General came to visit us, it was his birthday straight away. And the previous special envoy used to celebrate his birthday every month."

■ ■ ■

President Aslanov was extremely surprised when he heard what the presidential envoy had done with the present that the premier had given him.

"Perhaps he prefers jeeps?" he asked, "and we gave him a sedan."

His son objected:

"How can you give someone an armoured jeep? An armour-plated car has to be a sedan, any child knows that. Because when they blow it up, the shock wave strikes upwards.

Aslanov's son had been blown up three times, and he considered himself an expert on the subject.

"He's a Russian and he doesn't understand the simplest things," replied the second son, "but if he insists on a jeep, we'll have to give him a jeep."

■ ■ ■

Vladislav Pankov got into his car at nine in the morning. He smelled pleasantly of expensive eau-de-cologne, and he had spent almost ten minutes in front of the mirror, selecting and knotting his tie. Usually his wife did that, but she was holidaying in St. Tropez at the moment, and Pankov liked his tie to match his suit impeccably. The car set off smoothly and Pankov dialled a number on his phone.

"Igor," he said, "this is Vladislav. I'm firing the construction minister here. I saw him shooting at another man with my own eyes. Now they're suggesting I should split the ministry into three. Why's that?"

"Because three men have paid the president money for the position."

"Does the head of the government have any connection with the president?"

"He's married to his niece."

"Damnation! When are you going to get here?"

"On Friday."

Five minutes after this conversation finished, a printout of it was lying in front of President Aslanov and his two sons.

"So that's why he didn't take the car!" said the president's younger son.

"He wants to make him the head of the republic!" exclaimed the elder son.

■ ■ ■

Akhmednabi Aslanov waited for Vladislav Pankov in the residence of Pankov's predecessor, which was a luxurious mansion on the seacoast. The floor of the mansion was paved with marble, and every toilet in every bathroom was gilded. There were seventeen gilded toilets in all.

The previous special envoy had formerly commanded a combined forces group in Chechnya, becoming famous for repelling a Chechen incursion into the territory of Northern Avaria-Dargo in 1999. And the envoy had performed this outstanding feat of arms without once assuming a vertical position or detaching his lips from a bottle of expensive Avar cognac.

The residence itself had a remarkable history.

When he arrived in the republic, the previous special envoy had discovered that the accommodation allocated for him by the federal authorities was not appropriate to his status, and he had shared this misfortune with the republican president's son. The envoy had assumed the latter would give him one of his own seaside mansions. However, the president's son did something different. That very day he took the envoy in his car on a tour of a dozen houses. The mansion that the envoy finally settled on belonged to the minister of agriculture.

Then the president's son had suggested to the minister that he should sell the mansion for fifty thousand dollars. "I need to give a good man a present," the president's son had explained. The minister had been outraged and demanded a million. They'd carried on haggling until some Wahabis blew up the minister, and then his bereaved family had sold the house quickly.

The mansion had been given to the then special envoy, and he had taken such a liking to it that he hardly ever left it, and even held all his official meetings at his residence.

President Aslanov was already sitting in the summer dining room. With his grey hair, immaculate clothes and erect bearing, he looked more like an English lord than a former secretary of the Central Committee of the Communist Party who had returned to power after the *perestroika* period. In fact, as we have already remarked, the republic actually had two President Aslanovs.

One of them was 1.8 metres tall, weighed around 100 kilograms and was waiting for Pankov at a table set for a light breakfast of 28 dishes. The other was 2.8 metres tall, weighed three hundred kilograms, and was standing on a pedestal two metres high in front of Parliament House, gesturing broadly in greeting to the blue Caspian and the people climbing up the steps from the embankment.

One president was a jovial fellow, a joker who doted on his three children and seven grandchildren; the other never left his place of work and constantly pointed the way forward to a bright future.

This wasn't the only monument to an Aslanov in the republic. Immediately after the guard-post, the entry to the city from the Baku highway was adorned with a white marble monument to the celebrated educator of the Circassians, Lezghins and Avars, Saparchi Aslanov. Beside the town hall on the embankment there was a monument to Asludin Aslanov, who had been the first secretary of the Republican Communist Party up to 1937, and in front of the Gazi-Magomed Aslanov Drama Theatre there stood a monument to Gazi-Magomed himself, who had been the theatre's art director from 1961 to 1965.

But the most interesting monument was the one to Ramzan Aslanov. Before the war, thirty-two-year-old Ramzan had been a labourer on a collective farm, and until 1997 nothing was known about him, except that he had been killed at Stalingrad in 1943. Soon after Akhmednabi Aslanov was elected president, one of the newspapers in Torbi-kala printed an article about the heroic exploit of his great-uncle, who had blown up a fascist tank single-handed. A month later, another article made it clear that there had been two tanks, and three months after that the newspaper *The Heart of Dargo* had discovered that there had been four. The argument had been settled once and for all three years ago by the well-known local historian and parliamentary deputy Mukhtar Meerkulov. He published an article in a scholarly journal, demonstrating that there had been eight tanks. After that, a six-metre-high granite monument to the war hero Ramzan Aslanov had been erected on the side of the mountain Torbi-Tau, and Mukhtar Meerkulov had become the vice-speaker of parliament.

The door opened and the special envoy burst into the dining room. President Aslanov noted that the Muscovite almost bounded along, not like an important official, more like a kitten chasing a ball of wool. Aslanov rose from his chair in a dignified fashion, embraced Pankov and kissed him, in the Eastern manner.

"You cannot imagine," he said, "how glad I am that you have come to us. Because what is going on in the republic is quite intolerable! Wahabism is on the advance in the republic! Terrorists openly drive down the streets, every week someone is blown up! We have more bombs here than in Chechnya, and who can stop them? Only the federal authorities! What does the army do? Nothing. And what did the previous presidential envoy do? He drank. He drank cognac, and by the crate, let me tell you! By the crate!"

The president was not exaggerating in the least. A crate of cognac from the state company "Torkon" had been delivered every day to the home of the previous special envoy. The head of the company happened to be a nephew of the president.

"You took the step of arresting Magomedsalikh Salimkhanov. You arrested him because he was beating the vice-speaker of parliament in front of the television cameras. But did you know that this man took part in an attack on a federal guard-post? And he was in a vehicle that belonged to a guerrilla leader known to everyone?"

"When was that?" Pankov asked, astonished.

"Two weeks ago. Just imagine the scene: an armed column of vehicles passing through a federal forces guard-post on the border with Chechnya. Three vehicles, ten men, fifteen gun barrels. The most important terrorist in the republic is in one vehicle, a man who has repeatedly been declared wanted for various crimes, including ten murders. The captain of the Interior Ministry forces halts the column, and the terrorist offers him money to leave him alone. The captain fears an exchange of fire, because he only has the same number of men as there are in the vehicles, so he takes the money, but he phones the next guard-post and tells them to stop the column.

"Then what do you think happens? The column passes through the second guard-post! And then it turns round and heads back to the first one! They disarm the interior ministry soldiers and take all the money they've collected during the day! They drive them into the hut and say: 'We're going to burn you informers alive!' and this man and Magomedsalikh beat the captain, they break his ribs and tell him: 'If you write a complaint, we'll kill you!' "

"But why didn't they simply kill the soldiers?" Pankov asked in surprise.

"If they don't kill someone today, they can always kill him tomorrow!" the president replied. "This man's very teeth are stained red with blood, let alone his hands. He barters people with the Chechen bandits, he even stole my sons once!"

"When?"

"Nine years ago. I wasn't yet president of the republic, but my sons were successful businessmen. Very successful, without any help at all from me. And this man constantly terrorised them and extorted money from them! He could turn up in their homes with his guns at three o'clock in the morning, he used to get my sons out of bed at gun point. And he kept saying: 'Where's the money? Where's the money?' But they were honest businessmen, and they refused to pay him, and then they were stolen. My sons were stolen by a Chechen, Arzo Hadjiev, and he demanded seven million dollars from them!"

"And what did the first bandit have to do with it?"

"The first bandit was in league with Arzo, and he

supposedly freed my sons! It was all a trick. After that, they were in debt to him, not the Chechen!"

The special envoy paused before he spoke.

"What are your sons' names?" he asked.

"I'll introduce you personally," the president exclaimed warmly and gestured to his head of security.

A moment later the door opened and the president's sons came in. The younger son was about thirty-five. Despite the heat, he was wearing a light-beige jacket with a pearly tie. His small head had begun balding from the front, and his restless eyes flickered from side to side, like chickens pecking up grain. The elder son was wearing a blue-striped suit. He had grown enormously fat since the last time Pankov had seen him and panted noisily as he moved, every now and then wiping the sweat off his forehead. The expression in the large eyes set on each side of the swollen, cherry-red nose, had become even more hazy; his fingers were so fat that couldn't clench into a fist.

"Gamzat," said the president, introducing his younger son, "chairman of the board of directors of the Avar National Bank. You know, the banks keep on failing one after another! So I was forced to put my son in the job, to stop the state's money evaporating! And he's up to his eyes in work already – a parliamentary deputy, head of the equestrian sports federation and goodness knows what else! And head of my personal bodyguard!"

The senior banker and senior bodyguard of the republic held out his cold hand with narrow fingers to Pankov in the European manner.

"Gazi-Magomed," said the president, introducing his elder son, "the general director of Avar Oil and Gas. The devil only knows what's going on in the republic, little private refineries all over the place, I had to appoint someone I could trust. We'll burn them out! Beat them and put them in prison!

Thank God, the times are gone when any bandit with a pistol could try to extort money from my sons!"

"And what is this bandit's name?"

"Niyazbek," the president replied.

"An evil man," added Gamzat, "a terrorist!"

"And how is your wife getting on?" Pankov asked Gamzat.

The younger son started.

"What wife?"

"This terrorist's sister. Remember when you said he ought to steal me and he hit you and told you to shut up? He called you his brother-in-law."

Gamzat's narrow face turned the colour of a raw potato. The president looked at his sons and became even more like a bronze statue.

Pankov rose sharply to his feet and walked out of the dining room.

■ ■ ■

The morning of the fifteenth began with an expanded session of the parliament. Pankov sat on the right of the speaker and listened as the Interior Minister reporting on the progress achieved in the struggle against terrorism.

Progress had undoubtedly been achieved. A successful operation had been held the previous night. The special forces of the Interior Ministry had surrounded a group of armed men led by the well-known terrorist Waha Arsaev and raked them with light-arms fire and grenade-launchers for five hours. Two bodies had been found at the site of the battle, one of which was presumably Arsaev's,. The Interior Minister proudly declared that the band had been wiped out.

Pankov didn't pay much attention: during the previous

seven months Arsaev had been killed eight times. He was exterminated as regularly as a car's oil is changed when it's serviced.

An economist by education, Pankov was particularly concerned with one question. The republic produced a million tons of high-grade light oil every year, and at least half of this output was exported by road in oil trucks. As far as Pankov could judge from the report in front of him, not a single oil truck had been burnt in the republic during the last six months. Interior ministry vehicles had been burnt, barracks had been burnt, the week before someone had doused the building of the public prosecutor's office in the Shuginsk district with petrol and set it on fire (the files on fifty criminal cases had been burned to ashes, and the event had also figured in the report as an act of terrorism) – but the oil trucks drove round the republic just as if they were in Kansas.

If Pankov had been a terrorist, he would have burned oil trucks, not cops, and he was curious as to why Arsaev didn't do that.

Pankov sat in the presidium, listening to the speaker and occasionally glancing at his watch. It was one forty, the Moscow-Torbi-Kala flight ought to be just about to land, and the special envoy's cortege was already waiting for Igor Malikov at the airport.

■ ■ ■

The scheduled flight from Moscow with Igor Malikov on board landed on time, and when Igor stepped out on to the gangway, he saw below him a black armour-plated "Merc" with federal license plates.

Igor Malikov walked down into the hot, white skillet of

the airport. Colourless prickly plants bristled in the joint between the concrete paving slabs, and immediately beyond the slabs there was a jack pump, with a fat red turkey wandering around it. A woman in a shapeless yellow dress and white headscarf was chasing the turkey. The sun was beating down mercilessly, and in the distance the colourless, flat surface of the sea faded into the colourless peaks of treeless mountains. For a second Malikov thought that hell must look like this, and then he remembered that this was his homeland.

"Salaam Aleichem, Ibragim! They say you're going to be president!"

Igor glanced round. A short queue of officials and businessmen had already formed beside him, stopping the women dressed in black with bundles on their shoulders from leaving the plane. Almost everyone had congratulated Igor during the flight, but those who hadn't had a chance approached him now.

"Ibragim Adievich," the minister of communications said warmly, "you have no idea what things are like in the republic..."

The special envoy's bodyguards politely but firmly hustled Igor off. He dived into the cool interior of the armoured Mercedes and immediately his ears were struck by the sound of the *azan*: the republic's most popular radio station was broadcasting the daily prayer.

■ ■ ■

Rustam was sitting in his Zhiguli beside the level crossing when his mobile phone rang abruptly. "Okay," said Rustam, and got out of the car.

The level crossing, or rather, the open railway line

running across the highway on its way to the oil tanker terminals in the port, had always been considered a convenient spot.

First, cars inevitably slowed down at the crossing. Second, the wall of the seaport began literally five metres away from the crossing and it provided ideal cover for a sniper. It had been used in this way five times already, and the people in Torbi-kala joked that it was time to put up a sign at the crossing: "Caution, hit-men".

This time it was simpler. Rustam didn't even have to shoot. He lay down on the sun-baked earth and felt for the wire leading to the standard army detonator. Rustam had an automatic rifle hanging on his shoulder, but the gun wasn't needed right now. It might be needed later.

The sun beat down mercilessly on the highway; off in the distance there was a white boat sailing in the sea, and through the open windows of the Zhiguli the radio announced the time for daily prayer. Rustam frowned. It was a great sin to miss prayers on a Friday.

The cars appeared five minutes later. There were two of them; one a black, armour-plated "Merc", the other the silver Land Cruiser of the escort.

When the first car slowed down at the crossing, Rustam pressed the button.

■ ■ ■

The Interior Minister was already concluding his report when there was a boom from somewhere in the distance, and several white flakes of plaster fell from the ceiling.

Pankov turned his head. The speaker, Hamid Abdulhamidov, who was sitting on his right in the presidium, became anxious and went out. He came back a minute later and put down a white sheet of paper in front of the Interior Minister.

The Minister read the note, cleared his throat resoundingly and announced:

"Comrades! As I have already informed you, our ministry has achieved decisive successes in the struggle against terrorism! During the most recent period a hundred and forty-five members of illegal armed groups have been arrested. Two hundred kilograms of subversive literature has been seized. And as a result, at least a hundred and forty terrorist attacks have been foiled! But the enemy is ever vigilant. The terrorists who spill blood and spread hate in our republic have just committed another heinous crime! In broad daylight, on the Baku Highway, they have detonated an explosive charge and destroyed five vehicles travelling from the airport!"

■ ■ ■

Beside the main road to the airport, at the intersection of Lenin Avenue and Shamil Avenue, there was a new mosque that could hold five thousand people and, as always on Fridays, it was crowded. A tall man wearing blue jeans and a long-sleeved white shirt was praying one metre inside the door.

The boom of the explosion was three kilometres away from the mosque, and many people came running out at the sound, but the tall man did not even turn his head. A few moments later a friend of his called Djavatkhan walked up to him and said:

"They've killed your brother."

The man carried on praying.

"They've killed your brother," Djavatkhan repeated.

Then, in a break in his prayer, the man turned his head and said:

"But Allah is alive."

And he carried on praying.

■ ■ ■

When Pankov arrived at the site of the explosion, the stench of burnt steel and flesh still hung in the air above the road. Immense traffic jams had built up on both sides of the highway, and the Interior Minister trembled with zeal as he reported to Pankov that they had found the terrorists' car abandoned by the old mosque. It had also been burned out.

Pankov ran forward.

The shockwave had sheared the armoured Mercedes in half, like a sardine can, and thrown the two halves away from each other. The charred human debris had been thrown out of the car, together with the seats and the engine. Igor Malikov had been a tall man, almost two metres in height. All that was left of him now was a smouldering brand one metre long. It was lying on the asphalt like a big black doll, and Pankov couldn't tell if it was lying face-down or face-up.

The railway line had been severed by a crater three metres wide, and a little distance further on the remains of the bodyguards' Land Cruiser and a little white Moskvich were still burning. There were bodies in camouflage suits lying in a heap beside the jeep.

Pankov went down on his knees beside the body and saw that Malikov had not simply been burned to death: a piece of armour plating torn off by the explosion had sliced through his neck and was still protruding from the wound.

An eternity passed before the fair-haired Muscovite

raised his head. The bodyguards' car had already burned out, and the sun had moved on a little closer to the sea. There was a man in blue jeans and a long white shirt standing behind Vladislav. He had an automatic rifle hanging at his side on a wide canvas strap, like a postman's bag. Pankov looked up at him, and seen from below the man seemed very tall, even taller than he had been nine years earlier. The powerful fingers with white half-moons on their nails held the gun's magazine in a casual grip, and an expensive watch glinted on his wrist where it emerged from the long sleeve of his shirt. He had regular features with thick, black eyebrows and a flat nose that looked as if it had been broken, and his moist, plump lips stood out clearly on the smooth-shaved skin of his face. The face had not grown any older, but it seemed coarser and harsher, and small scar had appeared on the neck, starting just below the firm, square jaw and running in under the collar of the shirt.

There was a resounding silence on all sides, and all the security men who had flocked to the scene had moved two metres away from the body, the special envoy and the man with the automatic rifle.

"Were you going to make him president?" asked Niyazbek.

His highlander's accent hadn't softened at all: he still hammered the consonants into each other.

"No."

"The entire republic knew he was your friend. The entire republic knew you'd written a recommendation. Even the sheep in the mountains were gossiping about it."

"He refused. Categorically."

Niyazbek looked the Russian in the eyes, and Vladislav made an astonishing discovery. Niyazbek's eyes were the same colour as Arzo's: not quite black, but closer to dark-brown, like onyx, with red sparks glittering in their depth as if from the depth of the ocean.

"You killed him," said Niyazbek. "I saved your skin, and you killed him, as surely as the men who paid the hit-man. It's a pity you weren't added to Arzo's collection of specimens."

He turned and walked away.

■ ■ ■

Ibragim Malikov was buried in the mountains, beside his father and grandfather, according to Niyazbek's instructions. The body had been taken away immediately – Islamic custom required it to be buried before sunset, and the village lay a hundred and twenty kilometres away, over bad mountain roads.

After a brief argument with his security men, Pankov flew to the village in a helicopter. The only street was packed solid with vehicles, and there was a genuine traffic-jam running back along the road. Ibragim had not been in the republic for twenty years and all this obviously had less to do with him than with his younger brother.

Pankov was surprised to notice that not one of the vehicles was armoured. It was only afterwards they explained to him that it was almost impossible to drive around in the mountains in an armoured car. When they set off to the mountains, almost all the influential people in the republic drove in their own armoured limousines for about fifty kilometres, and then switched into jeeps. Pankov tried to imagine the scene if Malikov had been buried in the city, and realized it could easily have ended in a riot.

Pankov walked up to the cemetery with the other men and stood there, clumsily hiding his hands while the others took their leave of the dead man to the sound of the Imam's rapid recitation in Arabic. As he surveyed the graves, Pankov couldn't help noticing there were no surnames on the gravestones, only patronymics. The cemetery was located above the village, and from there he could see the peaks of the nearby mountains and the tables set out on the square in front of the mosque.

Pankov was told later that while he was in the cemetery, President Aslanov had driven up to the village with his cortege. Niyazbek and his men had come out to meet him and told him to turn back. "I swear on Allah, I didn't do it," the president had said, and Niyazbek had replied: "Go away, or I'll shoot." The president had gone away.

From the cemetery Pankov went to the Malikovs' house. It was on the edge of the village, a surprisingly modest new stone building two storeys high, sheltered behind a wall more suited to a fortress. The house was quiet and empty, the crowd of people was outside. But Pankov noticed two tough-looking young guys standing beside the rack for automatic rifles and looking bored.

Pankov walked past them into the main room, where the floor was covered with red and green carpets, and there he saw Niyazbek praying with his face turned towards Mecca. His Kalashnikov with its broad grey strap was lying beside him on a low, flat couch covered with carpets. The table in the main room was spread with simple food: flat loaves of bread, greens, red-cheeked tomatoes and plates with large chunks of boiled meat.

Niyazbek finished praying, stood up, folded away his prayer mat and put on his socks. Then he sat down on the couch without speaking.

Pankov sat down opposite him.

"Did you love him?" Vladislav asked.

"He was my elder brother," Niyazbek replied patiently,

as if the Russian had asked a childish question. He thought for a moment and then added: "He raised me. He was seven years older than me."

"Did you see him often?"

"The last time was nine years ago. I went to his housewarming in Moscow. His friends were there, and the director of his institute, and my brother started shaming me in front of them all. He said he was a Duma deputy, that he he'd got this flat and a driver, and the institute where he used to work paid him five hundred dollars a month as a consultant. "It is possible to live a worthy life without killing people," he said.

Niyazbek paused, and Pankov saw the scar on his neck suddenly inflate like a cobra's hood.

"I left the flat with the director of the institute. When we got down to the next landing, I started beating him, like a dog, and said: 'I give you two thousand, why do you only pass on five hundred to my brother? I'll get rid of you."

"And then what?" asked Vladislav.

"My brother also came out to see the director off. They were friends. He heard me hitting him. He came down and asked: 'Is the flat from you too?' – 'Yes,' I said. A month later he went away to America. I never saw him again."

"And did you give the director a really good beating?"

"Not as good as he deserved."

They sat without speaking for a few seconds. There was the crackle of automatic gunfire outside, in honour of the deceased.

"The head of the local Federal Security Service swears he was killed by Vaha Arsaev's group. And even my... experts don't exclude that possibility," Vladislav said eventually.

Niyazbek laughed.

"The killers abandoned their weapons. And they burned their car. Why would Vaha abandon his weapons? The cops know what he looks like. If they catch him, he'll be dead before they've taken him ten centimetres. A gun gives him a chance to survive. Why would Vaha burn his car, when the cops already have his fingerprints anyway? Abandoning the weapon is the way hit-men work, not Wahabis. A Wahabi would have hung on to his gun and his car. He doesn't have money to spare."

"But ..."

"Do you still have any illusions? Ibragim Malikov was your friend, and his brother saved your skin. What is the president of the republic supposed to think when you're appointed as special envoy? What is he supposed to think when he invites you to dinner, and you ask him: ;Where's the canteen?' What is it that every man wants, Vladislav?"

"To hold on to his job?" the Moscow official asked.

Niyazbek couldn't help himself, he burst out laughing.

"Every man wants to live. President Aslanov knows he won't survive even a month after he's removed from office. And his sons won't survive a single day. Don't deceive yourself, Russian. In the Caucasus that can cost you your life."

The door creaked open and a girl appeared, wrapped up in a black shawl so that only her face and slim hands could be seen. She put a large china bowl on the table in front of the men. It was full of broth, with the white crescents of *khinkali* dumplings floating in it.

"Eat," said Niyazbek, and Vladislav suddenly realized he was hungry. He hadn't eaten much since the day before – some kind of beetroot salad in the canteen at the House of Parliament. He would have been glad of a drink to go with his food, but for some reason there was no alcohol on the table.

The *khinkali* dumplings were hot and delicious, and Vladislav ate a whole bowlful, followed by some hard, dry-cured sausage.

"After that time nine years ago, I was ill for a long time," said Vladislav. "It might surprise you to know that some people have a thing called nerves. I spent three days in that basement, and I was under treatment for six months. Then I was in the USA for two years, as Russia's representative at the World Bank. When I tried to find the man called Niyazbek, they told me you'd been killed."

Niyazbek absentmindedly chased a piece of *khinkali* round his bowl with his fork.

"The doctors told me I should forget the Caucasus," said Vladislav, "and I did. After I was appointed the presidential envoy I learned a curious fact. I discovered that your new president was elected in 1998, five months after you got me out of the basement. And that his sons were called Gamzat and Gazi-Magomed. I was told that Gamzat and Gamzi-Magomed were involved in a lot of business dealings, dirty business. That they were always making problems. Forgetting to pay their debts. That if it hadn't been for their friend Niyazbek, they would never have survived, and president Aslanov would never have become president, because it was Niyazbek's men and their guns who made sure the votes were counted the way he needed. I also discovered that a week after president Aslanov won the election, Niyazbek's car was blown up by a landmine. So there'd be no need repay any debts. What are you going to do, Niyazbek?"

The highlander looked at Vladislav with his dark-brown eyes and replied:

"Nothing I'd want to tell the Russian president's special envoy."

Vladislav said nothing for a few seconds while he plucked up his courage. Just then the door slammed loudly and several men appeared in the main room. They were all brawny, with dark hair, some wearing black shirts, some dressed in camouflage suits. They took turns embracing

Niyazbek, and then the highlander turned and introduced the first of them:

"Djavatkhan."

Djavatkhan had a remarkably open face with olive-coloured features framed by a short black beard. By local standards he could equally well have been a government minister or a bandit, or both at the same time.

"Hizri."

Hizri leaned on Djavatkhan's shoulder as he walked, and Vladislav realized he had an artificial leg. He was painfully thin. The eyes glittering in his sallow face were as black as exposed film.

"Vaha."

Vaha was about forty. He had the flexible strength of a chain, with curly, greying hair and cruel eyes that were surprisingly blue for a highlander.

The fourth visitor turned to greet Vladislav and he involuntarily jerked his hand away as if he'd stuck it into a furnace.

It was Arzo Hadjiev.

The field commander had aged a lot. His clean-shaven face was wrinkled all over, as if he'd been dropped on to red-hot wire mesh, and the empty left sleeve of his camouflage jacket was pinned in at the waist. Hadjiev had three stars on his shoulder-straps. Vladislav knew that Hadjiev had gone over to the Russians five years earlier; now he commanded the "South" special task force of the Federal Security Service, and his brother represented Chechnya in the Federation Council. Vladislav knew he had been bound to meet Hadjiev sooner or later. But at the moment he froze in fright, gazing at Hadjiev as if he were expecting the Chechen to hit him.

Hadjiev laughed, exposing his strong, yellow teeth, and embraced Vladislav with his sound right arm.

"It's time I was going," said Vladislav.

No one tried to stop him, and he realized he was doing the right thing. The five men needed to talk, and even if they spoke to each other in Russian (and they would, because Arzo was a Chechen), no Russian would ever be able to understand what they were talking about.

In the hallway Vladislav ran into the girl in black. She was carrying a stew pan full of meat, and Vladislav asked:

"Can I help you?"

The girl glanced round, startled, and Vladislav suddenly saw the regular features of her amazingly beautiful face, with the thick, dark eyebrows like Niyazbek's and the deep, black pools of her eyes. Not even the baggy clothes could conceal her lithe, slim figure. The girl first looked at the fair-haired Russian in his Saville Row suit, then at the armed men in the hallway (there were quite a few more of them now) and said in a low voice he could hardly hear:

"No, no. You mustn't. You're a man."

Vladislav watched as she slipped through the doorway into the drawing room.

It was dark when his helicopter took off. In traffic-jam on the mountain road all the cars' headlights were lit up. The special envoy closed his eyes, going over in his mind the conversation he'd just had, then suddenly jerked upright, as if he'd been jolted by an electric shock.

"What's wrong, Vladislav Avdeevich?" his security chief asked, startled.

Vladislav put his hand over his eyes and saw the faces of the men who had come to see Niyazbek as clearly as if they were still there in front of him. The shock of meeting Arzo had driven every other thought out of his head. That was unfortunate. He didn't know who Djavatkhan and Hizri were, although he thought he might have seen Hizri at the economic forum. But he did know the face of the man who had been introduced as Vaha. They'd never met, there was no way they could have, but it was the same face that had stared out at him from the file of the criminal investigation opened on the most important terrorist in the republic, Vaha Arsaev, in 1997, when he and seven cutthroats armed to the teeth had hijacked a plane on a scheduled flight from Torbikala to Moscow.

Translated by Andrew Bromfield

& PEACE

OLGA SLAVNIKOVA

MARIA GALINA

MARIA RYBAKOVA

MARIA ARBATOVA

MARINA KULAKOVA

OLGA SLAVNIKOVA

THE SECRET OF THE UNREAD NOTE

A Literary Case History

A certain young lady, a student, who went by the nickname of Mouse (we shall not mention her real name even once all the way through our tale) used to earn a bit of extra money as a marriage broker. Not that Mouse was desperately short of money, although she could always do with a bit more, like all the rest of us. It was something else that was lacking in her life.

It should be said that a cursory glance at my heroine would have suggested her nickname was entirely unsuitable. That was just something you had to get used to. Mouse was about one metre and eighty centimetres tall and when she stepped out through the puddles in her heavy, granite-coloured Stewards, it was as if a telegraph pole had come to life and set out along the road. She probably got the nickname Mouse because she was so white. Like some laboratory specimen, she had almost completely white hair that looked starched, eyelashes of the same colour and even a pale, thin moustache above her upper lip, as if she had just been drinking milk. An attempt to try her luck in the modelling business was a complete and utter flop, quite literally — Mouse actually fell off the catwalk and landed at the silk-stockinged feet of the woman who owned the agency, after which she limped out without a backwards glance, slamming doors along the way. Nothing on earth could have made her go back. Ever since then she hadn't really cared whose face she found herself looking at, as long as it wasn't her own in the mirror. Cultured old ladies who looked like dilapidated little plush teddy-bears addressed her as "young man". In short, the nickname Mouse only had the right kind of ring to it if you were one of her close friends — and the number of those could be counted on less than the fingers of one hand.

The point is that Mouse had a secret that wasn't entirely real. But at the same time, for her it was the very essence of reality. Dealing with this secret required a special skill. It is possible, for instance, to conceal some act or crime, to provide misleading testimony to a police investigation or to bury the material evidence in someone else's vegetable garden. It is possible to conceal a physical defect, to conceal a scar and the origins of a scar. It is far more difficult to hide *nothing*. Mouse had no young man, male consort, boyfriend — that is so say, nobody loved her and nobody wanted her. There was nothing but emptiness. Whichever way you looked, Mouse was spotless, pure as the driven snow. Not a shred of *material evidence*. Nothing but emptiness, which had to be concealed from outsiders. And it wouldn't fit in her handbag or her pocket.

Instead of love-making, Mouse had to be content with *nothing*-making. Making nothing come of nothing. She was already familiar with the weird sensation of walking without knowing where you were going and seeing nothing but your own boots striding along. Sometimes everything around her became a game. Mouse's neighbourhood, Krylatskoe, looked like a gigantic Tetris screen that only stayed upright without collapsing through the ground because of the empty gaps it still had in it. People in the metro performed dance movements to the music from Mouse's earphones. Everything around her became a pantomime. This *nothing* gave Mouse a right and a duty to be idle, but her parents didn't understand that: for them every single moment was precious. Even when they lectured Mouse on proper behaviour, they kept trying to sneak a glance at their watches, as if they had an itch up their sleeves.

Time, by the way, really was passing — and not only on her parents' watches. Age was beginning to tell, no matter what you might say. The years were beginning to repeat themselves. While once nothing had seemed fresher to Mouse than the slightly bitter school scent of a new autumn, this favourite scent now smelled no different from the last time around. The leaves were torn from the trees and after that, sprinkling quietly down from the sky as if it had just been shaken off the frozen groceries, came what was obviously last year's snow. And then one day Mouse betrayed her *nothing*. As she strode around Moscow like an astronaut moving across the surface of the moon, she wandered into a side street where the clumpy, tight-packed houses looked like Russian stoves. And there she stumbled upon the "Ludmilla" introductions agency, which set Mouse's thoughts moving in a new direction.

Despite its European-style decor and its dossier of eligible foreign bachelors, this was a good old Soviet-style institution, that is, it was formal, dull and totally useless. Having intuitively divined this fundamental characteristic, Mouse acted like her heroic old granny, who had not become an actress, but the deputy director of a delicatessen. In order to get anything worth having out of the "Ludmilla" agency, you had to be standing on the business side of the counter.

Mouse's duties included conducting the initial discussions with clients, preferably on a heart-to-heart basis, and helping them to fill out the appallingly complicated forms that were like mazes for trained rats (90 per cent of the information didn't even need to be entered into the computer). Only in a spot like the "Ludmilla" agency could the initial contact with these anxious ladies and gentlemen possibly have been entrusted to a creature with the appearance of a soldier and a most unladylike vocabulary — but that is precisely the kind of spot it was. Before they took a seat in the Italian armchair facing Mouse, the men hitched up their trouser legs with an obsequious gesture, as if they were preparing to curtsey. Solitary girls of various ages laid out the laminated snapshots of candidates from other cities and foreign countries with the same air as if they were ordering things from a catalogue and could take several items at once. A bored Mouse assigned the "goods" — i.e. the photographs — to albums bearing the imaginary stamps "Freaks", "Idiots", "Kind of Average" and "Old Fogeys"; the hypothetically possible album "Top Secret" was missing, because Mouse could not see anything suitable for herself in the assortment on offer from "Ludmilla". After that she had to take a haphazardly assembled group of clients to parties in a rented restaurant. The clients made a sincere effort to relax, but there was some kind of embodied steel reinforcement inside that wouldn't let them. The couples danced stiffly, as if they were stools. The men brought along vodka for courage, and if the assembled company was not already entirely decrepit, after a short while the toilets would be veiled in the blue smoke of the joints they had smoked.

As far as Mouse could observe, the "Ludmilla" agency's clients were exactly the same as all other people. That is, not part of a pair by definition. Rejects, you might say. Odd off-cuts of material that had been made up into clothes. As if the genuine, true humanity had to be somewhere else — and in some metaphysical sense the presence of the off-cuts actually proved that it existed. But they were really no good for anything. And Mouse knew the reason why this happened to the men and women in her country. It was simply because they all studied Russian literature at school.

Actually, Mouse didn't really have anything to say against Pushkin, Turgenev and Tolstoy. She was even rather fond of Chekhov and his old-fashioned pince-nez. The true enemies of humanity were the teachers of literature, who were distinguished from ordinary physics teachers and botany teachers by the special authority they possessed. The love that the classic writers had written about was their exclusive preserve. It was their mission not to let love through into modern life. In other words, not to allow the pupils of secondary schools to profane what was sacred by making themselves out to be genuine Rostovs or Bolkonskys. Modern boys and girls were unworthy of the classical storylines and were altogether very suspicious. Mouse had heard from someone that in former times not everyone was allowed to draw portraits of Lenin, even if they happened to have the rather strange desire to do so, only special artists on approved lists could do it. It was exactly the same thing here. If a relationship developed between two members of a class (and not just sex while the parents were away at the dacha for the summer), it was always the literature teacher's business.

Life had probably handed Mouse one of the most malicious specimens. Naturally, Zoya Viktorovna, known in the vernacular as Zuya, whose tightly belted waist and sagging behind made her look like a wasp, could not possibly have failed to detect the electricity that was crackling between Mouse and the athlete Terentiev. Everyone could see that Terentiev and Mouse suited each other: they were the only two in the class who were that tall. All of a sudden the moment arrived when Terentiev became a special person for Mouse. Suddenly she found it interesting to hang about in the courtyard in the evenings, because she might accidentally meet Terentiev there. She fell in love with his sweaters and his two velvet jackets in a way that she had never felt about a single rag of her own. Through him she came to understand how the other girls felt about fashionable frippery from Mexx and Benetton. Through him she could have loved all the rest of humanity, including even Zuya, with her reverence for Pushkin and that tight bun of dyed hair on her learned little head.

The relationship developed slowly, the way they do in four-volume nineteenth-century novels. Terentiev walked around on his own with his hands stuck in his pockets and smiled dreamily. According to the laws of the genre, the moment for the declaration was drawing near. And at long last, during a literature lesson (it just had to happen like that, didn't it!), Mouse saw a genuine, classical note from Terentiev travelling through the rows of desks towards her. All the thoughts in her heard immediately arranged themselves in a rainbow. Borne on the crest of a wave of helping hands, knowing glances and quiet smirks, there was happiness surging towards her through the classroom. And up ahead of her Terentiev was sitting perfectly calm, but his ears were blazing like two big velvet roses.

And then came the appalling sound, like nails being hammered into a coffin, of clattering heels. For some odd reason pulling her sleeves up all the way to the elbows, Zuya snatched the note. While she was reading it, with the piece of paper held up close to her misted-over spectacles, the classroom fell silent. All of them realized that was the way someone looked when they just couldn't believe their own eyes. Zuya's face altered from the bottom all the way up, then from the top all the way down. Finally she crumpled up the note, reducing Mouse's happiness to a dry, tight little ball.

"Terentiev, out of the classroom," she declared menacingly, standing there like Mother Russia in the poster, with her clenched fist raised.

And the athlete Terentiev, with slouching shoulders and a smile stretching all the way to his left ear, walked out of the classroom — and out of Mouse's life, of course, because there was no way things could be put right after something like that. And that was the beginning of Mouse's ***nothing*** — after all, you can't really make a something out of a super-brief relationship with a dim-witted jerk high on grass who utters pronouncements like "Sex is just a chance to show your style, babe." Mouse, as always, couldn't give a damn for style, and the jerk, who in dim light couldn't tell the difference between her and a pillow that had fallen on the floor, instantly pissed her off. But now that she had aged from sixteen to twenty, Mouse was hoping for something again. The "Ludmilla" agency had led her into temptation. From somewhere or other Mouse developed the firm belief — as complete and joyful as her certainty concerning the contents of the note — that, having been left without her, sooner or later the lonely Terentiev would turn up at the introductions agency. Everything pointed to the fact that these business premises, with those vulgar little armchairs and that gilded clock with hands that looked like Cupid's arrows, was the absolutely perfect place for her to wait for Terentiev. So she did wait, disdaining the other eligible bachelors — when she looked down on the top of their heads she could see the little bald patches that even they didn't know about.

And then one fine day Mouse did get a visit from someone she knew. Only not from Terentiev. It was Zuya, dressed in broad daylight in some kind of dusty old velvet with sequins, who sat down in the seat facing Mouse for an interview. Zuya had tried very hard to change her appearance: the tight little dyed bun had been transformed into a froth of curls, the eyes without spectacles were so heavily outlined with make-up that Zuya seemed to be looking out through the slits in a half-mask. As she peered short-sightedly at the massive young woman behind the desk, she must have vaguely recognised something — but she was afraid to acknowledge what she recognised.

"Hello, Zoya Viktorovna, I hope you're well?" The feeling expressed in Mouse's voice might have been taken by some outside observer for genuine joy at meeting her favourite teacher. Zuya started so violently that her bony knees knocked together under her velvet skirt.

"So here you are," thought Mouse, gloating to herself. It felt as if Zuya were performing her fidgety movements to Mouse's inner music. Mouse wanted to yell out loud so everyone in the office could hear: "Take a good look at what you've done! All these crazy men and women who come here or are too shy to come — you did that. You've made the biggest ***nothing*** in the world. And now you don't want to obey your own rules? Now you want to have your very own old, bald Terentiev? Perhaps, Zoya Viktorovna, you even want ***happiness***? Don't you think you're asking a little bit too much for yourself?"

"Rychkova?" said short-sighted Zuya, leaning forward. "So this is where you work..." She tried to conceal her embarrassment and assume a pedagogical air, fastening all the gold buttons of her tight-fighting jacket.

"Don't be nervous, Zoya Viktorovna," Mouse said in a honey-smooth voice, which made her colleagues glance round in surprise. "All of us here are working to help you. First we'll just have a little talk about the details of your private life. That's the only way we'll be able to choose someone worthy of you. Our firm is well known for the high-quality service it provides."

"Couldn't I just take a look at the photos first?" Zuya asked with an effort, her crimson velvet attaching itself once and for all to the nap of the green armchair. "Perhaps I might see what I need for myself. Without all this bureaucracy and red tape..."

"Of course, Zoya Viktorovna!" Mouse responded happily. She had the dossiers stamped "Freaks" and "Idiots" ready as if she had just been expecting this moment to arrive. In the confident belief that her hand was acting as the agent of justice and following the bidding of Fate, Mouse handed Zuya the collections of snapshots that she thought resembled vacuum-packed slices of salami, ham and dry-cured sturgeon. Unfortunately for short-sighted Zuya, she had come without her spectacles, so she wouldn't see anything but nightmarish blobs — and that was really all that she deserved.

"Here, take your Pechorin. Here, take your Bolkonsky," Mouse repeated again and again inside her head. "And you'll still end up telling me all about yourself anyway. About your first sexual experience. About your divorce. All your secrets will be mine."

"Ah, what a fool you are, Rychkova..." the unfortunate Zoya Viktorovna was thinking in the meanwhile. She didn't have the slightest intention of revealing the secret of that memorable note to her former pupil. "You've no idea what kind of obscene filth your adored Terentiev wrote to you. And that's the way it should be. There are many things in life that it is best not to know, because what you learn won't do you any good."

At this point we shall abandon our two heroines, as Pushkin once abandoned Onegin in his painful moment of crisis —

and in somebody else's mansion too. Let us merely observe that, strangely enough, justice actually does exist. On the sixth page of the photo album that Mouse, who was indeed acting at the behest of Fate, handed to the teacher of literature, there was a snapshot of a good-hearted Italian man — no prince, but he did own a modest car repair workshop. And several months later this widower with three children carried the happy Zuya away to the shores of the Bay of Naples. Mouse herself would go on hanging about for a while until she met two non-Terentievs and the choice between the two of them became the central theme of Mouse's life for the foreseeable future. Which leads us to conclude that not knowing something is not necessarily bad. Sometimes it might even be a good thing.

You won't find the "Ludmilla" agency any more. In its old place there's a rather nice coffee bar where they brew strong coffee with garlic. Only for some reason the bar still has the same old green armchairs with the fuzzy nap, and the clock with hands that look like Cupid's arrows, which occasionally broadcasts a high-pitched chime above the customers' heads, but the number of strokes never corresponds to the time shown on the dial. Perhaps it shows a different kind of time, the time that it would still be if the "Ludmila" agency had continued to exist. But then again, it's quite possible that the author simply borrowed these items from the coffee bar for the requirements of the present story.

Translated by Andrew Bromfield

MARIA GALINA
THE END OF SUMMER

While he was swimming the weather took a turn for the worse and the sky became obscured by a dull, white haze. As he clambered out on to the bank the clayey soil still felt wet after the night, it was slippery underfoot, trying to push him back down into the greenish water. The sight of the dragonflies perched on the sedge stalks sticking up out of the water, fluttering their transparent wings and creating tiny glassy clouds around themselves, and the water boatmen skimming across the surface of the creek, leaving a faint triangular trail behind them, suddenly gave him a bad feeling — the alien life swarming all around was rejecting him: isolated here, all alone under the pale, indifferent sky, he was no longer a man, the crown of creation — for this wordless place he was merely a receptacle for bacteria or food for worms.

On his way he called in to see Vasilievna, and as he opened the gate at home, he carefully held out one hand, clutching the litre can with fresh milk splashing about inside it.

Sveta met him on the porch — she was hanging out the washing.

"I'm worried it won't dry. It's going to rain again," she

said anxiously. "You've brought some milk? That's good! Let's go and have lunch."

His bouquet from the morning looked resplendent in a clay jug in the centre of the table. He sat down and enjoyed watching Sveta lay the table for lunch; how lightly she moved around the room — the floorboards didn't even creak!

He'd been looking forward to a peaceful summer day — one of those long days that only happen in childhood, or out in the countryside, where time isn't measured off by hours, but by natural phenomena: when the cock crows, it's morning; when the nightshade opens up its gramophone-like flowers, it's evening.

But today it had never even got light — quite the opposite, in fact, the sky had gradually turned darker and darker, hanging down lower and lower over the river, the distant edge of the forest, the badly rutted dirt highroad.

"Just look at that, will you?"

He jerked the cotton print curtain open. The rain was really lashing down now: there were broad puddles under the windows, with colourless bubbles erupting from them. He sighed: somehow he'd never expected they would have to live through endless evenings like this, with a solitary light bulb glowing dimly and the wet porch gleaming as it reflected the colourless sky, and water mingled with some kind of fine litter sprinkling down from the trees. When there was nothing to do, and just the sight of the files of *Ogonyok* magazine for 1975 made you laugh, and the vague misery kept gnawing away at you, and a man torn out of his usual surroundings was no more than a physical body occupying an insignificant sector of ambient space.

"Can't you stop walking around like that?" asked Sveta... She'd installed herself in the old rocking chair, sitting there with her tongue stuck out like a diligent schoolgirl, knitting a bright-coloured little square.

"Self-service, is it?" he asked, surprised.

"Vasilievna taught me." She held her hand out in front of her, examining the fruits of her labour with satisfaction. "You know, it's not really difficult at all."

The indifferent space outside the window suddenly looked frightening, and he pulled the curtain shut again. The twilight was thickening fast, soaking up with water, and he thought he could make out a quiet whispering in the darkness, almost like speech.

He had a vague, uneasy sort of feeling.

He went over to Sveta, stood behind the chair and put his arms round her shoulders. There it was again: there was something wrong — instead of pressing against him in the usual way, her body tensed up under his hands.

"There's someone there," she said softly. Once again he was amazed by how sensitive she was — she seemed to be able to sense events that hadn't even happened yet: as if they were gliding towards her and the waves they made rippled out like circles in water, gently flowing over and around her.

"You just..." He stopped when the boards of the porch gave a quiet creak.

She turned towards him, her face glimmering softly in the semi-darkness of the room.

"Maybe it's Phil? He keeps asking if he can come round for a game of preference."

"Who else could it be? You know how early they all go to bed round here."

There was someone dawdling on the porch, trying to make up their mind to come in.

He flung the door open with a jerk. A bright rectangle of light spilled out on to the wet boards and skipped down the steps to where the sharp line between light and shade blurred, scattering across a multitude of water-filled potholes.

Sveta put down her knitting and went out on to the porch after him.

"Seryozha," she said in a whisper, "look."

There was a tiny figure cowering against the log wall of the house.

"Hey there," he said in a quiet voice. "Who do you belong to?"

The little girl moved away from the wall. Now, when she stepped into the strip of light, he realized she was older than he'd thought at first: about ten. Skinny and frail, you could almost see right through her. The fine drops of water glinted and shimmered in her straight, dark-blond hair.

"Come in then," he said, stepping aside to make way. "Don't be afraid."

The girl slipped into the house without speaking. The dress clinging to her scrawny body was so wet he couldn't even tell what colour it was.

He caught Sveta's surprised glance and shrugged without saying anything.

"Who do you belong to?" he asked again.

The girl looked at him with transparent, almost vacant eyes.

"Oh, leave her alone, will you," Sveta said irritably. "Just look how wet she is. She's cold!"

She spoke to the girl: "Get that off, quick now."

The girl turned away and obediently pulled the darkened, shapeless mass of material up over her head, leaving herself in just her linen knickers. Her back was completely untanned, with protruding shoulder blades and sharp little vertebrae.

Sveta took the wet bundle of material from the girl, then took his favourite bathing sheet down off its hook and threw it over her. She wrapped it round her and started rubbing the skinny body.

"Don't get carried away," he commented, "her mother must be looking for her."

He turned to the little girl:

"Where's your mummy?"

She looked back at him with vacant eyes.

He sighed: "She's a bit... Maybe she's the local idiot?"

"Have you seen her before?"

"No. But every village has its own idiot."

"Don't be silly," she said with a shake of her head. "We know everyone round here."

"Maybe it's someone here on holiday?"

"Do you think someone else might have arrived? Right this evening?"

He went out on to the porch again. The rain was splashing down into the puddles like thousands of toads — the air was filled with a constant rustling, but there weren't any other unusual sounds. No engines rumbling, no doors slamming, no voices. And it was dark all around — as if time hadn't even begun yet — not a single bright window, black leaves stirring sluggishly under the blows of the watery lashes, against the background of a black sky.

He went back in and shook his head in reply to Sveta's inquiring glance.

"Nobody there."

Sveta gave the girl a worried look.

"Perhaps... you ought to walk round the village?"

"What's the point? If the parents have any brains at all, they'll find us themselves."

"But perhaps she doesn't have any parents?"

"Come on, there has to be someone."

"Maybe she's from Rozhdestvenskoe? Run away from home?"

"Perhaps. We can't throw her out, she can stay the night here. I'll go over there tomorrow. First thing in the morning.

Her parents must be going out of their minds. And why doesn't she say anything, dammit?"

He turned and spoke to the girl again:

"Listen, can you talk or not? You live in Rozhdestvenskoe, don't you?"

Her pupils were wide open, making her colourless eyes look almost black. She stared hard at him and the faint shadow of a smile flitted across her face.

"Daddy," she said.

He sat down on a chair.

"Well now," he sighed, "how do you like that!"

He strained wearily on the pedals on his way back. His trip hadn't produced any results. The local policeman sitting in the white single-storey building with the sign on the wall that said "Administration" — it also contained the post office, the telephone centre and, oddly enough, the dry cleaner's — had just shaken his head:

"No, we haven't had any reports. And anyway... If anything had happened, then I'd know about it. We don't have that many folks round here, everything's out in the open."

"Will you take her?"

"What would I do with her?" the policeman had answered, annoyed. "Move her in with me, should I? I've got three of my own at home already. You leave your address and I'll get in touch with the district office. Or call back yourself in a couple of days."

"What about the girl?"

"She can stay with you for the time being. Where else can we put her?"

But then the policeman had suddenly been struck by something:

"Listen, maybe she's from the home?"

"What home?"

"The children's home. There's a children's home not far from here. For backward children. You said she was a bit odd, not all there."

"Yes," he said thoughtfully, "that sounds about right."

"But then, they'd have notified me... try going over there anyway."

The children's home stood on the very edge of the village. After it there was nothing else, just hills receding into the distance, criss-crossed with ravines and dotted with little groves of trees that gradually fused together into the solid blue wall of the forest on the horizon. The iron gates in the blank wall were closed, and so was the side gate — he had to press the bell button for a long time before it finally opened.

"Who do you want?" asked the elderly woman wearing a headscarf right down to her eyebrows.

"I'd like to see the director."

"Are you a dad?"

"What?" He didn't understand.

"Parents' day is tomorrow."

She shot a disapproving glance at this irresponsible father who'd got his parents' days mixed up.

"No, no," he said hastily, "I'm not a father. I just wanted to know... You see, a little girl has strayed into our house."

She looked at him even more suspiciously.

"Maybe she's yours? I mean, from your home?"

"I don't see how she can be, I don't think anyone's gone missing."

But even so she moved aside and let him through.

"Matveevna!"

Another elderly woman came over, this time with a tight, curly perm.

"This man here," said the woman on duty, jabbing a crooked finger at him, "says he's got this little girl..."

"Enrolment was in June," the new woman said in an incorruptible voice, "and anyway, there aren't any places."

"No, no," he said, setting the old, familiar record turning yet again. The speech ended with "... and your local policeman said she might be from here".

"From here?" She shook her head. "No, ours are all where they're supposed to be."

Some children were walking through the yard, probably on their way to the dining hall. They were walking in an uneven column, in pairs, holding each other by the hand and obviously trying very hard to keep in step, but always losing the rhythm. In the hot, quivering haze of the vapours rising from the ground, they looked like aliens from another planet, the way they're usually drawn — with big heads, eyes sunk deep under their foreheads and disproportionately tiny little hands and feet.

He shuddered despite himself.

"No," he said, "ours isn't like that. She's... a normal girl. Just a bit strange."

"All ours are strange," the director said severely, "they make little monsters when they're drunk, and then dump them on us."

As if by command, the round heads turned towards them, the mouths opened slightly...

"She's not one of yours then?" He shivered again in the suffocating air. "No? Okay, I'll be going."

He almost ran to the exit, feeling the director's disdainful gaze on his back.

He spotted them straightaway — in the garden: Sveta leaning down over a flowerbed, working away precisely with a small hoe and the little girl squatting down and tying up the frail green stems, painstakingly sticking in the thin sticks of wood beside them.

When the gate squeaked, they both raised their heads at the same moment and gave him equally fleeting smiles.

"Well?" Sveta asked, taking him aside and wiping her green-stained hands on the bottom of her dress. He shrugged.

"Nobody knows a thing. The policeman says he'll get in touch with the district office. Perhaps they know something there."

"A-ah." Had he imagined it, or had he really heard a note of concealed satisfaction in her voice? "All right, then."

"There's a home there. A children's home. For all sorts of..." He shook his head, driving the memory away. "I'm glad you didn't see them!"

"You thought... that was where she was from?"

"No, of course not! She's nothing like them. They're all, you know... And the director says nobody's gone missing there."

The girl grew bored of carrying on with the monotonous work on her own — she got up, dusted off her knees and ran over to them.

"Are we going to the river?" she asked.

Her voice was high but soft — not wheedling, not begging, simply asking.

He looked at Sveta.

"I wouldn't mind going. I've sweated myself to death on that blasted bike. It's so incredibly stuffy..."

"I'll get the towel, shall I?" asked the girl, and she ran up on to the porch, skipping every second step, and disappeared into the house.

"She's a bright spark," he remarked disapprovingly.

"You take care over there," said Sveta, "if anything happens to her..."

"What could happen to her? Unless she decides to go running off again."

Sveta gave him a strange sort of look.

"She's quite a nice girl," she said after a while.

A half-smile — or more the shadow of a smile — lit up her soft features just for a moment. He suddenly noticed that she wasn't looking well: her face was so pale it looked transparent and there were deep shadows under her eyes.

"You're looking a bit green," he said, gazing at her anxiously.

"It's nothing... it's just so close. I've got a bit of a headache."

"I should think so! You've been hanging upside down all morning. Who's all this stupid weeding for anyway? We're going home in a week."

"It was her," said Sveta, nodding towards the little girl, who was standing on the porch, painstakingly cramming the towel into a plastic bag. "She kept saying: 'The flowers feel hot too'."

"Never mind what she says! Yesterday we couldn't get a single word out of her. And by the way, what's her name, did she condescend to tell you?"

A smile flitted across Sveta's face again, reflecting her thoughts rather than her words.

"Her name's Katerina. Katya."

"Is it now? Did she mention her surname as well?"

"I asked. She just laughs."

"She is an idiot after all," he sighed. "Maybe that director woman's lying? She didn't keep a proper eye on her, let her get away, and now she's lying."

"She calls me mummy," said Sveta, not listening to him, and her smile broke through even more brightly this time, like a light bulb when the current is gradually turned up.

He sighed, shrugged and turned towards the girl.

"Let's go," he said curtly.

She darted after him, still hopping and skipping. Her

bouncy way of walking irritated him, and he lengthened his stride, knocking the heads off the thistles with the heavy plastic bag as he walked along.

She didn't fall behind — she just worked her little legs faster, sometimes breaking into a run.

"Daddy!" she called out eventually.

He didn't realize straight away that she was calling to him. When he did, he asked wearily:

"What do you want?"

"Daddy! Is a daisy white?"

"Yes," he confirmed.

"Then why did you tell me there's no such colour as white?"

"When did I tell you that?" The oppressive heat before the storm was pressing down on him, making it hard to think.

"Last year. Or the year before. I don't remember."

"Well actually, the colour white isn't a colour at all," he agreed. "It's simply a mixture of all the colours. There are seven of them. That's..."

"I know, I know," she said, running along beside him, trying to catch hold of his hand, "red, orange, yellow..."

"Maybe she's not really an idiot, after all," he thought. "Just a bit peculiar. She's run away from home and made up all sorts of crazy things..."

The water was slumbering under the steep, sticky earth bank — no, not slumbering, it was waiting, there was a dark, ominous menace stirring under the surface. For a moment he even thought that if he stepped into it, disturbed its peace, it would grab hold of his ankle with chilly blue fingers and never let him out.

The girl spread the towel out on the grass, folding up her dress just as carefully — now that Sveta had dried it and ironed it, it was pink, with small purple flowers — and set off towards the water. She walked with her toes pointed funnily, as if she really was a little girl from a good home who'd been dragged off to dance classes almost as soon as she was out of nappies, and now she was trying to delight her doting parents with her skills.

He sighed:

"Do you know how to swim, at least?"

She giggled:

"You spent all that time teaching me..."

"Last year?" he asked resignedly.

"Nah, I already knew how last year. Probably the year before."

She slithered down into the water and started swimming along the bank, stroking with her arms and legs in a funny way, like a frog. In the water her body had a transparent, strangely morbid vulnerability, her light hair spread out on the surface like a bunch of rotting waterweed. All of a sudden he felt a strange desire to turn his back and tiptoe away, then run and keep on running until the doors of the Moscow train slammed shut behind him. It made him feel ashamed.

He took a run and jumped off the bank into the water. It closed over his head for a moment to form a glassy, swaying ceiling that immediately shattered into a thousand tiny fragments when he burst back up, gasping and snorting, on to the surface.

The disturbed water was simply water, there was nothing hiding in it apart from a school of startled minnows, which immediately darted off in all directions.

A few sweeps of his arms — and he set his foot on the slippery bottom, shuddering as he felt the silt slithering between his toes, and climbed out on to the bank. The girl was already sitting on the towel, wringing out her light hair. Damn, he thought, she's just an ordinary little girl. What on earth got into me?

"Get up," he said curtly.

She jumped to her feet, picked the towel up off the ground and ran across to him.

He opened out the towel and started drying himself without speaking. The sky hung low over the earth, pressing down on the back of his neck, and he was suddenly overcome by a nauseous feeling of unreality.

Nothing that was happening felt real. It was as if he hadn't actually climbed out the water, but was still moving through it — in slow motion, struggling against the resistance, the way things happen in dreams.

The little girl watched him anxiously.

"Did something make you feel frightened?" she asked eventually.

"Frightened? What the..." He checked himself. "Why do you think that?"

"You came up so quickly. Is there a catfish sitting down there?"

"Let's go home," he said. "What catfish? There aren't any catfish in there."

"You remember, you told me. When you were little, a catfish grabbed hold of your foot."

He suddenly saw that black, slippery body again quite clearly, spinning round and round in the water like a car tyre inner tube, and he felt the sudden, sharp pain in his foot — as if someone had scraped a small grater over it — and saw his foot covered in small, bleeding scratches.

"When did I tell you about that?" he asked slowly.

(The humiliating, choking fear, his own sickening screech still ringing in his ears... he never told even Sveta about that... And the sudden sharp spasm, and the warm little cloud between his legs, and the feeling of shame...)

She giggled.

"You said you were so frightened you even peed yourself."

"The catfish got left behind in a hollow," he said thoughtfully, talking to himself more than the girl, "on the bed of the river, under a snag, and when the water level fell and the river turned shallow, he couldn't swim away. He was very big. And he must have been very hungry."

The girl nodded:

"Aha... and you told me when they caught him, it took two men to carry him, and his tail still dragged along the ground."

That strange feeling of resignation came over him again — as if he really had told her something he'd never told anyone, and from somewhere deep in the vaults of his memory he heard his own voice say compliantly: "I was just walking along the bottom, and I fell, whoosh, into that pit! Can you imagine it? And then the way he came for me! And I didn't know how to swim properly, either. You be careful when you go swimming, you never know what might happen!"

He shook his head, trying to dispel the delusion, and automatically lengthened his stride.

She skipped along behind him — a friendly pest...

"Have a good swim?" Sveta asked when she met them on the porch. "Come to the table, then."

How quickly she's adapted, he thought. Perhaps that's a general female characteristic — to adjust to everything.

At dinner the little girl chattered away without stopping — the usual sort of nonsense children talk. Her high, thin voice was like a mosquito buzzing round his head; it was just as if the pane of glass in the veranda window, with the grey moth sleepily beating itself against it, was jingling in its frame.

When he finished eating he was all set to help Sveta, but she pushed him away gently:

"No need, we'll manage on our own."

She turned to the girl and said:

"Let's show how good we are at keeping house..."

The unspoken word "daddy" was left hanging in the air.

The evening was drawing in. The rain still hadn't come on, although the dark clouds, as heavy as lead, were heaped up on top of each other above the forest.

They'd drawn the net curtains across the windows to stop the mosquitoes flying in, but even so there were little creatures of some kind fluttering round the lamp. He sat there watching the two figures bustling round the table, noticing how remarkably well-coordinated their movements were, as if they really had known each other for years and years: the girl took the wet plates from Sveta, wiped them carefully with the towel and stacked them in a pile.

He felt out of place in this female realm, an outsider, and he was actually glad when the steps of the porch creaked again. For some reason he immediately thought it must be the policeman from Rozhdestvenskoe. But why didn't he hear the motorcycle?

They'd found the parents after all...

When he saw Phil the disappointment was like a sharp blow. Phil paused in the doorway for a moment in casual surprise.

"I see you have an addition to the family?"

"Uhu," Sergei agreed. "An incredible stroke of luck."

Sveta's reproachful glance brought him up short.

"Where did she come from?" the student asked casually.

"Ask me another."

Phil squatted down and pulled a fierce face. The girl giggled.

"She's a pretty thing," he said.

"Oh, is she now?"

"Oh, stop it," Sveta intervened in a conciliatory tone.

She turned to Phil and explained: "He's still a bit shocked, you know. It was so unexpected."

"Just appeared from out of nowhere, did she?" asked Phil, ruffling the girl's hair as he stood up. "Have you contacted the police?"

"What police? There's no one but the local man, and he's stuck over in Rozhdestvenskoe."

Sveta gave the girl a hug round the shoulders and pushed her towards the door into the tiny windowless extension, where they'd set up the folding bed.

"Go to bed now."

"Oh, mum-my," the girl whined.

"Wow!" Phil said. "It didn't take you long to break her in."

There was an odd guilty expression on Sveta's face.

"I came to give you back your salt," the student explained. "And the matches. I finally bought some. I was beginning to feel awkward, borrowing from you all the time."

"Don't be silly," Sergei said magnanimously. "It's only a bit of salt... How's the work going? Any progress?"

"Once I get the roof finished, that'll be it," Phil said proudly.

"Well, that's good," his host responded indifferently.

But instead of going, Phil hung around by the door. He obviously didn't feel like going back to someone else's half-finished house.

"Well, shall we deal out the cards?" he suggested. "You wouldn't mind, Sveta, would you?"

Before Sveta could answer, Sergei shook his head and said:

"Not today. I'm feeling a bit tired. I rode all the way to the village and back, and I've got to go back again in the morning."

"A-ha," Phil drawled, disappointed, "well then, be seeing you..."

He went out of the door.

Sveta lifted her head from the ball of bright-coloured wool.

"Knitting again," he said, "you'll only ruin your eyes."

She hesitated, not knowing how to begin.

"So you're going to Rozhdestvenskoe tomorrow?"

"Of course. I told you, the policeman promised to phone the district centre. Maybe they've found out something. We can't keep her forever."

"Listen," she said in a quiet voice, "maybe you shouldn't?"

He didn't understand straight away.

"Maybe I shouldn't what?"

She looked away.

"Maybe... if there's no one looking for her... She could stay with us until... until everything's sorted out."

He gaped at her. Until what was sorted out? Had she lost her mind?

"We're leaving in a week," he said as gently as he could. "Are you going to drag her along with us? To Moscow?"

"Why not?" She was looking straight at him now, and there was a clear note of defiance in her voice.

"Because... She's strange. Really strange. You should be more careful with her."

"You're talking nonsense," Sveta said coldly.

He hesitated, not knowing how to begin. Jesus, she'd think he was raving!

"Sveta," he said eventually, "listen, there's something not right about her. It's not just that she's a bit strange... She... She knows things about me..."

"What things?" Sveta asked suspiciously. "You're just imagining it."

"Things that happened to me when I was a boy. And in general..."

"You must have told her yourself."

"When could I have told her?"

I've never told anyone about that, he thought. It's a load of nonsense – what's there to be ashamed of in the whole thing anyway, but all the same!

"Maybe..." he said. He didn't believe in all that rubbish, of course, he had to force himself to say it: "Maybe she's psychic..."

"Good grief, Seryozha!" He saw the absolute amazement in Sveta's eyes. "What's happening to you? You always used to laugh at me..."

"Yes," he admitted wearily, "I know. But all the same... Listen, let's test her!"

"How? Are we going to buy a crystal ball?"

"We'll just ask her... You know... Something about us."

"Seryozha," Sveta said uncertainly. Are you sure we need to? Perhaps you just imagined it?"

"I'm damned sure I didn't!" he said, striding determinedly towards the extension.

"At least let's wait until morning," Sveta suggested.

"She won't be asleep yet," he retorted. "She's lying there in the darkness, grinning."

He suddenly had a clear vision of himself backing away, avoiding turning his back to this alien creature, going down the steps, slamming the gate shut and running, running until the doors of the train clattered shut behind him.

He opened the door carefully and sprang back.

"What is it?" asked Sveta, looking at him anxiously.

"She's not there!"

He shook his head, concealing his relief.

"She must have run away again."

"Seryozha," Sveta said patiently. "She couldn't have run away. There aren't any windows in the extension."

She pushed him aside and swung the door open resolutely. Then she turned to him with a puzzled look.

"There she is! What on earth's happening to you?" He glanced over her shoulder into the extension. The girl was sitting on the folding bed. She looked at them without saying anything. He shook his head, trying to dispel the delusion.

"Let's ask her," he said again, "let's ask her about something!"

He shrugged Sveta's pacifying hand off his shoulder and stepped into the extension. The girl was still sitting there without moving, with the beam of light slanting in through the door picking out one half of her transparent face — the other half blended into the log wall of the extension.

A little lunatic, he thought. He called to her in a quiet voice:

"Hey!"

She turned her face slightly — now it was a bright spot floating in the damp semidarkness.

"Do you know who I am?"

"Yes," she answered in a thin, surprised voice, "you're daddy."

No chance, he thought.

Somehow he couldn't bring himself to sit beside her on the folding bed: he lingered in the doorway.

"What's my job?"

"You're a programmer," the girl answered quietly.

"I see. And what about... mummy?"

"She collects songs. And sayings. No, proverbs... No sayings... I've got them mixed up again."

"Well," he said, turning to Sveta. "Did you tell her about your job?"

"Yes," said Sveta, surprised, "just a bit."

He thought for a while.

"What can we ask her about... Ah! The place where I live in Moscow, can you describe it?"

The girl frowned hard, knitting her light eyebrows together.

"Ooh... It's a funny kind of name... Perkhushkovo, that's it! A big tall house. Beautiful, with balconies. On the sixth floor. And I've got a room of my own, pretty wallpaper with little dinosaurs..." She paused and added happily: "We put it up together."

He shook his head.

"There, you see," Sveta said in a conciliatory voice. "And you were imagining God knows what."

He relaxed a bit.

"Yes," he admitted, "she got that wrong."

He spoke to the girl:

"You're just making things up, you silly thing. I live near Mayakovsky Square."

"But you told me yourself they were going to move everyone somewhere else soon," Sveta interceded unexpectedly and entirely illogically.

"What of it?" he shook his head. "They're moving everyone around these days."

She wasn't clairvoyant, she was just a little fool or a dreamer. Maybe the whole thing was no more than a coincidence? He couldn't be the only boy who'd ever been attacked by a catfish, could he? Jesus, why couldn't he make himself look into her face? Why did he shudder at the accidental touch of her defenceless little child's body? As if she weren't a child at all, not even human, but something born out of the blind, damp twilight, hatched out of a shapeless mass, a mixture of water droplets, grass and the damp earth teeming with worms...

"Now tell me this..." he said, casting about feverishly for the right question. A question that would settle things.

"That's enough for today, Seryozha," Sveta said quietly but firmly.

He gestured in weary submission and had already turned to walk away when he was suddenly stopped by the girl asking in a clear, curious voice.

"Daddy, why did you shout at Mummy about Uncle Phil? It made me run away and hide."

He stopped with a jerk.

"When did I shout at her?"

"Yesterday..."

He shook his head:

"You imagined it."

But she went on:

"You said it wasn't the first time and you'd had enough..."

"Listen," he said wearily, "stop."

"... and you knew why she wanted to come to this dump every spring."

He took a step towards the dark silhouette on the bed, felt for the skinny little body and started shaking it with almost all his strength.

"Shut up, I said!"

"Seryozha," Sveta said quietly behind his back, "you were the one who started it."

He let go of the girl, took Sveta by the elbow and led her out of the extension, closing the door firmly behind him.

Sveta gave him a puzzled look.

"You're behaving oddly," she said eventually.

He almost laughed out loud.

"Me? I'm behaving oddly?"

He squeezed her elbow tighter.

"Listen, don't you see anything at all? This nonsense she spouts... there's no sense to it, no logic, but she's creeping... yes, that's it, she's creeping into our life... she... God only knows where she came from, but look how quickly she's managed to bewitch you."

"Well, she invents things," Sveta said gently, "she tells fibs, but you're acting as if she were some kind of monster, not just a little girl."

"Exactly."

"You're just jealous," she said unexpectedly.

He gaped at her.

"Me? Jealous?"

"You're used to everything revolving around you, and now someone else has appeared and demands attention, you're kicking up a fuss. Stop going for her like that, please. Otherwise..."

"Otherwise what?"

Sveta just shrugged and turned away. They didn't talk to each other again until the morning. They didn't even talk in the morning, when he got up, drank a cup of cold but strangely tasteless milk and rolled the bicycle out of the shed.

The road had turned soggy and he had to press harder than usual on the pedals: he was soaking wet when he left the bicycle outside the low, white building with the sign "Admnistration" and went in.

"Well," he asked from the doorway. "Did you call the district office?"

The policeman raised his head, pulling open the drawer of his desk at the same time.

He's probably reading a thriller, Sergei thought.

"I did," the policeman answered, sounding annoyed. "What's the point of coming here every day? I've already spoken with your wife."

"When was that?" he asked suspiciously.

"I called in yesterday. I was passing, so I called in. I wanted to take a look at the little girl, but you were down at the river. I didn't go inside, but your wife came to the gate. I told her the district office hadn't received any reports yet. I said you could put her in the children's home for the time being — I made arrangements. But she said there was no need. Said you were going to adopt the girl, if the parents don't turn up."

Seeing Sergei's bemused expression, he stopped, then asked:

"You mean she didn't tell you?"

"No..." Sergei looked away in order not to see the look of sympathy on the policeman's face and added: "Perhaps she forgot."

The policeman sighed:

"Obviously she made her mind up without consulting you. That's the way women are. Act first, think later."

"Yes," Sergei muttered, "yes, I suppose so... I'll have a word with her."

The bicycle had got so hot that it burned his hand when he touched it. He pressed on the pedals, bouncing over the bumps and potholes... so, Sveta had decided to keep the girl. And she hadn't said anything to him — as if he were some kind of empty space. Just what was so special about this snot-nosed kid to make her take such a liking to her? And why, why did he feel so reluctant to go back into a house with that pale little alien creature wandering around in it?

He left the bicycle at the gate — how had he managed to miss the treadmarks left in the clay by the motorbike's tyres yesterday? — and went into the house.

Loud peals of happy laughter assaulted his ears while he was still on the porch. The girl was laughing, Sveta was laughing, and there was another strange voice was laughing with them.

Phil was standing blindfolded in the middle of the room, trying to catch the two idiots, who kept dodging away and squealing. They were having so much fun, they didn't even notice him come in.

The girl darted in one direction and Sveta darted in the other, but Phil stretched out his long arm and managed to catch her and she struggled to beat him off, tossing her head to shake off the hair that had fallen across her face.

He coughed.

The happy squealing stopped and the room was suddenly silent.

"Am I interrupting anything?" he said coldly. "I beg your pardon."

Two equally flushed faces stared at him, and for the first time he noticed how much alike they were: as if the girl were mimicking Sveta, copying the features of her face, the way a flounder reproduces the colour of the stone that it's resting on.

Phil pulled off his blindfold and stood there, blinking his colourless eyelashes in confusion.

At the sight of that confused expression something inside him burst, like the shimmering film of a bubble on the surface of a puddle, leaving nothing but emptiness and a strange, nerve-jangling feeling that all this wasn't really happening.

"Get out!" he yelled. "Clear out!"

(Jesus, is that really me shouting like that?)

"You're always hanging around here! Now I know why."

"Seryozha," Sveta interceded timidly.

"And you..." he said, turning on her, "you slut!"

Phil grabbed him by the shoulder, forcing him to turn round. The skin on the student's face was bruised and broken, there was blood dripping from his nose on to his shirt. Had he hit him, then?

"What's got into you? What are we supposed to have done?"

"I'll tell you... I'll tell you what it is you've done."

"Phil," Sveta said in a quiet voice. "Leave it... we'll sort it out... you'd better go..."

"I..." Phil started, then gave up, edged past him

awkwardly and made for the door. In the doorway he looked back, trying to catch Sveta's eye, but she was looking away. He shook his head and walked slowly down the steps.

"Seryozha..." Sveta said quietly, gazing at him wide-eyed. "What's wrong with you, Seryozha?"

"With me?"

He grabbed hold of her hand, but she broke away and gave him another frightened look.

"And what's wrong with you? All it takes is for some snot-nosed kid to turn up, and for her sake you're ready... It doesn't bother you that the sight of that creature makes me sick, go on... go on, take her back to Moscow. Why not? Phil's taken such a liking to her... Uncle Phil — well, well, well."

He swung round towards the girl:

"What do you know, you viper? Out with it! And where did you spring from anyway? Who are you? Tell me. Who are you?"

Her head wobbled backwards and forwards on her thin neck — he was shaking her in desperate fury, as if he were trying to shake the truth out of her.

Then Sveta came to her senses.

"Let her go! Let her go, you..."

She grabbed hold of the base of his neck, her fingers felt cold and sharp, he struggled to tear the strange hand away, but it stuck to him.

Eventually he managed it and twisted round, hitting her in the solar plexus with his elbow. She gasped and recoiled. He swung his hand through the crimson twilight again, feeling his fist sinking over and over into something soft.

"Dad-dy!" the little girl screamed piercingly. He swung round towards her, realizing that this shrill, repulsive voice was the reason why he couldn't think straight.

"Shut up, you monster!"

She carried on yelling — something appalling,

unintelligible, on and on, with her eyes goggling wildly, turning her distorted and unrecognisable face towards Sveta, who was writhing in the corner of the room, clutching her stomach with her hands.

He flung aside the skinny rag doll of a body and dashed over to his wife, but she instinctively cowered away. As the girl's face changed, losing its newly acquired likeness, its own features re-emerged — it was her usual face, but it was pale and tormented, there was terror pulsing in the staring eyes.

"That wasn't me..." he said, struggling with the words, "it wasn't me... forgive me... I'm sorry..."

He lifted up her head and pressed it against himself.

"What?"

"Seryozha... I'm hurt... quick..."

He let go of her and ran out on to the porch — the lanky shadow was still loitering at the gate.

Biding his time, the bastard, he thought in passing, but he shouted out:

"Phil, help me..."

"What's happened," the student asked in alarm.

"I don't know. Help me, I say..."

He dashed back into the house and appeared in the doorway again, holding Sveta in his arms. She looked so pale, she seemed to be trying to dissolve into the fading daylight, her head was lying feebly on her shoulder, her hand was pressed hard against her stomach, crumpling the bright-coloured material of her sarafan.

"Hold the bike, damn you!"

She got on to the crossbar with a struggle, holding her arms round his neck. Phil ran alongside, keeping one hand on the handlebars, and they moved along the road, balancing like that for a while, pursued by a gradually fading, spine-chilling wail that didn't sound human.

"What's she doing?" he asked Phil, who was still running alongside, keeping them upright.

The student understood what he meant.

"Standing on the porch and yelling."

"Damn her to hell," he muttered, then he finally got his balance and pressed down hard on the pedals. Phil was left behind, the screaming behind him faded away, and now he could hear Sveta gently moaning in a regular, hopeless rhythm.

The evening had come and gone. The attendant in the reception area was mopping the floor, and the squeaking of the sponge on the linoleum was unbearable — he wasn't thinking about anything any more, all he wanted was for that sound to stop, it made the hairs on the back of his hands stand up on end and his mouth fill up with saliva.

The attendant finally went away, pulling her mop along behind her and dragging her feet in the blue felt slippers. Then he regretted that the sound had stopped. The silence was far more frightening.

"You ought to go home." The woman in the white coat who had appeared in the doorway looked to him like a copy of the director at the children's home. Even the white coat was the same — grubby, with some of the buttons missing.

"But... how is she?" he asked, struggling to get the words out.

"She's sleeping. Come back in the morning. Bring her some underclothes, a mug, a toothbrush..."

"What's wrong with her?"

"A miscarriage. And soap. We don't have any soap."

"She was pregnant?"

"Yes, that's what I'm telling you. In her third month. There's heavy bleeding. But everything will be all right. She's young and strong."

"I don't..."

She pushed him towards the door.

"Go now, go. Nothing's going to happen to her before morning."

He set off along the road, pushing the bicycle — a solitary streetlamp lit up the metallic leaves and the insects fluttering in the cone of light were like falling snow.

He dumped the bicycle by the gate — the prickly bushes by the fence seemed suddenly to have grown, he had to force his way through them, and the long, parallel scratches on his hand stung. There was no light in any of the windows in the house. Surely she couldn't have gone to sleep — not after all that... He'd have to take her to the hospital, damn her, the little monster, but if Sveta wanted him to... Since she'd taken such a great shine to her. He suddenly realized he couldn't remember her name, even though Sveta had told him, hadn't she?... Valentina? No, that wasn't it...

He deliberately made a noise stamping up the steps — so she would hear.

"Hey," he said, "it's me."

The door opened without a sound at the touch of his hand. The room was empty.

He pulled a chair out from under the table and sat there for a while without moving, leaning back with his legs stretched out. Then he stood up, took a plastic bag and started gathering together the pitiful collection of things she needed: a change of underclothes, a mug with a chipped edge, a little mirror, a comb... He moved methodically, calmly, trying not to forget anything on the doleful list. When he was finished, he put the bag down carefully on the chair, leaned his hands on the windowsill and looked out into the darkness. Beyond the black garden there was not a single light shining all the way to the distant sea of the forest. Just the hills, with their criss-cross ravines, and the slow rivers, where the dark, taciturn fish surface at night from the deep pools...

He stood there for a while, feeling the black-red space pulsating through him...

"Would you believe it," he said to the gloom all around, "she's run off again..."

Translated by Andrew Bromfield

MARIA RYBAKOVA
A STING IN THE FLESH

I. This was the last attempt. If it failed, there wouldn't be any more. Because the glass would break. Varvara Petrovna reached out for the glass of water on the little bedside table. The trembling fingers gripped the glass with surprising firmness, and the hand only shook slightly as it carried it to her mouth. The old woman drank the water in small sips and put the glass back just as slowly. The job was done. There were some things that she could see through to a conclusion, after all, some things that she could completely consume. First the water was there — and then it wasn't. It was all drunk. It had been necessary for Varvara Petrovna's life to continue. Thirst. The water disappears. That was how you existed, by destroying something. The air in the room was probably stuffy. But she didn't care. It wasn't likely to improve her condition if the room was aired. When the curtain was pulled back, she could see the tops of the trees. They were still bare — it was spring. Her favourite time of year. How good it was that time had started moving so slowly again, like when she was little. This winter the snow had seemed to go on falling for years. Or perhaps she had just happened to see a blizzard outside when the curtains were open, and then the sight had come back to her over and over again in her dreams. She didn't sleep at night, the way she used to before, only in short, frequent bursts, so that the days were broken up into lots of little sections and became all confused. And the same thing happened with the nights. The numbers that she'd once had under such masterful control had escaped her now. If you asked her how many years she'd been lying in this room, she wouldn't have been able to tell. Maybe ten years, maybe five. Maybe even less than that. But hardly more. Sometimes (it must be when she was only half-awake) she used to ask herself: was there ever anything else? Or had she spent her entire life lying on a big bed in a room full of furniture, looking out through the window at the tops of the trees? Had she never been able to get up and walk across to the wardrobe to see what was hidden in its dark depths? Had she never thrown the windows open, since there probably wasn't anything outside anyway? What if no other life existed apart from hers? But then there was that nice young man who came and showed such concern for her. He couldn't just be dismissed out of hand. Sometimes she became oblivious of everything and stopped noticing that he was there. But then she came round again, and she felt ashamed for having forgotten about him. That meant she couldn't really be all alone; and since the young man came from somewhere and went away to somewhere, she concluded that there must be some other world that she had never visited — there outside the windows. Sometimes (once again, when she was only half-awake — nowadays she only ever had any thoughts during the transition from sleeping to waking — it must be because her mind had become so lazy) she didn't recognize the room and wanted to run off back to her job — the sun was already shining brightly, and she might be late. She had had bad dreams, about having grown old and become bedridden, that was probably because she was so terribly tired and she needed to take a break, but that was all right, the working week would soon be over. It took her quite long to remember. About thirty seconds. When the most frightening part was already over and she had more or less understood everything, she tried to convince herself that she didn't care about her old life, and trying to remember the names of the people she used to work with. She could still remember one or two of them: the rest had all been erased because she had no use for them. She had never been able (while she had still been healthy and strong) to endure the idea that people existed entirely apart from her, without caring about her life or feeling any need to inform her about their own, rejoicing without her, grieving for reasons that had nothing to do with her. That was why she'd always tried to be a focal point of rumours-she had managed to invent at least some-and set people against one another. But now she couldn't remember their names, she didn't know what these people were doing, or if they were still alive. And the strangest thing of all was that she didn't care. Perhaps, as the end of her life approached, she simply didn't need anyone any more. She had always envied people who weren't like children, who didn't try to play with other people as if they were toys. Who were contented with just themselves. Now she was complete in herself too. The only difference was that there was nothing left for her any more.

And yet life remained interesting. For instance, she'd never noticed that vase shaped like a huge wine glass on the table by the window. The rounded, gleaming object of transparent glass had only caught her eye recently. She must have bought it herself at some time or other, where else could it have come from? If she concentrated, she'd be able to remember. She'd went... She'd walked... The memory of how she bought the vase was somewhere very close, but it was eluding her. How could she have forgotten everything? How could she have only noticed the vase now, after all these years? A ray of sunlight had lit it up in some special way, or the young man had wiped it with a damp rag when he was removing the dust from every surface in the room with such thoroughness. Hello vase. Perhaps you were never there before. Perhaps the fairies brought you, and the elusive memory of buying you was no more than a trick of the mind, nothing but an invention. The geranium beside you is so bright and gay — there's no way anyone could forget that. Ten years ago, or perhaps two, she would have called herself an old fool. You stupid old fool, you've forgotten where your spectacles are again. But then she'd stopped talking to herself like that. She'd stopped talking to herself at all. If you were an old fool that meant there must be those who are young and clever. But they'd all disappeared somewhere, and now she couldn't tell where Varvara Petrovna ended, and where the "all the rest" began. After all, the table with its lace tablecloth, the iron bedstead and the window frame were almost part of her. And as for the sounds — for instance the trains rumbling by in the night — they were her as well, to a certain extent. The young man who came to help her, he had nothing to do with her. But he came to fluff up her pillow and prepare her food, so she was still the focus of everything. Everything centred round her. All those years, and she hadn't realized what an important person she was. But now at last, she had. She didn't watch the television any more — she had a different way of entertaining herself. There was a large clock standing on a shelf, and it had a dial that wasn't round, but a rhomboid shape, with flat hands made of yellow metal. It wasn't that she really cared what time it was. She still sometimes got confused between the left side and the right side: four o'clock or eight o'clock? What interested her was that the hands moved. Everything else in the room stood still; sometimes she would get the sudden feeling that something in the corner had moved, as if a chair taken a step forward, or something small had darted across the floor. She only had to turn her head just a little bit (slowly) to see quite clearly that everything was still the same. But the hands of the clock moved all the time. Sometimes she could even notice the little jerk that edged a hand along. The clock was such an amusing and sad device. All those screws and little wheels, a well-adjusted mechanism, but displace just one little spring and time came to a stop. She would have liked to make a map of everything around her. The entire landscape of her present existence shrunk to the size of this room... What made a map a map were its parallels and meridians. The grid drawn on the surface of the earth. The cell that we are in. Her present location looked like this. First, there was the land of the wallpaper. Little bouquets of flowers, not all the same at all, because the colour had been printed carelessly and the outlines of the elegant buds rarely coincided with the colour that filled them. At one spot the wallpaper had warped, forming a bulge. There were irregularities in the ground. Sometimes she wanted to pat the bulge with her open hand to smooth it out. She would have liked to put everything right, to arrange everything the way she wanted. That was quite impossible now, but little things like that irritated her — only a bulge in the wallpaper but it couldn't be put right. Perhaps when the next owner redecorated the room he would smooth out the bulge. Yes, of course, he would tear down all the wallpaper and re-plaster the walls, or whatever it was they did. Second, there was the ceiling. The cracks in the ceiling. There weren't many, she would have preferred not to notice them. She had always hated cracks, because they put her in mind of an earthquake. That must be the way the earth cracked open when it tried to devour everything that was alive. She had never seen any earthquakes, only read about them, but she had always been afraid. A crack was always a cranny leading into hell. She tried not to look at the cracks in the ceiling although they were right overhead.

The spider was a different matter. A spider had spun a web in the corner farthest away. The young man had wanted to kill it in the course of his zealous cleaning, but she had stopped him. Leave me the spider — that was what she had said to him. If they opened the window, the web started trembling in the wind. What skill it must take to make something so fine and at the same time so strong! The spider was alive. Clever spider. A spider was a sign: it meant there would be a letter. There must be some news waiting for her. Third, there was her body. She spent much time inspecting her hands and could still never see enough of them. Loose, flabby skin covered with brown blotches, but there hadn't been any of that before — no flabbiness and no blotches. She couldn't understand where they had all come from, all these unwelcome changes, and why they had come in this particular form. When she had seen old people earlier, she used to think they had always been like that — and she would never be like them. Her body had always seemed so perfect and unchanging, she had controlled it with such confidence, but they had crept up on her somehow, so that she hadn't noticed — this flabbiness and these wrinkles. And it was so completely senseless. Like all the changes to her body, it made no sense at all. Her fingers would hardly bend at all now, and they were very difficult to unbend as well. And yet she had managed to keep hold of the glass of water. But she had very quickly become used to the fact that she couldn't lift or hold anything. It was strange even to think that once things had been different. She had hardly any memories left of movements that were free and strong. Instead, all the frustrations and helplessness of childhood had come back to her. People were born that way and lived that way until at a certain moment they suddenly got grand ideas about themselves: "I am strong!" Then after that they went downhill. What a good thing it was that she had a clean nightdress. White and fresh, not like her own skin. She had torn the previous nightdress herself. One clumsy movement of her old body and — oopsa-daisy, a hole in the side. Cheap material. There were some things even more fragile than an old woman. The nightdress had been thrown out and now Varvara Petrovna was lying on the pillow, gazing at the tops of the trees outside. Some of the things that surrounded her would reach the end of their days sooner than she would. So there. Her helplessness was not absolute, there were still some things that she could do, she wouldn't go without a fight. She tried not to look at her feet. Terrible, huge, swollen feet that looked as if they didn't belong to her at all, but to some sick giant. If the blanket slipped and exposed her feet, Varvara Petrovna didn't even realize straight away that they were part of her. It was many years now since her feet had swollen up, but she still couldn't get used to it. They must have died already. Her father's feet had swollen up too, six months before he died. When she noticed that it was happening to her, she had been too afraid to ask the doctor what was causing it. She had promised herself that she would never look at them, as if they didn't even exist. Are those swollen stumps mine? No, no, you're mistaken, there's nothing wrong with my feet — they still walk, after all, although they are slow and, to tell the truth, it hurts to step on them — I never look down, because I don't have any need to, after all, if someone's healthy, they don't even notice their own body. There's something terrible down there. Don't look. She was waiting for the young man. Soon she would hear his steps, and his key turning in the door. I smell the blood of a human soul. The handsome young fairytale hero would arrive any minute. Only he would be the one who fed her and put her down to sleep, and she wouldn't be able to advise him about which way to go, which turn to take, who to fire his arrows at. She didn't know anything, at times she even forgot her own name. He had held a mirror up to her face once and she hadn't recognized herself. She'd been surprised, wondered who it was, the face had looked mysterious to her, but after a while the sense of mystery had passed and she'd recognized herself from the set of her eyes. It had been a brief moment of insanity. All those years looking at those features in the morning, only finally to forget, completely forget who they belonged to! Her head must be busy with very important thoughts now. What a pity she couldn't recall her first impression of that strange face. She had thought it looked mysterious but what else? Had the woman in the mirror looked sad, cunning, reconciled? She could have learned a lot about herself but she had missed her chance.

Kirill turned the key in the door and stepped out of the darkness of the hallway into a square of bright light. The air in the room was stuffy, he ought to open the window. Right, now the window was open. He had brought a bouquet of flowers with him, now he would cut off the ends of the stems and put them in water. The pink heads of the buds swayed against each other, some of them were ready to open. The water refracted each of the thorn-covered stems. There was a geranium in a pot beside the vase. It needed watering. Varvara Petrovna had drunk her water and put the glass back. That was good. At any age it was healthy to drink a lot of fluids. He went into the kitchen to put the kettle on. Any water she drank had to be boiled. The tap water was full of bacteria. Through the window he could see the bare yard clear of snow, the naked trees and bushes. In spring there was too much rubbish on the roads, the gutters were full of water, the light was harsh. Kirill really disliked that bright spring light. Give him the soft light of autumn, the brief light of winter, even the summer sunshine. But just now everything was so bright and at the same time so empty, the earth had been freed from the snow, and the air from the cold, but what had arrived to take their place? Emptiness, emptiness everywhere, and that's why the sunlight seemed so unbearably bright. He came to see Varvara Petrovna: an old person couldn't be harsh, shallow and pitiless. Old people were warm. Kirill had set himself the task of loving the old woman simply because she had already lived her life and now she was close to death. He had missed his chance with his mother and he hardly ever spoke to his father. One day the sense of guilt would probably overwhelm him. But for now he had a ship in a safe harbour — Varvara Petrovna. It was good to watch the storm and the sinking ships from the safe shelter of the dry land... He had read somewhere that the universe was constantly expanding and in the same gradual way — he thought — people moved away from each other forever. He was sitting on the edge of the universe, looking into the distance, and the people he used to know were already blurred dots on the horizon. Every time the young man looked at the old woman it was as if he were trying to discover something. But what was it that he wanted to discover? Nothing came to mind, and he stopped thinking about it and started cleaning and tidying. Then later, on his way home or in the evening, before he fell asleep, he would remember her face and think that he ought to have asked her about her imminent departure from this world which constantly amazed him. He needed to ask, to discover everything about a life slipping away. It was impossible to get used to the impermanence. To the fact that not everything could be mastered. He would have to ask her about her childhood. Then he would remember it, and there would be something left. But once he reached Varvara

Petrovna's place, he felt timid and he couldn't bring himself to ask. So now Kirill arrived there knowing nothing, or almost nothing, about her. The old woman was the physical expression of his "love thy neighbour", or rather, of his attempt to love his neighbours. Because he cared for her without asking anything in return. It made him happy to think that he had made her life easier. Because she was old and helpless and he was young and strong. And he used his strength and his youth to help this old woman. The room looked nicer because he had put the flowers in the vase. He enjoyed being here. The chairs with the curved backs and the thin legs looked frail, but in fact they were very strong, and so was the table. It was as if a small herd of gazelles had been transformed into furniture. The massive mahogany wardrobe pushed up against the wall was rather too large and oppressive for the room. Its left door was decorated with carving reminiscent of architectural details, and the right was covered with a huge mirror that reflected the bed standing opposite it. There was a large, black keyhole in the left door, but the wardrobe was never opened.

Varvara Petrovna looked at Kirill from under her half-opened eyelids. He was still a boy, he couldn't even be seventeen yet. He always came wearing the same sweater, silvery-grey with a high neck. The sweater was stretched tight across his broad, over-square shoulders. Sometimes, if it was hot in the room, he would bend over and pull the sweater off with a rapid movement and then hastily tuck his shirt into his jeans, as if he were embarrassed. She didn't really like Kirill's face, she'd have altered it a little bit. It sagged somehow, like wet cloth. The eyes were big but watery and static. But the lips were always moving, stretching out in a smile, pursing up tightly, bending their corners down. As if someone had put a mask with huge eyes and a bulbous nose over the face, but the lips had been left free. The whistle of the kettle roused Kirill from his reverie. He went into the kitchen. Varvara Petrovna felt for the stick leaning against the bed and slowly got up to go to the toilet. She needed to go to the toilet more and more often nowadays. Almost nothing would stay inside her. There now, that was already enough reason to look forward to the end. Because it was intolerable to know that every half hour, like a faithful dog, you had to go running to answer the call of nature, which was so stupid and so absurd and, what's more, unlike the dog's master, it couldn't care less how difficult it was for you to get up. There now, that was another argument in favour of the existence of the soul, after all, the person that Varvara Petrovna thought of herself as being couldn't possibly be the same person as the decrepit body that could barely walk a few steps and couldn't even hold its urine.

II. The church was like a forest. Every time Kirill came in here, he felt afraid of getting lost. The church was even darker than a forest: it was a forest at night, its gloom seeming all the more intense by comparison with the little islands of candles. Every one of the burning candles must be someone's life. Kirill sometimes caught himself thinking that he wanted to blow one of them out, but of course he never gave way to this impulse. He had never lit a candle himself. He liked to look at the icons-barely illuminated by the lamps burning in front of them the icons gleamed in the darkness. He could only make out the vague outlines of the figures, but he could imagine the details for himself. That was what he enjoyed — imagining the invisible. Only rarely did he understand what the priest was saying. The words from the pulpit sounded like an incantation, and it was up to Kirill to give them meaning.

At prayer, he was immersed in the incomprehensible and the invisible, and he flickered like a candle flame. The feeling was most powerful in the evening, when the flames of the candles were reflected in the dark window of the church. Nothing came to him directly, only as the reflection of a reflection, an incidental harmony, a chance link between disparate elements. "Now, in days to come and to the end of time." The reflection of light in dark glass and, if the next pane was ajar, a multitude of reflections, and Kirill's double could reach out his hand to every one of them to cover the flame with his palm — that was what "to the end of time" meant. He prayed for those travelling by sea and by land, for those who were in sickness and suffering. With its old women and children, the church set off on a voyage across the ocean of the city's streets, with the singing of the crew echoing the noise of the waves, and the priest came out on to the captain's bridge. Now he would swing his censer, scattering a gentle scent, just as the sea scattered its salt spray: when the spray of the incense reached Kirill, he would have to perform the strange ritual of crossing himself, raising three fingers of his right hand to his forehead, to his chest, to his right shoulder and then his left. Sometimes he went on crossing himself for a long time, until his arm felt tired. At first he'd felt awkward that these movements were so contrived but now he found their constant, sweeping repetition pleasant. There was a young woman standing beside him with a light-coloured headscarf worn right down to her very eyes. She was standing absolutely still. She must be so absorbed in the prayer that she had forgotten to cross herself and bow. She had the face of a young nun, Kirill thought: arched eyebrows, a straight nose, lips pressed together. Kirill wanted to catch her eye, so that he could guess what she was saying to God. But the girl was looking down and off to one side. Quite probably the young woman

Kirill had taken for a nun had only come here by chance. She had thought that attending church would bring her relief, but now she was simply feeling bored and hot. She wanted to go, but it seemed impolite to her to leave in the middle of the service, she was waiting for it to end. The girl tried to leave the church without attracting attention. Kirill followed her out. They walked along the asphalt-surfaced lane, planted with poplar trees that were bare at this time of the year — the same road that Kirill walked along on his way to see Varvara Petrovna. Kirill had no idea why he was following the girl, her white scarf was leading him on. The girl entered the house next door to Varvara Petrovna's. Kirill looked to see in which of the windows a light would go on, but his wait was in vain. Her windows probably looked out from the other side of the building. He turned back and went home. That night he dreamed of a big wardrobe with a mirror on its right-hand door. The wardrobe was spinning around as if it was suspended in a state of weightlessness, but its doors were securely locked. He could hear a girl's voice from inside it. Kirill tried to hold the wardrobe still, he braced his foot against one of its doors and pulled on the handle of the other. The wardrobe wouldn't give way and carried on spinning just as if it were being sucked into a whirlpool but without moving from the spot. Sometimes Kirill felt the door beginning to yield slowly under his fingers, and then he felt worried. Who knew what might be concealed in the wardrobe? Perhaps it was something he didn't want to see at all? He stopped tugging. His fingers clutched the handle of the door feebly. Suddenly he felt a jerk from the inside. The door began opening of its own accord. And now Kirill pressed his entire weight against the wardrobe, trying to stop the doors opening. He could hear dull thumps from inside, no matter how hard he resisted, the door begins to open. It cost him an immense effort to close it again; there was a force inside resisting him, trying to break out. I mustn't let it out, thought Kirill, I mustn't see what's inside, and as he threw himself against the wooden board with a groan, he woke up.

III.

Varvara Petrovna was afraid of many things. You might have expected that, as the end of life approached, fears should pass away; but no, they multiplied. In the darkness she heard the rustle of steps, as if there was someone walking about in the hallway. There was someone pacing across the kitchen, as if it was a cell. She propped herself up on her pillows, waiting for the criminal to come into the room. The steps died away, and then after a while the rustling started up again. Perhaps it was the rustling of mice. But she was still afraid there was someone there, and she lay without sleeping, holding her breath, expecting the terrible creature to come into the room any second. Or she would suddenly take a nervous breath in, because she thought she could smell gas. Any moment now there would be the boom of an explosion. One, she counted, two, three, four — but no explosion came. She was all ready to get up and go to the kitchen to check if the cooker was switched off. But this time she was paralysed by fear of her nocturnal visitor: as soon as she had hobbled to the kitchen door with her old woman's walk, he would throw himself on her out of the darkness. Her fears were always imaginary, she always invented something for herself to be afraid of. It was pointless for her to seek the source of her fears in something that had once happened to the neighbours, or in the newspaper she had read. Her fears came from within herself — like satiated flies leaving an animal's eroded carcass. Was she afraid of Kirill? No. He was kind and still just a boy. She could tell that he was a little bit afraid of her. No, of course, it wasn't her he was afraid of (she was too helpless for that) it was her age. It seemed to her that the young man would do almost anything she asked. Perhaps the stranger the request, the more willing he would be to carry it out.

Kirill believed that Varvara Petrovna knew some secret that attracted him and made him almost submissive. Not long ago he had asked her if she had ever been happy. Only the callow banality of youth could have asked a question like that. But she had known how to answer. Yes, she said definitely, she had been. He had asked her to tell him about it. She had danced with a lieutenant at a New Year ball. There had been something special about the way he moved and looked down at her without taking his eyes off. She had looked up at him and moved in rhythm with his steps. He had held her very close to him, so close that for years afterwards she had wanted to cry when she remembered that dance. Then they had seen each other for six months, they had even wanted to get married. But it hadn't worked out. Kirill had looked away. This wasn't the story he had wanted. She had made a second attempt, trying to hold his attention. Once she had gone to a holiday home with her colleagues from work. At night, when everyone was asleep, she'd been walking along the corridor for some reason and suddenly she'd stopped and listened. She could hear sleepy breathing from behind a door — she didn't know whose. The quiet breathing of people sleeping. She had stood and listened. Kirill had liked that a lot more, it sounded as a genuinely happy experience to him.

Varvara Petrovna had been angry with herself for saying too much and because the young man understood so little. Her story hadn't had anything to do with anybody's soul. The breath escaping from half-parted lips, the hot body of a man dancing — how could this youth understand such things when he still wasn't even aware of his own body and was in no danger of losing it in the near future? But her train was already gathering speed on its way out of the dirty but familiar station, full of smells, touches and handshakes. Soon she would lose this body, these legs and arms she was so used to, the skin covered in goose bumps, the stomach, the grey hair, the wrinkles, the skinny neck. Everything that she hated about herself and everything that she was proud of. She wanted to howl, like a faithful dog being parted from its master. "What do you keep in that wardrobe?" Varvara Petrovna smiled. The wardrobe was as big as a little room. Varvara Petrovna imagined how children could hide inside it, as if it were a cave, and look through the big keyhole, watching what was happening in the room as in a book she once read to a neighbour's son. Nothing special would be happening but the world seen through the keyhole would have seemed a lot more interesting. And whoever they were observing would have looked at himself in the mirror on the right-hand door, quite sure that only he could see himself. "I won't tell you," Varvara Petrovna answered. She wanted to sound mysterious. Everything had always turned out not quite right. Even though she had always worked out so carefully how she would appear in the eyes of people around her she had never achieved the effect she wanted. But now she had a sixteen-year-old youth with her (she had forgotten about her own eighty-seven years) and she didn't want to part with her little mystery just yet. Varvara Petrovna slowly shook her head, and the flabby skin trembled on her old neck. She wanted to get up and have a cup of coffee, she wanted movement, laughter, gossip, flirting, kisses — but there wouldn't be any more of that... If I only have a few days or a few months left, thought Varvara Petrovna, and if I don't do anything else, at least I must think about all the things I've never seen. She closed her eyes and saw snow-covered mountain slopes in front of her. The sun must be blinding her eyes, she needed to put on her dark goggles, to push off with her sticks and glide downwards on her broad skis, tracing out wide zigzags. When the picture became too real, when she could almost reach down and touch the snow with her mitten, Varvara Petrovna began feeling unwell and she started to think about something else. People were standing crowded together on the deck of a ship, gazing up at bursts of red, green and orange light. "The northern lights," the passengers said to each other. The entire sky was covered by rays of coloured light. Varvara Petrovna suggested that the cold made the lights brighter, and the person standing beside her nodded in agreement. No, she really mustn't give way to melancholy over what she had missed. She had assumed that her thoughts would be glad to be lost in dreams: in actual fact every dream was one more stab to the heart, if the heart was already exhausted. She should have done it earlier, earlier, while she still had the strength, if not to do something, then at least to say to herself: it's not that important, not such a great loss. But now she couldn't possibly deceive herself. She had so little strength left for herself; it didn't matter if the others weren't alive. There weren't any other people in the world apart from her, and this solitary human presence would soon disappear. Kirill and the others (there weren't actually any others) were puppets dancing around her in a ring. When she stopped existing, the puppets would lie in a dark cupboard without moving, like in the fairytale about Pinocchio. But now she would take them out, paint their faces, dress them up in strange costumes. Knights and ladies would meet each other. Every colour and every gesture would have a meaning. She was drifting into sleep. It seemed to her that she was pulling the puppets' strings, and they were singing and dancing. The sounds they made were as sweet as the singing of angels — Varvara Petrovna was amazed at how she had managed to make them sing.

IV.

Kirill opened his eyes in the dark room. His earliest memories were coming back to him — from that early childhood when even things that have really happened still feel like a dream. His nanny was putting on his green sweater in the hallway. His nanny was promising him a wonderful treat. Kirill suspected that he had been evicted from home and he was trying to break free and run back in. But his nanny was holding him tight by the arm. He didn't remember the front of the building they went into. There was a big crowd of grownups inside, and every one of them turned his back if Kirill tried to approach him. The child had realized that what came next would be the total loss of his name and identity; that he had been brought here in order to grow up, that is, in order to become one of these preoccupied, noisy people who turned their backs on him. Kirill had gone dashing to where he thought the way out ought to be, but during the last few minutes left and right had changed places. The entire space of the vast room had been reversed, there was just his nanny's hand that had appeared out of nowhere and grabbed him by the collar. He had been led for a long way and made to sit in an armchair where he had frozen, motionless, when he saw the two trees in front of him on a platform and beyond them the wall of a house with a window and a door. There was no one near the house. The entire crowd of people had receded behind Kirill's back, so that now he was closer than any of them to the miraculous trees and the house. But even so he couldn't have got to them, because the platform raised them high above his head. Even if the child could somehow have got up there, he couldn't have failed to sense the prohibition that was hanging in the air. Kirill leaned back in his chair, although what he wanted to do was go down on his knees and ask what they had all done wrong to be put in this pit and forced to sit there quietly; he wanted to beg to be lifted up there, to the motionless, bright-green trees, to the wooden house where no one lived. "You'll see everything now," his nanny had said. What she had actually said must have been: "It's going to start now," but he had taken the words to mean that soon they would explain to him why he had been brought here. He had frozen in anticipation. Everything had suddenly gone quiet and then he had heard music playing, but no one had explained anything to him, they'd simply frightened him to death. Instead of words his ears had been filled with silence, and then with music that had no words and was even more frightening. The child had realized there was not going to be any explanation and within these walls all the rules that he knew so well had collapsed. Suddenly a figure had appeared in the doorway of the wooden house high up on the platform and moved forward to the edge with light, slow steps. "Mummy!" Kirill had called out. She had left the mysterious house to come to his help. His nanny had shushed at him threateningly, his mother had pretended that she hadn't noticed anything. He had been about to call out again, but his nanny had tugged him by the arm and hissed that he mustn't dare, that "it had begun already", and now he had to keep quiet. The child had understood and turned away. So that's it, he had thought, now I know the answer to the question that wouldn't let me sleep at night. And no matter how frightening it might be, it was still better to have seen and remembered the motionless leaves of the trees and the gaping window of the house, the music, the crude platform and the crowd of people at the entrance than to suffer the torments of uncertainty at night, curled up in a tight ball on his bed. It was clear to him now that his mummy had died: he had looked at her through his tears and thanked death for allowing him to see her in the world into which she had withdrawn. She had spoken words that had no meaning (even now her words still seemed meaningless to Kirill, like the speech in a dream when we remember it in the morning) and the child had pitied her in her incoherent isolation. Speaking in a whisper, or perhaps just to himself, because a loud voice might frighten away the dead women, which was why his nanny had hissed at him the first time, he had promised his mother always to remember her as she was when she came out on to the platform looking so very beautiful in the smart dress and grand hairstyle of her other existence.

Other people had appeared beside her, dark and light shadows who had held senseless conversations with her and made strange gestures with their arms. Kirill had realized that they were the mothers and fathers of the other people who had come here. He had realized that when they were jostling each other in the other room, these people had behaved rudely because they were so saddened by the loss of someone they loved, and they had turned their backs on Kirill so that he would not see their tears — and he had forgiven them. All of them together had revelled in what was surely a final meeting. At the end, the people on the platform had linked hands and bowed in farewell, and the people who were sitting down below had clapped, trying to make as much noise as possible — so that those other ones would remember them. "Look, it's daddy!" his nanny had said and pointed to a man who had gone up on to the stage. It really was Kirill's father, but just the same as he always was. There was nothing strange about his face or his movements, nothing exaggerated. "Why's he there?" the child had asked his nanny. "He produced it. Don't you understand? Well, he thought the whole thing up..." — "So it was him!" Kirill had exclaimed so loudly that the fat man beside him had turned his red face to look. The child hadn't been able to say any more, but now, many years later, Kirill spoke for him, saying what had been left unsaid. So his father was the force that had killed his mother and the relatives of all these other people? So he had made them die, and now he was showing them to us, almost as if he was deliberately mocking us — we couldn't go up there and touch them, could we? There he had stood, triumphant, the only living person allowed to climb up on the platform, and there he had stood, smiling, while we obsequiously applauded him, there he was, the lord of our life and death! The child had wanted to brandish his fist or call out, but there had been no time. Clutching his nanny's hand, he had left the hall and submissively allowed himself to be taken home.

"You want to know what's in the wardrobe?" Varvara Petrovna was holding Kirill's hand in her own and he was sitting on the edge of her bed. Kirill nodded. The young man was really interested as if someone had promised to reveal to him the secret of the spark that crossed from the old woman's hand into his own when they touched each other. There exists, he thought, a certain impulse that cannot be described in physical terms, that animates everything alive: and perhaps, by an effort of will, it can be transferred to inanimate nature too... Varvara Petrovna took a key out from under her pillow and handed it to Kirill. He went over to the wardrobe, glanced at his own reflection in the mirror and turned the key in the keyhole. The doors swung open. The space inside the wardrobe proved to be even larger than he could have suspected from the outside. There were clumps of dust lying in the corners, and dangling from a solitary hanger there was a yellowish dress that had once been white. "Do you remember I told you how an officer once courted me?" Kirill waited for her to say: Things were different in those days. "Of course, in those days, the relations between young people weren't what they are today." He gave me flowers... "He gave me flowers, we went for walks along the embankment, we talked a lot, such a lot." And then, of course, he had seen her home. "Then he used to see me home, and we would kiss each other goodnight — on the cheek. You know, it's a pity it was all so modest. We did plenty of talking, God knows, but nothing else. He used to say such strange things. He didn't like our songs or our films. He said they were too optimistic, they tried to stop people being afraid of all the things they ought to be afraid of. I used to object: How were we ever going to achieve anything if we were afraid? Well, if you want to achieve something, he said with a wink, then forget about frightening things, but I'm still interested, even if it kills me. You read that somewhere, I said. He smiled and took hold of my arm and we carried on walking. He told me a lot of other things as well, but I've forgotten them." No, she hadn't forgotten, but how could she tell them to a callow youth for whom all old women's tales were the same? It was impossible to describe that precise shake of the hand, that precise voice without using other people's words. "I was so happy" and "he was so polite and intelligent" and "we were very young then" — those words left no space at all for what belonged only to Varvara Petrovna. "And then what happened?" — "A week before the wedding he suddenly said it was impossible. He didn't explain anything. At first I cried, and then I stopped. Are you getting bored?" Kirill stepped inside the wardrobe and closed the doors behind him. The darkness enveloped him. He reached out his arms and felt for the walls. The keyhole was his only source of light, and it was an automatic response for him to put his eye to it. He saw Varvara Petrovna's hand pulling the blanket up to her chin, he saw the smile on her face. She guessed that Kirill could see her and beckoned with her finger for him to come out and sit on the bed again. "Listen, I want to ask you to do something," she said, speaking more quietly than usual. Kirill leaned closer in order to hear her. "I want to see you kiss a girl." He started back. "You know, I've got so little time left... And I'm so bored. I sometimes feel as if I'm already dead. But if I could see two young people kissing, that would give me strength... I don't have anyone except you, you're almost like my son or my grandson. Think how glad your mother would be to see you with a girl. You can't imagine what a delight it is in old age to see proof that life goes on, that young people love each other — all the things that are beyond our reach. There's really nothing strange about what I'm asking." Kirill turned his eyes away from Varvara Petrovna's face. He was beginning to feel rather upset.

V. "... fulfilling thy desire in heaven: thy youth shall be renewed like an eagle..." But nothing happened. No matter how long Kirill listened to the priest's bass voice and the high voices of the choir, his life was not renewed. He was still the same as before. He felt as if in his unrenewed state he ought not to have crossed the threshold of the church, but here he was standing by the wall on the right, the same youth who had been inspecting the pimples on his face that morning. And yet he still believed that his present face and present way of thinking had not been given to him for ever: either he would make a great effort and change, or some external force would transform him. The burning candles and the singing always created a festive atmosphere, but just at the moment Kirill felt depressed. He was thinking that his mother had died and become a pale mask in a coffin five years ago. Before that he had never even imagined his life without holding his mother by the hand every day — and now it was impossible even to imagine that he would ever touch that hand again. He thought about how his father had stopped being the person that Kirill had known in his childhood. All that was left of him was the name that theatre people still remembered and a grey tailored suit, the only one left now, dirty and torn — his father fell asleep on the floor, in the entrance, out in the street. At school they had tried to trip Kirill on the stairs, and he had staggered but straightened up and then looked down on them again. Kirill didn't want to rouse anyone else's pity. The feeling had crept into his heart anyway (he had hoped his contempt would conceal it) and made him pity others, but they must never pity him — never!

Kirill was thinking about Varvara Petrovna, her outrageous request and her pitiful body. He suspected that his concern for her was not sincere, that he admired himself for helping her. Nothing ever turned out the way he imagined it would. There was nothing touching about it, there was just a bad smell and weakness and fragmentary words. Sometimes it seemed to him that the old woman didn't feel any gratitude at all, but was angry with him for some reason — probably because he was so young. But he couldn't just take his own youth and give it to her. And would he have done it if he could? He pictured the old woman's trembling hand taking a glass of water and raising it to her lips, trying not to spill any. Every time Kirill was afraid she would drop it and the glass would break. His thoughts were as heavy as storm clouds, as strong as a gale, blowing him off his feet. But during an especially strong gust, when Kirill swayed and almost fell, he suddenly found himself leaning against something firm. Like a man standing on a bridge with the river seething below him, Kirill stood there and knew that he was safe, because Christ was a wooden parapet. And wherever a man might go, he could always lean on it. Kirill felt happy. He thought the singing had got louder and the candle flames had got brighter. People were praying and crossing themselves, bowing down and then straightening up again. Their faces were all turned in the same direction, they were contemplating the same performance that had been played out every day for many years. If it had not been repeated, they would not have come here. They needed to know that something happened over and over again: that was their way of touching eternity. Immediately in front of him, Kirill could see a white headscarf, the edge of a forehead and cheek. He realized it was the same girl he had noticed a few days before. He didn't need to see her face, he recognized the way she was standing, she wasn't bowing and she was hardly even crossing herself, she just lowered her head slightly, she was so completely engrossed in the prayer. She was wearing a grey coat with a little fur collar. Kirill could see her elbows: she was standing with her hands pressed to her breast. Something caught his attention: her black fishnet stockings and old, scuffed shoes.

VI.

It was dark inside the wardrobe with just a narrow strip of light making its way in through the keyhole. She sat on a small chair with a low back. The important thing was to sit there absolutely stock-still. To keep her eye pressed to the keyhole. And observe. The bed was opposite the keyhole — and everything was going to happen on the bed. She couldn't really see all that much through the keyhole. But what she could see seemed somehow new. As if it wasn't her room at all. Or as if someone had only just moved in and the room hadn't been arranged yet; or as if the previous tenants had left their furniture behind. Such a small, unfamiliar space. It made her feel faint just to look at it. But she didn't feel guilty. Perhaps what she was doing was wrong, but she had a right to do it. All her life she'd done nothing but good, at least she hadn't spoiled things for anyone. But now she had so little time left to live, and so little strength, and she couldn't do anything that was really bad: she would just get a little enjoyment out of it, what harm was there in that? Nothing would happen afterwards, she wouldn't go anywhere, she wouldn't meet anyone else, she would just stay lying here until she gave up the ghost. Why shouldn't healthy young people let her take a sly peek at their life — oh, and what a life!

There was a noise in the hallway. Two voices, one Kirill's and the other a girl's, unfamiliar. The young man had kept his promise. He had put the chair in the wardrobe for Varvara Petrovna and got everything ready. But he had started looking somehow sadder than before. She must have disappointed him with her request. He obviously hadn't expected to encounter such desires in old people. "So this is where your grandmother lives?" — "Yes, she's gone to visit relatives in Ukraine, and I come to water the geranium." — "Her room's very beautiful. Look at the chairs." — "You'd better sit on the bed, the chairs are nice but their legs are flimsy." Varvara Petrovna saw the girl sit down on the bed. She had large features, a round face and light-coloured hair. She had a blouse with flowers on it and a straight-cut skirt, with fishnet stockings. Her shoes were dirty. Never mind, Kirill would wipe the floor. Afterwards. Now she had to look. "Would you like some tea or coffee?" — "No." Kirill sat on the bed beside the girl and took hold of her hand. She pulled her hand out from under his. She wasn't looking at Kirill, but he was looking at her intently. He had one hand propped against the bed behind the girl's back, so that he was sitting half turned towards her. They didn't say anything, so Varvara Petrovna could hear them breathing. They must be feeling tense. It seemed so easy to make a movement forwards, towards another person, but at the same time it was very frightening, after all, the first touch had to be followed by another touch — and once you had touched, it was impossible to pretend that nothing had happened. The girl turned her head towards Kirill, at the same time leaning it back, so that their faces were not too close, and asked: "Do you go to church every day?" — "Every day since my mother died. I have the feeling that if you stand and listen very carefully and follow what's happening very closely, then perhaps you can understand the mystery of the resurrection." Don't get distracted, please, Varvara Petrovna wanted to say. She could see the girl's arms relaxing and her head swaying gently. But Kirill was not looking at her any more, his gaze was directed straight ahead, to where the old woman was sitting. "What creepy things you're saying! If there were dead people who'd come back to life everywhere, there's not much chance that we'd love them. What incredible fantasies you have!" — "Are you frightened?" asked Kirill, putting his arm round her shoulders and pulling her towards him. Now there was no way back. The old woman watched with bated breath. They only had to cross a tiny gap, the final resistance of their souls, because their bodies were already drawn to each other. The girl's face was still expressionless, but Kirill was already moving his lips close to hers, and now they had met. Firm at first, her lips became softer, then they parted, and at the same time her eyes closed. Both of them had their eyes closed: Varvara Petrovna's eyes were fixed on them as they kissed. They had closed their eyes in fear and, no doubt, in shame, hardly in pleasure. The old woman was afraid that a single awkward movement would spoil everything. The youth and the girl were excited, but if only they could have known how still the heart of the woman watching them was. What if they bumped awkwardly against each other, or there was a sudden sound outside the window — then they would shudder and pull away from each other. But Varvara Petrovna could see that Kirill was holding the girl and she was pressing herself against him. Varvara Petrovna watched Kirill's hand, those five slim fingers, and she felt as if she were moving his hand by remote control. The hand touched the girl's waist; then it moved higher, higher — up to her breast. The girl tried to move away, but Kirill wouldn't let her go, and she moved back towards him. He slowly unfastened the top button of her blouse, then the next one, exposing what had been hidden — not for himself, but for the old woman hiding in the wardrobe... "I think I'd better be going," said the girl, freeing herself from Kirill's embrace. She fastened the top buttons of her blouse, looking at Kirill reproachfully, but with a smile, as if she weren't sure whether she ought to be angry or glad, probably she was glad, but she was making herself feel a little bit angry too. And Kirill obediently lowered his hands and glowered at her sullenly from under his brow. The girl got up off the bed and the old woman noticed the flush on her cheeks; he brought her coat and helped her put it on; before he went out, he cast a quick glance at the door of the wardrobe, then he turned away and went out after the girl, to see her home. Varvara Petrovna opened the door of the wardrobe and greedily breathed in the air in the room.

The two of them walked as far as the crossroads, then they stopped, he took out his wallet and counted out the money and she winked as she put it in her pocket. Then they walked on. The girl walked with a firm, quick step, without looking at Kirill, and he looked at the fluffy headscarf that was tied round her head, at the strand of light-coloured hair that had fallen out across her forehead, at the eyelashes with their thick coating of mascara, at the straight nose. Sensing his glance, she turned round and gave a quick laugh, then turned away again and carried on walking. She was like an animal, thought Kirill, she was a lithe, uninhibited animal. He was attracted to people like her: to people who were confident in their movements, who answered you quickly, without pausing for thought. His spirit was weak, and the girl lacked that weakness. Just look at the brisk way she walked and spoke, without pausing to think, the proud way she turned up her nose and the haughty way she twitched her shoulder, she always knew best: from lower down, where she lived, the world could be seen in more precise perspective. Kirill wanted to wind himself around her like ivy, so that she would carry him away with her into the caves of human life, into dark flats with mattresses on the floor, into corridors and alleyways, unnatural sleep with sudden awakening. Kirill left the girl at the next crossroads. He had to go back: there had been a smell of urine from inside the wardrobe. They arranged their next meeting, The girl kissed him on the lips, the way she kissed every one when she met them or parted with them, waved her hand as she crossed the street and walked on without looking back. Kirill wanted her to look back — that would have meant she was remembering him and thinking about what had happened. But she had already forgotten Kirill and the flat, the things he had told her and his face. She walked straight on, screwing up her eyes against the sunlight.

They were a long way away now. They must be walking in the park. Or along the river. The old woman would have liked to get a glimpse of them. The ice had probably melted already. The water was high, almost level with the banks, its surface so smooth it looked as if you could walk across it, a strange reflective substance. Two people walking along the bank, and down below, in the watery realm, their doubles following them. Then the youth and the girl would walk on further into the city — but where would the ones in the water go? Or perhaps the river was still covered with ice, the sun hadn't melted it yet, and it had turned cold and dull outside, and the people walking along had to protect each other against the wind? The trees were bare and black, the crows flying between them were black too, black tears. The water was dirty-brown under the ice. The two of them were wandering along with the wind fluttering the flaps of their clothes. The stronger its gusts became, the lower they bowed their heads, the more stubbornly they walked towards their goal. She would never be able to join them. She was drawn to young people by envy and sadness, but that was not all. There was some third thing mingled with the first two, a strange kind of curiosity, like the way healthy people feel about the deformed, the way successful people feel about homeless tramps, as if youth were a sickness. Varvara Petrovna's thoughts were becoming confused. Supposedly she wanted to watch them kissing, because she would enjoy it. She couldn't very well hug and kiss herself. Or was it because she wanted to prove something to herself — as if she were telling herself; that's all impossible for you, watch and suffer? She had wanted to play at dolls. But had she wanted to cry? She had wanted to look where she should not look. No one could see except God and her. After all, she was going to die soon, take pity, good people! Some kind of indulgences had to be allowed, if you had to go through something like that. She had wanted to amuse herself a little bit just for the moment. But while she was sitting in the wardrobe it had become clear that she had simply made herself suffer one last time. For some reason or other she had wanted to see two healthy young people making love to each other in front of her, while she could never have even the tiniest little bit of their health or the tiniest little bit of their love. If only she could have a piece of other people's bliss! There was a time when she had hopes. Now it was too late. In any case, her wish hadn't really made much sense. But wasn't that the way life behaved — and Varvara Petrovna was only imitating it. What if an old woman had made a strange and cruel demand on young people — hadn't life made the same kind of demands on her? The way Kirill brought her tea or soup or a bouquet of flowers for her vase, the way he handed her a shawl when she felt cold and told her fairytales when she was bored, it all reminded Varvara Petrovna of how the officer had courted her a long time ago. The old woman was frail, but when she accepted her shawl from Kirill she felt frail in the way a girl did. Look at the way things had turned out: in her old age it had happened all over again — the care and attention, a young man. The touch of his hands reminded her of those old, half-forgotten touches, and they resurfaced out of oblivion, the past returned. But there was no more desire. Desire had died on that day when the officer had come to her and said in a firm voice that she must forget him, that the wedding was impossible. He had stood there for a moment without saying anything. Varvara Petrovna had been too shocked to speak, and so she had not asked him the reason. He had put on his cap and left. She had never met him again, although for a long time she had expected to see him: surely he must be waiting for her round the corner, or standing on the doorstep when the bell rang? Varvara Petrovna used to swing the door open, but the officer always turned out to be a postman or a neighbour, and round the corner the street was deserted. Varvara Petrovna simply could not believe that all there had been between them had been no more than a joke, and she could not believe that he had simply gone away either. She had tried to invent a reason: he had been posted to the border; he had been arrested; he was a spy; and she had even attempted to cry, but her tears had dried up, because she knew that none of these reasons was true. The only explanation was that there were no obvious reasons for the most important things that happened to people. And so Varvara Petrovna did not feel any resentment for the officer, she felt angry with destiny, and that was the way things had always been in her life: she had never directed her reproaches at people, but higher, waving a clenched fist: why should this have happened to me? And she had never found an answer, as if someone up on high had kept repeating to her: that's none of your business — when he obviously didn't know himself. Nobody would ever convince her that she had deserved it all. She hadn't done anything wrong. Except, perhaps, fail to understand something. Perhaps she ought not to have been seeing the officer from the start. All those dances had been too grand for her, she had been far too happy. Strong feelings were strange and novel; she hadn't been able to tear herself away. They had been strolling in the park and as she pressed herself against him, she had said: "If I weren't still a virgin, I'd give myself to you." She wished she hadn't seen his eyes. Or perhaps it was just the impression she had got in the darkness that he was staring at her in fright and confusion, when she had only wanted to please him. Well, never mind. What had happened was all past and gone. And what hadn't happened would never pass.

Varvara Petrovna had once gone back to the places where she had spent her childhood. She had a curly perm and was wearing shoes with high heels. She had had to step in the mud of the badly rutted road, and walk past local people who hadn't recognized her and had stared at her sullenly.

Opening the gate, she had walked up on to the porch of the house with boarded-up windows and looked around. She had felt a cold shiver because she recognized everything – the barrel in the garden, and the sagging step, third from the bottom – and yet even so, everything was unfamiliar now, shrouded in the mystery of things that have lain abandoned for many years. She realized she could no longer wipe away this dust of time that had made the close and familiar strange. On the other side of the fence someone called chickens to be fed. A mother walked past the gate with a stubbornly resisting child, on the next street two harsh voices – a man's and a woman's – called to each other. For those who had carried on living here, the close and familiar had remained close and familiar, because time changed things so gradually that people didn't notice. The place where she had been a child still existed – but not for her: she had been away for years and she had let the little town escape, like a bird. She had stepped slowly down from the porch and set off through the garden again. The garden was overgrown, with branches felled by the wind lying on the ground. In some places she had had to part the bushes with her hands. The little brook by the fence was covered over with green slime now, like a little swamp in a forest. With an effort, she had swung the gate on its rusty hinges – this time in order to leave.

Varvara Petrovna's mind suddenly started working clearly. She pushed against her pillows and raised herself up a little. You remember things and you suddenly realize that everything you used to feel then was absolutely wrong. As if someone was giving you hints but you never caught on: it's not until years later that it becomes clear what they meant. She ought to have locked the gate — from the inside, not the outside — and tidied up the garden. The rake and the broom would have swept away the veil of strangeness from things that had been waiting for her arrival but had merely witnessed her flight. When she was a child she had enjoyed digging in the garden. She thought then that she would be a gardener, but by the age of fifteen that had been completely forgotten. Now she had gone back into the garden, she had stood there and listened as the voice inside her said: take the watering-can and the rake. It had all been foreordained, and she had smugly turned round and walked away — in some sense she abandoned herself. That is, she had lived a life that wasn't hers. And the life that ought to have been rose up with perfect clarity before the eyes of an old woman astonished by her own blindness.

VII.

Kirill woke up when it was still dark, but he could tell it would soon be dawn because the gloom outside the window looked lighter. Kirill never closed the curtains: even at night he did not wish to be cut off from the streets. He wanted to know everything that was happening in the city, even the dark happenings of the suburbs at night. During the day he often wandered about aimlessly, guessing about the lives of people he met from their faces. He left his curtains open at night so that the headlamps of passing cars cast fleeting patches of light across the walls of his room, and he listened to the roar of an engine, to someone's voice, to the bang of a slammed door, trying to find a reason for each sound. He felt the same passion as those who once invented the gods and composed plays: for him, like them, his own life was not enough, he needed to multiply himself over and over, he filled the world with deities in his own image and people who did not exist. These were the games Kirill played before he went to sleep, indulging his fantasies.

But if he happened to wake up in the middle of the night, he had other things on his mind. The day he had lived through came back to him, but all the events of that day were grotesquely exaggerated and they frightened him. Often when he recalled an absolutely insignificant event, Kirill would suddenly experience a strong feeling of guilt and even as he felt it he was already surprised that this feeling, so distinct now, would disappear almost without trace in the morning. Another such nocturnal visitor was pity — for someone he hardly even knew or, on the contrary, a genuinely painful pity for his own father, or sometimes regret when he'd given something away as a present.

He woke up and thought with horror about what he had done and what he was intending to do in Varvara Petrovna's room that smelled of medicines and old age. Kirill could not understand what had made him kiss a girl with a hidden witness watching. The old woman had wanted to see how two young people made love, and he had been willing to go along with her. In order to fulfil the old woman's wish, he had also had to deceive her — he had paid the girl so that she would agree to go with him. A pathetic show, even two shows. Kirill only hoped that no one would ever find out. But then, that's not the important thing, he thought. It had always been important to him that people find out about him. Not necessarily what was true — better, in fact, if it was something that wasn't true — but something he wanted them to know. He made no secret of the fact that he went to church, for instance. Once, when he had seen girls from his class there, he had started bowing right down to the ground. Afterwards, though, he had felt ashamed. He hadn't told anybody that he went to see Varvara Petrovna. That was his secret trump card. But he wanted to tell someone sooner or later: in the first place, he thought he was being unfair to other people by making them think he was worse than he really was; in the second place, he wanted to astonish them. Many people would laugh at him, but he wanted that too because their laughter did not humiliate him, on the contrary, it elevated him above them. He told himself sadly: I'm nothing but show. But now his audience had all disappeared, they were not what mattered, only Kirill, the old woman and the girl mattered now or, rather, only Kirill. The old woman was no longer responsible for anything: when you got old, your mind got weak, and your will got even weaker. The girl was doing her job, earning a living. Kirill was the only one who had accepted everything voluntarily, not for the sake of money and not because he couldn't resist a desire.

But why had he really allowed himself to act like that? From the very beginning he had sensed that there was some secret hidden in every old person that could not be put into words, that did not even fit into the concepts used by people who were still young. This secret knowledge had to be derived from the fact that old people were forced to understand and accept the inevitable to which young people found it impossible to reconcile themselves. They could not reconcile themselves to it — perhaps because death was still far away, or was it because the non-acceptance of death was a sign of innocence? When Kirill had learned about certain sexual perversions, he had been amazed that people would allow others to do those sorts of things to them. This was the same thing, except that it was sanctified by nature: every human being belonged to this unnatural act and had to regard it as natural: to wait for his or her own killer and not complain. A thought: what if Varvara Petrovna still hadn't reconciled herself, what if she hated what must soon happen to her, and she hadn't forgiven the killer at all? In that case Kirill coming to see her with his Christian spirit was simply absurd. Her eyes, gazing into a distance that he tried in vain to penetrate, held a genuine power over him; and perhaps their power derived from the fact that they were the eyes of the first woman who had ever been alone with him. He had thought he was going to care for some one who was helpless but Varvara Petrovna had proved too much for him: a pitiful invalid, and the old woman his mother could have turned into if she had lived long enough, and the decomposing stump of a human being, and a half naked female body that he had to clean and dry and turn from side to side. He hadn't been able to work out what was most important for him, who he was coming to see and what he was feeling. Had it really been pity, or fear, or perhaps revulsion had been most important, or love? But it had all been so simple when he started taking care of her, so good and simple, he wished he turn back the clock. But he had already stepped across a line that perhaps he ought never to have crossed, and now he couldn't even enter the church with the ease he had before. Kirill ought to have behaved differently from the start. He ought to have read to her from the Bible, for instance, tried to find some consolation for her. Of course, that raised the question of who he was to be offering her consolation, when he was so very young and still hadn't seen anything of life. But then, if he had tried to justify death, Varvara Petrovna would have regarded him — and quite rightly — as an ally of the force that was preparing to exterminate her and she would have hated him for it. And it really was true that Kirill could only have told her: "this is the way it should be, and therefore there is no evil in it," if he himself believed that. Kirill had come to Varvara Petrovna with this idea in mind, but when he had seen her helplessness and her desire to live, he had begun to have doubts. What he felt like doing was bursting into tears and shouting out that life is unjust and death is repulsive — and then the old woman would have nodded, he would have helped her by doing that.

He felt that she had asked him to do something unclean and by agreeing he had become disgusted with himself. He imagined how he would have refused: "I can't possibly do it. It contradicts all basic moral principles. I spend a lot of effort trying not to think about things of the body, and you want me to seduce a girl, to exploit her for a purpose — for your purpose: you want to watch. At the end of your life you wish to descend into the very depths of baseness — and I am supposed to indulge you?" But he was going to do what she wanted, and not even out of submissive obedience, or out of pity, but out of the wish to console and amuse her even in this strange fashion. Kirill was on Varvara Petrovna's side in opposing the natural course of events. It was clear that what they had planned was bad: but they said that there was no evil in it. It was clear that the death of an old woman was not a crime committed by anyone, it was inevitable: but they said it was murder, and they would fight against this evil. Perhaps Varvara Petrovna didn't look at things this way at all. No doubt all this were just his own fantasies. He had invented his own defiance, his outrage, his struggle and, before that — his religion. The old woman was simply suffering because her legs could hardly walk and her insides refused to function; she wanted to take a look at what had been taken away from her, as if life were still carrying on. In actual fact, it was impossible for him to find out what she thought, and even if she thought anything at all. Even if he asked her, even if she answered, and even if she answered sincerely, it would be nothing at all like the reality.

It was true that another person's soul was a dark mystery, a terrible dark mystery. And he wanted very much to get a glance inside. He would need a lamp, but the fearful shadows of the old woman's soul would flee from its bright rays. If only he were a creature of the darkness, who could see through the murk without a light, then he could probably have glanced into people's souls. Kirill was going to do what she had asked without even knowing why. There would be nothing for him to be proud of because it could never be classed as a good deed. But he wouldn't feel ashamed either. Standing in front of Varvara Petrovna's bed, he felt guilt because he was young and shame because he could not help. These feelings were so strong that he had stepped across a line into a place where there was no more guilt or shame or kindness. That was why Kirill no longer understood himself; but he could see that he was a remarkable and mysterious being.

VIII.

Everything was pregnant with anticipation, they ought to arrive soon, very soon. Kirill had already been there, he had helped the old woman into the wardrobe and closed the doors; hidden her away like an old treasure, a gold ingot, a rare manuscript; hidden her the way people hide jewellery, stolen items, compromising documents, the way they hide the corpse of someone they have murdered. Now she had hunched down and gone quiet, pressed one eye against the keyhole and screwed the other one shut — she was a bird of prey, the barrel of a rifle. Now the mystery would be played out before her: copulation giving birth to the world, copulation celebrating a mystery, but this mystery was not concealed from her — she was present! She was initiated! Oh, how artificial all existence was, what an unnatural performance with the scenario known in advance, oh the repetition after repetition: monotony was immortality. It seemed to Varvara Petrovna that Kirill and the girl had already walked into the flat a hundred times and spoken words to each other —

always the same ones. And the gestures, their gestures — movements repeated again and again, bodies bending, the sweet, frightening curves that the old woman wanted to see, the straining muscles — she could make out every one of them, her eyesight had not grown any weaker. She could see well, she just couldn't do anything else: Varvara Petrovna had become one big eye, a concealed eye watching what was not allowed to be seen. It seemed to her that in every flat, in every nook and cranny, there was an eye avidly observing life, and nobody realized it was there.

The time has come, Varvara Petrovna told herself, when I can do anything. After all, it was bad to watch people in secret (who was that whispering — reason, conscience, good taste?). But she still had to take her revenge on them (now whose voice was it — envy, old age?) Revenge! For the way they must be walking round the streets now with their arms round each other, chattering and twittering away: cheep-cheep-cheep-cheep, as if they were talking the language of the birds that she didn't understand. For the fact that the two of them were together and she was alone and no one doubted that was the way it ought to be. Rot, you old woman! You've had your life, now move over. Give others a chance to live. And what if I haven't lived? If I don't want to move over and make way? Nobody's asking you. But then, I won't ask you how I should treat you. And I'll destroy you. Life was returning. As unexpectedly as a spring torrent, life flooded into her veins. The ice had broken on the river and the floes were crashing against each other, her teeth were chattering, there was a trembling awakening, her body was shuddering like a volcano. There are some people who flower late, suddenly start dancing and building pitiful sand castles (only in their imagination, because they are exhausted), pitiful phantom dancers in a pitiful late youth. She had arranged all this out of a desire to humiliate two young people who were not guilty of anything and one of whom took care of her. If she had had any children, she would never have allowed anybody to treat them like that. She had never known pity except for herself, or any concern, except for herself. But what if the lives of those whom she was going to pervert in this way would be more terrible than her life and her old age, what if their existence would be transformed into an unbroken chain of pain that started here, in Varvara Petrovna's flat? Old age should not be so pitiless. Her request had been dictated by a momentary eclipse of reason. Soon her request would be carried out, the youth and the girl would come and do what she had asked. But she could not imagine watching them with her newly clear eyes, eyes that were no longer clouded by death. Varvara Petrovna wanted to stop Kirill. To go down the stairs to meet him, take them both by the hand, lead them into the kitchen and give them tea. Who could tell, they might even get talking with her. There was an aloe plant on the windowsill, it gave the entire kitchen a cosy feeling, and you could use it for treating all sorts of coughs and colds in winter. Remember, Kirill, after I'm gone, you can break off a branch and drip the juice into your nose if you get a cold. The three of them would have sat there, the others would have laughed as she told them all sorts of stories... But they wouldn't understand her stories. For young people everything was cut and dried, old age had to be kind, helpless and touching. She wished she could subscribe to these false truths, but she was going to tear them to pieces.

With his arm round the girl's shoulders, Kiril talked and couldn't stop. She was already wondering why he had really brought her here. She kissed him and ran her hand over his body, trying to imitate innocence, as they had agreed. He held her hand in his and kissed it, but did not look into her eyes. He began undressing her, but stopped in order to finish saying something that he just couldn't finish, that he didn't want to finish, didn't want to think through to the end, and he kept on saying it over and over again. "You fragile living creature, I have never caused anyone pain, never killed birds or frogs, but if only you knew what strange fantasies I have had in my dreams. The most harmless of people have the most terrible thoughts; I was so surprised by my own cruelty that I've always felt sorry for everyone, as if I'd already done them harm. Listen, perhaps it's something left over in men from prehistoric times, when they must have killed one another as a mater of course. Always the same feeling: there's someone breathing and then they stop breathing — because of me. I felt so ashamed, if only you knew, I tried to make myself out to be a defender of the weak, but you see, the defender and the killer are almost the same, because the defender has the strength to kill. I felt so ashamed, so ashamed that I chose myself as my only victim: let someone torment me, I thought — but what for? I can't torture myself: that would be entirely artificial, it would be absurd. So now I'll fall in love with you and I'll suffer so much it will drive me mad." Kirill spoke words, but he heard only sounds. The hot body was breathing beside him. He carried on talking until he was totally exhausted, until it was totally impossible to say anything else.

The beginning had dragged out too long. As if they realized this they got undressed and lay down beside each other. Varvara Petrovna watched, fascinated. But Kirill saw a woman in white bed sheets that weren't very clean. It seemed to him that he had known this body before. Soft, white arms covered with brown blotches. He kissed the breasts and stomach, and under his lips the skin turned loose and flabby. The legs swelled up. They were so shapely a moment ago, and now they were red, weak, lifeless. She smelled bad. Kirill noticed red blotches on her side. He tried to look at her face, but the wrinkles made it too recognizable, he couldn't force himself to kiss the bags under the eyes, the sunken cheeks, the folds of flesh beside the lips, the almost toothless mouth. What had been a girl groaned and croaked in a sudden fit of old age. She reached out her arms, but dropped them back on the bed again, shook her head, coughing, and the dangling skin on her neck trembled, a hand with crooked, twisted fingers covered her mouth, her shoulders were shaken by the cough. Revulsion and pity took away Kirill's strength. Just as this girl is unattainable to me, so everything I ever desire will crumble at my touch.

Kirill saw that the girl would inevitably become an old woman and he would never do more than watch the girls walking by, without approaching them. He saw couples on benches in the park, lovers walking along the embankment, he saw husbands and wives walking arm in arm and himself walking past. From out of the darkness of the street he peered into the light of the windows, making out shelves and carpets in the rooms, an armchair and a lampshade, a table and the people sitting at the table: but he didn't join them — he was impotent. The young man lay there beside the girl, gazing at her in confusion. He stroked her cheek, with her head lying in the crook of his arm. This would be the way forever now. He was sure that it was forever. He raised himself up slightly, still hoping, but shook his head and turned away. He was left alone with his "forever". He thought very rapidly about all his life to come, as if this were the right moment. Others would gallop on the horses invented in his mind and open the stage curtains beyond his reach. Others would walk along the streets with their arms round each other, they would bawl out songs at the top of their voices, but he would remain silent, he would walk away into a side street. He saw people shaking each others' hands, congratulating each other, doing good, he saw some going to church and others sacrificing themselves. Some he saw setting out on distant journeys, and some constantly inventing new games — but he could no longer make himself out, he had merged so far into the darkness, shrunk away and hidden himself — and he was watching intently, with his arms lowered along his body and his shoulders hunched over. Just as the girl's body aged at the touch of his fingers, so everything he strove for was bound to turn to dust: but when Kirill was left alone, an even worse fear would steal up on him. And it would seem to Kirill that he himself no longer existed, and there was nothing but the window and the tree outside it, the cloud in the sky, the pain in his scratched finger, the draught from the open window. There has to be someone to see and feel all this, Kirill would tell himself, but the sum of sensations does not mean at all that I am still here. His stomach would feel hunger, his ear would hear sound, his foot would stumble, but Kirill would no longer exist. He wanted to say, "Get dressed," but he didn't say anything.

The girl had already understood everything herself. She was pulling on her bright green underwear, so beautiful that her heart rejoiced every time the silk slid across her skin. She put on her skirt and stockings and started buttoning up her blouse. Well, it happens sometimes, it's perfectly understandable. But he'll still have to pay. Perhaps he really will fall in love with me. Or maybe he won't want to see me at all now. No, he'll probably start pestering me: "It's not that I can't do it. I don't want to, because my feelings for you are so divine." "He can give me perfume. I realized he was that kind straightaway, he went on talking for so long. The old woman's probably angry. It wasn't a very interesting performance. I wonder if she's paying him for this? He'll have to give her back her money. Or maybe he isn't taking anything?" The girl tied her shoelaces and stood up. Kirill forgot to hold her coat for her and she put it on herself.

Kirill stood there, numbed, still not believing that it was all over. He wanted to start everything all over again, to lead the girl into the room, embrace her without saying a word, undress her and kiss her, closing his eyes so that her body would remain unchanged, a lithe body that aroused desire. But he had realized too late, he ought to have thought about things less, the girl was leaving the building and he was following her out, without his cap. The girl who had been with him only a moment ago was walking quickly down the stairs, moving further away with every step, and Kirill was falling further and further behind her.

So that was how it was. You spent your life racking your brains over a riddle, you suffered and you howled — and this was the answer. The pitiful, meagre explanation of your grief. Life had been such an incomprehensible, cruel force when it made the officer leave Varvara Petrovna. Everything had seemed meaningless, but therefore profound; it was unjust but she could still shake a fist and shout at heaven. But now everything was clear, and so there was no one she could blame. He had left her because he could never have been a husband. Many years ago his leaving had cancelled the rules that a young woman had thought were immutable. Varvara Petrovna had spent the rest of her life outside the law, in a dark country where right and left had swapped places, the grid of coordinates had shifted and the sky seemed to have collapsed on to the earth. But now the lights had been turned on, and the old woman had found everything back where it had been. From now on everything would be simple. A wardrobe was only a wardrobe, and not a hiding-place for a peeping eye, and a geranium was not a remnant of a lost garden but only a plant in a pot. Varvara Petrovna had thought before that some terrible power had parted her from the officer and fogged her reason. But once her reason had worked things out that power had proved to be a weakness, an inability. She had been left by a man who was not a whole man. That was all. The life she had lived fell away and lay at her feet like restrictive clothing. Varvara Petrovna could see his face. I know everything, she wanted to say, don't go. There is nothing apart from us. We invented impossible destinies for ourselves, but everything's much simpler than that. No, he replied. Don't be tempted by explanations. Between the rational and the nonsensical, always choqse the nonsensical. We are close because we shall never see each other. And every time you remember me I shall be going away. The hall door opened. Someone came in: he stamped his feet and wiped them. Then he stopped making any sound. Now she would get up and go to meet him, without leaning on her stick. Life was like the sky-blue balloon in the song, floating above her head. The springtime of her old age was beginning.

Translated by Andrew Bromfield

MARIA ARBATOVA
MY LAST LETTER TO A.

Why write letters to someone who doesn't exist? Or to be more precise, he exists physically, and by reading this letter is compelled to become that person you are writing to, and which also frustrates both him and you, given the awareness of the ironic distance between the real him and the him, who is reading this letter.

The man in question has emigrated in order to sever what you, at least to some extent, have managed to sever while staying put. And if you love him with that cosseting sisterly love, of the sort Russian women are traditionally prone to (involving everything from mild intellectual flirtation to erotic frenzy) then leave him in peace. He has nothing to feel guilty about, and has no wish to feel guilty about the way of life he has chosen. And leave yourself in peace too, you who have much of your life ahead of you, and a sufficiently sober view of the problems both solved and still in the solving. Say "thank you very much," and move on, because life is hardly likely to give you the chance to do as much good for this man as he has managed to do for you in his brief stopover.

Phallocracy has legitimized all forms of male introspection but denies the same rights to women. All these Henry Millers and their lesser brethren, whose writing elucidates with religious fervour their coming to terms with their genitalia, in which hierarchy genitalia enjoy the status of master and introspection that of slave. This hopeless male world, with the phallus at its centre, worn-out by the same macho civilisation, which long since ceased to be a means and became the end.

God forbid to be born male and have to measure yourself and universal harmony by this physiological yardstick. Look how stupid such a yardstick makes men, although we socialise with them within the same Procrustean space, share the same planet and even sleep in the same bed, whether out of duty or passion, depending on the conjunction of Mars and Venus in the sky.

How interesting to be a woman when you get to this point. The stages of the big journey when from a puny fragility you begin to fill out and this proves to be both uncalled for and painful because the school uniform has not been designed for it and the seams under the armpit dig deep red creases into your skin.

"I don't want to wear this uniform!"

"It's not a matter of what you want!"

"Well I won't!"

"They won't let you into school without it!"

"I'll wear an ordinary dress and the school apron over it!"

You can't bring yourself to say, "It pinches, it's too tight!" — "It's not too tight for anybody else, but it is for you eh? What's so special about you then?"

Later, in marriage, you can't bring yourself to say it: "It's too tight!" School aprons are a symbol of phallocracy. Black for every day. White for special occasions. You have to get sed to the apron from the start. And your hair has to be either in a ponytail or a pigtail. But if you give in on your hair you give up having a mind of your own. Like having your head shaved for the church, army, or prison!

"What's that? Get out of this class! Tidy up your hair! You know where you'll end up if you wear your hair loose like that? I would say it out loud but there are boys in the class!"

Or: "I will not start this lesson till you girls take off your rings and earrings and put them away into your pencil boxes. I refuse to teach in a brothel!"

That hysterical envy of the young gipsy girls who have their ears pierced in infancy. And that fearful image of the prim, asexual teacher, before whom you are made to feel ashamed, who would mow the class like a lawn with garden shears, but who at night weeps into her pillow bemoaning her unclaimed femininity.

Just what am I writing? Is it prose? "Is that what we are speaking?" asks Molière's M. Jourdain. Writing prose is like talking. Writing a play is like telling a story. To write a poem, that's sensuality.

I don't like it when they try to sell me learning as sincerity. It reminds me of adolescents with their under-developed erogenous zones, who having dipped into pornography consider themselves fully accomplished at the real thing.

And is this prose? Thus writes A., to whom this letter is addressed, but A. has gone far, far away and is not planning to return. I am ordinarily touchy but existentially cautious, and in the balance between my touchiness and caution there materialises his insane laughter and honey-coloured eyes.

Back with the stages of the big journey... In school, at break time: "That Lena, from 7A told us in the toilet today that she became a woman yesterday. With that tall lad from Grade 9. Right there on the football pitch where the grass starts... painful she says, like having a tooth out, and the blood!"

"It hurts? Maybe you should take some sort of painkiller. Like when you have a tooth out!"

Everybody rushes to examine Lena, who became a woman yesterday. We're all still in the fourth grade, and just lost our baby teeth.

"They'll chuck her out now! In the upper grades the gynaecologist has everybody X-rayed and if it shows she's not a virgin, she's expelled straight away. No college will accept her. Only the Tech."

Then at fifteen, everybody cuts loose, and those who can't, get hang-ups. Those who don't make it, end up henceforth drifting between loneliness, cancer clinics, and unhappy marriages, while piously reciting a history of parental prohibitions.

One depressing symbol of Christian culture is the love-barren prostitute, who offers love for money to a loveless client. Remove the money from this equation, allow this wretched pair to enjoy the bounty that nature has so richly invested in them, much too abundant for mere procreation but adequate enough for them, having constructed a culture of denial, to become utterly deformed. Leave them in peace. Concentrate on the ones who kill and abuse.

"No! We won't. We have to draw the line somewhere, because we too suffer from repressed sensuality. Even at 90 we dream of young bodies and their symbolic substitutes. No we won't give. We won't let them. Mankind is on the brink of an AIDS pandemic!"

It was a youthful romance with a famous television superman. Strolls by the Baltic Sea, reciting Pasternak to the shrieks of seagulls, seaside bars saturated with the smell of coffee and expensive perfume. Then a sudden early morning departure and a strange note. And about five years later, a chance meeting at a party, where neither could put a lighter to a trembling cigarette.

"I couldn't understand what happened?"

"The point is...The point is I realized I was not up to the mark in bed."

Not up to the mark – what does that mean? And where is the mark? What's with this insane masculine world in which you treat the sexual act as a Leninist exam, in which you don't do it for your partner but to earn a good mark for your performance. Because with your partner you are never left tête-a-tête. Around your bed, or a park bench, a glade, a car, in which you are both transfixed, enchanted by tactile contact, there is an invisible panel of judges chanting in sexless voices: "Get on with it old chap! We are watching you! Don't let us down!"

I long ago lost interest in being cannon fodder for justifying other people's expectations. Does it follow then that I have justified my own? Maurois used to say that no man, even the most brilliant, could be bored by a woman who remembered that he was a human being too. This principle works also in reverse.

A man is invariably attracted by the exciting medley of sin and innocence, as long as he is not sure in what proportion. Here lie his main erogenous zones. He wants simultaneously to debauch and castrate you. Run your finger over these zones and you will win everything: tenderness (if he has had a normal childhood), money (if this is what you want from him), soul (if you can summon up the experience and the nerve to have it in the context of a relationship) because it is not you he needs, but power over you. If through thoughtlessness or feminist orientation you happen to highlight your own intellect or your affections or both, then you have failed. Because in ninety nine cases out of a hundred, what interests him is not your delicate skin or the fragrance of your hair, but the hierarchy of power between you. He will wear the number of your orgasms with him like a row of medals. How sickening!

The exception to this rule is A. to whom this letter is addressed. But even if the panel of judges leave the scene when he fondles you, they will still remain inside that head of his, which is crammed with lines and rhymes, because he has decided to draw and write, instead of living a life. The judges of course have already bullied him enough. He has learned that he can only hide from them in a woman's body.

"What a view you have from this window!" I said enviously to a certain charming female journalist.

We were drinking coffee. And the window above her writing desk faced inwards from the Garden Ring Road, embracing the diversity of roofs in central Moscow.

"Yes it is beautiful. I've been here a month. It's my new husband's flat. And can you see over there — that grey building with its un-curtained middle windows? That's where my ex-husband lives. If you use these field binoculars, you can see everything inside in detail. He doesn't know I live here, and when he gets a new woman to visit him — which is about every three days — I ring him and offer him derisive advice. He's going spare. He concludes that since our divorce I have become clairvoyant. One time he even tried to curtain the window with bed linen, so I rang immediately and told him not to bother, because I can see through the sheets. Then he started to smash up the crockery. He stood there about twenty minutes smashing up this dinner service, which we had been given years ago. Poor old crockery!"

"Aren't you sorry for him?"

"Him? When we were together no woman could get into the flat without him practically screwing her on the threshold while explaining to me that I was inhibited and of no interest in bed. As a result I had a hysterectomy, and then met a man with whom I was both uninhibited and interesting."

She raised the binoculars to her eyes and grinned.

"He's got a brand-new one today. Looks pretty under-age to me. Want a look?"

When she grinned I could see a grey tunnel of heavy misery coming from her unhappy eyes to that distant blind window. I saw how terribly those people lived, how terrible it was for each of them now, without benefit of injury, because throughout that shared married life there hung a placard round their necks, which declared, "I was unhappy" instead of "We were unhappy, and it suited us."

But the saddest participants were the children in the photographs, earnestly trying to represent a happy childhood with their expensive toys. But what sort of childhood could it be if Mum and Dad are not hitting it off in bed; and not having become "man" and "woman" they cannot become true parents. Not having won membership rights in their gender community they must remain children. Most people I've met were the children of children.

My friend, a German from Cologne, and I were drinking champagne in a depressingly threadbare room, belonging to mutual friends. The German, as a matter of fact, lived in this room to economise on hotel bills, which enabled him to drink his money away in Moscow where his supply of German marks would buy him ten times more booze and a hundred times more conviviality than in Cologne.

"I feel depressed in this room before I drink myself senseless," he said. "As soon as I close my eyes I see white

rats running all over me. I jump up and wonder if I a[illegible]
the verge of suicide. I feel awful here, but I also feel aw[illegible]
Cologne, which I am accustomed to. I get up late, do a little work, then have a drink, work a bit more, have another drink, get in the car and visit various drinking establishments, talk with friends and pick up women. Periodically I drink myself senseless, and in the morning wake up with the feeling that I have just emerged from a cul-de-sac, and have the strength to live. I have a few friends in whom I can confide. This is very important to me because with us it's only acceptable to discuss spiritual matters with a priest or psychoanalyst. My favourite Chekhov quote, I'm not sure I translate correctly: 'The weather looks good enough for me to hang myself.' Ah yes, I have a daughter. I often visit her at weekends."

A., to whom this letter is addressed, and I were drinking wine in the bar of the Actors' Club, which was peopled by junior clerks and young typists of newly established firms.

"Finally I'm free, utterly free and single in Paris. I am finally living the life I have always dreamed about. Home-sickness has poignancy, but that does not in any way mean I must return. I have come to the end of my relationship with the geographical entity that you inhabit. While you are forever structuring your life I am just as constantly breaking the structure. I have my own lifestyle and I will not suffer any country, friend, or woman to make me alter it. I don't want to know how old I am, because in principle, time means nothing to me. You're telling me that in this country someone needs me? But just look at these people. They need nothing. They do not even need themselves; just like me by the way," he said, gloomily scanning the bar with his honey-coloured eyes.

Some men are superfluous by conviction. You love them because it's hard to help them in principle but they are easy to please. They have the ability to raise the temperature of short-lived happiness only to suffocate on it and run in disarray from themselves, and from their brief loves. The masochist derives from suffering not pleasure but a licence for it. However, the process of getting this licence so exhausts him that he stops deriving satisfaction from the licence itself. The Christian guilt complex has been reduced to farce. Happiness after all is simply a readiness for pleasure without any consequential pay-off. But that isn't in our culture, and if it should happen, it would be accidentally, in spite of everything, by deception. In each of their love affairs, like true travellers, in the morning they find a new town the most beautiful ever, but by evening find all towns pretty much the same. They don't really love anybody, themselves included, rather they are in love with love but this love is not reciprocated. Eternally adolescent, they blame every component of the universe except themselves.

"I bought an expensive cell phone," said my friend, a Russian woman writer, "but I can't understand the instructions. It can perform ten operations and I've only mastered two. I'm quite happy with that."

It seems to me that most men master two operations with a woman. So it's a complete mystery to him that there is a difference between a secretary and a director and the latter requires more investments from his inner resources. He wonders whether it is worth it. Or he understands, but hasn't got enough resources.

We master the same number of operations with our children.

A certain cultured middle-aged lady, agreeable in all respects and a trend-setter in one small branch of our cultural scene, once screamed during an editorial argument, "The most awful figures of our age are Marx and Freud! Marx loosed the Communists on the world, but Freud created a mass of young women without complexes. And people without complexes are people without moral standards!"

Insofar as I, for some reason, had been assigned the role — in her personal Table of Ranks — of "a young woman without complexes" no retort seemed feasible. The phrase expands like a rolling snowball, so that even the lady, who has given all of her sensuality to her native literature rather than to the opposite sex, is unable to retrieve the original snowball from the snowman. Without what sort of complexes? Without superiority complexes? What are the moral standards for the different complexes: of inferiority and superiority? And by what right can the inferiors prescribe for the superiors?

I very much want freedom, which is bound up with a sense of high self-esteem, and wish the same for everybody else. I fight my way through the concrete walls of the family scenario, through the serfdom of the Soviet marriage experience, through those iron bars of totalitarian prohibition, that riddle my body.

"Human rights..." I whisper piously, as if it were a prayer, but I doubt this makes me deviate from moral standards, for how can I possibly love mankind while having a wretched view of myself?

And I implore my psychoanalyst to peel away from me all those layers of ossified complexes, like a snake sheds its skin, so I can emerge renewed, shaken by the discovery that the sun and the grass are bright and clear as in childhood, and I regain a child's taste of an apple, the scent of flowering maple and the roughness of its bark.

"Can that happen?" I ask.

"Of course" my friend replies, "a convalescent patient moves back to the healthy world."

"Can everybody move back?"

"No! Only those, who really wish it. Basically people wish to be unhappy. You've left this scenario and fate raced to meet you bearing gifts. People prefer to live within a parental mould; they talk, think and act in pre-formed blocks. There are few who choose their own scenario for each day, or even for life, not because it's hard, but because it's terrifying not to be like everybody else."

I fell in love with A. to whom this letter is written, because he spoke and acted "like a fool fresh from the frost", to quote my linguist friend. He never uttered a single trite word, never offered a view that had not fed through his heart. It didn't work for him. He looked like a real man among automatons.

My favourite poet and friend Alexander Yeremenko wrote the following lines:

They called it all a kindergarten,
That felt like a kind of a mould:
One large duty-nurse there to prune
All that did not fit the pattern.

Oh, how much I studied the gestures and gait of those duty-nurses! How easy it was to read the type by their asexual open faces and voices, tense with their gospel truths. The one who used to go on about Marx and Freud also belonged to that type. I know practically everything about her. She studied diligently, was well-behaved and proud with that pride that comes not from generosity but from poverty. Nobody ever asked her to dance, but she was best prepared at exams, feared fashionable clothes, darkness and loneliness. Struggling with the flesh had not been a problem for her, since in her pre-puberty years her parents had weeded out all of it and only collected editions of the classics remained on the empty lot. Her husband derived from the same sort of stable, and was a potential loser. Sadistic-masochistic feelings affected the sexual. Any romantic affairs were doomed from the start, as are all affairs, which begin with pangs of anxiety rather than spasms of voluptuousness. I never saw her children, those poor wretches who had to work through her problems, and the most awful thing that childhood can offer you is a mother with repressed sensuality, who delivers you into a plastic world.

A. for whom this letter is meant, escaped these nannies, and chose a lifestyle that would have irritated them no end. Now he strolls along French streets with his white bullterrier, conversing in English and writing in Russian. That's insane, but then, as they say, "that's how a poet must live", and who else is a poet if not a youngster, who did not have his fill of play in childhood.

It is with great suspicion that I view unrequited love. To romanticise unrequited love is to romanticise self-destruction. It is people with a low sense of self-worth who love unrequitedly, they choose the unrealistic alternative, because it nourishes their lives with negative emotionality. To them it is more natural to implement their sensuality while suffering, and should the object of this sensuality turn suddenly to face them, they wouldn't have the faintest idea what to do with them, because their parents and mentors never supplied them with a licence to allow them to deal with happiness.

I don't believe in a love, in which the partners don't contribute equally. A relationship between the two should be like a moneybox, into which both throw in the coins, and when it fills and is opened, there is only a jointly owned

Thank-you!

sum to fund mutual trust; otherwise any union would become a list of mutual debts. And nobody can win because vampires are always unhappier than their victims.

A., to whom this letter is written, having read a story dedicated to him, said that if he had written this story himself everything would look the other way round. Why? No truth is ever born of an argument. Nothing is born of an argument, only pain! Especially where love is involved.

With A., to whom this letter is written, I had a mother-of-pearl relationship. The word "mother-of-pearl" rolls like a wave, as if pouting its lips for a kiss. It holds a ripple of watercolour and a dance of lights as in a turning seashell.

Short-lived affairs exist so that people emerge from them more protected than when they went in. They are not powerful enough to change the lives of the lovers, but have sufficient means to change the levels of their self-esteem. They were devised as a celebration, but a celebration is something that builds, not demolishes.

At about seventeen I was tutored by a famous middle-aged writer. He took trouble over my poems, supplied me with samizdat literature, and drew me into adult company. One day I met a young chap who looked so familiar to me that I suggested we must have met before. "It's funny," I said, "but I know your body language and your manner of speaking, the way you smooth your hair. It reminds me of this writer Y."

"He's my father," said the chap, after a prolonged and heavy pause.

"How odd! He's never talked about you. Only his daughters."

"He doesn't know of my existence. But I know of his. I've followed his career, read all his articles..."

"Listen, Y. is a man of genius! We'll come and visit you tomorrow."

"You mean you really can introduce us to each other?" He opened his eyes wide.

"Yes, it's simple. I'll ring now and he'll come like a shot!"

"No, no, not now. Better tomorrow. I'll have to prepare myself."

"What did you say his surname was? Yes, yes... It could be," said Y. yawning in response to my rather hysterical phone call. "There was that unattractive woman from the editorial department... She disappeared suddenly. It was rumoured that there was a child. Eh! Looks like me? Go and see him? You can forget that. We've got on famously without each other so far and can do the same in the future. He's proud of me? Let him be proud of me if it suits..."

"But you have always bewailed the lack of a son! You've always longed for an heir! He has such a forlorn look! He does so need you!" I wailed, and he finally gave in.

Next day we went to see him.

The room was packed with people and the table was laid with food and drink. My friend had invited everybody to whom he wanted to show off his father. In the hallway he and Y. had shaken hands, terrified. Y. performed non-stop all evening. He shone, and the son bathed in his reflected glory. He feasted upon the father with eyes welling with tears of adoration. When everyone had departed. Y. held out his hand in farewell.

"I... I was, well sort of hoping for some advice," said the son, in a voice, stiff with anxiety, "It's been suggested I do some postgraduate work... But I..."

"Yes, yes," Y. replied in a chilly voice. "I'll give you a ring sometime," and made off towards the lift.

On the return journey he said, "I don't find the boy at all interesting. But that wife of his looks a bit of all right. I wouldn't mind having a go at her. Mind she's got a biggish nose."

They never saw each other again. Some years later the son emigrated. And soon after, Y. died. He was placed in a sealed coffin, because he had lain almost a week in his flat, surrounded by antiques, before his ex-wife and multiple lovers got round to looking for him.

The relationship between children and parents is a most disturbing subject, trickiest, with its "what can we do" and "who's at fault". I have a woman friend who looks after the disabled with missionary zeal, who set me a problem to which I periodically return, without any hope of solving it.

Two wheelchair-bound young people got married. The woman became pregnant, and the administration at the home where they lived, demanded that she have an abortion.

The poser is: which course of action would violate human rights most?

If abortion is enforced?

If the child is put in an orphanage because the parents can't take proper care of it?

If somebody else (a charity, the State?) could guarantee their parental rights without recognising their parental obligations? I don't know the answer.

Should people, unprepared for adulthood have children? Where is that borderline beyond which adulthood begins? Is it not at the point where a sense of self-worth develops? When they approach love and procreation without the need to patronise and perfect, without crushing one another, because they trust their creative instincts and because they view their way to perfection as a way to freedom and not to mere convenience.

All rather banal perhaps.

"Don't be afraid of banality," said Matisse painting his primordial complex-free children's world.

A., to whom this letter has been written, will read it with no less perplexity than the reader. He will be looking for a subtext, and I am sure he will find it, though I wonder what sort of subtext there could be, given that the text itself is nothing special, and especially as it is by no means the last in that eternal genre of women's letters addressed to their long-lost lovers.

Translated by Richard Cook

MARINA KULAKOVA
ALIVE AGAIN

- Breaking Ground, Making a Display
- well known already when this story was published.

Author's note: To some, this story may seem too terrifying, too far fetched. But the thing is that it not made up. It's true. All this actually happened to me. This is part of my life, exactly as it happened. And if this story can be defined as a thriller, then it's a sort of non-fiction thriller. Non-fictional horror.

I didn't tell anybody about this for a long time. But now I've decided to tell my story. Why? Because I live, like we all do, in a violent world. Because I know through my own experience that violence can be and needs to be confronted. Because I want to warn people about the real, non-fictional dangers we face in our quiet lives. Quiet women's lives, in particular. Forewarned is forearmed.

CHAPTER ONE
THE MAN BEHIND MY BACK

So a bit further on, I turned from the road into the alley and dived into a tunnel carved out of treetops. I was taking a short cut home. After a few seconds I heard hurrying footsteps behind me and I suddenly sensed danger. It engulfed me in a wave of horror and I quickly and instinctively, not looking back at the source of the terror, turned to the left to... to what?

I intercepted the stab under my left shoulder blade; I "caught" it with my left arm. His knife slashed right through my venous plexus and blood gushed out. But I didn't feel any pain. I just felt the knife. Another stab, I intercepted that one too, bringing it down and cutting my palm on it, the knife pierced my thigh. He — I didn't see his face — grabbed me by the arm, trying to push it behind my back, and hit my temple with the handle of the knife. I couldn't dodge it and just gasped. "No use screaming," rushed through my mind, "it'll be over in seconds..." Another blow, I was fighting him. Two more blows to the stomach, one after the other. I blocked them, intercepted them. Then one more to my groin. I didn't feel the pain. Fear cleared my mind. What does he want? It suddenly came to me: money! My bag? I had maybe twenty rubles.

"I have nothing," I muttered, choking, trying to shout.

"I don't want anything."

Then I realized there was no way out. The voice that said: "I don't want anything," was not the voice of a human being. It was the voice of complete and utter emptiness, completely devoid of intonation. I couldn't even make out if it was high or low, loud or quiet. I only knew that this was it. Game over. He wanted to kill me.

And then I felt ashamed, unbearably ashamed that I was now being slaughtered so repulsively and so senselessly, and tomorrow Nika, pregnant Nika would see my bloody body, and even if she didn't see it, they would tell her about it in detail, and what had she done to deserve that? And what about me...

I screamed. At least I thought I did. I screamed out

"Help!" and he pressed his hand over my mouth, I managed to move forward and screamed.

Amazingly the fight only lasted several minutes. I stopped feeling the stabs, my right hand was so sliced up that my palm was a bloody mess. When he got me down on the ground, I still struggled against him. He stabbed at me persistently and chaotically at the same time. He actually seemed to like cutting through my body. My clothes, a light blue blouse and white trousers were already cut to ribbons, and my whole body was bleeding. My left arm, from which blood had started spurting, was now almost numb. We were fighting on the ground two steps away from the path when I noticed a young man walking along, he saw us, and walked straight past, frightened. I tried to break free again and call for help but he put his hand over my mouth. The passer-by sped up away from us.

"That's it." I thought. And as if to confirm it, he finally managed to get hold of my arms and press them down, then he cut through the remaining clothes on my chest, and I felt the knife under my left breast.

All of a sudden everything ceased to exist, came to a standstill, died away... How long did it last? I don't know, not that long, but it felt like forever. So I missed them coming up behind him, my senses had been stretched to their limits. They appeared from out of nowhere.

CHAPTER TWO
NO EXCUSES ACCEPTED

He hadn't heard anything either (how could he?). They had pounced on him from both sides. It was useless to resist.

I tried to get up; only now my whole body was pierced

with pain from the cuts which zigzagged across it like flashes of lightning. I held on to my chest. Almost simultaneously the beams from several torches crossed over me. I could hear restrained horrified gasps and lots of swearing; I was bleeding from everywhere, blood was even dripping from my hair. I heard the muffled sound of blows; they were beating him up, right there on the bloody grass. Some people came up to us. I remember a woman who was quite young helping me to get up. Her husband was there too, but he kept at a distance, he was scared. Five minutes ago she had called the police. There had been several calls at the same time; the nearest house had heard it all, and the local police department's patrol car was nearby and ready, really close. Everything had happened in a matter of minutes, even seconds.

It would have been like a fairytale rescue if there hadn't been so much blood. The Police came. Five minutes later the ambulance arrived. I had a strange feeling that I was looking at everything from somewhere far away. The afterlife? Maybe... but was I still alive?

I saw the stretcher and shook my head; my whole body hurt but it felt like it would be too painful to lie down. In any case, I was now so far removed from earth, from these people, that I didn't know how to come back, how to live or where to go. They quickly put a tourniquet on my arm and bandaged it up. "I guess this is yours?" asked the woman, holding my bag up to me. "Yes" I said. She offered me her hand. I stepped towards the car and turned round.

The police were standing around him. I hobbled over to them. They parted in front of me. One of them swore at him again, and said to me: "Don't worry, madam; he'll get what's coming to him." "Show me him," I asked, my voice was hoarse and wheezing. The beam of light shone on his face, and I shuddered.

He had a very large mouth, and tiny eyes. Maybe it was the light, but he looked monstrously deformed. He had sharp disproportions in his features, the shape of his head, and the outline of his figure; it seemed like he had an abnormally large head. I shuddered literally — it was at that moment that I started to shake uncontrollably.

"What... what..." I whispered, not managing to put into words what was droning in my head and tearing me apart, smashing me up, and dulling my conscience.

And suddenly he spoke as if he were returning from somewhere far away, in a kind of otherworldly, terrifying, deadly voice:

"Forgive me, my wife left me..."

If I had had the strength I would have burst out laughing. And so my battered mouth twitched into a weak smile, and it was as if all the cuts and wounds on my body also smiled which immediately caused them to sting sharply, and my head was spinning. The doctor and the nurse came to my side, and in a minute the ambulance was driving out onto the road. The young doctor asked me something cheerfully. I muttered something back. My strength finally abandoned me and I closed my eyes. "Hey, don't close your eyes!" I heard sudden worry and fear in the young doctor's voice and that frightened me. So it wasn't a dream. I couldn't go to sleep and wake up afterwards in my own bed.

Ridiculous. Absurd.

No. No. This was no accident. No way.

The ambulance flew through the empty streets of night-time Moscow.

CHAPTER THREE
THE BLUE CORRIDOR

In the reception ward where they brought me, nothing happened for a long time. A really long time — half an hour at least. The "sympathetic" young doctor, who was hugely relieved (that I didn't die on him in the ambulance, I now realized), had handed me over to the nurse on duty who was annoyed at being disturbed at such a late hour. She had gone somewhere. I sat, in anguish, on the shabby hospital couch, putting pressure on the bandages on my arm, they had quickly got soaked with blood. Someone badly wounded could easily die here before he got attention — it was a hospital but there was no one around. Behind a screen, a man was groaning and convulsing heavily.

Then a sullen looking nurse and a tall orderly in blue hospital overalls came in. The nurse brought me a hospital gown and shirt, and pointed to the next room.

"Get undressed," she said, looking suspiciously at me. "Don't you have any slippers?"

"Slippers? I hadn't really planned on coming here."

"Get undressed! Well I never, look at these rags; they are all covered in blood."

"Can I wear my sandals?"

She muttered under her breath and flung a cloth on the floor. I wiped the soles of my sandals, wincing with the pain. Any movement or effort I made was excruciating, I bent over, clutching my stomach. The man behind the screen groaned even louder.

"What's wrong with him?" I asked, shivering from the cold in my gaping shirt which smelt of chlorine.

"Stones." The nurse said curtly, paying no attention to him whatsoever.

The sleepy orderly wrote something down and, grabbing

some paper said: "Let's go". He had a kind of a "virtual" air about him. He seemed to keep aloof of what was happening around him in this hospital. Maybe, deep down, he was experiencing something much more important to him.

The walk took a surprisingly long time. We went through some corridors, lit by long "fluorescent" lamps, and then went down a basement tunnel, where there were blue light bulbs — it was an eerie sight. The further we walked, the more anxious I felt. If half an hour ago I had more than anything wanted to lie down on a bed and finally drop to sleep, after all this nightmare, which had receded into the past, now I was frightened again. The orderly walked with big strides, I could only just keep up with him. In the blue light his pale blue uniform suddenly changed colour: it became a bright violet. At some point he halted and glanced back. He had dark circles under his eyes. I also slowed down in confusion. Once certain that I was following him, he carried on. I was somewhat relieved but not quite. I realized that I shouldn't be following him, not at all. But where else was there to go?

The strange violet-blue deathly light flooded this long underground tunnel with old pipes running along the low ceiling. There was a smell, not just of earth, of underground, but a scarier smell of hopelessness, sheer animal hopelessness, of a terrible veterinarian clinic. It reminded me of my childhood, of something that I'd tried to forget. But I suddenly realized what it was. "Hell," I thought, "Is this hell, or just the road to hell?"

Finally we started to climb some jagged stairs. I almost cried out from the pain as I bent my knees, but my guide didn't look back nor did he slow down. Clutching at my wounds, I was incredibly relieved to see the stairs leading upwards. We emerged from the frightening blue basement.

The hospital now looked like a hospital should look.

When a duty doctor appeared to examine me at long last, I suddenly resisted with all the strength I had left in me.

"Where does it hurt?"

"Nowhere. I want to sleep. Leave me in peace."

"We need to examine you and put dressings on."

CHAPTER FOUR
MORNING

When I opened my eyes, there was someone from the Criminal Investigation Department sitting by my bed.

The sun was shining through the window. I remembered everything that had happened that night and huddled up miserably.

"How are you feeling?" The official politeness and slightly embarrassed sympathy did not mix well. I had always been sensitive to intonation.

"Thanks. I can still feel."

My "unorthodox" answer made the young officer quickly gather himself and he became all official and disciplined.

"May I ask you a few questions? It's for the investigation. I won't take up much of your time."

"Ask away"

"Your name?"

"Marina Kulakova."

"Age?"

"I'm twenty four."

"Are you working? Studying?"

"Finished university, worked for two years on an assignment, just got back from the country."

"What were you doing there?"

"I'm a teacher. I was teaching Russian language and literature."

"Do you live in Moscow?"

"No, I live in Nizhny Novgorod. I'm just visiting, staying with some friends."

"So, yesterday, on the night of the first of August, where were you coming from?"

"I came out of the Rechnoi vokzal metro station and was on my way home, to my friends' house."

"Can you give me their names and address please?"

"I'd rather not. My friend is eight months pregnant. I don't want her to worry."

"I'm afraid you will have to tell me that. Did you know your... the person who attacked you?"

"No, I had never seen him before."

"Are you sure that you had never seen him before?"

"Yes, I'd never seen this person before."

"Do you have any identification on you?"

"No, my passport is with my stuff where I'm staying."

"We will have to go and meet your friends. Don't worry though; we'll try not to concern them."

After a few minutes when the man who I had called an "investigator" had left to "investigate", the nurse came in and gave me some tablets.

"What are these?" I said, casting a suspicious look at the dish.

"Sedatives for the stress, and anti-inflammatories."

"Thanks."

My fellow-patients looked at me with some alarm. In the ward there were four other beds: two along the wall, and three at right angles to them and parallel to each other. The dishevelled and puffy hospital inmates began to exchange the usual morning niceties. When the nurse had gone out, I tried to get up.

My skin stretched painfully over my whole body. Over the last twelve hours the coagulated blood had stuck my wounds together and now I was disturbing them and blood was starting to ooze again in places.

"Lie down, lie down," said the woman on my left (I was in the middle), "We'll get breakfast for you. I'll bring it over, lie down."

But I got up. I felt anxious. For some reason, I didn't feel safe here.

I wasn't yet aware, or hadn't realized yet, that after that night my body, all punctured, all cut to pieces, had become incredibly sensitive. It had been like that before, but now my body was unbelievably more sensitive to everything. I suppose it was proportional to the number of injuries I had sustained. I'd been over-sensitive before as well, but I thought that's the way it should be. How could you not feel that the hunt was on? Get out of here. Leave. As I stood up, this feeling prevailed over a multitude of other feelings. In the space of a few minutes it had formed itself into words, it was done.

Get out. Leave. But how? In hospital garb? They'd think I'm a lunatic, but then it made no difference really what they thought of me. Who was I now anyway?

Wincing, I reached with my bandaged hand for my bag. There were traces of dried blood and grass stains on it. Inside there was some cheap makeup: mascara, lipstick, a hand mirror. I glanced at myself in it: it was like something out of a horror film. The whole right side of my face was bruised, under my eye a blackish-bluish haematoma had broken out, my mouth was smashed up, and my neck was covered with deep scratches with freshly clotted blood. My tangled fringe was stuck together with dried blood.

Where could I go looking like this? I sighed. I looked in my bag again, pulled out my foundation and sunglasses.

A few minutes later I was making a call from the hospital phone on the landing, having covered the picturesque part of my face with a hospital towel.

"Sergei?"

His familiar voice was such a relief after the terrifying string of unfamiliar faces, sounds, voices and events that I almost wept. It was as if he had finally brought me back, or at least a bit closer, to my former life.

"If you only knew how glad I am to hear your voice... only please don't tell Nika... I have had a bit of an adventure..."

"Where are you? What's happened? Has something happened?"

"Yes, something has happened. Someone from the police is on their way to you now. Or someone from the Criminal Investigation Department, I don't know where they are from. Please, you mustn't worry, I am alive."

"Where are you?"

"In hospital. Listen, I need to ask you a huge favour — I urgently need some of my clothes. In my bag I've got a red T-shirt, and on the chair next to the bed there are some jeans. Please could you bring them to me?"

"Of course, of course, I'll bring them. Are you injured?"

"Can you do it today?"

"Today? Today I'm on duty. No, today I can't. Maybe Nika can..."

"No! No! Don't tell her, or rather, don't tell her what's happened. Oh God! She mustn't come. What about tomorrow?"

"Tomorrow I can, definitely. First thing."

"Ok, I'll be waiting for you. I'll tell you more when I see you. Write down the address..."

I stood for a minute leaning against the wall. My head was spinning a bit, but Sergei's voice rang in my ears, it was the same as two days ago, a week ago, the same as a year ago... time was restoring everything. It was restoring it in fragments, pieces, silently. The pictures were emerging from the past. I was alive. Alive again.

I washed for a long time. My right arm was bandaged. My left arm was in a sling so it made it hard work. A huge rainbow coloured bruise stretching up almost to my shoulder was showing from my bulkily bandaged elbow. (It had been the first stab, to the vein, and I felt sick as I remembered.)

With the cold water and hospital soap, I tried to wash the blood out of my hair. Pale women with indifferent suffering eyes glanced at me as they shuffled in to the toilet. I was in the therapy department; they had put me where there was a free bed, waiting for doctors' orders.

Having returned to the ward, I lay down and closed my eyes. So, it's time to sum it up. Is life trying to get even with me? What have I done? Time will tell. What has really gone on in my life?

Let's start from the beginning, from the very beginning.

CHAPTER FIVE
A GIRL AND DEATH

I was four years old when I was sent to a summer kindergarten in the countryside. There was an older girl there who read my palm. "Here you have the letter L. This means Life. And here is a D, it means Death. You will have a short life, well, not very short of course, well... a normal life." I looked at my palm, there were a lot of narrow criss-cross lines ending abruptly... Death. I imagined death. I'm not there, I don't exist, just don't. I wandered in the dusty roadside grass. I was choking away the tears, trying to make a little bear out of burdocks. I don't exist. And never will. Evening began to fall. I was scared of going to sleep — like I was scared of dying or disappearing forever. Me... and what am I? Who am I? I looked in the mirror at the tearful short-haired girl with full lips in a pinafore dress. It's me. I don't believe it. I don't want to be like this. I want to be something else. To be, to be. I wanted so much to be with grandma, not even with my mum but with my grandma, everything was calm and simple around her. I wanted so much to be reassured, but I said nothing. My pillow was soaked with tears. I cried silently.

My mum and dad came on Sunday. They were very busy with each other. My dad didn't live with us: their painful relationship could never be described as a family. I understood straight away that they didn't care about me. And they didn't care about death. They were really full of life. My handsome young father and bright proud mother, always pleased with herself. I asked if they could take me to grandma's. No, they wouldn't. I cried. That summer I had become a real cry-baby, I didn't used to be like that at all.

I was preoccupied with death more than with any of my close friends that summer. More than with my closest relatives. Thoughts about death were with me, inside me, because death itself was close.

Finally the summer camp finished but the summer was not yet over. Mum took me on holiday with her. She rented a room in a country holiday village.

There was milk and berries, the wild strawberries had almost finished but you could still find some late July berries. There were also bilberries. The forest with clearings full of berries began right at the gate. The landlady's son, a smart, dark-eyed boy, who couldn't sit still for a minute, was watching as I stood for a long time by the water barrel or looked into the horses' eyes. It was so nice not having to have a set timetable or take an afternoon nap. I had stopped crying.

"D'you want to go berry-picking?" He suddenly suggested.

"Where?" I asked.

"There," he waved his arm in a direction that I had already been to with Mum. "I know where there are a lot of bilberries."

"OK, let's go," I agreed. Mum had gone somewhere and I wasn't doing much until she got back. I liked playing with dolls in the evening, but the forest always beckoned me. There was so much life in there but I always had to sit on a mat with my mum and not move from it on my own.

So I, being an obedient little girl out of habit from kindergarten, held the boy's hand. We walked down the road, down the sunny forest path, holding hands. There wasn't much around the village, just a few wooden houses dotted about among the trees. The right hand side of the path was lined with high bushes and thick ferns.

I wasn't really paying attention, and hadn't noticed the two men that had appeared behind us, how long they had been following us, catching up with us. Two grown-ups. Only afterwards, a lot later on, did I realize that they were young men, maybe around twenty. They were chatting. One of them had his shirt unbuttoned; it was he who suddenly picked me up. Before I knew what was going on he put his hands inside my panties and touched me where it is "shameful". Mum had always told me that down there, under the pants it's shameful to show, shameful to see and shameful to touch. I had known this for a long time. I was ashamed, and blood rushed to my face.

I lashed out, digging into the man's bare chest with my hands and looked him in the face. He didn't look at me and kept saying through gasping, heavy breathing, "It's OK, don't be scared." Then he said something else to the other one, encouraging him, trying to persuade him, "Let's go, come on, let's go."

I was terrified. The boy, my "chaperone", was just a little boy; he got scared too, sensing the evil, his eyes welling up with fear. He cowered like a wild animal, but muttered "Mum! Our mum is here! I'll call her!"

Not looking at him, he held me tightly and pawed me. "Call her, call your mum," he said in an expressionless, low voice. Nothing was going to stop him.

The boy rushed away. After him the other man retreated, muttering something and swaying, giving it up as a bad job. My abductor (the word "Murderer!" – crossed my mind, who else?) turned sharply into the bushes, the branches scratched my face. I felt smothered by the forest.

I started to groan out of fear rather than pain. I wanted to cry but couldn't. I pushed with my hands and kicked with my feet, but it was clear that nothing was going to help me now. The man was strong. I could smell something sickly sweet on his breath. "Come... Come..." he muttered. Holding on to me tightly, he put me on the ground, on the patchy grass with some moss scattered with old pine needles. He pinned me down with his knees and started to undo his trousers. "A knife," I thought. He's looking for a knife. Now comes the knife. His hands were shaking.

He still avoided my eyes. But I stared straight at him, terrified out of my wits, ashamed and in pain. He had pulled my knickers off, and it felt like he wanted to tear me in half with his knees and hands. Why was he taking so long to find his knife? The knife that he was going to murder me with.

"Are you going to kill me? (For some reason, I had decided that I could chit-chat with my murderer. Or maybe something in me wanted to quicken the proceedings.) Why do you want to kill me?"

He stopped muttering for a second and looked at me with his yellowish dull eyes.

"My mum's here," I carried on, "She isn't far away. Let me go, I want to go to my mum. Don't kill me."

"You'll go soon... Come, come..." He started muttering again.

But something happened. He glanced back.

"Please don't kill me. I don't want to die. This hurts." I pushed at his hands, trying very hard to free myself from this hot dangerous weight that was on top of me, and trying not to look at where his trousers were half undone.

He suddenly got up. Only then I started sobbing quietly. He rushed away, almost running back to the village. He nearly bumped into my mum who was running towards me, pale faced. Her legs gave way.

I trudged along the road, sobbing quietly. I was overwhelmed. I was alive. Now I think: I was saved by words. My words.

In the winter of that year I started writing poems. One was about a snowflake:

Snowflake, snowflake, where have you been?
I was living on a white cloud high in the sky.
Snowflake, snowflake, where are you off to?
I'll be landing on the ground, where the kids play.

CHAPTER SIX
BEING ILL

"Lunch! Lunch!" We were informed from the corridor.

Opening my eyes I saw that I was surrounded by dilapidated hospital walls, lying on a bed with a sagging mattress. Lunch. Just think of it! Isn't it amazing? Concerted shuffling of many feet in the corridor. Some kind of force gives out food, and they, the patients, obediently take it. They must be hoping that this force will cure them. Inhospitable hospital.

I was ill a lot during my childhood. I had problems with my ears. I had to have injections, which hurt. I had a sore throat. But I never experienced more pain in my childhood than my first operation, when they took my tonsils out. This was real torture, and I, normally obedient and quiet, broke free from the doctors' hands, spilling and spattering blood everywhere. They shouted at me, put me to shame, tied me up. They strapped me to the chair. The torture continued. My oilskin bib had slipped down, and there was blood all over my white top. I screamed and coughed up blood, pleading with them: "No more! Please no more! That's enough! No more!"

Before the operation they promised that they would give me ice cream straight afterwards. It was to be a consolation prize. But it was still scary. The children who had had their operation before me were coming back, quietly choking back the tears, or in a state of silent stupor. And they didn't want any ice cream. They really did offer ice cream. Afterwards. But you really didn't want to eat it. It hurt to swallow. For a few days I could only manage to drink and eat baby food that my mum would bring.

Maybe this is why I hate hospitals so much.

When I have to see a doctor face to face I always carefully study their faces, hoping to find sympathy. Something about their faces gives hope. Inspires trust, maybe. In what? I don't know. But how can these people stand to see this pain, this endless suffering every day? Yes, it's part of their job, a professional skill. But how is it possible not to be effected by it?

After lunch we had a newcomer in the ward. The stout woman took a long time to settle down on the springy bed, she tossed and turned and couldn't get comfortable. Eventually she sat up. She had a kind, round face with an unhealthy redness to it. She was breathing heavily. "Ooh." She said as if apologising, "I don't feel well..." "Lie down, lie down," responded the good-natured neighbour on my right. "None of us feels well here. They'll give you medicine. They'll put you back on your feet..."

It was as if the mishmash of medicinal smells in the air made everyone drowsy. After a few minutes the sounds of gentle snoring and heavy breathing could be heard from all around. Our new Mrs Panin also finally settled down and seemed to doze off.

I couldn't sleep. I could see green trees and a bit of sky through the partly opened window. I could see the green of the trees and a little bit of sky through the slightly open window. And there seemed no connection at all between the sickly peace of the hospital, and the twittering, radiant, living peace blowing in from outside.

I craved peace, that living peace. But it hadn't happened. Never in my life. Why? How come? Maybe there is something wrong with my thinking? Or maybe I don't ask the right questions? For example, how come? How come all this has happened to me? Let's say it was a test. A test? Why? What for? Who has been testing me so painfully for so long? Why is this turning into some kind of persecution?

I closed my eyes, knowing I wouldn't be able to sleep.

CHAPTER SEVEN
JAWS

"Go! Go!"

A terrified dog.

An awkward looking man in a trainer's suit is waving his arms and hitting the dog's snout with his long wadded sleeves. He keeps on hitting the panic-stricken young sheepdog. The dog is hysterical. It bites out at the sleeve and lets it go with a whimpering bark. The man again provokes the dog to get hold of the sleeve and tear it to pieces. The man is teaching the dog to be vicious.

They say that a dog is man's best friend. The dog does not understand the banality or the irony of this: it's just a friend, a devoted friend, and it's not easy to break this friendship. Forcing your dog to bite and tear at human flesh is very difficult after centuries of "friendship and devotion". Dogs will gladly bark at strangers — particularly if it is to protect their owner's property. But they would just bark at whatever. Dogs even go for cats, not because they are real enemies, but just for show. Everybody — dogs, cats, people — they all understand that it's a tradition, a game. A dog's teeth are a weapon. But the dog's jaws and teeth can only become a "weapon" by man's will. In order to bite, and moreover, to bite a human being, a normal dog needs to have been driven to "insanity".

It happens, there is special training for it.

After a few shocks my sheepdog guessed that it was a kind of a game. She guessed that the long armed scarecrow with a quilted jacket wanted her to bite at it. After a few days she had dutifully pretended to be a "very vicious dog". She tugged at her lead and barked "ferociously". The harder I tugged at her lead with a special teasing gesture, the harder she raged, tearing up the quilted sleeve with vehemence. I knew that she didn't have it in her to bite anyone. But her appearance had to show that she could, as it should do. She was a guard dog after all.

At the dogs' training ground, out of a few dozen dogs, there were two or three that were properly mean, dangerous even. Among them one dog stood out — a black one, with handsome reddish spots on powerful paws and a huge strong head. In a few months he had grown from a clumsy, good-natured puppy, the same age as my Kerry, into a beautiful but terrifying brute.

They said that he could tear a cat in two. He catches them and bites them with a crunch.

His owner was an elegant boy of average height with dark wavy hair and a purring voice. It wasn't the first time I had heard his voice behind me. I started to notice that I was being observed.

That summer I wore out my last children's dresses; short, made from bright cotton. I didn't want to part with one of them in particular, the green-and-red one. For some reason this dress seemed to symbolise my childhood — green and healthy, making all the wounds and burns better. With it went the country sunset, field strawberries, river sands, books, sorrel and plantains. A lonely childhood full of lots of different smells and people — a lonely, powerful, proud childhood. Something moved me to tears — I couldn't quite put my finger on it.

The previous summer, after my seventh school year, I went to summer camp. It wasn't the first time, but it seemed like the first time I had seen those athletic boys and girls with their dogs. They stayed separately from us, on the other side of the river, in tents. "Amazons" in T-shirts with dogs' heads on them. And the boys, the kind who always win at sports. They played adult, hard games on the other riverbank.

I looked at them and knew that in a year I would be with them.

And it happened.

At that age my mother's prohibitions, like all adults' words, no longer mattered to me. I had dreamed of having a dog for a long time, all my childhood, and now I just brought her — my future sheepdog, with still innocent, childish eyes.

My silly Kerry grew up quickly. Soon we caught up to each other's ages. We were probably very similar in some ways. She never came to terms with the fact that she had a master, but she didn't mind pretending, especially in front of others. She happily and graciously obeyed all the commands at dog shows, winning us gold medals and other awards. But to make up for it she'd be let off the lead on a walk, obviously thinking of commands like "Come here!" or "Heel!" as some kind of nonsense. She didn't think they were necessary. And I, having let her off the lead on a walk, often came home alone. She came back later. She scratched at the door, with an obsequious guilty smile, and her ears pulled back. She lay down, closed her eyes and muttered something — trying to vindicate herself, expecting a thrashing. I was seething with rage. Thrashing her wouldn't change anything. What she needed was to familiarize herself thoroughly with her surroundings, including the local rubbish dumps. This was absolutely necessary to her.

We were probably quite alike. I didn't believe in "The Master" anymore. Not one bit.

My teachers annoyed me.

At school the boredom was unbearable. I had dyed my hair a mahogany wood colour with toxic shampoo, and my skirt was "too long". It covered up my shapely long legs but somehow seemed a lot more provocative than a short one.

That summer I finally had to part with my little girl's

dresses. They became tight around my chest. My body was ripening like a fruit. And it hurt, either from the daily training sessions, or from the sun.

My body was suffering; it was being stretched. My eyes shone and smiles gleamed, and my voice sang. My body was taking shape, feminine shape.

I didn't like my body, it was too soft and wobbly, it was changing all the time, and I was never satisfied with it. If I ever saw a reflection of myself, it wasn't me. Except my own reflection in someone else's eyes, which was invisible but precise.

The kiss was like something alive. A living thing, something being born, a newborn. And it was hardly pleasant, it was actually rather frightening. It was a smothering, pressing closeness from another, with something else lingering behind it, dangerous and heavy. My body locked, tensed up. I felt numb. We had nothing much to talk about as it was, and now I had dried up altogether. Another kiss. My chest hurts. I push away his groping hands. They tighten their grip. I move away and see his eyes, tormented, bloodshot. A stream of his desire washes over me. It feels like the wind. I move away, trembling, snapping, fuming inside. I turn away to leave. I try to leave, but can't. There's a tight lead on me, you can't see it, it blends into the ground, the grass and autumn dampness. The lead is made of damp leather. A collar.

I twist off the lead, and bite at the collar. Growling rather than whimpering, although in my intonation there is a definite plea: let me go, while the going is good. Stand back! He won't let me go. And in the background are the hillside, the autumn, yellow grass, and the wall, there behind my back, a reliable, ancient, everlasting wall. I'll run off, I have somewhere to go, someone to rely on; my grandmother. She doesn't ask questions, only consoles me, and I have a room there. I try to tear myself away from him and cry. I want to break free, run away. Day after day.

In the winter, on the lead, in someone else's room, away from the cold, from the cruel frost. My blue coat, with a belt, a synthetic "sheepskin". The bitter frost carries the same wind I failed to recognise; it's exactly the same. It makes me numb and roots me to the spot. I don't know what to do but his greedy paws know, they grope while his cooing voice gets harder, like the wind and the frost. "Get undressed! Get undressed!"

He turns the light off, but it's only dark for a second; the light is coming in through the window, strong, bright moonlight. He quickly undresses to his trunks, gracefully, confidently. I remember this body from the summer on the riverbank; the olive-tanned body of this strangely cynical boy. I turn away.

He approaches me with a towel round his waist. He's tied the towel round his waist. I feel hot, very hot, how strange — it was frosty winter really not that long ago, only an hour ago. He moves confidently and naturally as if he has done it a hundred or a thousand times before.

I'm far, very far away from home, I don't have a home anymore. Did I ever have one?

We trained our dogs and he told me that he used to go hunting on the embankment.

"In the evenings there are lots of drunkards there, I let him loose on them. They wouldn't complain."

I didn't understand at first.

"Let him loose? With his muzzle on?"

"No, without. If a dog isn't used to snatching and biting human flesh, it will never get really vicious."

He grinned.

"It was funny yesterday; I set him on a man, let him go and waited till the man started to shout." He grabs the dog by the scruff of its neck, its ears pinned back, and its tongue hanging out of the half open jaws. "He tears him apart but the bloke just waves his hands. Just waves them and says nothing. I get closer and found he was a deaf-mute."

I stepped back and smiled stupidly.

Years later his dog died a painful, excruciating death, from a disease rare in dogs: he died of dropsy.

He was going on about something... Something had worried and angered him, I didn't fully understand what. Had I done something? In a year he joined the army with his beast. He was in the internal convoy troops. When he returned, he proposed.

"Dinner!" they announced from the corridor. The early hospital dinner was a sign for visitors to leave. I lay there, hiding behind a newspaper, to avoid embarrassing looks. Mrs Panin, who had only been brought in a few hours ago, had visitors: her round-faced domestic husband and a daughter to match. The Panins talked quietly, taking out jars of homemade food. You could see that they had temporarily moved their house here. They played house all together, paying no attention to what was going on around them.

After dinner, on the way back to my ward, I was a bit dizzy and my head was spinning. I told myself it was the loss of blood, and leaned against the wall. This contact reminded me of something, but what was it? I got back to my bed, and softly touched my right eye. Now I understood how a black eye felt. It was a massively bruised eye. I was a pretty frightful sight.

But then, even without doctors' diagnoses, I knew I would live. I would live again.

It was clear, and yet my head was buzzing like I needed to realize something, make a decision or understand something. It was like I was facing an exam: I'm almost prepared for it but my head is crammed with too many things. I haven't slept the whole night, it's as if need to read everything in just two days. Well, nearly everything. Is it really possible that I wouldn't pass the exam?

CHAPTER EIGHT **UNTITLED**

Our honeymoon in Tallinn turned out to be a disaster. Unjustified jealousy and ugly public scenes. The cake he had bought for me ended up on the floor in seconds, covered in snow and brick-dust. He stamped on it in childish hysterics. Fresh cream and nuts on his black boots — wasn't it funny? But his eyes were red with anger. Passers-by turn their heads in interest. They disapproved. The reticent Estonians understood that something was badly wrong. I was unbearably ashamed. But I could never understand the reasons for his sudden outbursts of irrepressible rage.

Then he would passionately, demandingly ask for forgiveness and "love". His desire for me was inexhaustible. And I couldn't forgive or forget the slap — he had hit me once before we were married. In fact it had happened too many times already. His reasons were imaginary. I could never understand them. What was this all about?

"She doesn't want me...she doesn't like it...never wanted it...the others just beg for it themselves...that chick, the team leader...she crawled up herself, and the little one, she gets a move on, wow... how she moves... and those girlfriends... they grab it themselves, shove it in themselves, don't stop moving their hands... rubbing-pressing-bending... moving their thighs... a-aaaaa trembling, and this bitch, no and no.... all lies, maybe not... just wants another one...found someone... if I find out, I'll kill you... what do you want?... All bitches moan... and this one reads books, the princess... studying, studying... go study, study, you studying bitch, you dumb whore."

That night I took all the tablets I could find at home. I didn't want to live anymore. After having woken up with difficulty twenty four hours later (it was mainly sleeping pills) I accepted chaotic apologies "Never, never again! This won't happen again."

What will be will be, I was pregnant... and in a state of nightmarish semi-consciousness for my wedding.

I avoided being alone with him. He got worse and worse.

"I'll kill you! I'll kill you!" I heard again and again. My blood ran cold, not out of fear so much as out of contempt for him. I had done nothing and so my indignation froze me to ice. Drove me to an icy outrage. I only wanted one thing, for him to leave me in peace. "I'll kill!" He was programming himself. His fantasies about murder became more intricate, more bloody and more detailed. More and more often "brains" figured in them. This word annoyed him, as did the word "poetess". I protected myself with silence, studying, and keeping busy. But his outbursts of monstrous aggression got more dangerous. I knew anything could happen.

In the end, he killed a woman. With an axe.

CHAPTER NINE
THE SECOND NIGHT

A quiet groan made me open my eyes. I glanced at my watch; it was a few minutes after midnight. Everyone was sleeping around me. The dim nightlight in the corridor came through the little window into the ward. Mrs Panin was moaning softly, pressing her hand below her chest.

"What is it?" I asked in a whisper, "Would you like some water maybe?"

"No, thanks," she said, shaking her head.

"Did they see you today? What did they say?"

"They said it's an ulcer. They're going to do more tests. Oh! They gave me some medicine. But I feel sick again. Oh God, God..."

Her voice was muffled. I could barely hear her. She sat up, massaging her chest.

"Oh God, oh God."

Then she lay down again but her soft groaning made my muscles tense up. Something alarming and distressing silently began to pound in my chest, and distinctly, slowly and resonantly my heart began to thump. She was moaning quietly.

I got up trying not to creak the bedsprings and, holding my stomach, walked towards the door.

"I'll get someone."

She didn't answer, just breathed heavily.

There was no one in the dimly lit corridor. The table where the nurse was supposed to sit was empty. I waited at the table, glancing both ways. One way the hospital corridor got lost in the darkness, the other way was longer and lit up.

I hobbled down to where the light was. At the end of the corridor there was a door with a sign saying "Treatment". Knocking gently, I opened the door. The light was on but no one was there. I looked miserably at the jars and bottles, idle instruments and tiled walls. I breathed in and out the thick medicinal smell, like a night-time cocktail, and closed the door. The bathroom and toilet was next, the light was on and there was no one in there either. So I went back.

Everyone was asleep in the wards. In some places there

were grunts and coughs, but they were all asleep. And only as I approached our ward did I hear that quiet groan which made me freeze at first and then something inside began pulsing desperately, in my chest and in my stomach. I sped up and helplessly went back into the ward. I patted her hand.

"There's no one there, but I'll try again."

I went out again, now in the other direction towards darkness. The corridor bent round and continued endlessly on and on. There was no one there either. Not one living soul. I went further, got to another table where there should have been another nurse, and there were traces of someone having been there: the logbook was open. There was an entry for the 1st of August. There was a fountain pen. But no one was there. I looked around in anguish. Should I shout? I remembered how twenty-four hours ago, for some reason it seemed like ages ago, I was going down the endless blue-lit underground corridors in this hospital, and no one had been there. The orderly wasn't there either. He had been where the doctors and nurses were: on the other side of life. They were not here on our side.

I rushed about hearing that groaning which I wasn't really registering anymore. Going back, I ran down the stairs and went to another floor. Another department? What was the difference, I should be able to find someone here. Oh, thank God, there was a girl there. "Please, please, please come with me!" I pleaded, grabbing her hand, hoping to convince myself that she was real and not a mirage. "Please, there's something badly wrong with Mrs Panin."

"Which ward?"

I told her.

"That's not my department. Where's your duty nurse?" She looked sternly at me.

"Oh God, if only I knew! Please let's go, she's really bad."

"Go back to the ward. I'll call the doctor."

She picked up the phone. I took a few steps back, but I didn't leave: I knew that no one would answer the phone.

"Go, go on."

"Please come with me, she needs help."

Having waited a few minutes on the phone, she picked up her stethoscope and followed me.

As she sat on Mrs Panin's bed, took her blood pressure and gave her some medicine, I didn't lie down, just sat down holding on to the iron bars of the bed. I was shivering.

Then I lay down, wrapped up in a blanket. Mrs Panin also quietened down. I think she had given her a sleeping pill.

It had started to get light.

CHAPTER TEN
WHO?

All this time I was consciously chasing away the memories and visions of the previous night and particularly of the "main character" I had seen in the torchlight. But it was impossible to forget and effectively chase away that horror. All the more so because the idea of victimization and deadly danger became even more evident to me. I was increasingly aware that this force that was persecuting me was able to take (however absurd it seemed) different human forms.

But that face, what was it? Who was it? How could a creature so repulsive, so deformed, be able to walk the streets?

"Thermometers!"

Throwing off my blanket, I felt hungry for the first time in twenty-four hours. Porridge and nice semolina pudding brought me back to some kind of reality.

Gently knocking, Sergei glanced into the ward. With his blond-bearded face he seemed angel-like to me in the sunlight. He was a bit confused when he saw me.

"Hi, how are you feeling?"

"Brilliant. So you know all the details then?"

"Yes, they told us. We know what happened."

He sat down on the chair next to the bed and put a bag down next to me. The clothes, (hurray!) were my key out of here. Trying to hide my joy, I slowly got up.

"Wait, I'll just..."

In the toilet, having waited for all the patients to come out, I quickly put on my T-shirt, pulled on my jeans, rolled them up a bit, and hid my clothes under the long wide hospital gown. A thick layer of foundation and dark sunglasses made my appearance look not exactly normal but acceptable, at least. I wouldn't stand out in a crowd.

I went back satisfied and sat on the bed so as not to attract attention. I didn't hide the fact that I wanted to leave (I had the right to do so, hadn't I?) but I didn't want to advertise it. I had long wanted to be inconspicuous. It's understandable why: it would take a while to get over all the attention.

"How is Nika? How is she feeling?"

"She's fine, everything is fine. You know, you'll be surprised, it is really odd... Such a coincidence..."

I looked at him happily. Any information coming from Sergei, particularly now as he was guaranteeing friendship and freedom, a messenger from a happy world, where there were thoughtful husbands and pregnant wives, literature and music, dreams and plans... I looked at him happily.

"Yeah, you will be surprised, but we know this man, the man who... well we even went to his house a few days ago... He rents an apartment nearby. He seemed so nice to us then."

I didn't understand straight away who he meant and

carried on looking at him happily. I don't know what expression I had on my face, but after a few seconds I got it. I finally understood who he was talking about.

"He seemed what? Nice? What? Nice???!"

I froze.

"Yes, we thought he was rather charming, we even talked about it when we got home."

"Charming?!"

I was lost for words. This information I was hearing and what had happened didn't go together.

"Yeah, we talked about music with him, he's a musician."

"A musician?!"

I didn't say anymore. I didn't repeat the words he was saying, didn't ask any questions. I couldn't laugh or feel surprised or cry. K.O.

I closed my eyes. After a minute I forced myself to remember that I had to leave. Getting up, I took my bag and nodded to my fellow inmates, as if implying: "I'm going to see him out." Sergei and I went outside. I left the hospital gown on a windowsill near the exit.

The hot August day took me back, I was glad I had my sunglasses. Glancing around the hospital grounds, which seemed huge with several buildings, I thought with relief that I would never come back here again.

I was wrong. I did come back, and very soon.

PENULTIMATE CHAPTER

The next day a "Please present yourself at the following address" letter arrived for me. Another investigator wanted to ask me some official questions in his office. I waited a long time in a queue for this. Sitting down, I looked around, and sniffed. There was a disturbing smell. It was my first time in a police station, apart from the passport office.

This time I was treated differently at the police station. I had the status of a victim "earned with blood". More than that, I was the main witness in an attempted murder. On the one hand, the case had already been solved: the criminal had been caught. On the other hand, it seemed that he was also a suspect in the murders of two other young women. They took evidence from me for a long time and in great detail.

Finally I decided to ask a question.

"Tell me, is it true that he is a... my friends told me... he is a musician?" I waited for an answer and was watching, almost praying, with hope, that it wasn't true, it was maybe a little mistake, a blunder that would take away part of the heavy weight, of the bleak absurdity of recent events in my world. A world, which I'd always seen as light and beautiful. A world where music and people linked to music (there were many such people among our family friends and relatives) were associated with enlightenment and beauty.

"Yes," the investigator answered gloomily. "His parents are also musicians, professional musicians."

I froze looking ahead of me fixedly.

"So, Marina Olegovna," he said, bringing me back to reality, "You discharged yourself from hospital without permission. I'm pleased that you're feeling better, but we will need to go back there tomorrow. The clothes you were wearing at the time are evidence of the crime."

"What's left of them," I muttered.

"What's left of them," the investigator calmly agreed, "is evidence."

"Cut up, bloody rags."

"Even so, we need them."

"Take them, why do I need to go there?"

"They won't give them to us without you. They are your

belongings. You need to identify them, to make sure that no one has tampered with them or replaced them. You just need to be there."

I shrugged.

"Well, if needs must."

"Tomorrow at 9.00 I'll meet you here and we'll go to the hospital. See you tomorrow."

"OK, see you tomorrow."

I left the office, breathing in the smell of the police corridor, the smell of mistrust and wariness, the smell of forms and protocols. People there, who'd apparently been through the mill, were giving me knowing looks, both those in the queues and officials coming out of the offices. Someone in dark glasses and bandaged hands wasn't unusual here, but their looks still expressed some guarded professional interest.

Going down the stairs, I pushed open the heavy door and went out into the street, relieved. The hot August air embraced me. To the right there was a balding middle-aged man sitting on a bench, his head bent, his hands covering his face. I lost my breath for a minute: above the man there seemed to hover an almost visible cloud of suffering. He was cloaked in grief. His grief was so dense that it seemed to push me away from him. He lifted his head.

A few days ago I would have probably got involved. Now, I knew that I didn't have the strength. I wanted to avoid him, turning away. I walked past.

"Marina?"

Flinching, I stopped. I looked back. He slowly got up to meet me. He had expressive eyes and a pleasant face.

"I'm... I'm his father. So sorry. How do you feel?"

"Um... fine, thanks."

"I wanted to ask you, is there anything I can do for you? Something to help?"

An unbearable heaviness poured onto me from him, adding to my own which was already too excessive, trying to merge into me, but not managing.

"Thanks, but there is no need. It's unlikely you can help me."

"You know, Sasha... he's not such a bad boy..."

I looked him in the eyes, turned and walked away, almost hobbling. Behind me, he sat back down on the bench, put his head in his hands and broke down crying.

CONCLUDING CHAPTER
THAT'S THE LIMIT

The next morning I was back in the police station. The investigator on the phone was trying to explain that we needed a police car, that he was accompanying a "victim". It was easy to understand that he was told there wouldn't be a car for the next three hours. There was a whole heap of problems and circumstances. Finally he put the phone down and looked up.

"We'll have to take the bus."

"I'll manage."

We walked to the nearest bus stop.

Both in his office and outside I had tried to answer questions and not ask them. Something strange happened: I was losing interest in the case. I was increasingly overcome by a heavy, unending fatigue. And almost by momentum, out of habit, questions were popping into my head only to dissolve there. I didn't want to speak.

But here, on the way to the bus, maybe to take away the awkward silence, he started talking about how many cases he had, besides mine. Criminal cases. He was tired and troubled. Thinking that I was no less troubled I suddenly decided to share my trouble with him.

"You know, this isn't the first time that someone has tried to kill me."

And immediately I wanted to take back what I had said. But it was too late.

"Then they'll get you one day for sure."

These words sounded ordinary, simple and substantiated. My heart sank with anguish and hopelessness. I looked at him: a tanned face full of life. I turned away. He regarded me without any sympathy and continued.

"It must be your own fault. We have such a notion in criminology: " a psychological victim". Criminal psychologists say that victims themselves attract criminals through their own behaviour."

"But I never wanted to be a victim."

"It's not important whether you wanted it or not. People often do not know themselves what they want, particularly women."

I fell gloomily silent. We had already pushed our way onto the bus and looked for a corner where it would be comfortable to stand up. My travelling companion tried to protect me from the shoves and prods from the sweaty moody crowds. People were obviously scowling at me. Of course, I was being accompanied by a policeman and wore bandages, but all the same...

"Why are they looking at me like that?" I whispered, speaking through half closed lips, hiding behind the broad back of my investigator. He grinned and nodded towards my bandaged up elbow and my arm in a sling and easily visible bruises.

"They think you're a drug addict and I'm taking you to get more."

I choked and went red, casting him a helpless and

despairing look. I had not thought of this. It wouldn't have even occurred to me.

I have to say that I've never been indifferent to what people thought of me, I had never been one of these people who didn't give a damn about anything. I stared out of the window in thorough despair and didn't say another word for the rest of the journey.

Soon I was walking once again through the buildings and down the familiar corridors of the hospital. At the reception desk they said that to "remove evidence" we needed the permission of the head doctor. On the way to the doctors' office, we split up for a while. "I am just going to my ward for a minute, to say hello to the girls." I said. "OK, I'll be with the head doctor, I'll be fifteen minutes max. I'll need you after though, to identify your things." You'll be lucky to get it done in fifteen minutes, I thought, knowing this place and the usual waiting times, but didn't say anything.

I glanced into "my" ward.

"Hi!"

"Hi, where have you come from? Back again?" The hospital "regulars" brightened up. There was a fair-haired girl sitting on "my" bed, a new girl who looked at me with surprise, she didn't know me. The bed alongside the wall was made up.

"No, I'm fine, just here to do with the case. Where's Mrs Panin?" I nodded at the made up bed.

"She... Oh, you don't know..." the woman's voice suddenly broke, "She died, that night, that day, in the evening, the day you left."

"How? How did she die?" I climbed on to the nearest bed. "Why did she die? What happened to her?"

"Heart attack. She was misdiagnosed as having a stomach ulcer. She had a heart attack. It should have been treated and they treated her with..."

"I know how they treated her." I said slowly, almost physically feeling my eyes go dark. Slowly I left the ward and went down the corridor. She had died.

I walked to the head doctor's office, like a zombie, and stared him in the face. The doctor was rapidly explaining something with his heavy Caucasian accent and face to match, but he stopped when he saw me staring. He lost the thread and looked at me questioningly. Then he started once again to make his point to the investigator. I interrupted him.

"Why did Mrs Panin die?" I asked quietly but clearly.

"Mrs Panin? Which Mrs Panin? What's your name?" He fired back, looking from me to the investigator and back again.

"Why did Mrs Panin die?" I repeated quietly, persisting.

"Mrs Panin..." He looked down, "Mrs Panin had a massive heart attack."

"A massive heart attack." I repeated, provoking his eyes. "Massive, eh?"

His eyes rushed around the room, then he leapt up and was gesticulating furiously.

"Do you think I can discuss and keep up with all the patients at the same time? Particularly those who run away from hospital? And their things?!"

The investigator, who didn't know anything about Mrs Panin, and who had enough problems without her, put his business card on the table.

"Call me when you find them. The victim was delivered here to you from the crime scene. You don't have the right to discard or lose any blood-covered items from the crime scene. They are needed as evidence. They need to be examined. Let's go."

This was to me. He walked towards the door, glancing back. What was there left for me to do? What could I prove to this doctor and other doctors here? Who was I to Mrs Panin? Mrs Panin who was no longer with us? I was alive, but what could I do?

"Bloody hell," the investigator said, but I kept silent. I didn't feel like discussing it. He looked at his watch, and took large steps on the pavement.

That's it. Time out. I couldn't take any more in. The End. I felt nothing.

Translated by Lucy Watts

ABOUT THE AUTHORS

ARKADY BABCHENKO, born in 1977, lives in Moscow. Winner of the Debut Prize for his cycle of first-hand accounts of the Chechnya campaign which is both a fictionalized documentary and narrative non-fiction. The stories are united by the same characters, the same place and time. Babchenko was drafted from Law School and sent to Chechnya after a brief course of training. On discharge he finished his education and wrote a cycle of graphic stories about his war experiences so as "to get the war out of my system". Currently he works as a journalist on the opposition paper *Novaya Gazeta*. His book *Alkhan-Yurt* came out in Russian in 2006. *A Soldier's War in Chechnya* will be published in book form by Portobello and Grove Atlantic, and is also coming out in France, Germany, and Italy.

"Babchenko has learned his craft as a writer with the great master Chekhov, as demonstrated by his very deliberate shaping of paragraphs, sentences and phrases in a way that is calculated to produce maximum emotional effect," says Rosamund Bartlett, Chekhov biographer.

DENIS BUTOV, born in 1975, lives in Krasnoyarsk, Siberia. He spent two years in active service in Chechnya. He is an IT specialist by training and currently works as Chief Information Officer at the Light Industry Factory in Krasnoyarsk. His war stories have appeared in various collections and magazines.

ROMAN SENCHIN, born in 1971 in the Siberian town of Kyzyl. Later the family moved to Minusinsk where he lived until recently before moving to Moscow. Winner of several prestigious literary prizes he is one of the most talented and expressive spokesmen for his generation. His work has been translated into German, French and other languages. His most celebrated novel, *Minus*, written in colourful and rich language, shows a bleak portrait of provincial life today. It is an autobiographical story of a trapped soul desperately trying to change his life. All of Senchin's writings give you information that cannot be found in guidebooks. Each character represents thousands of people living their lives in small villages and towns in post-Soviet Russia.

DMITRY BYKOV, born in 1967, is the author of several prize-winning futuristic novels and alternative histories invariably inspiring heated debates in the press. He is also a noted poet with eight poetry collections to his name and author of the definitive new biography of Boris Pasternak.

A famous TV presenter and journalist he is a deputy editor-in-chief of the *Sobesednik* weekly and a prolific essayist and critic contributing to Moscow's leading periodicals.

JULIA LATYNINA, born in 1966, a Muscovite, comes from a famous literary family. She is a topmost business journalist, with a Ph.D. in Economics and Philology, and is a prolific writer widely known for her "economic" thrillers and futuristic fantasies — more than 20 titles in all. By wrapping fiction around facts and real people, she can tell the real story behind Russia's often misleading appearance. "When it comes to interpreting the Russian economy, Latynina is, to borrow Isaiah Berlin's term, both a fox and a hedgehog, and that is what makes her books so fascinating." (*Globe & Mail)*

OLGA SLAVNIKOVA, a leading name in Russian letters today, rose to fame as a writer back in her hometown of Yekaterinburg in the Urals before moving to Moscow five years ago to coordinate the Debut Prize for young writers. She is the author of five prize-winning novels and is noted for her highly individual style and psychological depth. Critics praise her for her exceptional power of imagination and precision of comparisons. Her books have been translated into French and Italian.

MARIA GALINA, born in 1960, is a poet, critic, translator, and science fiction writer with ten SF books to her credit. A graduate from Odessa University majoring in marine biology she took part in several sea expeditions. She has been a professional writer since 1995. She has won many prizes for both her prose and poetry. Her fiction contains a strong element of magic realism while gender issues have always been the focus of her attention.

MARIA RYBAKOVA, born in 1973 in Moscow, comes from a famous literary family and has become a star herself with her prize-winning books. She has always been fascinated with the mystery of death which is a constant presence in her work. Her first novel *Anna Grom and Her Ghost* — an epistolary novel written by a soul travelling in the underworld — was published in 1999 and translated into German and Spanish. *Losers' Brotherhood* (2005, French translation 2006) focuses on a character daydreaming about China but never actually going there.

Rybakova is currently teaching Classics at the California State University Long Beach. She was a writer-in-residence and Capstone Scholar at Bard College in Jan.-Dec. 2005. She has received several literary awards including the Sergei Dovlatov Prize for the best short story (2004).

MARIA ARBATOVA, born in 1957, is a novelist, dramatist, noted public figure and leading activist in the feminist movement in Russia. Her 14 plays have all been staged in Russia and some in the USA, England, Sweden, and Germany. She has seven novels and a collection of short stories to her credit published in hundreds of thousand copies. Her books are all based on personal experiences from her private and public life. *The Moscow Times* called her "The Erica Jong of Russian literature," and *World Literature Today* wrote about our women's collection: "Arbatova's two selections are reason enough to read this collection of Glas."

MARINA KULAKOVA, born in 1962, is mainly known as a poet and critic. She lives in Nizhny Novgorod on the Volga where she teaches at the local university and edits the philological journal ORBI. She has five collections of poetry to her name and numerous publications in various literary journals. Recently she started writing prose, which won her immediate critical acclaim.

BEST OF THE BACKLIST

Sigizmund Krzhizhanovsky, SEVEN STORIES
[a rediscovered classic from the 1920s]

THE SCARED GENERATION
[short novels by Vasil Bykov and Boris Yampolsky]

CAPTIVES, *a collection*
[victors turn out to be captives on conquered territory]

Alan Cherchesov, REQUIEM FOR THE LIVING, *a novel*
[extraordinary adventures of an Ossetian boy against the background of traditional culture of the Caucasus]

STRANGE SOVIET PRACTICES, *a collection*
[fiction and non-fiction illustrating some typically Soviet phenomena]

Nikolai Klimontovich, THE ROAD TO ROME
[naughty reminiscences about the later Soviet years]

Nina Gabrielyan, MASTER OF THE GRASS
[long and short stories by a leading feminist]

Nina Lugovskaya, THE DIARY OF A SOVIET SCHOOLGIRL: 1932-1937
[a real diary of a Russian Anne Frank]

NINE OF RUSSIA'S FOREMOST WOMEN WRITERS, *an anthology*

Alexander Selin, THE NEW ROMANTIC, *modern parables*

Valery Ronshin, LIVING A LIFE, *Totally Absurd Tales*

Andrei Sergeev, STAMP ALBUM,
A Collection of People, Things, Relationships and Words

Lev Rubinstein, HERE I AM
[humorous-philosophical performance poems and essays]

Andrei Volos, HURRAMABAD
(Tajik national strife after the collapse of the USSR)

A.J.Perry, TWELVE STORIES OF RUSSIA: A NOVEL I GUESS

20TH CENTURY RUSSIAN CLASSICS
represented by the FTM Agency, Moscow

Anna Akhmatova (1889-1966), *one of Russia's greatest poets*

Pavel Bazhov (1879-1950), *famous for his tales based on the Urals folklore*

Vasil Bykov (1924-2003), *Byelorussia's greatest writer*

Kornei Chukovsky (1882-1969), *the first modern children's writer in Russia, critic and essayist*

Lydia Chukovskaya (1907-1996), *writer, poet, essayist*

Nikolai Gumilev (1886 – 1921), *poet, founder of Acmeism, husband of Anna Akhmatova*

Yuri Olesha (1899-1960), *avant-garde novelist, poet, dramatist*

Boris Pasternak (1890-1960), *poet and novelist, Nobel Prize winner*

Boris Pilnyak (1894-1937), Symbolist writer.

Andrei Platonov (1899-1951), *one of Russia's greatest writers* (Foundation Pit, Chevengur)

Varlam Shalamov (1907-1982), *writer and poet best known for his* Kolyma Tales *about Soviet labour camps*

Evgeny Schwartz (1896-1958), *dramatist, children's writer*

Victor Shklovsky (1893-1984), *novelist and critic, a major voice of Formalism in the 1920s.*

Nikolai Zabolotsky (1903-1958), *poet, member of the OBERIU group*